THE *Canterbury Tales* AND
THE GOOD SOCIETY

PAUL A. OLSON

The
CANTERBURY TALES
and the
Good Society

PRINCETON, NEW JERSEY

PRINCETON UNIVERSITY PRESS

1986

Library of Congress Cataloging in
Publication Data will be found on
the last printed page of this book.
Publication of this book has been
aided by a grant from The A. W.
Mellon Foundation. Clothbound
editions of Princeton University
Press books are printed on acid-
free paper, and binding materials
are chosen for strength and dura-
bility. This book has been com-
posed in Linotron Janson

ISBN 0-691-06693-0

Printed in the United States
of America by Princeton University Press
Princeton, New Jersey

For my family
Betty
Andrew   Ingrid
Lars

Contents

PART I

Chaucer, Social Theory, and Fourteenth-Century History

PART II

The CANTERBURY TALES *on Temporal Lords:*
Tales of the Court and Country

PART III

The CANTERBURY TALES *on the Spiritual Power*

CONTENTS

List of Illustrations

[ix]

Abbreviations

BIHR	*Bulletin of the Institute of Historical Research.*
Bonaventura	Bonaventura, *Opera Omnia*, ed. Aloysius Lauer, Quaracchi, Coll. of St. Bonaventura, 1898.
Brown, *Mézières' Order*	*Philippe de Mézières' Order of the Passion: An Annotated Edition*, ed. Muriel Brown, Lincoln, unpublished University of Nebraska diss., 1971.
Chess gloss	*The Chess of Love*, ed. Joan Jones, Lincoln, unpublished University of Nebraska diss., 1968.
C.P.R.	*Calendar of Patent Records*, London, Eyre & Spottiswoode, 1900.
CR	*Chaucer Review.*
CT	Chaucer's *Canterbury Tales.*
FA	Chaucer's *The Former Age.*
Foedera	Thomas Rymer, *Foedera conventiones literae et cujusque generis acta publica*, London, 1740.
HF	Chaucer's *House of Fame.*
Higden	*Polychronicon Ranulphi Higden*, ed. J. R. Lumby, London, Rolls Series, 1886.
Hist. Ang.	Thomas Walsingham, *Historia Anglicana: 1272–1422*, ed. H. T. Riley, London, Rolls Series, 1862–64.
Knighton	*Chronicon Henrici Knighton*, Ed. J. R. Lumby, London, Rolls Series, 1895.
Lyndwood	William of Lyndwood, *Provinciale seu Constitutiones Angliae*, Oxford, 1679.
LR	*Chaucer Life Records*, ed. Martin Crow and Clair Olson, London, Oxford University Press, 1966.

Montaiglon and Raynaud	Anatole de Montaiglon and Gaston Raynaud, *Recueil Général et Complet des Fabliaux*, Paris, 1872–90.
PF	Chaucer's *Parlement of Foules*.
PL	*Patrologia Latina*, ed. J. P. Migne, Paris, 1866.
Pol.	John of Salisbury, *Policraticus*, ed. Clemens C. I. Webb, Oxford, Clarendon Press, 1909.
Robinson	*The Works of Geoffrey Chaucer*, ed. F. N. Robinson, 2nd ed., Riverside, Cambridge, 1961.
RP	*Rotuli Parliamentorum*, ed. J. R. Lumby, London, 1767–77.
Wyclif, *English Works*	John Wyclif, *The English Works of Wyclif*, ed. F. D. Matthew, London, 1880.

Preface

The first draft of this book was completed in 1962 under a Guggenheim fellowship. Unfortunately for it, I was at the same time asked by my professional societies and the United States Office of Education to work on projects for the reform of English in the public schools and the reform of the education of teachers. Ultimately, I was to lead a USOE Study Commission on the latter subject. This work took me away from concerted work on Chaucer for the better part of twenty years though I continued to teach seminars and direct dissertations on him, and some of the conclusions that I had reached in the early 60s found their way into print in articles that I and my graduate students wrote. As time went by, the flood of Chaucerian studies of the last twenty years produced books by D. W. Robertson, Bernard Huppé, Judson Allen, Jill Mann, Paul Ruggiers, Alfred David, Donald Howard, V. A. Kolve, Alistair Minnis, and others who reached many of my conclusions independently. However, when I finished my educational work, I felt that pulling together my own "tales" of the *Canterbury Tales* might be of some use as an analysis of genre, structure, and intellectual milieu, particularly my analysis of Chaucer's immediate court environment.

I see Chaucer as a poet who addressed the immediate intellectual and social discussion of his age and his court more than do most Chaucerians. I have read most of the accessible books and lesser works written by well-known intellectuals at the courts of England, France, and Burgundy from the fourteenth century and by the Italian figures whom Chaucer knew; I have examined from a Chaucerian perspective as much of the court art as I could lay my hands on. I believe that literary analysis can be enhanced by attention to the specific temporal or ecclesiastical courts for which the major literary and artistic figures worked. The techniques of analysis of social discourse found in recent studies in sociology, anthropology, and philosophy carried out by Harold Garfinkel, Kenneth Pike, and the British analytic school assisted me with certain aspects of Chaucer that Marxist, structuralist, or traditional Chaucer-as-realist studies obscured (see Appendix). In 1980, I determined to finish the book.

In the initial writing of the book, I received help with canon-law technicalities from Father Donald Logan and with history from D. W. Robertson. In my revision, Professor Robertson has read the book, much of it twice, and given me dozens of pages of extremely learned, acerbic, and jocular notes, a labor sustained by our thirty years of friendship and argument. The book is not an "exegetical" book in intent, and I have not always accepted Professor Robertson's suggestions, but he has always sent me back to the sources. In addition, several other medievalists have read the book and given me extensive suggestions from which I have profited: David C. Fowler, Robert Haller, David Brumble, D. C. Myers, David La Noue, Kent Cowgill, Thomas Roche, and David Lampe. Professors Cowgill and Lampe have read the book twice, in various revisions. At an earlier time I profited from discussions with Professor Thomas Hatton. Professor Virginia Leland who is working with Professor John Crow on a biography of Chaucer, has given me help with the biographical and historical sections of the book. Several recent public presentations by Professor Anne Hudson and her students concerning Wyclif's educational program and the intellectual milieu of the late fourteenth century helped me to clarify the complexity of late fourteenth-century reform efforts. My wife, Elizabeth, has read the book twice and assisted me in clarifying many of its arguments. Kathryn Bellman, Karma Larson, and Ilene Hames have called my attention to

many editorial problems. Jerry Sherwood and Elizabeth Pow-
ers of the Princeton University Press have been unfailingly sup-
portive. For these helps, I am grateful. The book's failures,
substantive and editorial, are my own.

The research in this book has been supported by grants from
the Guggenheim Foundation, the Woods Charitable Fund, and
the University of Nebraska. Obviously, I could not have done
the work without their help.

PART I

Chaucer,
Social Theory, and Fourteenth-
Century History

On Looking at the Meaning of
Chaucer's Language

The first principle for understanding the language of another age or culture or writer is to look at its context. Only then can one see what the language "does," in Wittgenstein's sense (see Appendix).

Chaucer's language in the *Canterbury Tales* is language about society: about its estates, laws and institutions, about social obligation and its violation. This much is evident from the surface of the poet's writing and has been confirmed by numerous Chaucerians, however much they may disagree on other matters. The *Canterbury Tales* were also written in a period of extraordinarily intense debate about what constituted a good society—what the direction of European and English society ought to be. The poet who wrote them served a royal government in quest of social order, making sufficiently distinguished poetry to be recognized by both his contemporaries and immediate successors as a significant rhetorician, philosopher, and moralist or student of ethics.[1] In service to the government, he acted as a diplomat in the peace process from 1377 to 1387, a negotiator with Genoa in the 1370s, a controller of the King's customs in the port of London during much of the 1370s and 80s, a Justice of the Peace after 1385 when his jurisdiction, Kent, was threatened by French invasion and internal turmoil,

---

[1] Caroline Spurgeon, *Five Hundred Years of Chaucer Criticism and Allusion: 1357–1900* (New York: Russell & Russell, 1960), 1:x–xxi, 8–43; 3:16–17. Normally I give publishers only for books published after 1900.

and a member of parliament during the 1386 constitutional crisis between monarch and parliament. His later life led to positions of high responsibility, for example, Clerk of the King's Works in charge of the maintenance of Crown buildings. He knew the major issues of his age posed by the negotiations over war and peace with France, by the split in the papacy, and by the challenges to the authority of the Church made immediate in the Wycliffite revolt, to the authority of the state brought home in countryside revolts, and to that of the old agrarian system created by the new commercial and banking culture. He expressed his moral and social vision in impassioned ballades to Richard II, Phillipe de la Vache and others, and could hardly have ignored these issues when he created the larger canvas of his Canterbury poetry.

However, Chaucer's poetry is generally assumed to be detached from the issues of his day. Though the surface of his work refers to his period's names and faces, specific social problems and institutional changes, battles and revolts, modern readers tend to regard these now as mere "realism" or exotic decoration. We can, if we wish, identify the Knight's and the Squire's battles historically, the life stories of Giangaleazzo Visconti, Pedro the Cruel and Peter of Lusignan, the period when Stapler merchants desired to keep the sea safe between Middleburgh and Orewell, the time of the growth of the weaving industry near Bath and of the spread of the Lollards. We can identify technical legal concepts debated among the pilgrims which were also discussed in the councils of government. These events and concepts are part of the frame of reference of the poems, with most of them appearing in the 1380s, the period just before Chaucer wrote the *Canterbury Tales* (the fictive date of the pilgrimage is probably April 1387). Yet, for all the riches of Chaucer's topical or occasional reference, the prevailing view casts him as an ironist and disengaged comedian, something like

Joyce's artist imitating the God of creation by remaining within, behind, or above his creation—paring his fingernails. Part of the common perception of detachment comes from the geniality of the *Canterbury Tales.* How could the poet not break up his lines and weep if he saw what was going on around him? How could he fail to turn to the apocalyptic and complaint modes of Gower or *Piers Plowman* or Philippe de Mézières, in some moods, if he saw that his civilization was in jeopardy? When the *Canterbury Tales* were written, in the late 1380s and 1390s, England and France had been at war for more than fifty years and had bled each other white financially and physically while producing internal chaos accompanied by an uncomfortable centralization of the government. Their battle reflected itself in the battle between the two popes after 1378, Urban VI at Rome supported by the English and the Empire and Clement VII supported by France and its allies. Consequent to the papal split, the French-English war became a religious conflict in which the supporters of the two popes claimed the sanctions and indulgences of crusaders, rival claimants for bishop's seats appeared from the two centers of power, and papal discipline of the lower clerical orders suffered for fear of alienating one or another priest, prince, or province. While the two nations mounted their pseudo-crusades against each other, the Turkish army pounded up the Balkan peninsula relatively unchallenged and conquered most of it for Islam.

The internal governance of England and France was also unsound. Both were repeatedly discomfited by the plague after 1348 and lost perhaps half of their rural populations in some areas; partly as a consequence, both suffered countryside revolts directed at how the people were ruled, and both were riddled with brigands and marauding soldiers—particularly France and the English Gascon areas on the continent. At the same time, after 1380, both were led by child kings: France, by Charles VI who later became mad and occasionally howled like

a wolf or imagined himself made of glass; England, by Richard
II who was later as unpredictable as Shakespeare made him,
suspected by and suspicious of his magnates and given to ab-
solutist notions of the royal power. Weak kings and war prob-
lems led both countries into constitutional crises, the worst of
which led to Richard II's deposition in 1399. As a consequence
of real and imagined defects in Church governance, Wyclif
arose in England and began the process of criticism that led to
Hus and, indirectly, to the Reformation. Finally, and perhaps
most importantly, a money economy based on wool spread dur-
ing the fourteenth century through Italy and the Low Coun-
tries into England, becoming the basis of Chaucer's Merchant's
staple commerce, the Wife of Bath's West Country weaving in-
dustry, and the system of royal finance that made the English
part of the Hundred Years War possible. Obviously, old insti-
tutions and values could topple like Humpty Dumpty unless
the right words were spoken.

Chaucer's friends were interested in finding those words.
The immediate group to which he related and with which he
worked defines his intellectual milieu and tells us how he was
positioned in relation to the events of the time. It included peo-
ple like Usk, Gower, and Strode among court clerks but also
the knights of the Chamber (his diplomatic missions were car-
ried out under the auspices of the royal chamber) and related
diplomatic figures.[2] The Chamber knights who appear in

[2] Derek Pearsall, "The *Troilus* Frontispiece and Chaucer's Audience," *YES* 7
(1977):73–74; Derek Brewer, *Chaucer in His Time* (London: Nelson, 1963), p.
200; Derek Pearsall, *Old and Middle English Poetry* (London: Routledge and Ke-
gan Paul, 1977), pp. 194–97; Alfred David, *The Strumpet Muse: Art and Morals
in Chaucer's Poetry* (Bloomington: Indiana University Press, 1976), p. 122; Paul
Strohm, "Chaucer's Audience," *Literature and History* 5 (1977):26–41; Paul
Strohm, "Chaucer's Fifteenth-Century Audience and the Narrowing of the
'Chaucer Tradition,' " *SAC* 4 (1982):3–18 (Strohm's conclusions concerning
Chaucer's fifteenth-century audience are speculative given the record of fif-

Chaucer's life record are Sir Richard Stury, Sir Lewis Clifford, Sir John Clanvowe, and Sir William Neville. Three of them— Clanvowe, Stury, and Clifford—were active in the effort of the late 1380s and 1390s to achieve a peace with France, and Clifford was a member of the Order of the Passion, which did much of the negotiating. In addition, Chaucer praised, as the best

teenth-century manuscript ownership). For Gower, see John Hurt Fisher, *John Gower: Moral Philosopher and Friend of Chaucer* (New York: New York University Press, 1964).

Anne Middleton's location of the center of Chaucer's aesthetic in the new ascendant middle class ("Chaucer's 'New Men' and the Good of Literature in the *Canterbury Tales*," *Literature and Society*, ed. Edward W. Said [Baltimore: Johns Hopkins University Press, 1980], pp. 15–56) runs contrary to the internal evidence of Chaucer's poetry set forth in this book and assumes a separate, upwardly mobile, self-conscious literary class not evident in *any* fourteenth-century representation of social structure. Chaucer's associates were bound together not by class but by locus at the port or Chamber, bureaucratic responsibility to French negotiations, and service to the monarch. Some had common intellectual interests in Church reform that cut across lines of degree and estate. For example, Odo of Graunson, Chaucer's "flour of hem that make in Fraunce" ("Complainte of Venus," line 82), clearly a "maker," was also an evangelist for the conservative reformer, Philippe de Mézières. He died in an old-fashioned judicial tournament, and hardly stood, in any direct way, for the values of "new men" or aspiring classes. All Chaucer quotations and citations are from *The Works of Geoffrey Chaucer*, ed. F. N. Robinson, 2d ed. (Riverside: Cambridge, 1961), hereinafter Robinson. In general, the all-embracing concept of class is not appropriate to polyform medieval social groups—groups more properly described by the labels of degree and estate contained in medieval marshals' lists, estate lists, tax lists, and the like. I also believe that Chaucer's addresses to "lordynges" in the *Canterbury Tales* allow one to assume that the *Tales* were on occasion presented to genuine spiritual and temporal lords since no lords go on the pilgrimage save, dubiously, the Knight and the Prioress (B¹, 16, 20; B², 3429, 4515, and so forth); Richard Firth Green (*Poets and Prince Pleasers: Literature and the English Court in the Late Middle Ages* [Toronto: Toronto University Press, 1980], pp. 143, 166) treats Richard II as Chaucer's "patron"; however, Chaucer's remarks on the character of royal rule could also have been addressed to royal advisors and agents, given the corporate conception of the fourteenth-century Crown.

"maker" of French poetry, Odo of Graunson, one of the foremost exponents of the Order and one of its "four evangelists," and knew such people as Philippe de la Vache and Sir Thomas Clanvowe who were active in the French negotiations. He had himself been involved in these discussions from 1377 to 1387, when he went with Sir William Beauchamp to Calais to reestablish peace talks with the King of France, talks thereafter taken over by the Order of the Passion as part of its program to reestablish order in Europe.[3]

Chaucer's friends were also active in Church reform efforts occasioned by the instability of the times. Strode opposed Wyclif's ideas on Church property and power but did not deny the need for some reform. The Chamber knights, especially Stury, sponsored the 1395 *Conclusions*, "Wycliffite" statements calling for the abolition of clerical endowments, indulgences, the papal treasury of grace, the doctrine of transubstantiation, and chantry chapels. They condemned the priesthood and the disciplines of evangelical perfection, especially chastity, and condemned most wars as well, calling for complete pacifism unless the need for war or violence were sanctioned by God's special revelation, a position indicative of their disillusionment with the long war.[4] (Since these views partially contradict the Or-

---

[3] Paul A. Olson, "Chaucer's Epic Statement and the Political Milieu of the Late Fourteenth Century," *Mediaevalia* 5 (1979):67–68.

[4] For the Lollardry of the Lollard knights, see K. B. McFarlane, *Lancastrian Kings and Lollard Knights* (Oxford: Clarendon Press, 1972), pp. 139–226. Some other evidence concerning these knights puzzles one: e.g., in July 1380 "le Netherhall" in Norfolk, held by Sir Richard Stury, Sir Lewis Clifford, and other knights is one-third alienated to the prior and convent of St. Mary, Hykelyng, "for finding a lamp to be kept burning every day before the high altar in the priory church"; *Calendar of Patent Records, 1377–81* (London: Eyre & Spottiswoode, 1900), p. 525, hereinafter *C.P.R.* MacFarlane accepts the *Conclusions* as genuine (p. 177); Margaret Aston also accepts them as genuine in *Thomas Arundel: A Study in Church Life in the Reign of Richard II* (Oxford: Clarendon Press, 1967), pp. 328–29. For text of *Conclusions*, see H. S. Cronin, "The

der's ecclesiological positions and since Clifford's name is attached to both the *Conclusions* and the Order's *Ordo*, the Chamber knights may not have advocated all of the *Conclusions* but put them forward partly as matters for discussion. Still the *Conclusions* indicate the kind of talk that was in the air and that must have continued to be there from the time of Wyclif's retirement in the early 1380s to the Council of Constance in 1415.) Given this context, we should expect Chaucer to comment on the peace process and Church reform, using or refuting the ideas commonly discussed at his court to form his human comedy.

The climate of opinion at Chaucer's court is crucial—the intellectual patterns against which he could be relatively certain that his work would be seen. Much Chaucerian study has been dominated by the study of sources, but a source, though it may tell us something about the shaping hand of the artist, does not explicate a work's meaning, nor does it enter into the audience's process of discovering meaning unless it is also present in the audience's mind. An old work in a new political context, or in a new place in a larger work such as the *Canterbury Tales*, may mean something quite new. Thus, for example, Melibee's relatively obscure source probably did not affect Chaucer's audi-

---

Twelve Conclusions of the Lollards," *EHR* 22 (1907):292–304; cf. Wilkins, *Concilia Magnae Britanniae Hiberniae* (London, 1737), 3:221–23. If the Lollard knights held the pacifist position of the *Conclusions*, they must have come to it late since the Order of the Passion encouraged peace in Christendom but was not pacifist with respect to other civilizations. Moreover Clifford heard the appeal of a defendant in the court of chivalry on November 20, 1391 (*C.P.R.*, *1388–92*, p. 508); also a similar Scrope-Grosvenor appeal in 1389 (*C.P.R.*, *1388–92*, p. 159) and other similar cases in the same year (*C.P.R.*, *1388–92*, pp. 45, 130). For the word *Lollaert* in the Low Countries from 1340, see Ernest W. McDonnell, *The Beguines and Beghards in Medieval Culture* (New Brunswick, N.J.: Rutgers University Press, 1954), p. 267; for Clanvowe's remark that those who wish to live moderately are called Lollards, see *Lancastrian Kings*, p. 205. Harry Bailey, in a somewhat similar vein, calls Chaucer's Parson a Lollard for criticizing swearing (B¹, 1172–73).

ence's perception of its meaning, since the audience probably did not know the source. On the other hand, that the Melibee appeared during a time of peace negotiations suggests that Chaucer put it forward as a plausible definition of the way to peace. That he repeats his source, sometimes word for word, does not make his Melibee's words say less than those he invents.

Yet, some sources or subtexts would clearly have been available to Chaucer's audience as semiological controls: the lives of the saints, Biblical stories, common Ovidian and Virgilian stories and generic patterns, and the *Roman de la Rose*, at least in its more memorable scenes. Since the exegesis of the Bible was part of the process of establishing jurisdictions among various segments of society, Biblical exegesis became in fact jurisdictional debate; Chaucer's audience would have known, for example, what Judas's purse signified as to whether the Church could or could not have property.[5] Further, the men of the Chamber had to know the more common legal concepts and institutions basic to the administration of law; the Calendar of Patent Records makes clear that they carried out missions where such knowledge was necessary.

Using such patterns of thought as controls in interpreting a work is now fashionably called "privileging" one reading over another, but the "privileging" has in fact been done by the historical milieu. When one sees a Tennessee Williams play in which a son and mother obviously cling to one another, when one watches Olivier's Hamlet and sees him climb all over Gertrude in the great scene after the Mousetrap, one refers the scene and the acting to Freud whether one has read him or not. The talk of the day has exposed one to the pattern, and one in-

---

[5] See chap. 7 for a discussion of this particular item. In general, Chaucer scholarship may have concentrated too heavily on academic exegesis as opposed to exegesis used in controversialist contexts, especially in court debate.

stantly, almost intuitively, uses it as a control in interpretation.[6] Where Chaucer is interpreted by his glosses or his contemporaries, where he is interpreted by his early criticis, he is seen differently from the way we see him because the universe of discourse is different.[7] The business of historical criticism is to show what the universe of discourse was.

Two further examples may serve to clarify this issue. Chaucer often provides directions concerning the meaning of his own work that point to texts and events outside the work that are themselves significant in the social and intellectual life of the courts he knew. For example, astrology was being taken up by some members of the chivalric class in England and France, and Charles V of France employed Tomasso Pisano as the court astrologer in the 1370s. In attacking the cult of astrology, Nicolas Oresme tells the story of a king of Egypt who fled to Macedonia in the guise of a philosopher and offered to introduce Alexander the Great to the secrets of astrology. Thereupon Alexander pushed him into a fosse so that he broke his neck, a clear indication that he failed to see the future.[8] The Miller's Carpenter John retells the tale in a distorted form (A, 3457–60) to warn clerk Nicholas against astrology, but his greed still allows him to be taken in by Nicholas' astrological interpretation of the flood; whereupon, like the Egyptian king, he falls, breaks his

---

[6] See Laura Bohannan, "Hamlet and the Tiv," *Psychology Today* 9 (July, 1975): 62–65 for an illustration of the cultural factor in glossing.

[7] This is reflected in an upside-down way in Caroline Spurgeon's remark that "Chaucer's greatness as a literary craftsman" becomes apparent in the nineteenth century whereas in earlier periods he appears as a reformer, moralist, and satirist "who exposes and rebukes vices and follies" (Spurgeon, *Five Hundred Years*, l:xi, xix).

[8] Cf. G. W. Coopland's text and translation in *Nicole Oresme and the Astrologers: A Study of His Livre de Divinacions* (Cambridge, Mass.: Harvard University Press, 1952), pp. 70–72; cf. Eustache Deschamps, "Demonstrations Contre Sortileges," *Oeuvres Complètes*, ed. Marquis de Queux de Saint-Hilaire (Paris: Firmin Didot, 1878-1903), 7:192–99.

'bones, and thus repeats both the king's and his exemplum's pattern. However, Chaucer goes further. The astrological portion of the Miller's Tale in turn mocks the concern for the stars, providence, and destiny in the Knight's Tale and mistakenly treats the Knight, who is actually talking about natural law, as a ruler advocating rule by the stars. Oresme's scholarly anecdote serves at once to undercut the cult of astrology, to mock Carpenter John, and to expose the ignorance and rebellion of the Miller who believes that he has understood the Knight's philosophy of rule by natural law and can demolish it.

The Merchant's Tale furnishes another example of a historical situation used to give focus to a general Chaucerian point, this time about the new commercial culture. Chaucer negotiated with Lombard Genoese merchants on behalf of the King in the 1370s, and his Merchant attacks a Lombard knight in his tale, probably because English and Lombard merchants both sought to control royal finances and English trade after the 1340s collapse of the Bardi and Peruzzi.[9]

The Merchant uses a specific episode from the rivalry. In 1378 after Edward III's death and during Gaunt's period of control of the government, a Lombard Genoese nobleman mer-

---

[9] Martin M. Crow and Clair C. Olson, *Chaucer Life-Records* (London: Oxford University Press, 1966), p. 39, hereinafter *LR*; Benjamin Z. Kedar, *Merchants in Crisis: Genoese and Venetian Men of Affairs and the Fourteenth-Century Depression* (New Haven: Yale University Press, 1976), p. 31. The patent rolls contain numerous cases dealing with Genoese merchants: *C.P.R., 1377–81*, pp. 283, 307, 356, 360; *C.P.R., 1381–85*, p. 355; *C.P.R., 1385–89*, pp. 139, 165, 170, 255, 258, 265, 320, 324; *C.P.R., 1388–92*, pp. 27, 82, 85; *C.P.R., 1391–96*, pp. 38, 243, 282. In addition, numerous *C.P.R.* entries refer generically to the activities of Lombards or particularly to Matthew Cheyne. For a summary of earlier Lombard merchant activity, see Paul A. Olson, "The Merchant's Lombard Knight," *TSLL* 3 (1961):259–63, and "Chaucer's Merchant and January's 'Hevene in erthe heere,' " *ELH* 28 (1961):203–14. As controller of the customs, Chaucer represented royal, not merchant interest; cf. M. M. Postan, *Medieval Trade and Finance* (Cambridge: Cambridge University Press, 1973), p. 356.

chant named Janus Imperiale came to Southampton with a tarit called *la Seinte Marie*, perhaps the same tarit whose release Chaucer had obtained earlier, and received royal protection for two years to load anything at any English port and to skip taxation by English merchants at the Staple of Calais.[10] Instead, he was ordered to pay his royal taxes or "loans" directly to the exchequer. Gaunt and the other wool-producing magnates who controlled the government probably welcomed Imperiale as a device to break the local Staplers' monopoly which kept their prices down. But in August of 1379, Janus was murdered by John Kirby, mercer, and John Algor, grocer, who represented the great guilds of London which furnished the members to the Company of the Staple and stood to lose most by intrusions on their monopoly.[11] In his confession, Algor said that "he frequently heard from rumor and gossip in the households of Nicholas of Bramber, William Walworth, and . . . Richard of Preston and John Philpot . . . that the aforesaid Janus Imperial would destroy and ruin all the wool merchants in London and . . . within the realm of England [if] he could bring to a conclusion what he had in mind."[12] What he had in mind was a plan to acquire a Southampton castle for storage purposes and turn the harbor into the grandest in Northern Europe, one to which the Genoese could bring the exotic riches of spice and cloth of their Asian trade in return for privileged entry to the British

[10] *Select Cases in the Court of King's Bench under Richard II, Henry IV and Henry V*; ed. and trans. G. O. Sayles (London: Selden Society, 1971), 7:14–21, 40–41.

[11] For the importance of the London great guilds in the evolution of the Staple, see G. Unwin, "The Estate of Merchants, 1336–1365," *Finance and Trade Under Edward III* (Manchester: Longmans, Green, 1918), pp. 179–255. Cf. Maude Clarke, *Fourteenth Century Studies* (Oxford: Clarendon Press, 1937), pp. 36–52. For London merchants, particularly Brembre, as contributing significantly to royal finance, see *C.P.R. 1377–81*, pp. 24, 25, 280; *C.P.R., 1381–85*, pp. 164, 307; *C.P.R., 1385–89*, pp. 240–46.

[12] *Select Cases in the Court of King's Bench*, 7:41.

[13]

wool market. Ultimately, the murder was sufficiently an embarrassment to the British government to require an apology to Genoa, and Kirkeby and Algor, the murderers, were tried for treason because Imperiale was traveling under the King's letters of protection.[13]

Chaucer's Merchant's story of the Lombard, January, uses an attack by a British merchant on a Lombard commercial knight to mock the general possibility of creating a "hevene in erthe heere" through the search for private profit.[14] Its calendric Janus-January derives his topical point from Janus Imperiale, but even here Chaucer complicates things to comment both on Italian commerce and Italy's commercial rulers. Though January's tale is set in Visconti Pavia rather than in Genoa, the Visconti were the governors of Genoa between 1353 and 1356 and exercised influence there until 1396 when the city placed itself under the protection of Charles VI of France. The Imperiale name means that Janus belonged to the Ghibelline Pavian faction in Genoa.[15] Hence, Chaucer portrays January as a knight-commercial man who lives in a Pavian garden like that which Galeazzo Visconti developed and Giangaleazzo sustained, and includes in it a laurel tree (E, 2037) from which the Petrarch

---

[13] J. G. Bellamy, *The Law of Treason in England in the Later Middle Ages* (Cambridge: Cambridge University Press, 1970), pp. 129, 232–34.

[14] Olson, "Chaucer's Merchant and January's 'Hevene in Erthe Heere,' " pp. 203–13.

[15] For Guelph-Ghibelline relations in the city, see Kedar, *Merchants in Crisis*, pp. 6–9; see p. 180, n. 31. Not enough is known of the Imperiale family history to prove its Pavian or Ghibelline associations; however, the name is pretty good evidence. For Visconti Milan and Pavia as latter-day Ghibelline cities, see Daniel M. Bueno di Mesquita, *Giangaleazzo Visconti: Duke of Milan, 1351–1402* (Cambridge: Cambridge University Press, 1941). Merchants of Genoa and Piacenza are sometimes associated together and with Milan's and Giangaleazzo's interests in the period; see *C.P.R., 1385–89*, p. 324; *C.P.R., 1391–96*, pp. 38, 243. It seems probable that the Imperiale family was a Genoan Ghibelline family having a branch or strong connections in Pavia.

whom Galeazzo patronized might have plucked his crown.[16] January's interest in wealth, luxury, exotic spices, and gardens (E, 1770, 1805–11, 2029) links him to Asia and the Genoan-Pavian trade with it and provides Chaucer a particular exemplum which allows him at once to call into question Pavian rule, the malice of the Italian-English merchant rivalry and the culture of wool, commerce and banking itself (see chap. 9).[17] Chaucer's use of the topical to make a social and ultimately a philosophic point is almost always this elaborate and elusive.

In his own time, as I have mentioned, Chaucer appeared to be a great rhetorician, philosopher-poet, and master of the study of ethics.[18] The function of a rhetorician is to persuade people to new positions, of a philosopher to reveal the design of eternal sapience in specific historical moments, and of a student of ethics to show the ideal, as is done in Plato's *Republic*.[19] None of these tasks can be detached from poetic commentary on the state of the commonwealth. Chaucer's poetic associates and disciples also wrote commentary on the events of the day: Gower on the Peasants' Revolt in *Vox Clamantis* and on Richard's reign in the *Confessio Amantis* and the *Tripartite Chronicle*; Usk on his own demise in City of London politics in the *Testament of Love*, Deschamps on a thousand topical matters in his ballades and on the peace negotiations in his *Complainte de l'Eglise*.[20] Italy fur-

[16] For Petrarch, the Visconti family, and Pavia, see Ernest Hatch Wilkins, *Life of Petrarch* (Chicago: Chicago University Press, 1961), pp. 129–217.

[17] Cf. Olson, "The Merchant's Lombard Knight," pp. 259–63, and Olson, "Chaucer's Merchant and January's 'Hevene in Erthe Heere,' " pp. 203–14.

[18] Spurgeon, *Five Hundred Years*, 1:8–43, 3:xix, 1, 16–17.

[19] For rhetoric in the fourteenth and fifteenth centuries as political or social persuasion, see Martin Camargo, "Rhetoric," in *The Seven Liberal Arts in the Middle Ages*, ed. David L. Wagner (Bloomington: Indiana University Press, 1983), pp. 96–115, esp. 114–15; for the *Republic* as originating the study of ethics, see Hugh of St. Victor, *Didascalicon*, ed. C. H. Buttimer (Washington, D.C.: Catholic University Press, 1939), pp. 49–52.

[20] Murray Brown is preparing an analysis of Deschamps's role in the peace

nished Chaucer with the models of Dante, Boccaccio and Pe-
trarch, all of whom claimed for poetry profound civic func-
tions. And yet understanding the situational or topical in
Chaucer's poetry is not easy. When Hamlet says that the end of
playing is to "hold . . . the mirror up to nature, to show virtue
her own feature, scorn her own image, and the very age and
body of the time his form and pressure," he defines a poetry
that specifies types of social excellence and deformity as Chau-
cer's poetry does. But when he mentions showing the age and
body of the time, its "form and pressure," we understand him
because we can see Hamlet's Claudius wince at the Mousetrap.
We cannot see Chaucer's equivalent court figures flinch, though
glosses from Chaucer's own time may help in a few cases. Ac-
tually the General Prologue shows virtue's features through its
normative characters, the image of scorn through the other pil-
grims, and the form and pressure of the time through its con-
temporary references. These are then further elaborated in the
tales and the interplay among tales and pilgrims.

The Chaucer who emerges from such an analysis is a comic
controversialist. But recent Chaucerian criticism sometimes
discovers in Chaucer's Canterbury fictions the emergence of
controversial points of view belonging to the sixteenth, eight-
eenth, or later centuries, views opposed to the views of Chau-
cer's circle and of the rulers whom he served and contrary to
any conscious understanding assigned to the poet in his age.[21]

---

process, his relation to the Dukes of Burgundy and Orleans and the function of
the *Complainte de l'Eglise* at the negotiations at Leulinghen.

[21] For an example, see Stephen Knight, "Chaucer and the Sociology of Lit-
erature," *SAC* 2 (1980):15–51, esp. 21–22. Knight uses Marxist concepts of class
to describe Chaucer's development without reference to medieval self-descrip-
tion in the language of estate and degree or medieval descriptions of the deco-
rum of aesthetic modes; to assume a single feudal "hegemony" and pilgrims
playing out from under it (p. 39) runs contrary to our knowledge of competing
economic forces and systems in late fourteenth and early fifteenth-century cul-

Obviously controversy was much of Chaucer's life, but the controversy posited by modern criticism often argues issues of social class, capitalism, romantic love, and political marriage that no one articulated in Chaucer's age. When we find views from the eighteenth century and later in Chaucer, we should perhaps look twice to make certain that some fine Chaucerian irony has not escaped us. Indeed, when historical-sociological analysis is done meaningfully, the *Canterbury Tales* first receive what the linguist Kenneth Pike calls an *emic* description, one that examines Chaucer's language from within the linguistic and semiotic system available to the poet's court. Such analysis reconstructs the ideas of society that competed with his and on which he comments in the *Tales*: those of the Order of the Passion, of the Peasants' Revolt, of the friars and the English monastics, of the Roman papacy and English hierarchy. Each of these groups possessed its own idealism. Given this idealism, one reconstructs the meaning of Chaucer's images without imposing an *a priori* meaning, either patristic or modern.

Recently, Roland Barthes has argued that a poet from the past such as Racine "lends himself to several languages: psychoanalytic, existential, tragic, psychological [though] none is innocent."[22] However, the poet *lends* himself to such contemporary languages only as the borrower creates the loan, for to read as Barthes advocates that one read makes understanding poetry only an act of *seeing as*. It no longer requires *seeing*, to use Wittgenstein's phrase in the *Investigations*. If, as Wittgenstein ob-

---

ture. Cf. Fernand Braudel, *Civilisation Matérielle et Capitalisme*, 3 vols. (Paris: A. Colin, 1967), and Braudel, *Afterthoughts on Material Civilization and Capitalism*, trans. Patricia M. Ranum (Baltimore: Johns Hopkins University Press, 1976). Cf. D. W. Robertson, Jr., "Some Disputed Chaucerian Terminology," *Speculum* 52 (1977):580–81.

[22] Roland Barthes, *On Racine*, trans. Richard Howard (New York: Hill and Wang, 1964), pp. 171–72. Contemporary criticism might profit from Wittgenstein's distinction between "seeing" and "seeing as."

serves, to understand a language is to understand a way of life, then surely understanding Chaucer's language and system of usages requires understanding his way of life: his Parliament, Chamber, wool quay, the ecclesiastical and civil courts that he knew, and the assumptions of the poets and rhetoricians who defined how tragedies and epics communicated in his age. When we have achieved this understanding, we have done the critic's first job. We may then, if we wish, look at him with modern eyes and even decide that we despise his vision and dislike his artifice. We ought not flinch. Better so to reject the poet than to make him the Narcissus image of our own historical or semiological fantasies.

I

The General Prologue, the
Three-Estate Theory, and the "Age and Body"
of the Time

In his General Prologue portraits, especially in those details new to estate literature, Chaucer first introduces us to what Hamlet calls the form and pressure of the "age and body" of the time. The *Canterbury Tales* were immediately recognized in their own time as a three-estate poem by Lydgate who calls them tales told "of estatis in the pilgrimage" in which each person spoke according to his degree.[1] In the Renaissance, Speght recognized that Chaucer's tales show "the state of the *Church*, the *Court* and the *Country* [i.e., the three estates, italics mine] with such arte and cunning, that although none could deny himself to be touched, yet none durst complaine that he was wronged."[2] And these perceptions have been confirmed in the twentieth century by Frederick Tupper and, more recently, by Jill Mann; the latter's work is an exhaustive study of Chaucer's reliance on earlier three-estate complaints for the detail in the descriptions of most of his pilgrims.[3] However, none of the accounts clarifies how three-estate social theory undergirds the three-estate "complaint" included in Chaucer's prologue and tales, how Chaucer embeds new, contemporary details into his work to make it reflect the pressure and form of his time, or how

[1] John Lydgate, *Siege of Thebes*, ed. Axel Erdmann (London: Kegan Paul, Trench, Trübner, 1911), p. 2.
[2] *The Workes of our Antient and Learned English Poet, Geffrey Chavcer*, ed. Thomas Speght (London, 1598), sig. c4ʳ.
[3] Frederick Tupper, *Types of Society in Medieval Literature* (New York: H. Holt, 1926); Jill Mann, *Chaucer and Medieval Estates Satire* (Cambridge: Cambridge University Press, 1973).

the General Prologue works to determine the intellectual if not the physical structure of the remainder of the *Canterbury Tales*. None have shown how the visualization of society in the late fourteenth and fifteenth centuries took a three-estate form (cf. fig. 1), or how civic events and their visual representations commonly alluded to estate divisions which Chaucer also observes in the structure of the General Prologue and the tales (cf. fig. 4). In short, no one has shown what it is that Lydgate implies when he says that the *Canterbury Tales* are told by *estates* in pilgrimage.

In the *Parlement of Foules*, Chaucer sets forth a philosophy of the "estate" governance of social life germane to the speaking together and tale-telling of the Canterbury pilgrimage. In that work, the temple of Venus represents the voluptuous life— fallen mankind's pursuit of private libido and profit—with its associated impediments to community life: Cupid, Will, Fool-hardiness, Flattery, Craft, Priapus, Riches as Venus' porter, Bacchus and Ceres. On the other side of the garden opposite to Venus, Nature, as the reflection of the laws and harmonies in the natural world, ordains what natural law commonly ordained for the common profit, for mutual service and love in human communities. She requires the bird estates to organize their society into mutually dependent hierarchies (four, in the *Parlement*). She secures their right to property—or their own milieu—to free choice in marriage, and to free social assembly; she provides them opportunities for "speaking together" in *parlement* to discover what is most rational and in the common interest of the group, and she promotes what is most truly "human," given God's original design for mankind in the hierarchy of nature.[4] Chaucer's portrait of unfallen mankind in the "For-

---

[4] Paul A. Olson, "*The Parlement of Foules*: Aristotle's *Politics* and the Foundations of Human Society," *SAC* 2 (1980):53–69. This article documents Aristotelian late fourteenth-century natural-law social theory at length. The law of nature (or natural law derived from eternal law—law that signals to humankind what place it should occupy in the hierarchy of nature) should not be confused

mer Age" accepts the notion of an original golden age of common property, undifferentiated roles, and spontaneous social love, but all of Chaucer's normative works posit that fallen humankind requires hierarchy, role, property, and social assembly to create the social out of the selfish and violent. The Parson does say that grace may make the spirit of these institutions more the spirit of service than of violence, perhaps somewhat like the spirit of the golden age (cf. chap. 10). But Chaucer generally shows the discipline of grace to be difficult.

The theory on which the poet draws for the *Parlement* is not monolithic. Each natural-law right that the *Parlement* posits might be denied or modified by canon law or royal lawyers and asserted by others as the occasion demanded. Indeed, the poet's *Parlement* version of the three- or four-order idea belongs pecul-

---

with the disordered "law" of man's fallen nature or actual laws such as Nimrod's, derived from fallen exigencies; see St. Augustine, *De Civitate Dei*, 12.4–5; 14.11–13; 16.4; 19.13–15, for both concepts. The Old Law was given to correct fallen government which began with Nimrod, the New to interiorize the Old Law; King Alfred as a student of Augustine appropriately begins his laws with the ten commandments and precepts of charity. See John of Salisbury, *Policraticus*, ed. Clemens C. I. Webb (Oxford: Clarendon Press, 1909), p. 4, hereinafter *Pol.* Cf. John Alford, "Literature and Law in Medieval England," *PMLA* 92 (1977):941–49; Alford's analysis of the coming together of legal terminology and marriage terms involving marriage to God for those obeying eternal law relates to the end of the *Parlement* and its marriages under nature. Fallen nature or libido as described by Augustine in his marriage treatises is identical with Venus. See Judson Boyce Allen and Theresa Anne Moritz, *A Distinction of Stories* (Columbus, Ohio: Ohio State University Press, 1981), pp. 179ff., for a similar emphasis in the *Canterbury Tales* . My emphasis on Chaucer's interest in *parlement* or reasoning together suggests that he was interested in what Fortescue calls political, not royal, monarchy; Sir John Fortescue, *De Laudibus Legum Anglie*, ed. S. B. Chrimes (Cambridge: Cambridge University Press, 1942), pp. 31, 33, 41. Medieval parliaments were not "democratic," for the commons, generally swayed by lords, submitted petitions to be considered by the lords and, perhaps, passed on to the King; cf. Helen Cam, *Liberties and Communities in Medieval England* (New York: Barnes and Noble, 1963), pp. 1–32.

iarly to the English, urban, and late fourteenth-century world of his Westminster court. The hierarchies or estates that he defines include knights (eagles), clerks (doves), curialists (cuckoos), and commons (ducks and geese), groups commonly called together for the Westminster parliament of the royal government, and his own royal-court roots also appear in his unusual deference to temporal lords, in giving them first position in the marriage debate. He also treats the royal eagle with greater deference than he accords the other eagle lovers, but, in placing him under Nature's rule, he refuses to concede everything to the absolutists, for the king-eagle could not say, as Richard was to, according to his Lancastrian accusers, that the king wears the laws in his own breast. Nature clearly rules him. Finally, however, the *Parlement* celebrates the chaos of society and the uses of "speaking together" to discover what is nature's rule. Each estate discovers only some parochial part of this rule while awaiting Nature's own ruling requiring the upper aristocracy to wait for satisfaction and the female's choice. Only then can the rest of the members of society unite with a beloved. The poem's conception of the order of human community as rooted in God's eternal law manifested in the law of nature differs markedly from modern positivistic conceptions of the roots of law though it bears some semblance to the legal theory undergirding the Declaration of Independence and the Constitution. This conception informs Chaucer's art throughout the *Canterbury Tales*.

To understand Chaucer's position requires understanding his competitors. The *Parlement*'s estate theory forms part of a set of theories put forward at the time, some of which are satirized in the *Canterbury Tales*. George Duby argues that three-order theories were always, in the Middle Ages, used rhetorically—in their old forms, to justify the retention of an older order or, slightly altered to new forms, to consolidate the power of ruling orders coming to the fore. For example, the early eleventh-century formulations of Gerard of Cambrai and Adelbero of Laon were conservative efforts to protect in post-Carolingian times the Carolingian primacy of bishop and king, pope and emperor. The late twelfth-century reformulations of the notion served the power of the monastic and chivalric orders combined against peasants in the seigneurial world. The early thirteenth-century division of commons into city and country people, and the later development of definitions of the estates that left out the peasant altogether, served the cities.⁵ These formulations, resurrected in Chaucer's time, were again used to support enclave interests. For example, the Anselmian version of the notion that knights are to fight, clerics are to pray, and laborers are to work—one of the oldest of the three-order notions—is resurrected by Uthred of Boldon to support his conservative claims for monasticism's right to temporal rule.⁶

The most vigorous three-order polemics in Chaucer's period concern the monarchic claim to direct interpretation of God's will for temporal affairs, which royalists thought they found expressed in natural law, and the Church's contrary claim to the interpretation of the same will for both ecclesiastical and temporal affairs, which clergymen based on the Church's direct access to the divine will. To most fourteenth-century papal theorists, temporal power derives from spiritual. John of Legnano, whom Chaucer's Clerk praises, takes the Church's position in this matter;⁷ whereas the *Songe de Vergier*, written for the tem-

⁵ Georges Duby, *The Three Orders: Feudal Society Imagined* (Chicago: Chicago University Press, 1980), pp. 76–109, 271–92, 352, 354ff.

⁶ W. A. Pantin, "Two Treatises of Uthred of Boldon on the Monastic Life," *Studies in Medieval History Presented to Francis Maurice Powicke* (Oxford: Clarendon Press, 1948), p. 376; Uthred cites Anselm's formulation, "De Similitudinis," *Patrologia Latina* 159:679, hereinafter *PL*; cf. Duby, *The Three Orders*, pp. 238–42.

⁷ G. M. Donovan and M. H. Keen, "The *Somnium* of John of Legnano," *Traditio* 37 (1981):325–45. The Clerk by praising John of Legnano gives a dis-

poral court of France at the time of Chaucer's Bruges-Montreuil negotiations, debates the monarchic and ecclesiastical positions. The dream's Knight, speaking for the temporal power, and its Clerk, for the spiritual, join issue in the garden of the commonwealth and develop elaborate arguments which take up most of the jurisdictional debates of the day (fig. 2), including arguments of particular interest to the *Canterbury Tales*. Taking off from issues raised in the Anglo-French negotiations, the Clerk in the dream derives kingly power from the king's anointment by the Church while the Knight says that the Bible recognizes the legitimacy of the rule of pagan kings under natural law, a discussion which applies to the pagan Theseus of Chaucer's Knight. In other discussions, the two figures outline the two spheres of power as that of the "Knight"—which includes the body, the temporal power, the civil court, positive law based on natural law, and the enforcement of positive law through physical punishment—and that of the "Clerk"—which includes the soul, the spiritual power, the bishop's court, ecclesiastical law based on revelation, and enforcement of Church law through penance. At the same time, each debater takes his hierarchy's position on Hundred Years War rights in Brittany and Guienne, on whether nobility is based on blood or on virtue, on whether temporal kings who become tyrants may be overthrown, on how unjust excommunications are to be remedied, on whether God condones blood tournaments, and on whether God commands the poverty of the friars or allows ecclesiastical possession. These are topics that the *Canterbury Tales* also debate through the pilgrims' statements.[8]

---

tinctly clerical slant to the God-centered social theory implicit in his tale; see chap. 9.

[8] *Le Songe de Vergier*, ed. with an analysis by Durand de Maillane, 2 vols. (Paris, 1731), esp. 1:49–54, 75–78, 134–38, 147–70, 183–92, 212–15; 2:59, 82–91, 130–34. Cf. Marion Lièvre, "Note Sur Les Sources du *Somnium Viridarii*,"

In Chaucer's England, the same debates occur. In the 1370s, Wyclif, who was also a Bruges negotiator, sets forth his Erastian vision of a state-dominated Church within a three-order frame that is related to the Gallican picture of the *Songe*'s Knight. Simultaneously, the English hierarchy and monastic apologists make a strong case for the extension of ecclesiastical power to temporal affairs. The leaders of the 1381 Peasants' Revolt envisage a one-lord and one-bishop society and vary other basic three-order ideas to provide for radical land and legal reforms. Nearly every major governmental debate of the day ultimately becomes a three-order or two-swords debate, and the chronicle account of the Black Prince having four Latin debaters argue the issue before him, while probably fabricated, captures the spirit of the time fairly well.

The *Canterbury Tales* continue the *Parlement*'s analysis of estate debates, but their fictions, having human characters and historical references, permit a more particularized representation of the claims and inconsistencies of those who wished to rule Chaucer's crumbling world. The *Tales* begin with a setting similar to the *Parlement*'s in that spring comes in, the birds sing as Nature pricks their hearts, the estates of society come together and agree to a great conversation, and they consent to end their talk with a feast, one perhaps foreshadowed by the birdsong at the end of the *Parlement* and the feast that concluded the Westminster parliament.[9] Again, talk is to provide those

---

Romania 81 (1960):483–91 and Georges de Lagarde "Le Songe du Verger et les Origines de Gallicanisme," *Revue des Sciences Religieuses* 14 (1934):1–33, 219–37.

[9] Olson, *"Parlement of Foules,"* pp. 62–63, n. 15, and pp. 65–66; for the *Parlement*'s analogies to Parliament, see Willy Pieper, "Das *Parlament* in der me Literatur," *Archiv* 146 (1923):187–212. Parliament's estate terminology was fully formalized in 1421; see J. Enoch Powell and Keith Wallis, *The House of Lords* (London: Weidenfeld and Nicolson, 1968), p. 448; however, parliamentary seating and calls to assemble went out by estate; see fig. 4 and May McKisack,

who come together with enjoyment and direction, though the pilgrimage talk and direction are informal. The recent critical emphasis on the textuality of the *Canterbury Tales* tends to downplay their character as texts created to simulate and inspire talk, designed to be read both silently and aloud. That they are to be read aloud is clear from the direct addresses to an audience of "sires" and "lordynges" not on the pilgrimage. That they are to be read as a book is clear from the injunctions to readers to turn to another leaf if they do not like what they are reading. The *Canterbury Tales* are a simulated conversation designed to promote court conversation and reading and rereading. Though only the Franklin's Tale ends with a question, most of the tales pose a surface problem that can invite audience or reader thought and discussion: which lover got justice in the Knight's Tale? in the Miller's and in the Reeve's? how did the Wife's old hag become beautiful? And behind these questions lie the deeper ones pertinent to the governance of Chaucer's society and its *Parlement*.

These deeper questions can be posed in the *Tales* because the pilgrims who arrive together at the Tabard represent the fulfillment and inversion of social roles in a fully conceptualized social system having an ancient lineage and are not a random group of wanderers save at the very surface of the fiction. Their contest for the prize at the feast requires that they speak both wisely ("sentence") and entertainingly ("solace") in telling the *tally* or *tale* of their estate, a pun that the Shipman elucidates at the end of his tale.[10] But the character of the contest means that,

---

The Fourteenth Century: 1307-1399 (Oxford: Clarendon Press, 1959), pp. 388–89.

[10] For the tale-tally pun, cf. B², 1605–7, 1620–24. I have argued that the tales primarily reflect on the tellers and their estates in my articles on the Merchant's, Miller's, and Reeve's tales, cited in chap. 1 and 3. Harry Bailey sits as the parodic ruler during the pilgrimage; I have refrained from treating his functions at length because Professor Kent Cowgill has a study of this with which I am in

at least materially, the tale-telling will profit only Harry Bailey and one pilgrim. Most of the pilgrims will also serve self-interest by attempting to tell a tale that ostensibly reflects on someone else's estate, even if it actually only sets forth their own problem. The day is right for such a contest since the pilgrimage sets out on the day of the departure of the ark of Noah, recalled by the Miller's Carpenter John, whose three sons—Shem, Japheth, and Canaan—figured the three orders.[11] The journey also begins at the right place for an estate journey—in Southwark near the Belle Inn, an allowed stewhouse of the kind that John of Northampton made a political issue when he called attention to the Bishop of Winchester's holding of stewhouse tenements in the area. The penitential journey starts to the tune of the incontinent Miller's bagpipe as he leads the pilgrims out of town. Given the setting, most of the pilgrims talk about desire, marriage, and coupling—the commoners about common marriages, the knights about knightly ones, the contemplatives about "divine" marriages, and parish clerics about penance and its relation to marriage and fornication. The pilgrimage ends at the shrine of St. Thomas who was martyred for his insistence on the prerogatives of ecclesiastical law in the face of Henry II's temporal court challenges to it, an action that made him the patron saint of estate order in England.[12] Clearly, the question of

full agreement forthcoming in an issue of the *Journal of Medieval and Renaissance Studies*. Cowgill treats Bailey's relationship to the issue of estate order in great detail.

[11] Chauncey Wood, *Chaucer and the Country of the Stars* (Princeton: Princeton University Press, 1970), pp. 161–72; Duby, *The Three Orders*, p. 253.

[12] For the Belle as one of Southwark's allowed stewhouses, see Robinson, p. 668 (note on A, 719); for Southwark and John of Southampton, see William Page, ed., *The Victoria County History of London*, 4 vols. (London: Constable, 1912), 4:128; Donald Howard, *The Idea of the Canterbury Tales* (Berkeley: California University Press, 1976), p. 163; Hope Phyllis Wiseman, "Why Chaucer's Wife is from Bath," *CR* 15 (1980–81):21–23; Harold F. Hutchison, *The Hollow Crown* (New York: John Day, 1961), pp. 95–96; and Ruth Bird, *The*

the functioning of an estate society asserts itself at the beginning and continues throughout.

The significance of the pilgrimage's movement from the Belle and Southwark, where the Miller sounds his bagpipes, to Canterbury, where the shrine of St. Thomas lies, may be illustrated in fourteenth-century pictures. In a Harvard manuscript of Raoul de Presles's translation of the *City of God*, Adam and Eve, pushed down into Hell while the devils play the bagpipes, are contrasted with Christ as he liberates them. In Andrea di Firenze's illustration in the Spanish Chapel of the Church Militant and the Church Triumphant, a bagpipe leads revelers away from the Church Triumphant into a kind of pleasure garden of the voluptuous life. In contrast, in the Boucicaut Hours, one of Henry II's knights martyrs St. Thomas with a sword as he kneels before the Eucharistic chalice, symbolic of perpetual martyrdom, while another cleric wards off a sword-bearing knight with a cross which is placed at the center of the picture. Clearly the picture implies the triumph of the cross over the sword, of the martyr over the soldier, and of the first estate over the second as Chaucer's journey may also (figs. 3, 5, 6).

In beginning the description of the pilgrims, Chaucer asserts

---

Turbulent London of Richard II (London: Longmans, Green, 1949), pp. 63–65; for Thomas, see Lydgate's "Prayer to St. Thomas of Canterbury" which calls St. Thomas "protectour and diffense, / Of holy cherche the riht" who "maadest resistence / Ageyn the froward furious violence / Of tirantis . . ."; it asks that St. Thomas pray for the three estates ("Pray for the states of all hooly Cherche") and then prays for temporal lords, ecclesiastics, and commoners: John Lydgate, *Minor Poems*, ed. H. N. MacCracken (London: Kegan Paul, 1911), 1:140–43. For other significances of Thomas, see *Select English Works of Wyclif*, ed. Thomas Arnold (Oxford, 1869–71), 1:330–31; J. F. Davis, "Lollards, Reformers and St. Thomas of Canterbury," *University of Birmingham Historical Journal* 9 (1963–64):5–6; Walter Ullmann, "Thomas Becket's Miraculous Oil," *Journal of Theological Studies* 8 (1957):129–33. The patent rolls for 1397 also speak of the "special devotion of the king to St. Thomas the Martyr of Canterbury." *C.P.R.*, *1396–99*, p. 79.

that he will tell each pilgrim's "condicioun" (moral character or degree of dependency), "whiche" (vocation), "degree" (place within hierarchy) and "array." At the end he says only that he has told their "estaat," "array," "nombre," and cause of assembling (A, 35–42, 715–19). He leaves out *vocation* and *degree* and adds *estate*, suggesting that, though he does not assign his characters to specific estates, he assumes that his detail allows the reader to do so. Indeed, in the final section of the General Prologue, he also confesses that he has not set his pilgrims in strict ranks as some estate complaints would have done (A, 744ff.), apparently to call our attention to the work we must do to order the pilgrims by estate and degree.[13]

The seeming randomness of the order of the pilgrims in the prologue serves a further purpose in calling attention to the pilgrims not as characters but as sets of roles. The relationships among character, vocation, and estate are, in George Engelhardt's terms, relationships between the actual purpose and habitual action of a fictive person and his expected ethos or fulfillment of a role. The randomness allows Chaucer to inspect the estates and degrees as an interrelated system. He uses the estate stereotypes as the basis of his portraits, not simply as frames through which to observe the life of late fourteenth-century London and its environs, but as models of the strengths and liabilities of his time's whole social order.[14] The dramatized roles, the upright and perverse pilgrims, form a system showing how the common profit is sustained and love furthered on

---

[13] Mann, *Chaucer and Medieval Estates Satire*, pp. 6–7. I do not agree with Mann that the "haphazard" order uses the estate concept against itself. The order establishes Chaucer's critique of "present" estate practice. As this book shows, Chaucer constantly appeals to the paradigmatic and hierarchical to order apparent disorder; for a contrary argument, cf. Paul Strohm, "Form and Social Statement in *Confessio Amantis* and *The Canterbury Tales*," *SAC* 1 (1979):17–40.

[14] Mann, *Chaucer and Medieval Estates Satire*, p. 10.

the one hand, and how individual or "synguler profit" (*HF*, 310) is sought and malice fed on the other. The images of virtue are homologous with the images of scorn. In modern life the good accountant may be "honest and efficient," or "clever and efficient"; the bad one may be "honest and stupid," or "dishonest and efficient." The social purpose of the evaluator determines everything. But, in the estates literature, a role is subsumed under a concept of the estate's place in the morality of the total system. Chaucer's Manciple is worthless because he is dishonest and inefficient, given the purposes of the Inns of Court and of law in England. His or anyone else's private gain is no criterion of merit. A good manciple would be honest and efficient in relation to the assumed purpose of the Inns. Obviously, given such a system, neither the ideal nor its obverse can mean much, unless the poet can point to historical or probable reflections of both.

Both Jill Mann and Engelhardt admit that the pilgrims who represent the features of virtue are the Parson and the Clerk, the Knight, and the Plowman—at least one portrait of virtue in each estate; the Yeoman may also be such a character.[15] Were a three-order society to be made of such figures, its tellers of tales would, in Chaucerian terms, serve the common interest and not participate in personal rivalry over a prize that clearly is not worth fighting about. The pilgrims who are the scorned images of their estate follow individual profit as represented in the allegorical figures who cluster about Venus in the *Parlement*—riches, flattery, Bacchus, and willfulness. They also systematically violate the specific function assigned to the estate by Chaucer's ideal pilgrims. One must approach the General Pro-

---

[15] Ibid., p. 55; George J. Engelhardt, "The Lay Pilgrims of the *Canterbury Tales*: A Study in Ethology," *Medieval Studies* 36 (1974):283. For the Yeoman, see Mann, *Chaucer and Medieval Estates Satire*, pp. 172–73; D. W. Robertson, Jr., "Chaucer and the 'Commune Profit': The Manor," *Mediaevalia* 6 (1980):249, 258, n. 66.

logue with the assumption that Chaucer's portrait of the ideal and its obverse illumines his period's need for perfection within the specified roles requisite for the functioning of the three estates. For example, as a cliché, the second-estate Knight is powerful, worthy—physically strong and brave—but he also possesses the wisdom later defined in the Knight's Tale and the Melibee as the pursuit of peace through knowledge of God's laws for nature and man. He displays the fidelity, honor, liberality, and constraint of speech conventionally assigned his role while wearing the humble apparel of that "union of chivalry and monasticism" found in the chivalric orders,[16] perhaps the Order of the Passion or the Teutonic Knights. To him Chaucer ascribes perfection, not nineteenth-century perfectibility but the perfection of those who have undertaken monasticism's and knighthood's evangelical vows of poverty, cleanness, and humility, the better to know God. "He was a verray, parfit gentil knyght" (A, 72).[17] The line comes immediately after the poet has described the Knight's reputation for humility and cleanness. Perfection's battles are not designed to "evoke the exotic aspects of foreign travel" or the romance of war,[18] but to raise specific policy issues for Chaucer's court, debating the rival claims of the orders and related foreign policy, and they fall into three clear groups: "Way of Jerusalem" battles in the eastern Mediterranean fought by Peter of Lusignan and eulogized by Philippe de Mézières in his *Ordo* for the Order of the Passion subscribed to by Chaucer's acquaintances Sir Lewis Clifford, Odo of Graunson, John of Gaunt, and other of his friends and benefactors; "Way of Prussia" battles in the Baltic Sea against

[16] Mann, *Chaucer and Medieval Estates Satire*, p. 108. It seems possible that Chaucer presents the Knight as a member of a chivalric order to point to the Order of the Passion of Jesus Christ in whose model battles he has fought; see chap. 2. Mann plausibly suggests the alternative Teutonic Knights (pp. 109f.).

[17] Cf. Engelhardt, "The Lay Pilgrims," pp. 289–90.

[18] Mann, *Chaucer and Medieval Estates Satire*, pp. 111–12.

the pagan Lithuanians, urged as exemplary by the Teutonic Knights and by magnates who opposed a peace with France and sought to oppose paganism in Prussia and attack Islam eventually through its Asian flanks; and finally, battles against Islam in Spain in which Gaunt may have had an interest.[19] Since the "Way of Prussia" and the "Way of Jerusalem" constituted alternative policy directions for England in the period 1388 to 1396, especially in 1392–93, they may date the poem. The Knight gives dignity to both the "Prussian" and the "Jerusalem" past directions for English military effort.[20] However, Chaucer's first pilgrim also raises the future issue of whether England should continue to war with France and crusade in the Baltic or seek peace with France and crusade with the Order in the Mediterranean, an issue resolved in the Knight's Tale. Interestingly, the Knight has never fought in battles in France during the Hundred Years War, England's prime military effort in the period.

[19] The battles held up as model by both the Order and Chaucer are "Satalye" (A, 58), "Lyeys" (A, 58), "Alisaundre" (A, 51), and several other battles against "hethen in Turkye" (A, 66), probably the battles of Myra, Anamoir, and Anthiocete. Since these battles were not primarily fought by British knights, they do not reflect a British past so much as a British future proposed by Leo of Lusignan and the Order of the Passion in the late 80s and early 90s. Philippe de Mézières mentions "Sathalie," "Layas," and "Alixandre," and cites Turkey, Armenia, Syria, and Egypt; see Muriel Brown, *Philippe de Mézières' Order of the Passion: An Annotated Edition* (Lincoln: unpublished University of Nebraska diss., 1971), pp. v–vi, 34–35 (this edition, hereinafter Brown, *Mézières' Order*, stresses the Chaucer connection and literary background more than does Hamdy); cf. Thomas J. Hatton, "Chaucer's Crusading Knight: A Slanted Ideal," *CR* 3 (1968):77–87.

[20] Chaucer's inclusion of Prussian battles among the Knight's battles would satisfy those who favored the "Way of Prussia" such as Gloucester and also suggests an early-1390s date for the work when both the "Way of Prussia" and the "Way of Jerusalem" seemed viable crusading alternatives; cf. Anthony Goodman, *The Loyal Conspiracy* (London: Routledge and Kegan Paul, 1971), pp. 57–60, 78, 92–93. Robert Haller's forthcoming variorum edition of the Monk's Tale indicates that the Spanish battles were fought under Pedro the Cruel.

While the Knight has undertaken no crusades against Christians and no wars in France, and his perfection and lack of wife imply sexual restraint, his son, the "romantic" Squire, took part in the 1383 Flemish crusade of Christian against Christian which led to Bishop Despenser's impeachment. He wears a beflowered gown redolent of the voluptuous life and of the amorous month of May, and engages in the paradigmatic chivalric vice of "hot love," thought to reduce military prowess and leave one exhausted for battle.[21] The Squire's portrait contrasts with that given the Marshal Boucicaut in his hagiographic biography. He is said also to have dressed in fancy garb in the same period and fought in 1383 though on the Burgundian side. He also composed poems for his beloved, but he made her his image of virtue and, as a courteous lover, loved all persons for her sake. He sought distinction on the battlefield and in other virtuous actions to be worthy of her, not to have her hot love, a passion he mocked in his own troops.[22] In Chaucer's first two

[21] Alan Gaylord, "A 85–88: Chaucer's Squire and the Glorious Campaign," *Papers of the Michigan Academy of Science, Arts, and Letters* 45 (1960):341–60. For flowers and worldly love, see *Roman de la Rose*, 3:80ff., in Guillame de Lorris and Jean de Meun, *Le Roman de la Rose*, ed. Ernest Langlois (Paris: Firmin-Didiot, 1914–24); Jehan de Courcy, "Le Chemin de Vaillance," B.M. Royal 14 E II, fol. 49ᵛ; Jean Courtecuisse in A. Colville, "Recherches sur Jean Courtecuisse," *Bibliothèque de l'Ecole de Chartres* 65 (1904):526; John Trevor, "De Armis," *Medieval Heraldry*, ed. Evan John Jones (Cardiff: William Lewis, 1943), p. 135; Mann, *Chaucer and Medieval Estates Satire*, pp. 115–20. The *Chess* gloss also condemns foolish lovers who stay awake and dance all night. Cf. the gloss on the *Echecs Amoureux* contained in B.N. MS. Fr. 9197, in *The Chess of Love*, ed. Joan Morton Jones, 5 vols. (Lincoln: unpublished University of Nebraska diss., 1968), 4:814–17, 5:927, hereinafter *Chess* gloss. The association of the Squire with the calendric representation of the month of May comes from an unpublished paper by Robert P. Miller, presented at the 1984 Kalamazoo medieval conference.

[22] Boucicaut's early fifteenth-century biographer says that his hero dressed richly and participated in the Flanders campaigns. At the same time, he made the poems and songs of *courteous and chaste* love included in the *Cent Ballades*; cf. *Histoire de Marachal dit Boucicaut*, ed. Theodore Godefroy (Paris, 1620), pp. 29–

portraits, father and son, Knight and Squire, ride side by side as the feature of virtue and the mildly humorous face of scorn in the second estate and foretell what Chaucer will say about rulership and peace, the Turk and France, through the Knight's tale.

The same logic controls the relation of the images of first-estate perfection and imperfection reflecting the contemporary struggle over how the apostolic life was to be recovered. The Parson and the Clerk are simple, wise men, and the details of the Parson's figure, his caring for the sheepfold by staying at home with his parishioners, his generosity and reluctance to curse, his evenhandedness to the nobler estates whose confessions he hears, and the manifestation of the gospel in his work and action all reflect clichés of the first-estate ideal found in the complaints. But two lines of the portrait, perhaps the most important, have no obvious complaint origin:

> But Cristes loore and his apostles twelve
> He taughte, but first he folwed it hymselve.   (A, 527–28)

Gordon Leff has observed that nothing dominated fourteenth-century ecclesiological controversy more than the meaning of the historical apostolic Church for the medieval one, whether the primary significance of the former for the latter lay in its juridical organization or in its simple charismatic style of life[23]— whether bishops or friars were the true apostles. In setting down these lines about the Parson, Chaucer announces the ap-

---

31, 379–83. Though the style of chivalric dress and chivalric ballades changed in the 1380s and 1390s, I see no reason to believe that basic chivalric values also changed; these for some time included commitment to courteous love of the kind attributed to Boucicaut. For courteous love and contrasting hot love, see D. W. Robertson, Jr., *A Preface to Chaucer: Studies in Medieval Perspectives* (Princeton: Princeton University Press, 1962), pp. 454–66.

[23] Gordon Leff, *The Dissolution of the Medieval Outlook* (New York: Harper & Row, 1976), pp. 130–43.

ostolic theme that he will pursue in his clerical tales, where nu-
merous figures appear as "apostles"—Judas, St. Paul, St.
Thomas, St. John, or the twelve apostles considered collec-
tively. If making the Parson a true apostle allows Chaucer to an-
nounce a major theme of his whole work, then making him a
figure who both teaches and acts on Christ's word allows the
poet to define him as a "wisdom" figure, manifesting and acting
on divine principles after John 1 where Christ-as-Word speaks
and "acts" the same message.

The wise Clerk enters the General Prologue to allow the poet
to represent the Parson's estate at study, and he is again com-
pounded of estate clichés: the long examination of Aristotle and
logic idealized in the *Metalogicon* and common among the
schoolmen, speech sown with moral virtue indicating perhaps
a study of ethics and rhetorically proportioned speech: "Noght
o word spak he moore than was neede, / And that was seyd in
forme and reverence, / And short and quyk and ful of hy sen-
tence" (A, 304–6).[24] As a "philosophre," or lover of Wisdom, he
may have also pursued the quadrivium whose mathematical
disciplines were directed to detachment from the personal and
were absorbed in Wisdom's order of creation.[25] Aside from the
"philosophre" reference, however, Chaucer never specifies that

[24] For a general account, see Mann, *Chaucer and Medieval Estates Satire*, pp.
74–85; for the influence of John of Salisbury's *Policraticus*, see John Fleming,
"Chaucer's Clerk and John of Salisbury" *ELN* 2 (1964):5–6. Given Fleming's
evidence, it is appropriate that the Clerk answer the pilgrimage Epicureans (cf.
chap. 9, below). For the *Metalogicon* on the need for lengthy study of logic or
dialectic, see John of Salisbury, *Metalogicon*, ed. Clemens C. I. Webb (Oxford:
Clarendon Press, 1929), 1.24; 2.10. Since both Ariés and John of Salisbury
make clear that the liberal arts were not studied in a certain sequence, argu-
ments that the Clerk's long study of logic indicates defect of intellect or industry
are mistaken.

[25] Boethius argues that the quadrivium leads to wisdom; Boethius, "De In-
stitutione Arithmetica," 1.1 in *De Institutione Arithmetica: De Institutione Musica*,
ed. Godfried Friedlein (Leipzig, 1867; reprinted Frankfurt: Minerva, 1966).

CHAPTER I

the Clerk pursues the object of all learned study—"how to please God." He reserves this subject for the Clerk's Tale's attack on late medieval Epicureanism and its denial of the possibility of reaching Christ-as-Wisdom.[26] Communicating the nature of Wisdom, teaching "Cristes loore" as a "philosophre," defines both the Parson and the Clerk and directs the reader to contemporary dispute over the apostolic life and Wisdom's perfective means—chastity, poverty, obedience. One may expect lack of understanding of Christ's Wisdom and of His perfective means to characterize the scorned clerics as the abuse of power characterizes the Squire.

Finally, the Plowman's portrait centers in love rather than in the labor often described as "the first and often the only duty urged on the peasant by estates writers."[27] Chaucer's shift reflects a common change in emphasis in late fourteenth-century descriptions of the duties of the laboring estate away from *labor* itself to *love* as its motive: "Lyvynge in pees and parfit charitee" (A, 532). This emphasis, which does not have much precedent in estates literature from the earlier periods, clearly comes out of late fourteenth-century social unrest and is used by reformers such as the Wycliffites, Gerson, Pierre d'Ailly, Henri de Ferrières, and Philippe de Mézières to discourage it. The Plowman pays his tithe to the Church, does his manorial duty to neighbor and indirectly to lord, fulfilling the double love of

[26] Mann, *Chaucer and Medieval Estates Satire*, p. 76; cf. chap. 9, below.
[27] Ibid., p. 69. For contemporary definitions of the duty of commons to love and the duty of the estates to love and serve each other, see Nicolas de Clémanges, "De Lapsu et Reparatione Justitiae," *Opera* (Lyon, 1613), pp. 54–55; John Bromyard, *Summa Praedicantium* (Venice, 1586), 2:38; 1:13; *The Sermons of Thomas Brinton, Bishop of Rochester* (1373–1389), ed. Sister Mary Aquinas Devlin (London: Offices of the Royal Historical Society, 1954), 2:259–60; John Wyclif, *Tractatus De Officio Regis*, ed. A. W. Pollard and C. Sayle (Oxford, 1887), pp. 1–65. Gower's *Vox Clamantis* and *Miroir de l'Omme* are both built around the three-estate structure. Cf. S. B. Chrimes, *English Constitutional Ideas in the Fifteenth Century* (Cambridge: Cambridge University Press, 1936), p. 95, and A. I. Doyle, "A Treatise of the Three Estates," *Dominican Studies* 3 (1950):356.

God and neighbor. His peaceful life contrasts with that of the rebellious animals of 1381 of Gower's *Vox Clamantis* or of Chaucer's other third-estate manorial figures, the Miller and the Reeve. It forecasts what the *Canterbury Tales* will say of rural uprisings. However, since the discipline of the evangelical counsels is merely designed to make one perfect in the love of God and neighbor, Chaucer also tells us that the Plowman is as "parfit" as Knight or Parson, perhaps more so, thereby extending the perfective idea.

In emphasizing the sapient worthiness of the Knight, the wisdom of the Clerk and the Parson, and the love of the Plowman, Chaucer also suggests a position germane to his period. He departs from the old three-order picture of clergy as prayer people, knights as fighters, and commons as laborers and sorrowers and turns to a more recent version of the three-order analysis that the Wycliffites and the other reformers had formulated:

Almy3ty god þe trinyte, fadir, sonne and holy gooste, boþ in þe olde lawe and þe new haþ fowndid his chirche up-on þre statis, awnswerynge or acordynge to þes þre persones and her propirtes. So þat to þe fadir in trinyte, to whom is apropred power, awnsweriþ þe state of seculer lordis, fro þe hi3est kny3te . . . to be lowest sqwyer . . .

To þe secunde persone in trinyte, to whom is apropred wisdam or kunnynge, awnsweriþ þe state of þe clergy or of presthode; þe whiche by bissy study and contemplacyon schulde gete hem heuenly kunnynge, wherby þai schulde teche þe peple þe way to heuen and lede hem þer-inne . . .

To þe þridde persone in trinyte, to whom is apropryed true loue or goode wille to þe fadir & sonne, awnsweriþ þe state of þe comonte, þe which owiþ true loue & obedyente wille to þe statis of lordis & prestis.[28]

[28] John Wyclif, *The English Works of Wyclif*, ed. F. D. Matthew (London, 1880), pp. 362–63, hereinafter Wyclif, *English Works*. Anne Hudson's work on

However, things do not function so smoothly in Chaucer's mirror world as they do in the passage quoted, both because of his arrangement of the ideal estates and because of the vice he assigns their scorned counterparts. Though the Plowman and the Parson, linked as brothers, give the reciprocal services that the common profit requires of their estates in tithing and teaching, Chaucer's Knight, newly returned to England, has not been able to exercise his power in the internal construction of the commonwealth and does not interact with Plowman and Parson. This displacement of the Knight makes Mann argue that the ideal criticizes itself since the ideal characters appear to be "actors playing in a different style from the rest of the cast" so that "what makes the production hang together . . . cannot be the principles on which they, but nobody else, are working."[29] However, the "rest of the production" does not hang together within the *Canterbury Tales* or in the history of the period. England's knights were not stopping the Turk or conquering the Lithuanian, and England was frittering away her military strength in France while her demesne economy faltered and rural order declined, partly from absentee administration. If one is absent, one may be Chaucer's Knight and still do little good for countryside order. The decline of rural order

---

Wyclif has shown the English works assigned to him to be by other persons for whom I use the phrase "Wycliffites." Cf. Jean Gerson, *Opera Omnia* (Hague, 1728) 3:1431; Pierre d'Ailly, "Sermo de Sancta Trinitate," *Tractatus et Sermones* (Strassburg, 1490), sig. z2ʳ; Henri de Ferrières, *Livre du Modus et Ratio*, B.N. MS. Fr. 12, 399, fol. 101ᵛ–102ʳ; Philippe de Mézières, *Le Songe du Vieil Pèlerin*, ed. G. W. Coopland (Cambridge: Cambridge University Pess, 1969) 1:526–27. A speaker in the 1401 parliament compares the estates of the realm to the Trinity without attributing powers to each status; *Rotuli Parliamentorum*, ed. J. R. Lumby (London, 1767–77) 3:459, hereinafter *RP*. The notion of God the Father as Power, God the Son as Wisdom, and God the Holy Spirit as Love is set forth first in St. Augustine, *De Trinitate*, ed. W. J. Mountain (Turnholt: Corpus Christianorum, 1968), 15.7–24.

[29] Mann, *Chaucer and Medieval Estates Satire*, p. 85.

is obviously reflected in the lovelessness and malice of the Miller and the Reeve: the Miller, normally appointed by the lord or his steward, steals food from his clients and carries the weapons of the second estate to intimidate those who might object, while the Reeve, elected by peasants who dread him as the Black Death, deceives his lord and steals from everyone else. If the Knight is separated from the demesne society of the Plowman and Parson, it may be because Chaucer displays through the Knight, the Miller, and the Reeve, and their tales, the effects of second-estate rule *in absentia* and the processes by which future internal order and peace could be won in the countryside.[30]

Chaucer's clerical-estate portraits, using a somewhat similar technique, include phrases recollective of the negative arguments about the apostolic nature of the Church: for example, the Monk's "how shal the world be served?" reflects Wycliffite controversy over apostolic poverty and monastic occupancy of temporal office; the homosexuality of the Pardoner and Summoner reflects Wycliffite episcopal debate over the "hermaphroditic" commingling of temporal and spiritual power in the exercise of the apostolic office of the keys; the elaborate possessioner's clothing of the Friar reflects Wycliffite and Observant attacks on the Conventual friars. The Epicurean details of these clerics and of the Wife, the Merchant, and the Franklin associate their tales with growing controversies over the effects of commerce on the values of churchmen and laity. In short, the General Prologue sets up the possibility of a full poetic analysis of disintegrative forces at large in late fourteenth-century society.

Chaucer exploits the possibility he thus creates by presenting the pilgrims in an order designed rhetorically to appeal to a Westminster court dominated by temporal rulers. He moves

---

[30] See chap. 2 for a full discussion of these issues.

from court to city to country in concentric circles and from top to bottom in the moral order to show how confusion of role creates comedy and destroys society.

In the court group, he begins with the perfect second-estate Knight and his obverse, the Squire, and goes on to show us first-estate regular-order clerics-turned-courtiers, confused hobgoblins and "vile antitheses," the tender Prioress and the hunting Monk. Chaucer deliberately sets the Monk's fat horse against the Knight's simple one, the richly clad fat monk against the simple knight in fustian, the *manly* monk against the *worthy* knight. Using the rhetorical categories available to him and the concept of the estate rituals necessary to the correct use of power, he makes contemplative emulate courtier as appearance emulates reality, badly and always superficially, and he continues to play with this emulation in the tales.

In the city or town group, the description of the third of the regulars, the Friar who loves less unselfishly than the Plowman, forms the transition to a group of commoner burgesses whose roles were sometimes included in the "Fourth estate" with which the friar orders had an affinity. All three members of this group of commoners—Merchant, Lawyer, and Franklin—operate on the fringes of the temporal power: the wool Merchant as financier (the Clerk is attached to him to foreshadow the later juxtaposition of their tales), the Lawyer as bureaucrat and official of the King's law courts, and the Franklin as petty landholder and member of parliament. Lawyer and Franklin are paired as figures who operate in both the city and the country and who assist each other.

The rest of the "City of London" group, never fully developed in the tales and their prologues—perhaps because of the sensitivity of contemporary guild politics—includes the Guildsmen, the Cook, the Doctor, and the Shipman who moves between Dartmouth and Gascony for the London vintner's wine trade.

The General Prologue then moves to a country group, which we will examine in the second half of this book, centered thematically on the relationship of penance and wisdom and including both the first and third estates.[31] This group begins with the portraits of the Parson and the Wife of Bath, who is presented as a mock cleric in her prologue and tale,[32] followed by the Plowman with the Reeve and the Miller as his foils and by two clerics, the Summoner and the Pardoner, part of the Wife's following, who appear to operate primarily in the country.[33] The London Manciple is probably included in this group because Temple lawyers often tended the estates of rural lords. This group, for the most part, makes clerics behave as if commoners and commoners as if clerics. Thus, the overall development of the General Prologue moves from the center of the court's interest to its periphery with a few exceptions thrown in to convey an atmosphere of random verisimilitude and to set up ironic juxtapositions in the tales.

The ordering of the prologue predicts the literary artifice of the tales as well as their themes. In the process of telling their tales, the pilgrims who usurp the powers and properties of other estates tell stories that abuse a recognized decorum relating narrator, form, subject, and style. They use genres that do not belong to their estate and mock the forms that belong to other pilgrims. The concept of estate is a concept of decorum in duties, dress, and obligation that is intrinsically related to the

[31] These matters are discussed fully in chap. 5–10, below.

[32] One estate's virtues may be another's vices; e.g. Honoré Bonet's knight must not "till the soil, or tend vines, or keep beasts . . . or be a matchmaker, or lawyer. . . . And he should never, if he is a paid soldier, buy land or vineyards while he is in service." Honoré Bonet, *The Tree of Battles*, English version with introduction by G. W. Coopland (Liverpool: Liverpool University Press, 1949), p. 131. See Duby, *The Three Orders*, pp. 53–55, for precedent techniques used to comment on earlier political situations.

[33] See chaps. 7–9, below.

concept of literary decorum and genre. Geoffrey of Vinsauf, like his Renaissance successors, assumes that poets choose their genres on the basis of the stations of their subjects—epics being noble in style because they speak of military heroes, and pastorals low because they speak of humble shepherds—but John of Garland extends this notion, arguing that the choice of narrator as well as of subject is a stylistic consideration, so that a noble character should speak of a noble subject in a noble style. Chaucer uses John of Garland's idea in his Canterbury fiction,[34] importing into English the sense of social literary decorum, of classical genre, and of the language games through which genre communicates meaning traditional to Roman models as understood in his time. When Lydgate says that each of Chaucer's pilgrims speaks according to his degree, he probably refers to style as well as content. Thus, the Knight tells a tale of arms in the high style, a heroic poem mingling fable and history to pay tribute to a noble Theseus as master of arms ordering foreign affairs and internal strife. The strife-fed villains, the Miller and the Reeve, speak in the low to middle style of village characters, occasionally mocking the Knight's literary effects, while telling comedies, a form of *cantus villanus*. The Man of Law recites a history since lawyers were to study chronicles intensively; the Prioress and the Second Nun recall saints' lives after those studied and copied by monastics, and they pray as contemplatives should. In contrast, the Monk does not pray and speaks through rather thin tragedies, supposed histories, reflecting monasticism's interest in chronicle and the design of history. That he ignores the high style proper to tragedy should tell us something about his exercise of rule as well as of literary art. The Summoner and the Friar speak what is invective to them

---

[34] Edmond Faral, *Les Arts Poétiques du XIIe et du XIIIe Siècle* (Paris: E. Champion, 1924), p. 312; John of Garland, "Poetria magistri Johannis anglici de arte prosayca metrica et rithmica," ed. Giovanni Mari, *Romanische Forschungen* 13 (1902):920.

but is satire to Chaucer.[35] And so on. When Chaucer uses the classical genres, he uses them seriously and relatively straightforwardly save when a character aspires to a genre beyond his degree; on the other hand, when he uses the medieval genres of popular romance in the Thopas and allegorical romance in the Wife of Bath's Tale, he parodies or inverts them and shows himself to be a "medieval classicist" who discusses civic matters in the ancient idioms of civic or ethical poetic discourse.

The Prologue foreshadows Chaucer's choice of genre and style and also his structure. Recent years have seen renewed discussions of the Bradshaw and Ellesmere orders of the *Canterbury Tales* as keys to structure.[36] No doubt Ellesmere carries the most manuscript authority (though I cannot believe that Chaucer never had his towns on the way to Canterbury in the right order). The Bradshaw and the Ellesmere orders are alike

[35] John of Garland, *Parisiana Poetria*, ed. Traugott Lawler (New Haven: Yale University Press, 1974), p. 103. For full accounts of genre in medieval literary and exegetical theory, see Judson Boyce Allen, *The Ethical Poetic of the Later Middle Ages* (Toronto: Toronto University Press, 1982), pp. 21–29, 76–77, 85–87, 117–78; see A. J. Minnis, *Medieval Theory of Authorship* (London: Scolar Press, 1984) for a useful account of genre, the sense of author and Biblical commentary.

[36] For the Ellesmere order, see Larry D. Benson, "The Order of *The Canterbury Tales*," *SAC* 3 (1981):77–120; for additional articles favoring the Ellesmere order, see articles cited by Charles A. Owen, Jr., "The Alternative Reading of *The Canterbury Tales*: Chaucer's Text and the Early Manuscripts," *PMLA* 97 (1982):247, n. 1; for Bradshaw, see Robert A. Pratt, "The Order of the *Canterbury Tales*," *PMLA* 66 (1951):1141–67; Germaine Dempster, "A Period in the Development of the *Canterbury Tales* Marriage Group and of Blocks B² and C," *PMLA* 68 (1953):1142–59; Robert A. Pratt, "The Development of the Wife of Bath," in *Studies in Medieval Literature in Honor of Albert Croll Baugh*, ed. MacEdward Leach (Philadelphia: University of Pennsylvania Press, 1961), pp. 45–80; James H. Wilson, "The Pardoner and the Second Nun: A Defense of the Bradshaw Order," *NM* 74 (1973):292–96; J. M. Manly and Edith Rickert, *The Text of the Canterbury Tales*, 8 vols. (Chicago: Chicago University Press, 1940), 2:475ff.

save for the в² group, as Charles Owen has observed in arguing that the *Canterbury Tales* were never a neat pile of manuscript and that one cannot finally make interpretation rest on matters of order.[37] Whatever the original state of Chaucer's manuscript pile, arguments about order are now rather fruitless in view of the fact that the fundamental relationship that joins the General Prologue to the tales is the three-order intellectual structure and not any posited physical order. The tales are all elaborations of the prologue regardless of order. Almost all of the groups of tales treat the relationships of knights, clerks, and commoners to each other. Almost all contain some echoes of tales distant from them in the manuscripts. Hence, this book first discusses the tales that give a primary emphasis to court and country, then those that give primary emphasis to Church and country, without trying to establish some final Chaucerian intent as to ordering. The General Prologue acts as a "prologue" in the sermonistic or classical rhetorical sense in that it announces what Chaucer will pursue from then on:[38] his title, name, intention,

[37] Charles A. Owen, "The Alternative Reading," pp. 237–47.

[38] "Nam officium et lex prologi est prelibare et declarare materiam totius sequentis operis." Ezio Franceschini, "Il commento di Giacomino da Mantova al prologo dell' Andria di Terenzio," *Studi e Note di Filologia* (Milan: Pubblicazione dell' Università Cattolica del Sacro Cuore, 1938), p. 168. For additional commentary on the functions of a prologue from the sermon rhetorics, see Doris T. Myers, *The Artes Praedicandi and Chaucer's Canterbury Preachers* (Lincoln: unpublished University of Nebraska diss., 1967), p. 69. Cf. Allen and Moritz, *A Distinction of Stories*, p. 88. They also treat the prologue as forecasting the whole structure but with an emphasis different from mine, pp. 89ff. For Chaucer's General Prologue as announcing the *Canterbury Tales* as a *compilatio*, see Minnis, *Medieval Theory of Authorship*, pp. 190–210. The General Prologue also provides most of the information that Minnis attributes to the "Type C" prologue based on Boethius' introduction to Porphyry's *Isagoge*—namely the title of the work, the name of the author, the intention of the author (to create a *compilatio* of a story-telling competition), the subject matter (the pilgrimage), and order (the order of the tales, a "disorderly" order). Chaucer leaves to his reader the discovery of his didactic procedure and branches of learning; under *utility* he simply

order, and didactic procedure. If we are in touch with the idea of a prologue and the issues that his prologue raises, we know implicitly he will analyze what it means for the second estate to be worthy amid the Islamic invasions and French wars of late fourteenth-century Europe; he will scrutinize the wisdom of submerging members of the contemplative or clerical life in contests that strive for temporal or political sovereignty rather than for spiritual perfection; and he will question the effects both of commercial materialism on temporal and clerical rule, and of rural unrest on countryside justice.

The whole structure rehearses a sort of order. The poet begins the pilgrimage tale-telling with the Knight and claims of external order, ends it with the Parson and the claims of penance and internal order, and includes two prose tales related to many of the other tales through verbal and conceptual echoes: the Melibee told by a court servant about temporal governance and the Parson's tale told by a cleric about the government of the human spirit. The Knight intervenes twice to fulfill his estate role, once to protect the Church—in the form of the Pardoner—from harm from Bailey (C, 962), and again to stop the Monk from continuing to abuse temporal lords (B², 3957). The Parson intervenes once to stop a man from swearing (B¹, 1170ff.). At the beginning of the pilgrimage, the Miller, a rural fighter who is not a knight, leads the pilgrimage out of town with his bagpipes while the Reeve, whom the devil made to preach (A, 3903), brings up the rear. These two figures, standing for the abuse of the powers of the two ruling estates, both rehearse the order of the tales and their theme of violated de-

---

specifies that the tales are to be judged as to *sentence* and *solace*. For a useful argument, collateral to that developed in this chapter but elaborating Howard and David, see Elton D. Higgs, "The Old Order and the 'Newe World' in the General Prologue to the *Canterbury Tales*," *Huntington Library Quarterly* 45 (1982):155–73, esp. 169. However, Higgs ignores the topical character of Chaucer's General Prologue statement.

corum. The Knight, selected by "chance" to tell the first tale, tells of proper temporal rule as the pilgrimage leaves the unruly city of Southwark while the Parson reminds the group of spiritual order as it approaches the shrine of St. Thomas. All use of power by second-estate pilgrims, their commoner rivals, and their functionaries is measured against the Knight's and Theseus' use of power, and all search for penance and wisdom by the parish clerics and the contemplatives takes place against the backdrop of the penitential message and wisdom of the Parson. The tumultuous loves of the commoners in the frame story and the comedies must be seen by our inner eye in the context of their reaching or not reaching, with the Plowman, toward love of God and neighbor in the action of labor. All of these ideal and obverse images point back to the responsibilities of Chaucer's court in the world of the Schism, the Hundred Years War, the Peasants' Revolt, the Turkish advance, and England's constitutional crises in 1386–88 and 1399. Chaucer takes the clichés of his age's social construction of reality into the world of art and adds to them details and topical references significant to his theme and court so that the world of art may entice—may woo—the imagination of his time to seek a more artful, more graceful condition of life.

His wooing, as I hope to show, takes his reader or listener toward a royalist but anti-absolutist (pro-parliamentary) position in domestic policy and an "Order of the Passion" position in foreign policy, toward a Wycliffite analysis of Church abuses and an anti-Wycliffite analysis of the remedies for those abuses. To put it in another way, Chaucer makes the temporal ruler directly dependent on God and nature without clerical intermediary, but he makes the quality of his rule depend, like that of every other person, on inner perfection.

PART II

The
CANTERBURY TALES
on Temporal
Lords

TALES OF THE COURT
AND COUNTRY

2

The Order of the Passion and Internal Order

THE TALES OF THE KNIGHT, THE MILLER,

AND THE REEVE

Chaucer writes the *tales* in a variety of genres. If he also counts up the *tallies* of the realm of England in terms of its legal and societal debits and credits, his technique ought to be most apparent in the tales told by characters associated with the temporal court. We *know* what Chaucer did for the royal court and, to some extent, who his chivalric audience was. Moreover, next to the Knight's tale, the Monk's tale, which refers back to the Knight's tale and is stopped by the Knight, contains most of the clearly topical, contemporary historical references in the *Canterbury Tales*. The Group A tales are, therefore, a good test of contextual criticism.

Chaucer's tales dealing with the authority of temporal lords are told by the Knight, the Man of Law, and by Chaucer himself.[1] However, the Miller's and the Reeve's tales, told by indirection and in juxtaposition with the Knight's Tale, require consideration with it. Many other tales have temporal lords in them as characters, and some speak to the problems of the two swords, but they do not have the duties of the prince and of knights as their central focus. Typically Chaucer does not lay into contemporary figures or social forces with an obvious jab

---

[1] For useful analyses of the Knight's Tale, see Charles Muscatine, "Form, Texture, and Meaning in Chaucer's *Knight's Tale*," *PMLA* 65 (1950):911–29; Paul Ruggiers, "Some Philosophical Aspects of *The Knight's Tale*," *CE* 19 (1958):296–302; Wood, *Chaucer and the Country of the Stars*, pp. 69–74; David, *The Strumpet Muse*, pp. 77–89; John P. McCall, *Chaucer Among the Gods* (University Park: Pennsylvania State University Press, 1979), pp. 63–86; Alan Gaylord, "The Role of Saturn in the Knight's Tale," *CR* 8 (1973–74):171–90.

at them as Gower does in treating the Peasants' Revolt in *Vox Clamantis*. Rather he circles the problem or, to change the metaphor, reflects it in a complex mosaic whose "figure" is only clear after one has looked at its "ground," and after one has examined all of its parts in relation to each other, both close up and from a distance.

My first chapter argued that the General Prologue presentation of the Knight, Plowman, Miller, and Reeve foretells that the tales told by these characters will examine England's crusading goals, the war with France, the internal order in the wake of the Peasants' Revolt and related country uprisings of the 1380s and 90s. Disillusionment with the war and the internal uprisings against the magnates were related, and both grew out of disillusionment with England's Westminster leadership late in Edward III's reign and early in that of Richard II. This chapter examines how Chaucer in the Knight's, Miller's, and Reeve's tales uses his generic, philosophic, and historical tools.[2] It observes to what extent he shows an ancient natural-law ruler commanding peace to model how an English peace might be obtained. It questions to what end he presents the Miller's and the Reeve's tales as rivals to the Knight's—how he uses them to highlight England's internal disorder and, in relation to the Knight's Tale, to hint at possible sources of rural justice and order.

To understand the structure and meaning in the Group A tales requires a brief "chivalric" history of the problems of England's temporal court in the Ricardian period. If, in the General Prologue portrait of the Knight, Chaucer presents neutrally the "Way of Jerusalem" and peace with France, and the "Way of

[2] This chapter revises, somewhat, theses that I have previously set forth about the Knight's, the Miller's and the Reeve's tales but omits most of the detailed stylistic analysis; see Paul A. Olson, "Chaucer's Epic Statement," pp. 61–87; "Poetic Justice in the Miller's Tale," *MLQ* 24 (1963):227–36; "The *Reeve's Tale*: Chaucer's *Measure for Measure*," *SP* 59 (1962):1–17.

Prussia" and continued war, he clearly, in the marriage conclu-
sion of the Knight's Tale, rehearses a peace strategy based on
the grand design of nature, leading to a peace that would place
France under England and give the throne of both countries to
a joint "Athenian-Theban" house. The conclusion of the
Knight's Tale was interpreted in this way in the early fifteenth
century. In recreating the conclusion of the Knight's Tale at the
end of the *Seige of Thebes*, Lydgate makes the marriage-peace de-
veloped between Athens and Thebes reflect the treaty of
Troyes drawn up in 1420 to incorporate France within Henry
V's England. Lydgate places his Theban tale first in his account
of the return from Canterbury, pairing it with the Knight's
Tale and implying that the Knight's Athenian-Theban mar-
riage-peace represents the recently concluded peace between
England and France.[3] The appearance of a similar peace em-
phasis in the Knight's Tale should surprise no one, given the
General Prologue's listing of the battles in which the Knight has
fought. Though the magnates continued to be divided on the
peace question after 1388 and people like Thomas of Gloucester
sometimes sought a more militant French policy, after Rich-
ard's "restoration" in 1389 most of England's chivalric and bu-
reaucratic leadership moved steadily toward a French peace
treaty or, at least, toward the truce consummated in 1396.

In the creation of the new climate, Chaucer and his friends
played a role. The Bruges-Montreuil 1375–77 negotiations in
which Chaucer participated considered whether peace required
giving Aquitaine as an independent territory to Gaunt as the
vassal of France, or retaining it as the King of England's terri-
tory and requiring Gaunt to remain in vassalage to France, at
least in his rulership of Aquitaine.[4] After the failure of the 1383

[3] John Lydgate, *The Siege of Thebes*, 1:8–9; cf. Olson, "Chaucer's Epic State-
ment," p. 86, n. 40.

[4] J.J.N. Palmer, *England, France and Christendom, 1377–99* (Chapel Hill:
North Carolina University Press, 1972), pp. 28–42.

Despenser crusade against France, English negotiations resumed without Chaucer in 1383–84 over the same issues. As I mentioned in the Introduction, in 1387 Chaucer went to Calais with Sir William Beauchamp to negotiate a reopening of a free wool trade with the Flemish weaver cities of Bruges, Ghent, and Ypres.[5] The Flemish and English representatives asked that these negotiations be made official after November 20, 1387, when the magnates who had controlled the government, save for the privy seal, were to return Richard II to his full powers. Moreover, the Beauchamp mission also covertly opened talks with the French, an action that the Lords Appellant represented as possibly treasonable on Richard's part when they regained the control of the government in the Radcot Bridge civil war and gained direction of most of the government's functions for another year in order to renew hostilities against France. After 1387 Chaucer traveled no more in the cause of international peace.

However, the Lords Appellant won no particular military successes, and in the following year, Richard assumed his full adult powers. He sought the support of his uncle, Gaunt, and the help of the Order of the Passion to move England toward agreement with France. Chaucer's friends working on these negotiations included Sir Lewis Clifford, active from 1390 to 1396 and a member of the Order, Sir Richard Stury, active from 1389 to 1394, and Sir John Clanvowe and Sir William Neville, both active from 1385 to 1390. In addition, Philippe de la Vache and Odo of Graunson, Chaucer's acquaintances ad-

[5] Palmer, *England, France and Christendom*, pp. 107–15; 251–55; for background, see pp. 67–141, *passim*. Beauchamp witnessed for Chaucer in Cecily Champain's 1380 release (*LR*, 343–47), and Chaucer mainprised for Beauchamp in 1378 when Beauchamp was put in charge of the Pembroke estates (*LR*, 279–81); see Anthony Tuck, *Richard II and the English Nobility* (London: Edward Arnold, 1973), pp. 108–9. Chaucer's letters of protection to go with Beauchamp on July 5, 1387, were not revoked, and he appears to have made the trip.

dressed in his poetry, became significant parties in the negotiations (remember Odo was one of the evangelists for the Order).[6] Finally Sir Peter Courtenay, the poet's nominal overseer while he was deputy keeper of the Petherton Forest, fought a series of tournaments with the Marshal Boucicaut, one of France's most brilliant young soldiers who was also an advocate of the Order and a patron of the arts, tournaments that appear to have been part of the international festivities designed to promote a climate of peace.[7] Along with these tourneys went other conciliatory activities such as a plan for the joint building of a church, the Leulinghen festival events, and exchanges of tapestries and literary creations, among them Deschamps' ballade in praise of Chaucer, sent by the hand of Sir Lewis Clifford.[8]

[6] See Olson, "Chaucer's Epic Statement," pp. 67–68. For the membership of the Order of the Passion, see Brown, *Mézières' Order*, pp. 260–67. For Odo of Graunson and the Order, see Arthur Piaget, *Oton de Grandson: Sa Vie et Ses Poésies* (Lausanne: Librairie Payot, 1941), pp. 75–77; Boucicaut (Brown, *Mézières' Order*, p. 260) was also one of the primary advocates of the Order and to some extent carried out its purposes in the Nicopolis Crusade. For Clifford, see Brown, p. 263. For Odo's 1393 homage to Richard II, see Thomas Rymer, *Foedera conventiones literae et cujusque generis acta publica* (London, 1740), 7:761, hereinafter *Foedera*. The Order of the Passion list also includes Thomas West and John Harlaston as belonging to the Order, and both also appear in the Chaucer life-records.

[7] For Boucicaut's 1390 tournaments with Sir Peter Courtenay, see Rymer, *Foedera*, 7:663, 665. Deschamps also expresses sympathy for the peace program and wrote a major piece for the Leulingham negotiations, *La Complainte de l'Eglise*.

[8] Clifford's 1391 peace mission probably brought Chaucer's poetry to Deschamps; see Haldeen Braddy, *Geoffrey Chaucer Studies* (Port Washington, N.Y.: Kennikat, 1971), pp. 64–65. The Anglo-French negotiations of the 1390s included the important exchanges of fine works expressing court ideals, especially gifts by the Duke of Burgundy; see Henri David, *Philippe le Hardi: Le train somptuaire d'un grand Valois* (Dijon: Bernigaud et Privat, 1947), pp. 28, 32. Cf. Jean Froissart, *Chroniques*, ed. Kervyn de Lettenhove, 25 vols. (Brussels, 1867–77), 14:385; 15:109–10, 269ff., 285–306. For late evidence of English artistic ex-

Chaucer's work also included his role as Justice of the Peace in Kent. England's problem of order in the countryside was aligned with its problems with war finances, wartime exhaustion, and delay in negotiating a peace. The so-called Peasants' Revolt in 1381 was, in part, prompted by the 1380 passage of a poll tax, collected from all subjects save paupers, to pay for the renewal of the French war. The rebellion probably reflects as much a lack of confidence in the chivalric and spiritual leadership of the country in its dealings with France as a discontent with agrarian policy or the Statute of Laborers.[9] In early June 1381, the Kentish crowds released John Ball, a revolutionary priest, from his jail in Maidstone in Kent. His riming letters, presenting a description of Jack the Miller's work were sent across the country and signaled the start of the revolt:

> Iohan þe Mullere haþ ygrounde smal, smal, smal;
> Þe Kynges sone of heuene schal paye for al.
> Be war or ye be wo;
> Knoweþ ȝour freend fro ȝour foo;
> Haueth ynow, and seith 'Hoo';
> And do wel and bettre, and fleth synne,
> And sekeþ pees, and hold ȝou þerinne;
> and so biddeþ Iohan Trewman and alle his felawes.[10]

Knighton gives another version of the Jack the Miller material:

---

change with the Duke of Berry in 1397, see *C.P.R.*, *1396–99*, p. 174. There was also a plan for a jointly built church to be dedicated to Our Lady of Grace.

9 Edouard Perroy, *The Hundred Years War* (Bloomington: Indiana University Press, 1959), p. 181.

10 Kenneth Sisam, *Fourteenth Century Verse and Prose* (Oxford: Clarendon Press, 1921), pp. 160–61; Thomas Walsingham, *Historia Anglicana, 1272–1422*, ed. H. T. Riley (London: Rolls Series, 1863–64), 2:33–34, hereinafter *Hist. Ang.*; Thomas Walsingham, *Chronicon Angliae: 1328–1388*, ed. Edward Maunde Thompson (London: Rolls Series, 1874), p. 322.

Jakke Mylner asketh help to turne his mylne aright. He hath
grounden smal, smal; the king's sone of heaven shall pay for alle.
Lok they mylne go aright, with the four sayles, and the post stand
in stedfastnesse. With ryght and with myght, with skyl and with
wylle, lat myghte helpe right, and skyl go before wille and ryght
before myght, than goth our mylne aryght. And if myght go be-
fore ryght, and wylle before skylle; then is our mylne mysad-
yght.[11]

The meaning of Ball's work in *Piers Plowman* style is not en-
tirely clear, but it evidently calls the lower orders to arms and
unity and promises that the mill of revolt will grind the nation
fine. While leading the revolt, Ball developed an ideological al-
ternative to conventional three-estate thought that, instead of
regarding social hierarchy and authority as a providential re-
straint placed on man's froward will by the actions of Canaan,
Noah, and Nimrod (cf. *FA*, 58; 1, 765), treated it as without
providential content—the unique product of the particularly
evil men who emerged after the Fall.[12] Though Augustine had
explained that an evil Nimrod had founded a lordship allowed
by God to protect mankind from chaos, Ball's exegesis denied
this and promised a new "Eden" or golden age with the aboli-
tion of serfdom. Most magnates and ecclesiastical lords were to
be abolished and, in their place, was to go a three-order society
composed of one king, a Church without hierarchy save one
archbishop, and a freed commons. The man of law's office,
lawyers, and judges were to be abolished and new laws were to
be written. Urban monopolies were to be destroyed, and land

[11] *Chronicon Henrici Knighton*, ed. J. R. Lumby (London: Rolls Series, 1895),
2:138, hereinafter Knighton. John Ball knew only the A-version of *Piers Plow-
man* for which see David Fowler's review of Vincent DiMarco's *Piers Plowman:
A Reference Guide*, in *Analytical and Enumerative Bibliography* 7 (1983):131–55,
esp. 149–50.
[12] *Hist. Ang.*, 2:32–33.

reform enacted.[13] When Froissart rendered John Ball's sermon, he portrayed it as advocating a return to a primal communism probably based on the Golden Age, a primal communism that Chaucer presents as permanently lost to human selfishness and greed in his "Former Age."[14]

Ball's Kentish revolt, as well as revolts in the Oxford and Cambridge areas, in Norfolk, and in many other parts of England, lasted long and included many social groups and vocations—peasants, carpenters, armorers, chaplains, tailors, lawyers, sacristans, clerks, weavers, bakers, limeburners, cooks, and others.[15] The formal charges of causing insurrection extend from April 17 to August 5, almost four months.[16] A minor insurrection occurred in September of the same year,[17] another in 1388 to get Burley tried more quickly, and another in 1390.[18] The Jack Cade revolt of 1450 also took place in Kent. Chaucer was appointed Justice of the Peace for Kent when it was frightened by the 1385–86 talk of a French invasion and when many of its unpaid soldiers, stationed to resist an invasion, pillaged the countryside to survive.[19] Revolt again seemed possible, and it is clear that Chaucer served in office with people who had

[13] Rodney Hilton, *Bond Men Made Free* (London: Temple Smith, 1973), pp. 222–30.

[14] Froissart, *Chroniques*, 9:388–89.

[15] W. E. Flaherty, "The Great Rebellion in Kent of 1381 Illustrated from the Public Records," *Archaeologia Cantiana* 3 (1860):65–96.

[16] W. E. Flaherty, "The Great Rebellion in Kent," pp. 65–96.

[17] W. E. Flaherty, "Sequel to the Great Rebellion in Kent of 1381," *Archaeologica Cantiana* 4 (1861):75–6.

[18] Thomas Favent, *Historia siue Narracio de Modo et Forma Mirabilis Parlimenti*, ed. May McKisack (London: Camden Society, 3rd series, 1926), 37:21; *Polychronicon Ranulphi Higden*, 1381–94, ed. J. R. Lumby (London: Rolls Series, 1886), 9:220, hereinafter Higden; *Hist. Ang.* 2:196.

[19] *Calendar of Close Rolls, 1385–89* (London: Keeper of the Records, 1892–1963), pp. 187, 193–94; Knighton, 2:212–13; *Hist. Ang.* 2:145–46; for other possible sources of English unrest, see Froissart, *Chroniques*, 11:368–71.

gained experience in the post-1381 trials and commissions which examined the Peasants' Revolt. At the time of his 1386 appointment, the royal government also added to the panel Sir Robert Tresilian, England's most experienced jurist and organizer of the courts that dealt with the 1381-uprising, and gave to Sir Simon Burley, the constable of Dover organizing the Kentish defense against the autumn French invasion, a one-vote quorum if he chose to assert it.[20] Clearly England needed a peace not only because its military efforts were unsuccessful but because preoccupation with the war and the cost of the war were creating internal discontent. The royal government trusted Chaucer to be part of the peace effort in Kent.

The problems of the period were answered by literary-diplomatic solutions developed by the Order of the Passion of Jesus Christ which led the French-English negotiations from the late 1380s until 1396 and made an unusually comprehensive analysis of the interrelationships among Europe's problems. That is, Philippe de Mézières, soldier under Peter of Lusignan, tutor to Charles VI of France, and a Celestine monastic during

[20] Bertha H. Putnam, *Proceedings Before the Justices of the Peace in the Fourteenth and Fifteenth Centuries* (London: Spottiswoode Ballantyne & Co., 1938), p. xlix. For additional documents concerning the royal effort to punish the Kentish insurgents and pacify the countryside, see André Réville, *Le Soulèvement des Travailleurs d'Angleterre en 1381* (Paris: 1898), pp. 235-40; W. E. Flaherty, "The Great Rebellion in Kent," pp. 69-70; *C.P.R., 1381-85*, pp. 71-77; W. E. Flaherty, "Sequel to the Great Rebellion in Kent of 1381," p. 72. The memberships of the special royal commissions and of the Commissions of Peace in the period overlap. For the membership of the Kent Commissions of Peace in Richard's reign, see *C.P.R., 1377-81*, p. 44; *C.P.R., 1381-85*, pp. 253, 346, 503; *C.P.R., 1385-89*, pp. 81, 84 (Chaucer's first appearance), 253; *C.P.R., 1388-92*, pp. 137, 341; *C.P.R., 1381-96*, pp. 435, 728; *C.P.R., 1396-99*, pp. 228, 237, 437. Throughout the period the same names (e.g., Rikhill, Culpeper, Fogge) appear over and over; Chaucer was not the fixture on the J. P. Commissions which the Kentish squirearchy were. For Burley's one vote "quorum," see *LR*, pp. 351-54.

the period in question, created voluminous works, notably the *Songe du Vieil Pèlerin*, the *Epistre au Roi Richard II*, and the *Ordo* for the Order of the Passion, setting forth his analysis of the crisis for European civilization. In these treatises Philippe commonly bases his analysis on the notion that Western civilization has been overcome by the three temptations to pride, luxury, and avarice, and these have led Christendom to succumb to such other faults as the split in the papacy, the crusades of Christian against Christian, England's war against France, and Europe's failure to meet the Turkish threat in the Balkans, and hold the Christian eastern Mediterranean strongholds.[21] Further, the military crisis has led to a decline of sense of function in society, to a decline of estate order, and to a general spread of unruliness–what modern sociology would call anomie.[22] In the *Songe du Vieil Pèlerin*, Philippe scrutinizes each country in Europe, anatomizing its faults. For example, England, which has raped France in the French wars, has placed itself under Richard's uncles who do not want peace and under prelates who fight wars, while France, because of the war, has become impoverished and disorganized in each of its estates.[23] To rectify these faults, Philippe proclaims that Divine Providence has shown him the Order of the Passion of Jesus Christ to begin the fight against the three temptations with a new chivalric vow of perfection requiring humility (obedience to the commander of the Order) to combat pride, poverty (refusal of war booty) to overcome avarice, and married chastity to resist luxury.[24] By

[21] Brown, *Mézières' Order*, pp. 95–100; Philippe de Mézières, *Songe du Vieil Pèlerin*, 1:243–47, 307–14, 392; Philippe de Mézières, *Letter to King Richard II*, ed. G. W. Coopland (Liverpool: Liverpool University Press, 1975), p. 79, lists pride, avarice and envy, and love of transitory and temporal possessions as the equivalent for pride, avarice, and luxury.

[22] Brown, *Mézières' Order*, pp. 12–14, 95–98, 123–27, 158–59, and *passim*. Philippe's *Songe* and *Letter* make the same point.

[23] Philippe de Mézières, *Songe du Vieil Pèlerin*, 1:394–402, 442–636; 2:420–21.

[24] Brown, *Mézières' Order*, pp. 98–100, 107, 177.

[58]

married chastity Philippe means fidelity in marriage, not the abstinence that was the vow of the older crusading orders (Philippe somewhat whimsically observes that a vow of celibacy is unrealistic for knights going to the eastern Mediterranean where the warm climate stimulates hot-bloodedness).

Philippe posits that, after this moral change, the two kings can arrange a peace-marriage between England and France and a reunification of the papacy which their war had split. Further, once Europe orders itself internally, it can crusade under the leadership of the two young kings against the Turk and recover the eastern Mediterranean and the holy places. The joint crusade is to be modeled on the crusades of Peter of Lusignan who triumphed at Alexandria, Lyeys, Satalye, and the other Mediterranean battles in which Chaucer's Knight has fought. Peter was important to Philippe's rhetorical posture because his career supposedly illustrated Christendom's capacity to resist Islamic forces in a period when few victories came to the West. Finally, to remedy the decline of hierarchic order in European civilization, Philippe proposes that a model four-estate society be formed in the eastern Mediterranean according to which European society can reform itself. All of this is argued with elaborate literary allegories, similitudes, and spiritual journeys, devices that must have had some persuasive effect since Philippe achieved a following that included not only Chaucer's friends, Odo of Graunson and Sir Lewis Clifford, but also the kings of England and France, the chief peers of both realms, Giangaleazzo Visconti of Milan, and the Marshal Boucicaut of France. The success of his argument led to the 1396 marriage truce and in the same year, the Nicopolis Crusade against the Turk.[25]

Whereas Philippe is a French courtier and monastic, rhetorical and grandiose, full of a sense of the *gloire* of his vision,

[25] Ibid., pp. 259–67. Palmer's *England, France and Christendom* shows to what extent the Order received the support of the two kings during the early and mid-1390s and the events leading up to Nicopolis.

:er is a quick-witted, bawdy Englishman who tempers the
__ur of his vision with its potential comedy. Such differ-
ences in style do not prevent these two court figures from de-
veloping many of the same ideas. In the Group A *Canterbury
Tales* Chaucer takes up nearly all of Philippe's themes, perhaps
to encourage the Chamber knights and others carrying out Phi-
lippe's work and to persuade others at court to attempt it. Per-
fection appears in Chaucer's perfect Knight (A, 72) and in the
chaste marriage and piety of Theseus and his humble accept-
ance of advice. The conclusion uniting Athens and Thebes cel-
ebrates the sought-for marriage-peace; the Knight's battles un-
der Peter of Lusignan look forward to a Turkish crusade. The
estate order that Theseus establishes in his realm after finding
Palamon and Arcita's forest "rebellion" shows how order is to
be won in England, and Theseus' ordering execution first, and
then mercy, for the Theban knights who serve Venus and Mars
shows how the royal government ought to establish order when
concupiscent Millers and irascible Reeves raven on the rural es-
tates. (It also reflects, perhaps accidentally, the strategy used by
Richard's government to establish order after the Peasants' Re-
volt.)[26] The same root problems that Philippe finds to be im-
portant—the overwhelming power of the three temptations to
disorder society—dominate the Miller's and the Reeve's tales
and the actions of these two pilgrims on the demesne. But
whereas Philippe uses rather simple, extended dream allegories
to carry most of his statement, Chaucer used the Knight's com-
plex epic and the Miller's and the Reeve's comedies mocking it
to define chivalric obligation.

Chaucer also occasionally deviates from Philippe in sub-
stance. Though Richard was not the fool Whig historians have

---

[26] The Crown first proposed severe punishment for the rebels and did punish
the leaders severely but later granted mercy to the common rebel; see chap. 5,
below.

made him out to be, he was, as chapter 3 will indicate, unu-
sually ready to assert his right to rule by personal prerogative
without advice from parliament or the magnates, and he ex-
pected his lawyers to defend his rights and his trappings of
power. His failure to consult with parliament over the 1387
French negotiations created internal suspicions that did not
help his effort to bring about a peace, and Chaucer seems, how-
ever subtly, to emphasize the royal government's need for con-
sultation and attention to natural law. While Philippe describes
his monarchs, Richard and Charles, as sacral kings illumined
by God and His Divine Providence and pays little attention to
natural-law limitations on the monarch,[27] Chaucer presents
Theseus as much greater and more powerful than the *Parle-
ment*'s royal eagle, but still a natural-law monarch, bound by
the cycles of nature, deferential to his parliament and baronage
(A, 2970, 3096), and limited by his subjects' wills in marriage
matters (A, 3070ff.). Again, while the Order conceptualized an
orderly hierarchy of estates to be established in the eastern
Mediterranean which would constitute a model for European
reform, Chaucer takes the more practical direct approach of
"Reform now; reform within." He simultaneously undercuts
the dreams of absolutists around Richard who claimed unilat-
eral power for the king and the utopian dreams of reformers like
Philippe who posited that an ideal *res publica* created somewhere
else would remake Europe.

   To make his fundamental statement in his tale of knighthood,
Chaucer chooses a modifed version of the epic plot of the *Teseida*
and juxtaposes against it the two comedy or fabliau plots of the
Miller's and the Reeve's tales which "rebel" against its symme-
tries and sublimities.[28] Clearly the Knight's Tale is an epic or

---

[27] Philippe de Mézières (*Letter to Richard II*) ignores natural law and eliminates
any reference to restraint of Richard by parliament or council.
[28] Stephen Knight ("Chaucer and the Sociology of Literature," p. 33) ob-
serves that "the Miller retells the knight's plot in a different social location and

heroic song, as Dryden and Pope and a few modern critics have recognized. Even the Miller "recognizes" as much when he says that, in telling his tale, he will "quit" what the Knight has told—"By armes, and by blood and bones, / I kan a noble tale . . ." (A, 3125–26); "*Arma* blood-boneque cano"—while parodying Virgil and claiming epic grandeur for Carpenter John's broken bones. Here Chaucer gives the first hint of his classicizing program in the *Tales*, a hint based on Dante's remark that the high style is appropriate to tale of arms and on Boccaccio's assertion, after Dante, that his epic *Teseida* constitutes the first of the vernacular poems to deal with arms.[29]

Paul Strohm has argued that an untidy Chaucer never uses Cicero's three categories of *historia, fabula*, and *argumentum* for true, fantastic, and *true-seeming* stories. But the poet, in fact, uses precisely these three terms to define his classical generic program, and he uses them correctly.[30] He uses the term *storie*, derived from the Italian *istoria* or the French *estoire*, when speaking of events that happened, including the lives of the saints thought in the poet's time to be histories (A, 859; A, 3110–11; B¹, 1124; B², 1653, 3156–64; G, 78–84). He also uses it in referring to Theseus' history (A, 859). Theseus appears in the *Polychronicron* and other contemporary histories as the founder of knighthood,[31] the first philosopher-king, the founder of parlia-

episteme." For Chaucer's use of the *Teseida* and epic tradition, see John Kevin Newman, *The Classical Epic Tradition* (Madison: University of Wisconsin Press, 1986), pp. 340–71.

29 Olson, "Chaucer's Epic Statement," pp. 61–65. Bernard F. Huppé argues that the Knight's Tale is a comedy (*A Reading of the Canterbury Tales* [Albany: SUNY Press, 1964], p. 54), but it is perhaps better seen as a comic epic, leading to a heroic marriage but created without comedy's grotesques.

30 Paul Strohm, "Some Generic Distinctions in the *Canterbury Tales*," *MP* 68 (1971):321–22; contrast Olson, "Chaucer's Epic Statement," p. 65 and p. 81, n. 14.

31 Higden, 2:381–95. Giovanni Boccaccio, *De Casibus Illustrium Virorum* (Augsburg, 1544), pp. 15–16; Laurence of Premierfait, "Les Cas des Nobles

ments, a fighter who overcame the Minotaur, a butcher and wrestler. In Cicero, history contrasts with fable, which did not happen or even appear to be true; thus, the Physician says that his narrative taken from Livy's history is "no fable, / But knowen for historial thyng notable" (C, 155–56), and the Parson refers to fables, which are old wives' tales, untrue at all levels, whereas the Nun's Priest tells a beast-fable as if it were a history of the olden days when animals could talk (B², 4070–71) and includes the usual invitation at the end to see beneath the surface of the "folye," to find the corn beneath the chaff.³²

As to *argumentum*, the Cook, at the end of the Reeve's Tale, identifies its fictive mode as the Miller has the Knight's at the end of that tale. He calls the Reeve's work an "argument of herbergage" (A, 4329) that has a "sharp conclusion" (A, 4328) for

---

Hommes et Femmes," B.N. Fr. 226, fol. 17ᵛ; John Lydgate, *The Fall of Princes*, ed. Henry Bergen (Washington: Carnegie Inst., 1923), bk. 1, lines 4390ff.

³² For the Parson's distinction and the Wife of Bath, see chap. 9 and 10 below; Strohm ("Some Generic Distinctions," pp 325–26) wishes to deny the specific significance of the Parson's reference to 1 Timothy 4.7. But the Parson's "Fables and . . . wrecchednesse" from Timothy "weyven soothfastnesse" (I, 30–36) whereas the Nun's Priest assures us that his tale is not a "folye" (i.e., not foolishness or dissipation) but has a "moralite" (B², 4628–30) or truth in it. Actually he gives three complementary moralizations (B², 4616–22, 4623–25, and 4626–27); see D. E. Myers, "Focus and 'Moralite' in the *Nun's Priest's Tale*," *CR* 7 (1973):210–19. Chaucer's language is completely conventional for describing the allegorical understanding of Scripture or of fables; e.g., "Take of thys Psalme the moralyte" [Lydgate, *Minor Poems*, p. 90]; though "feinyeit fabils of ald poetre / Be not al grunded upon truth," yet the "nuttes schell" holds the "kirnill" (*The Poems and Fables of Robert Henryson*, ed. H. Harvey Wood [London: Oliver and Boyd, 1933], p. 3); an early fifteenth-century version of Fulgentius' mythology remarks that Fulgentius, "sub tegmine fabularum," describes the beauty of virtue and the deformity of vice and that unless fables are used to encourage moral action, theologians ought not to use them but "sicut vanos et frivolas devitare" (Fulgentius, *Mythologiarum* in Bod. Western MS. 2684, fol. 35ʳ). If Chaucer's aesthetic of the fable is unconventional, he certainly did not signal that in B², 4628–36. Cf. Minnis, *Medieval Theory of Authorship*, pp. 206–7.

the miller. Presumably this is the bang on the head which com-
pletes his plot. Since the tale includes no "verbal disputation"—
the other common meaning of argument—Chaucer, through
the Cook, must be identifying the work as an *argumentum* or
verisimilitudinous story, which would also make it, by defini-
tion, a comedy, the only genre commonly associated with the
argument plot.[33]

Beginning with the standard medieval interpretation of work
in the classical genres, scholarship can use these plot labels as
semantic controls indicating levels of reading required to con-
trol both over- and under-allegorization. Histories, including
the main plots of tragedies and epics, were commonly inter-
preted as exempla, as were arguments used in comedy, but
those fables which were not old wives' superstitions were seen
as allegories, a fact that the Nun's Priest takes considerable care
to reveal.[34] A heroic poem such as the *Aeneid* or *Thebiad* was, in
Chaucer's time, thought to use a mixed fiction composed of the
exemplary history of the hero and a group of allegorical fables
set in the fantastic loci of the hero's trip and in the councils of

[33] For *argumentum*, see *Ad. C. Herennium*, 1.8.13; Giovanni of Genoa, "Ca-
tholicon," B.M. MS. Stowe 981, fol. 72ᵛ; Franceshini, "Il Commento di Giaco-
mino da Mantova," p. 165; Giovanni Boccaccio, *On Poetry*, trans. C. G. Osgood
(New York: Bobbs-Merrill, The Library of Liberal Arts, 1956), pp. 49, 165.
Argument always describes comedy. See Allen, *The Ethical Poetic of the Later
Middle Ages*, pp. 21–22.

[34] Olson, "Chaucer's Epic Statement," pp. 63–65. This point is made abun-
dantly clear in Boccaccio's *On Poetry* in its treatment of history, argument, and
fable and in almost every interpretive effort attached to comedy, epic, and fable
by medieval critics. Cf. A. J. Minnis, *Chaucer and Pagan Antiquity* (Totowa,
N.J.: Rowan and Littlefield, 1982), pp. 7–30. Unfortunately, Minnis does not
recognize the genre of the Knight's Tale or its character as a mixed fiction con-
taining fable elements and their standard allegory pertaining to the passions.
The figurative content of this planet-passions fable Saturn explains directly in
A, 2453–78, ignored by Minnis, pp. 15–22. Cf. Allen, *The Ethical Poetic of the
Later Middle Ages*, pp. 76–77.

gods (who could stand either for the influence of the planets or for the human passions that they appeared to direct). The Knight's history of Theseus—the founder of knighthood and the originator of parliamentary and philosophic government— reveals its full meaning in the conversations of planetary gods and in the rich iconology of their temples, in the actions of minion furies (A, 2684–85) and bleeding trees (A, 2334–40), and in the phantasmagoria of the epic funeral that decorates the culmination of the historical plot (A, 2913ff.). These fable elements comment on the Theban lovers generally in an ironic-comic vein, and on Theseus in a more heroic one, making Chaucer's epic a serious critique on English policy to create peace within and abroad.

To make his statement about how peace is to be won, the Knight adapts the *Teseida*'s tale of reconciliation and makes Palamon and Arcita, representing the concupiscent and irascible passions, more explicitly comic and Theseus a more distant Ricardian figure.[35] The lovers' philosophic maundering undercuts them as they veer, Arcita first toward Saturnian determinism (A, 1081ff.) and then toward mouse-drunk "free-willism" (A, 1235ff.), Palamon first toward yearning love and then toward envying the beasts their lack of soul and afterlife (A, 1313ff.). The lovers see their whole future unfolded in the oracular temples at which they pray and yet fail to read a single oracular sign aright; they fight over a woman ignorant of their existence, bringing Theban disorder to the Athenian realm by fighting ankle-deep in blood while thinking to hide their fright from the very Theseus whose pillaging soldiers have earlier found them buried in a pile of bodies, half dead. Destiny, using the ancient epic's miraculous hunt, brings Theseus to the clearing as the lovers begin to fight, thereby stopping the rebellion at its

[35] Robertson, *A Preface to Chaucer*, pp. 466–68; Engelhardt, "The Lay Pilgrims," pp. 293–301.

start.[36] Chaucer makes his lovers also rebels, rebels against natural law in fighting for a Theban tyrant and rebels against Theseus in fighting in the woods without judge or officer.

And while the poet makes his lovers and warriors more ridiculous than Boccaccio does, he also heightens the dignity of Theseus as the judge and leader who controls them, making him more tapestry-like and hieratic in effect than Boccaccio's muscular figure. Chaucer may hint at Richard in making Theseus appear like a "god in trone" before the tourney (A, 2529; cf. fig. 8) and having him prefer temporal rulership's judicial to its warring functions when he turns the epic's battles into its games. Richard was not particularly effective as a warrior nor was he fond of tourneys. Though Theseus forbids useless and comic tournament weapons—the "shot . . . polax . . . short knyf . . . [and] short swerd" (A, 2537–60)—in the interest of preventing "mortal bataille," he clearly does not relish loss of life in tournaments, and no life is lost in the contest.

However, if Theseus' surface gestures sometimes present details that flatter Richard's peculiarities as a monarch, other aspects of his rule reflect a more consultative, conciliatory conception of the royal prerogative than Richard commonly exhibited. In pursuit of chivalric perfection, Theseus serves Diana (A, 1682), gives generously of himself, and is as humble as Dante's Trajan (*Purg.* x.7off.). He, like Trajan but unlike Boccaccio's Theseus, gets off his horse to comfort poor widows (A, 952). He listens to the plea of his wife and sister-in-law and forgives the Theban warriors in the forest as Richard, in Richard of Maidstone's account of a 1392 pageant, listened to the formal pleas of Anne of Bohemia as *mediatrix* and forgave the City of London. But Theseus, unlike the Richard of 1387–88,

---

[36] See A, 1681; since the hart is not in Boccaccio, it probably is modeled after the deer that appear to be providentially sent by Destiny to assist Aeneas in book 1; cf. *Aeneid*, 1.198ff.

does not try to arrange a peace after a long war without bringing parliament and the baronage into the process (A, 2970, 3076, 3096). If Richard said that the King wears the law in his own breast, Theseus clearly knows that the monarch and his society are subordinate to the law of nature which takes its beginning from the First Mover who "parfit is and stable" (A, 3009).

Theseus' perfective discipline leads him to completion in the perfect God who is the author of nature, not of revelation. This discipline affords the leader divine help so that he appears to know some of the future. He builds temples that contain murals of Julius Caesar, Anthony, Nero, Turnus, and Croesus, who lie in time ahead, comes by special providence in the form of a hart to the grove where the Thebans fight, and trusts the outcome of his tournament to the court of providence, God's "pryvetee," as the Miller calls it (A, 3163). But his insight, like that of Boethius' God, does not "cause" his subjects to act, any more than St. John's vision causes history to occur, as his open-handed gesture in the Angers tapestry makes clear (fig. 7). When his last scene comes, Theseus does not argue from oracles or special royal God-like insight but from Theban-Athenian history and from his knowledge of "the immutable order and regular motion of the heavens" whose meaning for human culture was thought to be available to sapient kings.[37] His knowledge in this last scene is accurate.

Charles Muscatine and subsequent Chaucer scholars have demonstrated how the whole of the Knight's Tale balances on

---

[37] Duby, *The Three Orders*, p. 45. Theseus, being a pagan ruler, has not been anointed with holy oil. The Knight in the *Songe de Vergier* (1:75–78) argues that just pagan rulers are legitimate and, therefore, temporal rulers generally do not require clerical legitimization. On the other hand, Dante—in describing Theseus's mercy and kindness, and Statius's conversion before writing about Theseus—implies that Statius anticipates aspects of Christian rulership in his portrait of the Athenian ruler. Cf. Allen, *The Ethical Poetic of the Later Middle Ages*, pp. 260–62.

a certain symmetrical order of contrasts: ruler-tyrant, mar-
riage-death, garden-prison, exile-prison, tournament-duel.[38]
Theseus uses these contrasting circumstances to make rational,
judicial determinations and properly to allot rewards and pun-
ishments to Creon, Palamon, Arcita, Hypolita, and Emelye.
Theseus' justice not only allocates due rewards and punish-
ments but makes his subjects better people.

This ordering and perfecting sense comes to focus in his final
speech, which places human culture and law within the cycles
of nature, and the lives of Arcita and Palamon and Emelye un-
der the demands of a culture fitted to nature (A, 3007ff.). Fol-
lowing the pattern of Chaucer's dream of Nature's court in the
Parlement, Theseus' speech begins with a presentation of a nat-
ural law moved by the First Mover or "Juppiter, the kyng" (A,
3035) who is above nature and binds fire, air, earth, and water
through a fair chain of love, like that of Nature in the *Parlement*
which knits together, hot, cold, heavy, light, moist, and dry
"by evene noumbres of acord" (*PF*, 381). The music and har-
mony of divine number and divine love puts all things save hu-
mankind in their places. As Nature in the *Parlement* establishes
the engenderings of things, so here Theseus' First Mover and
King establishes through nature's law (A, 3005ff.) the "speces of
thynges" (A, 3013) and their successions: He has set life and
death for Arcita, but His Necessity allows free choice. Theseus
sees that Arcita *chose* to die well. Indeed, the Knight makes him

[38] Muscatine, "Form, Texture, and Meaning," pp. 911–29; for an extension
of Muscatine's argument with which I disagree, see David Aers, *Chaucer, Lang-
land and the Creative Imagination* (London: Routledge and Kegan Paul, 1980), pp.
174–95. Aers' nineteenth-century view fails to place Theseus against Kanto-
rowicz's account of medieval theories of kingship or natural law; it reads the
Knight's remarks about Arcita's death (A, 2765–2815) apart from Ariès' account
of dying in the Middle Ages, and sees Theseus' promotion of a Theban-Athe-
nian marriage as "imperialism" though ultimately a Theban-Athenian house
will rule over Athens and a subinfeudated Thebes. Cf. Philippe de Mézières'
marriage proposal in his *Letter to Richard II*, pp. 7–10, 21–24, 33–42, less an im-
perialistic gesture than an effort to end an endless war.

do so by having him follow Aries' four-step process for a proper death—recognizing his faults, forgiving his enemies, reconciling them to his friends, and committing his soul to the mercy of the hereafter (A, 2808).[39] Arcita has made death's necessity his personal power or virtue by seizing on it as an opportunity to forego Mars and the fury that has killed him. Now, in Theseus' view, Palamon and Emelye should recognize that like power will come to them from making their Venerian and Cynthian "necessity" into a "virtue" through which they can enhance civic order and carry on nature's cycles. They must act where they have freedom to act—Palamon by transforming his Venus into a *marriage* and Emelye by transforming her Diana into a *chaste* marriage. As a member of Nature's court looking at the stars that influence his subjects and the cycles of all things that condition human culture, and mediating what he sees to the Athenians and Thebans, Theseus acts as the *Rex Imago Christi* who makes the natural law of desire into positive law to benefit the community. He speaks in the voice of the Crown which, by medieval jurisprudential fiction, has known necessity through eons of time.[40] With such knowledge, what forgiveness can there be for Theban lovers wading up to their ankles in blood over an Athenian princess who has not seen them? Yet, forgiveness based on a sense of comedy (A, 1785ff., A, 3093ff.) appears in the monarch. He is secure. Eternal law, manifest to him as natural law when he sits in council or parliament, permits him to reconstruct the externals of Edenic peace and joy for Emelye and Palamon, Athens and Thebes.

---

[39] Theseus' description of natural law and its relationship to divinity and kingship follows closely the *Parlement's*; for the stages in Arcita's death, cf. Philippe Ariès, *Western Attitudes Toward Death*, trans. Patricia M. Ranum (Baltimore: Johns Hopkins University Press, 1974), pp. 7ff., and *The Hour of Our Death* (New York: Knopf, 1981), pp. 14–19. Michael Boccia has an article in preparation on this topic.

[40] See Ernst H. Kantorowicz, *The King's Two Bodies* (Princeton: Princeton University Press, 1957), pp. 273–90.

CHAPTER 2

Within the fiction of the *Canterbury Tales*, the Knight tells his story to celebrate civic order and instruct those who do not understand it. Proper estate subjects for his instruction raise their voices in the form of the Miller and the Reeve, village followers respectively of Venus and Mars. Both apparently have the rule and the run of their estates and, in the pilgrimage, act out the woodland conflict of Palamon and Arcita to tell us how, in Chaucer's view, peasants unaccustomed to rule would rule themselves. Both emblemize the power of the three temptations with their arrogance, incontinence, and theft, and their tales tell of the same three: pride, luxury, and avarice in the Miller's Absolon, Nicholas, and John, respectively, and then again in Simkin's wife (A, 3950ff.), the Reeve's clerks, and Simkin himself.[41] Pride, luxury, and avarice overwhelm the worlds of the Miller's and the Reeve's manors and the Oxford-Cambridge "village" worlds of their tales as Philippe de Mézières had said they were, because of bad government, overwhelming most of Europe. In these tales, no Theseus comes to stop the fights and create justice; yet the tales have a kind of comic retributive or-

[41] For the Miller's Tale, see Olson, "Poetic Justice in the Miller's Tale," pp. 227–36; Simkin's wife is comically "proud" (A, 3950) and alert to her own "gentility" (A, 3965), the clerks are obviously luxurious, and Miller Simkin's avarice appears in his outrageous theft (A, 3995) and jealousy toward his wife (A, 3961), a passion commonly seen to be an aspect of avarice; for jealousy, see Paul A. Olson, "Chaucer's Merchant and January's 'Hevene in Erthe Heere,' " p. 206, n. 4. For the three temptation patterns, see Paul A. Olson, "Vaughan's *The World*: The Pattern of Meaning and the Tradition," *CL* 13 (1961):26–32. Kolve disputes this interpretation, but to do so, he has to ignore the sinister aspects of the Miller, the Biblical, hagiographic, and exegetical subtexts underlying Nicholas and John and their illustrative tradition (cf. figs. 10–23). Kolve denies the plain meaning of lines A, 3224–26, which say that John was jealous and feared that he might become a cuckold; V. A. Kolve, *Chaucer and the Imagery of Narrative* (Stanford: Stanford University Press, 1984), pp. 188–89 and notes on 440. Kolve does not reckon with John's invincible stupidity in trusting Nicholas or with Nicholas's need to get both John and the servants out of the way.

der that contrasts with the transformative order of the Knight's tale. Aristotle recognized that the *Odyssey*, with its conclusion restoring the marriage of Odysseus and Penelope, is a kind of comedy. If the *Knight's Tale* presents a marriage as the center-piece of its comic epic culmination, the Reeve's and the Miller's tales offer us the grotesques that usually surround comedy's courtship and marriage.

When the Cook identifies the Reeve's Tale as an *argumentum*, he also implicitly identifies it as a comedy, as I have mentioned. Not only is comedy the only recognized genre using the argu-ment plot, but in *Troilus and Criseyde*, Chaucer expresses the hope to write "som comedye" (bk. 5, line 1788) in the future. And Lydgate recognized that Chaucer wrote "fresh comedies,"[42] almost certainly, since he uses the plural, what we would call the "fabliaux." Calling these tales "comedies" may offend some scholars, but labeling them so denigrates none of the extensive, useful research on the fabliau. Chaucer's comedies obviously derive from the French fabliaux, but they also derive from, and are close relatives of, the more elaborate, twelfth-century Latin school comedies, written in the Orleanais region;[43] both the

[42] Lydgate, *The Fall of Princes*, bk. 1, line 246.

[43] For useful analyses of Chaucer's relationship to the fabliau tradition, see Charles Muscatine, *Chaucer and the French Tradition: A Study in Style and Meaning* (Berkeley: California University Press, 1957), pp. 58–69, 212–13; Thomas D. Cooke, *The Old French and Chaucerian Fabliaux: A Study of their Comic Climax* (Columbia: Missouri University Press, 1978). For useful general background, Per Nykrog, *Les Fabliaux* (Copenhagen: Munksgaard, 1957).

The fabliaux arise simultaneous with or after the twelfth-century Latin school comedies; see Gustave Cohen, *La "Comédie" latine en France au XIIᵉ siècle*, 2 vols. (Paris: Société d'édition "Les Belles Lettres," 1931). Peter Dronke, in relating the fabliau to Cambridge eleventh-century lyrics, a fabliau feeling, and "courtly love," ignores the fact that most of the archetypal fabliau situations are found in Roman comedy or Ovid's love poems, which were regarded as com-edy; Peter Dronke, "The Rise of the Medieval Fabliau: Latin and Vernacular Evidence," *Romanische Forschungen* 85 (1973):275–97. Jürgen Beyer has endeav-

Latin and French versions of the genre were being read in Chaucer's time.[44]

Chaucer's use of the term "argument" to describe his Reeve's plot places what we now call the fabliau in the tradition of classical comedy, as does his assignment of the Miller's Tale to a

---

ored to show that the fabliaux are a genre separate from the comedies because the "cunning woman" of the fabliau is unknown in elegaic comedy and is replaced by the cunning servant and because twelfth-century elegaic comedy uses school rhetoric, dialect, and so forth; Jürgen Beyer, "The Morality of the Amoral," *The Humor of the Fabliaux*, ed. Thomas D. Cooke and Benjamin L. Honeycutt (Columbia: Missouri University Press, 1974), pp. 24–25. However, for the view that the comedies and fabliaux have a close relationship, see Edmond Faral, "Le Fabliau Latin au Moyen Age," *Romania* 50 (1924):321–85; Larry D. Benson and Theodore M. Andersson, *The Literary Context of Chaucer's Fabliaux* (New York: Bobbs-Merrill, 1971), pp. 206–7; Cooke, *Old French and Chaucerian Fabliaux*, pp. 78–79. For rather standard fabliaux plots in twelfth-century comedy, see in the Cohen edition, the *Miles Gloriosus* (1:195ff.), *De Mercatore* (2:270–73), *Lidia* (1:225ff.), and *De Babione*, ed. Edmond Faral (Paris: Champion, 1948). Similar fabliaux include *De la Borgoise d'Orliens* in Anatole de Montaiglon and Gaston Raynaud, *Recueil Général et Complet des Fabliaux* (Paris: 1872–90), 1:117ff., hereinafter Montaiglon and Raynaud; cf. *Le Cuvier* (Montaiglon and Raynaud, 1:126ff.), and Thibaut's *Romanz de la Poire*, ed. Friedrich Stehlich (Halle, 1881).

Glending Olson, in "The Medieval Theory of Literature for Refreshment and its Use in the Fabliau Tradition," *SP* 71 (1974):291–313, shows that some fabliaux claim to entertain and little more; e.g., Laurence of Premierfait introduces his translation of the *Decameron* with the notion that the stories have a function of *solace* in a gloomy world bothered by plague; "Prologo di Lorenzo di Premierfait alla sua versione del *Decameron*," in *Studi sulle opere latine del Boccaccio*, ed. A. Hortis (Trieste, 1879), pp. 744–45. Obviously medieval people loved entertainment, but entertainment is not the only point of Chaucer's comedies as it is not the only point of classical comedy or of twelfth-century Latin comedy. Lydgate's attributing comedies to Chaucer, Chaucer's use of the comic character types, his use of the "argument" label from comic criticism, and other framing and internal features place his works in the tradition of instructive comedy more than the tradition of fabliau-as-pure-entertainment. They are obviously also jolly good fun.

[44] Gower retells the Babio story in "Confessio Amantis," 5:4781–4857; *The*

THE ORDER OF THE PASSION

"goliardeys," the standard mimer of classical comedy. His as-
signment of both stories to vulgar village harvest characters, the
putative originators of the comic genre in medieval criticism,
means that these tales do not belong to the aristocratic courts to
which Nykrog ascribes the medieval fabliaux, but to the vil-
lages of criticism.[45] No medieval definition of comedy requires
that it be acted, and the illuminations show it being read and
mimed (fig. 9). In the Renaissance, which had sharper eyes for
the comic genre than we do, Sir Francis Beaumont recognized

Complete Works of John Gower, ed. G. C. Macaulay (Oxford: Oxford University
Press, 1901); cf. Frank T. Cabral, The Prohemia Poetarum of Thomas of Wal-
singham and the Accessus ad Auctores Tradition (Lincoln: unpublished University
of Nebraska diss., 1974), p. 120. Both Gower and Walsingham interpret the
Babio moralistically.

   [45] Isidore of Seville, Etymologiarum, PL 82:658; Giovanni of Genoa, Catholi-
con (Mainz, 1460), no signatures visible, entry under comedia; St. Augustine, De
Civitate Dei, commentary by Nicholas Trivet and Thomas Walleys (Basil,
1489), sig. c[1ʳ]; Miroir Hystorial, trans. Jean de Vignai (n.p., 1495), 1:sig. bb3ʳ.
The harvest origin of comedy and its association with the village and villein in
the standard medieval comic criticism accounts for Chaucer's assignment of the
Miller's and the Reeve's tale to villeins; the assignment appropriately puzzles
Alfred David (Strumpet Muse, p. 116), given Nykrog's evidence that the fabliau
genre was an aristocratic one, but it should not, given the standard definition of
a comedy as a villanus cantus. Chaucer reflects here the expectations of art, not
life. That the Miller is a "goliardeys" (A, 560) relates to his "recitation" of a com-
edy, for Raoul de Presles argues that the bawdy theater of Roman comedy was
"la petite maison que estoit ou milieu ou ces choses estoient faites par les ien-
gleurs et gouliars qui contrefaisoient les personnages de ceulx de qui on iou-
voit"; Raoul de Presles, Cité de Dieu (Abbeville, 1486–87), 1:sig. B3ʳ. Chaucer
may have known Donatus on Terence directly (e.g., Nicholas de Clémanges,
who came to Chaucer's court, knew it) but more likely knew its concepts from
dictionary entries and glosses transmitted from earlier periods; see M. D. Reeve
and R. H. Rouse, "New Light on the Transmission of Donatus' Commentum
Terentii," Viator 9 (1978):235–49; for more general material on the medieval
Terence, see Paul Theiner, "The Medieval Terence," in The Learned and the
Lewed, ed. Larry D. Benson (Cambridge: Harvard University Press, 1974), pp.
231–48.

[73]

that Chaucer's characters included the standard comic types. In the Miller's and the Reeve's tales, one finds the *senex* (Carpenter John), the *juvens* (the clerks in the two tales), the *puella* (Alysoun and Malyne), the *matrona* (Simkin's wife), and the would-be village *miles gloriosus* (Simkin).[46] Comedy meant obscenity, which Chaucer defends by asserting that word must reflect deed (A, 742), exactly Augustine's defense,[47] but it was also insistently moralistic—each of its character types exposed common "village" flaws. Since the form can only be understood by those mature enough to understand the nature of the good, according to Oresme, the poet places his comedies after the Knight's picture of the good, has them parody it, and warns us against making "ernest of game" (A, 3186), turning the humorously grotesque into serious mischievous instruction, a charge sometimes laid at Ovid's door.[48] Finally, the best evidence that Chaucer's tales told by his villeins are comedies comes from their being more learned, more highly wrought, and more symmetrical in their poetic justice than anything in the vernacular fabliau tradition in France.[49] As the Roman and twelfth-cen-

[46] *The Works of our Antient and Lerned English Poet*, introduction by Sir Francis Beaumont, no sig. For the medieval conception of comic types, see Franceschini, "Il commento di Giacomino da Mantova," p. 165; cf. Mari, "Poetria," pp. 917–18; *Scholia Terentiana*, ed. Frederick Schlee (Leipzig, 1893), pp. 164–65.

[47] Augustine, *De Civitate Dei*, 21.8–9.

[48] Nicolas Oresme, *Le Livre de politiques de Aristote*, ed. Albert Douglas Menut (Philadelphia: American Philosophical Society, 1970), p. 338.

[49] J. I. Wimsatt ("Chaucer and French Poetry," *Geoffrey Chaucer*, ed. Derek Brewer [London: G. Bell, 1974], p. 111) observes that "Chaucer's style in his fabliaux is much richer than that which characterizes the French verse tales, and the stories themselves in the late fourteenth century were part of the common literary stock of Europe." Chaucer's richness of philosophy, pious subtexts, character types, and comic justice appear to derive from his sight of himself as writing comedies enriched in the way that the *Babio* and *Miles Gloriosus* and classical comedies are. Beryl Rowland ("What Chaucer Did to the Fabliau," *SN* 51 [1979]:205–13) emphasizes the development of the sense of vil-

tury comic writers draw constantly on classical myth to enrich and "philosophize" their ludicrous situations, so Chaucer draws on Biblical subtexts and epic parody to accomplish the same ends, as the Miller and the Reeve seek to displace the comic epic Knight's tale by imitating its loves and battles. The pilgrimage "Peasants' Revolt" comes about through generic and iconological attack.[50]

Robin the Miller, cousin to the revolt's "Jack the Miller" but seen through elite court eyes, insists on telling his drunken, rebellious tale in preference to some "bettre man" (A, 3130) in a three-order society—Bailey would like the Monk to speak (A, 3118). Robin will "quit" or repay the Knight's tale. Since the Knight has said nothing of millers in his tale and has been on crusade, Robin has no reason to pay anything back, but he is drunk and excited, and knightly order, even in literature, offends his taste for chaos and chivalric grotesquery. Belligerent and obstreperous, he assumes the knightly function of fighting—with his wrestling, knives, shield, and ability to knock down doors with his head.[51] Kolve makes quite a full analysis of

lage, of the verisimilar, and of irony from the fabliau—all features of comedy generic criticism.

[50] Knight ("Sociology of Literature," p. 33) observes that the "apparently threatening world of Miller and Reeve is, in consoling closure, shown to self-destruct." The perception, accurate enough, requires that one identify the character of the threat in its relation to peasants and the providentialist origin of the self-destruction in terms understood by Chaucer's court.

[51] In 1388, people who were servants in husbandry, laborers, servants of artificers, or victuallers were forbidden to bear buckle, sword, or dagger except when with their masters; *Statues of the Realm* (London: Record Commission, 1810–28), 2:57–58. For other references to weapons, see "Annales Ricardi Secundi, Regis Angliae," *Chronica Monasterii*, ed. H. T. Riley (London, 1866), 28:189; also Knighton, 1:303. The Statute of Trailbaston (1305) was designed to put down rural gangs, a complaint to Parliament in 1332 speaks of companies of marauders (*RP* 2:64), and the 1393 government issued a proclamation against "Insurrectiones, Congregationes, Conventicula, Assembleas, Routas, Seu Riotas, contra Pacem Nostram . . ." *Foedera*, 7:746. For a summary of the research,

the visual tradition behind the first five tales, but does not observe that Robin is grotesquely modeled after the medieval visual representations of Samson (figs. 10–14, 17) who protected an agricultural Israel from Philistine oppression. Samson worked as a miller after his Philistine enemies captured him and made him pull the millstone (B², 3264), and was a wrestler who also once knocked down doors with his head—at the gates of Gaza. Unfortunately, like Robin, he lacked interest in his wife's secrets (A, 3164) and so was deceived and "blinded," as Oswald shows Robin to be. Divinely blessed, Samson drank no wine, unlike Robin who ought to cry, with the Pardoner's drunkards, "Sampsoun, Sampsoun!" (C, 554). The Reeve's Simkin, created to mock Robin, has ample hair (A, 3935); he has a name that appears to diminish Samson's—Samson or Simson becomes Simkin—and he possesses a skill in letting animals loose in the fields to spite his "enemies." His name includes the *simia* or "ape" root, recalling Samson's juxtaposition with the ape which stands for fallen man in medieval art. He also ultimately falls from a great blow to the head. But Robin/Samson, without divine blessing or divine ruler, cannot act as Samson, the judge, or quit the Knight's tale save by writing comic graffiti over it to mock its myth of rule.[52]

As many critics have observed, the Miller retells the Knight's tale at a lower social level, but he also attacks it, instinctively making his story a picture of what the Knight's would be if told by Bacchus and Venus. Chaucer obviously understood the ex-

---

see the variorium edition of *The Miller's Tale*, ed. Thomas W. Ross (Norman: Oklahoma University Press, 1983).

[52] Judges 13–17. For Simkin's hair, see Walter Clyde Curry, *Chaucer and the Medieval Sciences* (London: Barnes and Noble, 1960), pp. 82–83. The Samson motif may begin with Arcita; see Allen and Moritz, *A Distinction of Stories*, pp. 28–29. For Kolve's interpretation of the visual arts and the Miller's Tale, see V. A. Kolve, *Chaucer and the Imagery of Narrative*, pp. 158–216. See also H. W. Janson, *Apes and Ape Lore* (London: Warburg Institute, 1952), p. 122.

1. The Three Estates and the author's presentation of his book. Lawrence of Premierfait's translation of Boccaccio's *De Casibus*; French, early fifteenth century

2. The garden of the temporal realm (Spiritual Power and Clerk, *left*; Temporal Power and Knight, *right*). *Songe de Vergier*; Flemish-French, 1378 (?)

3. The martyrdom of St. Thomas of Canterbury, with juxtaposition
of temporal and spiritual lords, sword and cross, along the central
axis. *Boucicaut Hours*; French, early fifteenth century

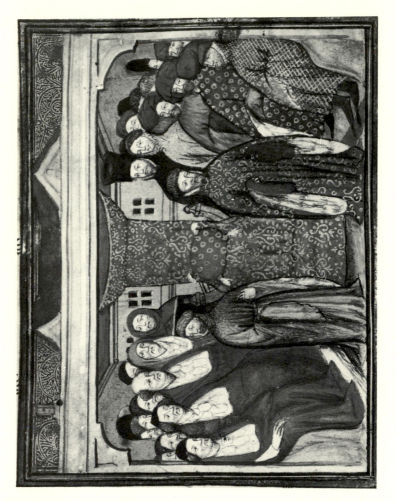

4. Henry IV and Richard II before Lords Spiritual and Temporal at the time of the deposition of Richard. *Histoire du Roy Richart II*; French, late fourteenth century

5. Adam and Eve falling, placed in hell, and harrowed from hell, while devils play bagpipes. Augustine, *Cité de Dieu*; French, fourteenth century

6. Andrea di Firenze's *The Church Militant (section)*, with bagpiper leading celebrators in an earthly pleasure garden away from the celestial city. Santa Maria Novella; second half of the fourteenth century

7. Apocalypse vision: St. John in present time, the great earthquake in future time, and Christ in eternity. Angers tapestry; Flemish-French, after 1377

8. Portrait of Richard II as "God in trone" (A, 2529), emphasizing Richard's interest in the analogy between earthly kingship and divine rulership. English, late fourteenth century

9. Terence, a Roman Chaucer, reading his
comedies to his audience while they are mimed by
joculatores (*upper section*). *Duc de Berry's Terence*;
French, early fifteenth century

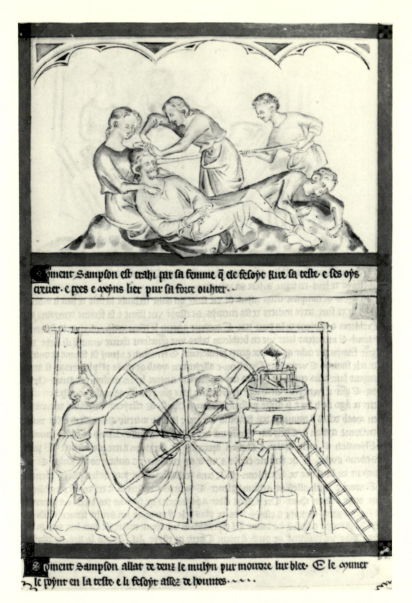

10. Samson blinded and made to mill. *Queen Mary's Psalter*; English, early fourteenth century

11. Samson as miller. *Giangaleazzo Visconti's Hours*; Italian, late fourteenth century

12. Samson loosing foxes, as the Reeve's miller looses horses. *Queen Mary's Psalter*; English, early fourteenth century

13. Samson wrestling the lion, also Robin's sport. *Queen Mary's Psalter*; English, early fourteenth century

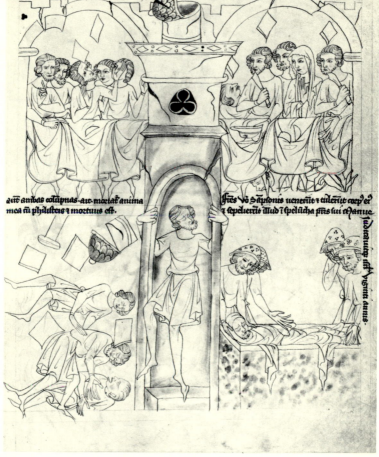

14. Samson bearded, pulling down the Philistine temple, about to be felled by "staff" pillar (cf. A, 4304), and being buried (*lower right*). *Velislay Picture Bible*; Prague, 1341–1351

15. The angel in St. John's *Apocalypse*, presenting John with a carpenter's rule to measure the temple. Angers tapestry; French-Flemish, after 1377

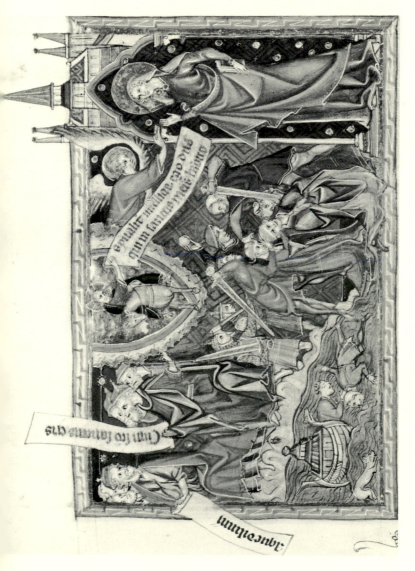

16. Noah and John: Apocalypse and deluge. *Apocalypse*; English, late thirteenth century

17. Samson with Gaza's broken gates on his head, acting a little like
Chaucer's Miller who heaves off doors with his head. *Giangaleazzo
Visconti's Hours*; Italian, 1370–1390

tent to which groups in revolt displace their rulers' stories of saints and statesmen and mock their decorum, social and literary, in the process. To breathe fire into his revolt, John Ball, according to the chroniclers, altered the functions Augustine assigned Nimrod, Noah, and Canaan; and Robin does the same thing by altering the functions and meanings of the Knight's set of characters and his story. He attacks the Knight's notions of hieratic kingship and faithful married love by making nature-interpreting, temple-building Theseus into a dumb Carpenter John who builds the three-tub arrangement, and gazes at the stars through Nicholas to see an apocalyptic future. He makes Theseus' faithful marriage to an Amazon (and Palamon's similar marriage to her sister) turn into an old man's cuckolding. John becomes so befuddled by the proposal to possess his Alysoun-Hypolita and the lordship of the whole world in the post-diluvian period that he forgets that the rainbow promise to Noah denies any future watery apocalypse. Hence he cooperates with Nicholas (A, 3547–3637).[53] Meanwhile, he ignores the fire between Alysoun and Nicholas which destroys his present "good." Combining Noah in his actions with the Apostle John in his name and carrying the trade of both (fig. 15), he fuses the first and last apocalypses literally, as the Berengaud commentary and illuminations do figuratively (fig. 16).[54]

As Robin is an upside-down Samson-the-Judge, so his tale is an upside-down Knight's tale filled with upside-down Biblical and hagiographic figures. St. Nicholas was conventionally the patron saint of innkeepers, of storm-tossed sailors, and especially of chaste boys and men like the Prioress' martyr (B², 1703–5). The Knight's concupiscent Palamon inspires Robin's

[53] Olson, "The Reeve's Tale," pp. 3–5.
[54] For Berengaud's commentary, the source of this illumination, see Pseudo-Ambrose, "Expositio super Septem Visiones Libri Apocalypsis," *PL* 17:822–23, which interprets the great sword of the red horseman as the flood and the fall of the city into the abyss under a rain of sulphur and fire in the Apocalypse.

CHAPTER 2

unchaste St. Nicholas (cf. B², 514–15), who prostitutes Alysoun instead of saving her, conjures up a false storm instead of calming a real one, and asks for his namesake's three tubs to ruin the craft of "herbergage" which his namesake patronized (figs. 18–20).[55] The Knight's long-haired, irascible Arcita (A, 2415–17) inspires a long-haired angry Absolon (fig. 21) with his Biblical namesake's golden hair and demagogic appeals to the populace. Absolon also vulgarizes the Canticle of Canticles "sung" by his Biblical "brother" Solomon in his whimper outside Alysoun's window.[56] At every stage, comic elements displace the epic and hieratic and abuse the devices of epic. Tubs replace temples and

[55] See Jacobus de Voragine, *Legenda Aurea*, ed. Th. Graesse (Breslav, 1890), pp. 22–29. St. Nicholas was a patron of sailors because he saved some sailors in a storm; see Simeon Metaphraste, "Vita S. Nicolai," *PG* 116:327; cf. Petrus de Natalibus' 1370 *Catalogus Sanctorum* (Lyons, 1534), sig. A6ʳ; Wace, *La Vie de Saint Nicholas*, ed. Einar Ronsjo (Lund: C.W.K. Gleerup, 1942), p. 122, 124–26. Several stories also describe Nicholas as relieving famine with supplies of grain, which may account for the Miller's choice of Nicholas as his hero; *Legenda Sanctorum*, comp. Bishop John Grandison, ed. Herbert Edward Reynolds (London, 1880), fol. 4. Pseudo-Richard of Maidstone, *Sermones Dormi Secure de Sanctis* (Strassburg, 1489), sig. B2ʳ, says that Nicholas brought sailors to extend a merciful measure of grain to Myra's starving; see *Early South-English Legendary*, ed. Carl Horstmann (London, 1887), pp. 243–44. W. F. Bolton's denial of significant relation to St. Nicholas seems doubtful, given the elaborate inverted iconography; W. F. Bolton, "The Miller's Tale: An Interpretation," *MS* 24 (1962):88. Cf. Ann Haskell, *Essays on Chaucer's Saints* (The Hague: Mouton, 1976), p. 38–43.

[56] Pierre Bersuire, *Opera Omnia*, 6 vols. in 3 (Cologne, 1730–31), 1–2:99–100; Nicholas de Lyra, *Biblia Latina* (n.p, 1502), 2:sig. [p4ᵛ]-[p8ᵛ]; Gower, "Mirour de l'Omme," 1468–70 and 12,985–87; Bromyard, *Summa Praedicantium*, 1:90ᵛ, 2:159ᵛ; Paul Beichner,"Absolon's Hair," *MS* 12 (1950):222–33; Kelsie B. Harder, "Chaucer's Use of the Mystery Plays," *MLQ* 17 (1956):194–95. Cf. Thomas J. Hatton, "Absolon, Taste and Odor in the *Miller's Tale*," *PLL* 7 (1971):72–75. Wearing clothes inappropriate to one's clerical estate was forbidden by the provincial constitutions of the English Church; see William of Lyndwood, *Provinciale seu Constitutiones Angliae* (Oxford, 1679), pp. 118–19, hereinafter Lyndwood.

[78]

councils of the gods, astrology replaces natural law, and Alysoun replaces Lavinia or Hypolita. The local blacksmith shop substitutes for Vulcan's forge, the plow coulter for the hero's armor, and the kiss, coulter burn, and fart for the usual three-stage battle. It is as if Chaucer created the "Byzantium" of the Knight's Tale to befoul it.

Yet the Miller's tale somehow cancels out its own chaos and asserts an order in the Knight's terms (as does the Reeve's narration also). Avaricious Carpenter John, deceived by wife and storm, gulls himself because he thinks that the storm will make him a world ruler like Noah and his wife (A, 3581–82), and his behavior recalls Robin's will to call the tune on the pilgrimage, determine its narrative order, and usurp the Knight's genre. It recalls "Jack the Miller" and his will to grind his country's rulers 'Fine, fine" in order to possess more of his world, particularly since Gower's *Vox Clamantis* had likened the Peasants' Revolt to a flood or tempest and the revolt did have millennialist elements. The Miller's incontinence is mocked by Nicholas who experiences lust's "rue rub," as Brathwait puts it, and is burned where he burns as the Parson predicts the luxurious will be; his arrogance is mocked by Absolon's fart in the face, the stench which the Parson predicts for the proud;[57] and his possessiveness by John's cuckolding. Divorced from any temporal ruler who can be the vehicle of a divine effort to harmonize humankind with the movement of the "stars" and the motions of nature, Robin knows an Oxford world that offers only retributive justice, not Theseus' transformative kind. Robin's kind of justice also promises punishment to him for his defeat by the three enemies who make him steal grain, pipe and tell goliardic

57 *Richard Brathwait's Comments in 1665 upon Chaucer's Tales of the Miller and the Wife of Bath*, Chaucer Society, 2d ser., 33, ed. C.F.E. Spurgeon (London: Kegan Paul, Trench, Trübner, 1901), p. 13. Cf. Olson, "Poetic Justice in the *Miller's Tale*," *MLQ* 24 (1963):234.

stories, and bear the proud arms of nobility.[58] It is not acciden-
tal that the tale is located in Oxford where revolt was particu-
larly intense.

The Reeve's tale, the product of Mars, carries the displace-
ment one step further as the effects of the three temptations are
again represented, now almost without parodic epic overtones.
Simkin, Theseus' new equivalent, is both dumb like John and
belligerent like Robin. Oswald's heroines are pretentious and
sluttish "Amazons." The vehicle of plot entanglement is not the
clever tubs but a baby's cradle, the clerks are merely vengeful,
and the battle merely a beating for poor Simkin. If Robin, in
unconscious self-mockery, exposes his Samsonistic will to rise
up and fight to displace knighthood, Oswald exposes his
Simkinistic will to judge. In the manorial economy, a reeve was
a peasant who represented other peasants to the lord or steward
at planting and harvesting time and adjudicated minor disputes
among the bondmen. Since he kept the tallies of the harvest, he
was often rather severely judged by his lord or steward for
stealing or losing track of grain.[59] But Chaucer's Reeve appears

[58] Ibid., p. 235. See figs. 5 and 6, this volume. For the bagpipe, see St. Au-
gustine, *De Civitate Dei*, Harvard College MS. XIV, Typ. 201, fol. 45ʳ (fig. 2); a
tempter with bagpipes leads people away from heaven in the "Triumph of the
Church"; cf. Piero Bargellini, *I Chiostri di Santa Maria Novella e il Cappellone degli
Spagnoli* (Florence: Arnaud, 1954), and fig. 2. See also Edward A. Block,
"Chaucer's Millers and Their Bagpipes," *Speculum* 29 (1954):239–43; Folke
Nordstrom, *Virtues and Vices on the 14th Century Corbels in the Choir of Uppsala
Cathedral* (Uppsala: Almquist and Wiksell, 1956), p. 95. The bagpipe appears
as the devil's instrument in folk tradition; see Alfred Oskar Dähnhardt, *Natur-
sagen*, 4 vols. (Leipzig: n.p., 1909), 1:189. Deschamps calls the bagpipes "in-
strumens des hommes bestiaulx" which enchant people and destroy their sense.
Deschamps, *Oeuvres Complètes*, 5:128.

[59] See H. S. Bennett, "The Reeve and the Manor," *EHR* 41 (1926):362–65;
Olson, "The Reeve's Tale," pp. 2–3; Robertson, "Chaucer and the 'Commune
Profit,' " pp. 249–50. Cf. James E. Thorold Rogers, *Six Centuries of Work and
Wages* (New York, 1884), p. 66.

to be above all this, having come into a sort of rule by frightening the peasants while bewildering his bailiffs and lord. A carpenter in craft, now a leader of farmers, he follows the two vocations practiced by Noah before and after the flood (figs. 22–23).[60] As Noah was an agent of God's judgment, so he, though mocked for assuming the role by Robin's Carpenter John, continues to play the agent of retribution against Robin. Though he claims that Robin can see motes in *his* eyes while ignoring beams in his own, his tale magnifies Robin's "faults" from motes into the phallic beams that Simkin's women enjoy. Robin's few weapons become Simkin's veritable arsenal, his petty theft becomes systematic and proud, and his drunkenness makes him a cuckold.[61] Robin's wife, apparently the basis of his indifference to the state of his wife's privities, becomes the smutty harvest of the local parson's sowing of wild oats in Oswald's account. In deference to her origins she is transplanted to a nunnery to be reared, and brought home to Simkin "proud, and peert as is a pye" (A, 3950) to lie in Clerk John's bed and be pricked "harde and depe" until Peter's third cock crows (A, 4231–33). As the beam and mote parable that the Reeve uses for the text of his tale promises, everyone in the tale gets measure for measure, reaping what he has sown (hence the tale includes a number of maxims presenting legal and Biblical versions of the measure for measure principle).[62] But the measure that the malicious reap is harsher than that which they sow: Simkin, contemptuous of the clerks for their northern dialect and clerical estate, sows estate hatred, theft, and the rent of his house and reaps the loss of the grain he has stolen, the cake he has baked with the stolen meal, and the pride of his daughter and wife. He pays triply for loosing the wild horses of the clerk's

[60] Olson, "The Reeve's Tale," p. 4.

[61] For more detail of stylistic analysis, see Olson, "The Reeve's Tale," pp. 14–16.

[62] Ibid., pp. 8–14.

passions.[63] Concomitantly, the harsh measure that Oswald exacts from his demesne underlings and promises to Robin, he also promises to himself at the hand of his manorial lord when the tallies are counted in the future, or at the divine hand from which comes the final measure.[64] The unrighteous steward of the Bible, whose lord discovers his mismanagement and judges him harshly (Luke 12.42–48), appears in one Middle English sermon as the unrighteous reeve whom God judges.[65]

Chaucer, through Theseus, shows providence halting the violence and injustice of Palamon and Arcita in the forest. He promises through the "providence" of the plots of his Reeve's and Miller's tales that Theban tyranny will not endure forever unpunished on England's agricultural lands, but he does not show directly how it is to be defeated. He handles his villein tales with the same symmetry and narrative justice with which he governs his Knight's Tale, but without a Theseus to administer the happy justice that reforms the characters. The countryside awaits the Knight to relieve it from threat and vengeance, theft and embezzlement, violence and blackmail.

It is natural to become indignant and sermonize about the injustice at large in Chaucer's demesne world. But one's laughter at the tyranny in the Miller's and the Reeve's worlds is so profound that indignation may not be needed. Theseus' laughter at the Theban rebellion leads him to remember his own foolish past, to offer mercy to the rebels, and to begin building the machinery of justice in the temples and the tournament,[66] a series of actions that again may model what Chaucer saw as appropriate court action.

[63] Kolve, *Chaucer and the Imagery of Narrative*, pp. 238ff.

[64] Olson, "The Reeve's Tale," pp. 12–13.

[65] Anonymous, "Mirrur of Sermons," B.M. MS. Harley 5085, fol. 115ʳ–115ᵛ.

[66] For the judicial tournament as a legal court, see Bonet, *Tree of Battles*, pp. 198–99; cf. G. D. Squibb, *The High Court of Chivalry* (Oxford: Clarendon Press, 1959), pp. 22–26.

Four hundred years after Chaucer, Wordsworth "laughed with Chaucer" beside the "pleasant Mill of Trompington" where Chaucer set the Reeve's Tale. Some few years later, he saw in Paris "The Revolutionary Power / Toss like a ship at anchor, rocked by storms." In Wordsworth's description of his own laughter, one encounters no indication that he senses that Chaucer wrote about a similar "Revolutionary Power." France's kind of revolt against bonded villeinage had occurred in England centuries before and had set the course of England unalterably away from the bonded system that was to characterize the French rural economy for centuries.[67] One can laugh at Trompington's farce, as Wordsworth apparently did, without understanding Chaucer's skepticism of what self-rule might become. Wordsworth probably did so because he had little appreciation for the generic basis for Chaucer's comedy of chivalric abandonment of rule. Born in an age that cast aside the generic and iconological conventions and social system of Chaucer's age, he did not observe how Chaucer's vision supported—as inevitable, natural, and required—the very same *ancien régime* that his own age discarded, in literature as well as politics. And so he may have missed the heart of Chaucer's comedy. If the Reeve and the Miller running amok through their estates reflect the perception that no Saturnian age of gold and communal benefit can exist without clear definitions of role and decorum, so also does the Knight's Saturn who slew Samson as he shook the pillar. Saturn, standing for melancholy and contemplation as well as the natural cycles, recites nothing but humankind's melancholy history and can promise, at best, the reconciliation of warring planets and passions, not their elimination. Peace is not Saturn's job now that the Golden Age is gone; it is the job of Jupiter, the King, and Duke Theseus, an idea that must have given a certain comfort to the experienced

[67] Hilton, *Bond Men Made Free,* pp. 230–32, 234–36.

[83]

servants of the Crown who surrounded the poet and for whom he tried to convey the meaning of his time.[68]

The genius of Chaucer's work in these tales resides in his presentation of lower-order rebellion as based on the systematic destruction of the decorum of established rule in life *and* in art. The Miller and the Reeve, as part of their rebellion, use their tales to overthrow established conventions governing temporal heroes, ecclesiastical saints, and literary genres. Chaucer makes such villein destructiveness laughable and impotent, but he does not ignore the problems that have led to the demise of internal order in England. His version of the Order of the Passion's vision demonstrates how peace within the nation and between nations may be established through language. As a poet, Chaucer recognized far more clearly than did Philippe that speech, words, and tales create the order and the disorder—in the *Canterbury Tales* and outside them. His next "tale" examines the disorder implicit in the absolutist view of British kingship with its dubious interpretations of history and its dependence on miracle and the constancy of the man of law.

[68] Allen and Moritz, *A Distinction of Tales*, pp. 122–23.

3

The Lawyer's Tale and the History of Christian English Law

The Man of Law chronicles the arrival of Christianity in Saxon England and the creation of civic order through a Christian king whose authority is theocratic and absolute. His view is the precise opposite of the Knight's. After the Knight offers his chivalric or baronial view of a just government growing out of the leader's consultation with unprotected widows, with his parliament, and with nature and history, the Lawyer presents his absolutist vision of governing based on a kingship directed and protected by God. Such government requires no consultation and may even destroy the monarch who ignores God's miraculous direction and follows the advice of his magnates or people. Kingship, to the Man of Law, derives its power from royal saints, miracles, and divine blessing—elements of kingship that, like the emblemology of the king as the sun, fascinated Richard as he considered his own role.[1] The divine blessing given at an English monarch's coronation was sometimes symbolized by anointment with holy oil like that used by the prophet Samuel, and when Richard was asked to abdicate, he responded that he could not, by the simple act of surrendering the throne, give up the spiritual role conferred on him by his anointing. The Lawyer argues for absolutist conceptions of royal power, like those which Richard espoused throughout his

[1] The magnates' sort of view may best be set forth in John of Salisbury, *Pol.*, 4.1–2; for Richard's absolutist views, see Richard H. Jones, *The Royal Policy of Richard II: Absolutism in the Later Middle Ages* (New York: Barnes and Noble, 1968), pp. 125–75; for 1388 Appellant views by essentially the 1386 group, see Kantorowicz, *King's Two Bodies*, p. 369; cf. pp. 364–72. For Richard's interest in the chrism, see Ullmann, "Thomas Becket's Miraculous Oil," pp. 129–33.

reign and which the royal lawyers defended in 1387, by altering the standard account of England's Christianization to make a theocratic king its central figure. At the same time, the Lawyer's story appears to undercut what he advocates, suggesting that Chaucer was not enthusiastic about either the theocratic view or its regalian promoters.

The absolutist view flourished under Richard II, partly because it was supported by his men of law. The royal lawyer was always expected to uphold the royal prerogative, but Richard tended to identify that with his personal prerogative. The issue of whether royal or political monarchy was to prevail vexed much of the fourteenth century in England, but never more obviously than in Chaucer's 1386 parliament and in the justices' responses in 1387 to its decisions, which illustrate the royal lawyers' attitude toward any restriction of royal authority.

The history of this parliament and subsequent events cast some light on the issues raised by the Lawyer, though I do not wish to claim that only these events motivated Chaucer to write the Man of Law's Tale. Suffolk, the chancellor, opened the 1386 session with a speech requesting additional levies to defend the nation and was greeted with angry criticism of his handling of the government, particularly his failure to implement the parliamentary reforms of 1385 calling for a reduction in the costs of the anti-French military effort and the Crown administration and for a commission investigation of royal finances.[2] Richard withdrew in anger from the Westminster session to Eltham palace so parliament could not function, but Commons, not intimidated, sent word that they wished Suffolk removed as chancellor. Richard shot back that that body could not make

---

[2] *RP* 3:216ff. J. S. Roskell, *The Impeachment of Michael de la Pole, Earl of Suffolk in 1386* (Manchester: Manchester University Press, 1984). J.J.N. Palmer, "The Impeachment of Michael de la Pole," *BIHR* 42 (1969):100–101. For the entire 1386 session, see *RP*, 3:215–27.

him remove "even a kitchen boy." Thereupon Gloucester and Thomas Arundel, the Bishop of Ely, went to Eltham for a face-to-face meeting with the monarch in which Gloucester, as described by Knighton (who may not be accurate), assured the King of parliament's respect for his dignity, property, and honor. But he also asserted that the ancient statutes and customs required an annual parliament in which equity would "shine like the sun at the meridian," reforming the realm and destroying its internal and external enemies.[3] According to the duke, the King could not separate himself from his deliberative body, save for sickness, and certainly not simply out of strong-headedness; after the King's absence of forty days, parliament could go home without acting on his agenda, including the tax requests. Implicitly, another session would have to be called that year. When Richard replied that, should the Commons and people of England rebel against him, he would receive help from the King of France, Gloucester reminded him of the war misery that France had caused his country already and went on to describe the impoverishment of the English realm caused by bad counsel. Finally, he reminded Richard of Edward II's deposition for following such counsel. Faced with this threat, Richard returned to parliament, allowed Suffolk to be removed and impeached, and surrendered many of his powers to a "great and continual council" which included the later Appellant group and more moderate magnates who were to rule the realm for a year until November 19, 1387.

The events of 1386–88 drew the strongest possible line between the absolutist and consultative views of kingship distinguished in the Lawyer's and the Knight's tales. Richard, unlike

---

[3] Knighton, 2:216–20; Kantorowicz, *King's Two Bodies*, pp. 32–33, n. 18. Richard emphasized the king as the "sol justitiae" in his general functioning when he adopted the sun symbol; Gloucester may have given the "sol justitiae" notion a narrower definition, connecting it to the King's functioning with the magnates and commons in parliament.

Gloucester or his 1386 council, favored the former view, and his countermove came in August of 1387—his famous ten questions to the royal judges who included Sir Robert Tresilian, first a sergeant at law and later chief justice of the common bench, three other justices of the King's common bench, and another sergeant at law. Tresilian and Belknap were also Chaucer's fellow justices of the peace for Kent. The intent of these questions was to make parliament an advisory body, perhaps the captive of the King, and to define its 1386 leaders as traitors. Since the judges were close enough to Richard to know that he was fond of the trappings of anointed kingship (fig. 6), we may suppose that they knew what answers were appropriate. Richard asked them whether the statutes, ordinances, and commissions of the 1386 parliament offended his regality and prerogative by forcing him to act against his will, and they replied that Gloucester and Arundel had so offended and deserved to be punished with death as traitors. Richard asked whether the King normally controlled the length and agenda of the parliamentary session, whether an officer of the King could be impeached by parliament, and whether the trial of Suffolk was authoritative. The judges answered "No" to each question.[4] Under later pressure from the Appellants, they were to claim

---

[4] Higden, 8:481–82. This volume of the chronicle is by the Higden continuator in Harley 2261, which goes to 1401, has no Latin original, and was probably composed circa 1440. See S. B. Chrimes, "Richard II's Questions to the Judges, 1387," *Law Quarterly Review* 72 (1956):365–90; cf. Roskell, *The Impeachment of Michael de la Pole*, pp. 52–54. Roskell (p. 54) says that the questions reflect "Richard's own personal devotion to a policy designed to demolish parliamentary control of government." My analysis is based on Chrimes but uses Kantorowicz's definitions of the language applied to kingship. This parliament also denied deputies to controllers (*LR*, pp. 268–69) and annulled controller life appointments which Chaucer did not have; cf. *RP*, 3:221–23; and *LR*, pp. 269, 368. Chaucer received a deputy on February 17, 1385 (cf. *C.P.R.*, *1381–85*, p. 532). During the period, Chaucer was associated with Scrope who defended Suffolk; see *RP* 3:217.

that duress prompted their answers; however, these answers were also generally traditional—the King *had* controlled the agenda and term of parliament and generally *had arranged* impeachments through Crown proceedings—but Tresilian was later executed by the Appellants for giving his opinions. Such was the intensity of feeling about extreme royalist or theocratic views of kingship that they led to the execution of one sergeant at law and eventually, of course, to Richard's own deposition in 1399 (Chaucer appears, by the way, to comment on these views in his two short poems to Richard II and Henry IV).[5]

[5] *RP*, 3:422–23; cf. "Annales Richardi Secundi et Henrici Quarti Regum Angliae" in *Chronica Johannis de Trokelowe*, ed. H. T. Riley (London: Rolls Series, 1866), pp. 259–78. Chaucer may deal with the same issue in "Lak of Stedfastnesse" which Shirley calls a "Balade Royal made by oure laureal poete of Albyon in hees laste yeeres"; Aage Brusendorff, *The Chaucer Tradition* (London: Clarendon Press, 1925), p. 274. Brusendorff places the poem in 1397 or after; I see no reason to dispute his and Shirley's conclusion, given the advice and iconology, on the basis of the assumption that Chaucer could only flatter Richard. For alternative views, see Geoffrey Chaucer, *The Minor Poems*, ed. George B. Pace and Alfred David (Norman: Oklahoma University Press, 1982), pp. 78–79. Chaucer appears to warn his absolutist monarch to hate extortion (line 23), though this advice is usually taken to mean extortion-in-others; Caroline M. Barron ("The Tyranny of Richard II," *BIHR* 41 [1968]:1–18) presents compelling evidence that the August 1396 blank charters, August 1397 loans to the Exchequer, and the 1397–98 Charters of Pardon were used to identify dissidents and enrich the treasury, that the "fines of pardon" were particularly extortionate, and that Richard's exoneration of the sheriffs of Hertfordshire and Kent from bad debts "was merely the cover for a piece of blatant extortion" of £1602 from Essex and an unknown amount from Hertfordshire (Barron, pp. 9–10). "Stedfastnesse" also asks the monarch to wed his people to steadfastness again; for the theocratic or absolutist implications of the wedding metaphor, see Walter Ullmann, *Principles of Government and Politics in the Middle Ages* (New York: Barnes and Noble, 1961), pp. 181–92, and Kantorowicz, *King's Two Bodies*, pp. 212–23; see also Walsingham, *Chronicon Angliae*, p. 159. Richard of Maidstone says that London, waiting for its king, "properatur ab urbe / Regis in occursum coniugis atque sue"; Richard of Maidstone, *Concordia Facta Inter Regem Riccardum II et Civitatem Londonie*, ed. Charles Smith (Princeton: unpublished Prince-

In the *Canterbury Tales*, the Sergeant at Law—eligible by role to be a justice of the King's bench or of the common bench but presently representing royal justice in the assize courts—presents the royalist, theocratic position. He does so in his Man of Law's tale which maintains a position like Tresilian's, not through the conventional image of a king anointed with holy oil and therefore knowing the divine answers, but through a narrative account, purporting to be history, of a model monarch married to the saint who converts England. She, in turn, has a model emperor for her son, and sanctions the rule of both king and emperor through repeated miracles legitimizing absolute rule.

Chaucer's Lawyer should make us suspicious of absolute rule since he has neither a good character nor an honorable practice. Chauncey Wood has argued that the diatribe against poverty in the prologue to his tale and its praise of rich merchants extends the suggestion of venality in adjudicating land disputes and accepting the robes mentioned in his portrait in the General Prologue; that his love of fee simple extends to his effort to control the transmission of his tale; and that his materialism resounds in his concern for Constance's material well-being.[6] He may represent just such a figure of corruption in the royal household as led to the 1385 concerns over its extravagance. If Chaucer's

---

ton University diss., 1972), p. 170.

In his poem to Henry IV ("Complaint of Chaucer to His Purse"), Chaucer recognizes Henry as "verray kyng" by lineage and free election but does not call him king-by-conquest though he is "conquerour." Again, Chaucer's subtle language reflects the parliamentary position; cf. E. F. Jacob, *The Fifteenth Century: 1399–1485* (Oxford: Clarendon Press, 1961), p. 15, and B. Wilkinson, "The Deposition of Richard II and the Accession of Henry IV," *EHR* 54 (1939): 215–39.

6 Wood, *Chaucer and the Country of the Stars*, pp. 192–244. For a useful discussion of the text of this section, see Charles A. Owen, Jr., *Pilgrimage and Storytelling in the Canterbury Tales* (Norman: Oklahoma University Press, 1977), pp. 25–30.

ironic claim for him—that he knows all of the cases since King William—derives from his making up legal precedent to tilt the scales of justice, then he predictably possesses such an uncertain grasp of history as would be gathered from itinerant merchants who come to the London wharf.[7] Sergeants of the law, who were supposed to be wealthy, were not to derive their wealth from such contempt for poverty as the Lawyer exhibits (B[1], 99–126), and ideally a justice's knowledge of history would come not from the wharf but from chronicle. Fortescue testifies that the festivities marking elevation to the sergeant's office in the fifteenth century could cost £266.13.4d, a "millionaire's" sum, signifying the dignity and learning of the office, and adds that a sergeant received his title only after sixteen years of study and that only sergeants could be installed as justices in the King's court of pleas or the court of the common bench where real property issues were pleaded. Sergeants were to wear a coif of white silk (Chaucer's sergeant wears a girdle of silk) which they were not to doff even when talking to the King.[8] The ceremony and wealth that surrounded their office were not to symbolize ill-gotten gain but an easy security above the concern for gain. Far from appearing busy, sergeants who sat on the royal bench were to hear cases only three hours per day and to spend the rest in meditation and reading the scriptures and the law. Fortescue also argues that the Inns of Court student is to spend

---

[7] D. W. Robertson, Jr., *Essays in Medieval Culture* (Princeton: Princeton University Press, 1980), pp. 275–79.

[8] John Fortescue, *De Laudibus Legum Anglie*, ed. S. B. Chrimes (Cambridge: Cambridge University Press, 1942), pp. 118–19, 125. Holdsworth posits no different pattern for the earlier period; W. S. Holdsworth, *A History of English Law* (Boston: Little, Brown, 1923), pp. 484–93. There was some complaint in the fourteenth century against abuses in the giving of robes, livery, or silver to Crown justices by interested parties; see Richard W. Kaeuper, "Law and Order in Fourteenth Century England: The Evidence of Special Commissions of Oyer and Terminer," *Speculum* 54 (1979):753–84.

much of his study time with chronicles.[9] In short, the dubious sources of Chaucer's Lawyer's wealth and intellectual authority may be expected to contaminate his tale's legal statement.

And they do. The tale distorts a history, given in Trivet's chronicle and in Gower's *Confessio Amantis*, of the Christianization of England and gives a *raison d'être* for theocratic kingship. Constance, being true to her name, represents a legal or political virtue that was required in good government.[10] St. Thomas Aquinas calls it the virtue that allows one to conquer the external impediments to the other virtues; Macrobius writes of it as one of a number of political virtues having to do with the conquest of external difficulties; and the *Miroir des Dames*, written for ruling women, asserts that a constant ruling woman will be firm and unchangeable as she deliberates over matters of justice and injustice, good and evil.[11] Constancy requires the following of a rule in difficult circumstances as is evident in the remarks of a speaker in a late fourteenth-century parliament who says that "where the Will reigns and Reason retreats, constancy flees."[12] And Chaucer's Constance clearly acts out what her name means as she faces external difficulty without flinching—

[9] Fortescue, *De Laudibus Legum Anglie*, p. 129. Wyclif, however, regards the lawyer's studies as contemptible: "Ex quo videtur quod legiste laborantes tam solicite propter questum et honorem mundanum circa tradiciones humanas putridas, que scienciam Dei cum aliis virtutibus excludunt, sepius sunt a Deo notabiliter increpandi" (John Wyclif, "De Magisterio Christi," *Opera Minora*, ed. Johann Loserth [London: C. K. Paul, 1913], p. 440).

[10] Constance as the daughter of the emperor may glance at Richard's queen, Anne of Bohemia, esp. B[1], 652–58; for Anne's interest in the empire and knighthood, see Bishop John Trevor's "Tractatus De Armis," written for her, in *Medieval Heraldry, passim*.

[11] *Summa Theologica*, 2.2, Q 137. Art. 3; Macrobius, *Commentary on the Dream of Scipio*, trans. William H. Stahl (New York: Columbia University Press, 1952), p. 122; Anonymous, "Le Miroir des Dames," B.M. Add. MS. 29,986. fol. 28[v]. As a historical figure, Constance is not an allegory as claimed by Huppé, *Reading of the Canterbury Tales*, pp. 95ff.

[12] *RP* 3:423.

the Syrian murders, the rough sea, the barbaric Northumbrian conspiracy, and Roman anonymity. Her life summarizes itself in her remark:

> He that me kepte fro the false blame
> While I was on the lond amonges yow,
> He kan me kepe from harm and eek fro shame
> In salte see, althogh I se noght how.
> As strong as evere he was, he is yet now.
> In hym triste I, and in his mooder deere,
> That is to me my seyl and eek my steere.　　(B¹, 827–33)

The Lawyer, because he respects Constance as a picture of what rule should be, never suggests that constancy apart from miracle and divine guidance may become mere stubborn insensitivity to the needs of the realm; similarly, the lawyers who spoke in 1387 failed to offer Richard anything beyond strict legal answers by pointing to what might be prudential for him, given the country's need for unity after the Peasants' Revolt and the French defeats.

In creating a history that is a flat melodrama, the Lawyer draws the issues as starkly as possible—as did the royal lawyers. He avoids cluttering his portrait of Constance with the complex iconography that Chaucer otherwise uses to decorate and place even his lowest characters: e.g. the Summoner's garlics, leeks, and onions; Nicholas's tubs, storm, and love rituals; or January's *Song of Songs* routine. A few references to the Bible place Constance beside such figures as Daniel or Susannah and invite brief comparisons to Christ or Mary. But the work is generally semantically flat and forces the reader to concentrate on the heroine's virtues and her relation to theocratic kingship. Constance's opponents, Islamic law and Anglo-Saxon lawlessness, are equally flat. Her first adversity comes from Islamic law characterized by the Syrian privy council as so contrary to Christian law that no marriage treaty is possible (B¹, 218–24).

[93]

The Islamic ruler's mother-in-law, perceiving a threat to the "olde sacrifice" required by Islamic law, feigns conversion to open the door for the destruction of Christian converts and to protect Islamic law defined as, first, sacrifice like that of Old Testament Judaism (B¹, 325), second, the rule of the Koran and Mohammed's commands (B¹, 332–33), and third, a law promising hell to Islamic converts to Christianity and encouraging killing the infidel without mercy (B¹, 337–57). This episode defines the Man of Law's theme in the relationship between a country's religion and its law.

In Northumbria, neither religion nor law exists. The period is dark, certainly bleaker than that described in Trivet and Gower, and more like that in the alternative version of the period's history in Bede or his followers among the late medieval chroniclers. Briton Christianity has gone underground. Only the bookmaking of the Britons has been preserved ("A Britoun book, written with Evaungiles, / Was fet," B¹, 666–67)—perhaps Chaucer had seen a manuscript such as the Lindesfarne gospels. Into Northumbria's night of murder, conspiracy, and manslaughter comes Constance to begin a work like that described in Acts when she gently and almost silently converts Hermangyld, the wife of the constable of Northumbria, who performs the conventional apostolic act of giving sight to a blind person, thereby in turn converting the constable, cornerstone of the country's political structure. When Hermangyld is killed and the crime attributed to Constance, another apostolic event occurs: as Alla as king forces the real murderer and Constance's accuser to swear on the Briton gospels, a voice like that heard at Christ's baptism sounds from heaven, declaring her a guiltless daughter of Holy Church and accusing the knight of slander as his eyes miraculously burst from his face. Neither jury nor royal consultation is necessary. In Chaucer, the king forces the confession and the miracle whereas, in Gower and Trivet, the figure equivalent to the constable does it.

These changes are very important to the Lawyer's message. When his king acts, faith creates justice, as faith earlier led to Alla's conversion, the Christianizing of the realm, and the civic bliss at the marriage of the king and Constance. Such a picture should have appealed to those who encouraged the young king to have faith in royal miracles, anointings, and proclamations that the king's law is in the king's breast.

The king, converted and blessed by God, in turn becomes the cornerstone of English order. The fictive Constance's period must be the late 500s. Chaucer, Trivet, and Gower all picture a Christian Roman empire still alive and governed from Rome, an Islam that has already captured Syria, and an England about to be re-Christianized.[13] Actually the historical Constance or Constantina lived when the Justinian line was ruling from Constantinople. The Justinian emperor, Tiberius II (578–582), mentioned in the early part of the tale, had a daughter, Constantina (or Custance) and was succeeded by Mauritius (582–602), our tale's Maurice. But historical lineage as we know it does not follow the paths described in the tale. Mauritius was one of Tiberius' generals and subordinates, and Constantina married him in order to solidify the succession. Thus, Mauritius was not her son nor Alla (or Allae, as Bede names him) her husband.[14] Furthermore, though England was probably first being converted during Constantina's time (i.e. A.D. 597), she had nothing to do with the conversion, and Islam was not to

---

[13] The Constance "history" of the conversion of England may not have existed before Trivet; see W. F. Bryan and Germaine Dempster, *Sources and Analogues of Chaucer's Canterbury Tales* (Atlantic Highlands, N.J.: Humanities Press, 1941), pp. 156–57.

[14] John W. Barker, *Justinian and the Later Roman Empire* (Madison: Wisconsin University Press, 1966), pp. 220–21. Capgrave's early fifteenth-century chronicle has the events in the eastern empire for the period set down approximately accurately, though sketchily; cf. John Capgrave, *The Chronicle of England*, ed. F. C. Hingeston (London, 1858), p. 93.

CHAPTER 3

conquer Syria for another generation or two (630s). Whether
Chaucer knew Constance's history to be inaccurate is doubtful.
Accurate or not, it clearly fits his Lawyer's purposes. Trivet
may have pieced the first version of the story together from cer-
tain suggestions in materials available to him and written it to
please the noble lady for whom he wrote the Anglo-Norman
Chroniques, creating an alternative to Bede's account which also
describes a ruined England prior to its Christianization, filled
with civil war, turned from truth and justice, and uninterested
in Christianizing the invading Anglo-Saxons. In creating his al-
ternative, Trivet made his account kinder than Bede's both to
Celtic Christianity and to the rulers of the old Saxon world.
Bede ascribes to Aethelferth, Northumbria's ruler, the killing
of more Christian Britons than to any other ruler; his successor,
Aella, our tale's Christian Alla, rules in a Northumbria in-
cluded in the kingdom of Deiri when St. Gregory begins to be
interested in England; after seeing two of the handsome Deiri
in the slave market in Rome, asking their kingdom's name and
being told, "De Iri," Gregory puns on it to make it say they are
snatched from God's wrath and prepared for his mercy. Hence,
he planned his mission to England and then assigned it to Au-
gustine of England when he became pope. Importantly, Bede's
story makes no particular point of the importance of good mon-
archs to the conversion of England and emphasizes Augustine's
conflicts with Celtic Bangor Christianity.[15] In contrast, Chau-

---

[15] *Bede's Ecclesiastical History of the English People*, ed. Bertram Colgrave and
R.A.B. Mynors (Oxford: Clarendon Press, 1969), pp. 67–69, 133–35. This
story was available in Chaucer's day; cf. Higden, 5:351–57; Matthew Paris,
Chronica Majora, ed. Henry Richards Luard (London, 1872), 57:1:254–60; *Eu-
logium Historiarum*, ed. F. S. Haydon (London: 1860), 9:2:366–70; Capgrave,
Chronicle of England, pp. 93, 101. For Trivet's account of Constance, see *The An-
glo Norman Chronicles of Nicholas Trivet*, ed. A. Rutherford (London: unpub-
lished University of London diss., 1932), pp. 199–226, and for the Britons,
192–93.

[96]

cer's royal lawyer uses the Trivet-Gower story of the Christian-
ization of England because his stable government emerges from
the ruler's conversion to Christianity, and because king and em-
peror have miracle as their sanction, following the theocratic
claims of Richard. For some reason he, unlike Bede, also wishes
to make Northumbria the source of Anglo-Saxon Christianity
rather than its enemy and to harmonize the Celtic and Roman
versions of the faith.

Trivet's Constance is a good source of power for a Christian
king in that before she marries anyone she studies the seven lib-
eral arts which were to lead one to a wisdom such as might be
used in directing nations.[16] Her father marries her to the Sultan
of the Holy Land to convert the Saracens and open pilgrimage
places for Christians, but providence, willing the movement of
the Christian dispensation to England, spares her from becom-
ing the sultaness and throws her on the waters that lead mys-
teriously to Britain and its conversion. Special providence
rather than her learning make her the consort of England and
the mother of Rome. The idea of a miraculous providence that
thrusts Christian rulership on England overwhelms any normal
sense of a causation in Trivet's story and makes the narrative
hard to remember, particularly in comparison with the
Knight's tale (cf. A, 3111–12). After Northumbria is converted,
Constance's enemies, in the king's absence, concoct the story
that she has given birth to a fairy-monster child and put her out
to sea where miracle after miracle occurs; then Alla kills his
mother in anger over her part in Constance's betrayal, pilgrim-
ages to Rome to repent the matricide, and is miraculously reu-
nited with his wife. He rules successfully in a Christian Eng-
land while Maurice, his and Constance's son and the most
Christian of emperors, reigns in Rome. At every stage in

---

[16] This is the subject of a study that I am presently preparing.

Trivet, Alla's Christianity depends on miracle—on Constance's Roman Christianity or Bangor's Welsh faith.

Trivet's story reflects the ideology of the thorough-going Augustinian royalist who wrote the extensive commentary on the *De Civitate Dei*,[17] and Chaucer's Lawyer heightens Trivet's emphasis. Augustine holds that history is controlled by general providence and miracles, that earthly rule is a fragile thing—rarely more than tyranny—that an occasional theocratic king or emperor may rule in a Christian way, and that Church and Empire alternately struggle and harmonize with one another as the salvation scheme gives history its fundamental meaning.[18] Such a random and unpredictable view of how things happen from the human perspective requires divinely inspired monarchs if government is to be effective. God must rule since nothing is patterned or normative in human action, and nothing can be read from nature. The Constance story, given the varying unwitting wisdom of villain and emperor in disposing of Constance, replaces the predictable natural law of the Knight's Tale with miracles; salvation comes first to Syria and then to England only because of a divine plan that moves God's blessing from the throne of Syria—the Holy Land and the object of pilgrimage—to England. One may contrast the Lawyer's conception of the ruler as the miraculous, divine vehicle with the

---

[17] For an account of Trivet's commentary on Augustine, see Beryl Smalley, *English Friars and Antiquity* (New York: Barnes and Noble, 1960), pp. 58–65.

[18] Augustine, *De Civitate Dei*, 5.24; 11.13; 12.11; 12.14; 19.17; 20.8; 22.30. Cf. Herbert A. Deane, *The Political and Social Ideas of St. Augustine* (New York: Columbia University Press, 1963), p. 204. C. A. Patrides speaks of the Augustinian Orosius' discerning, in the rise and fall of civilizations, "the hand of a divinity shaping their ends, now supporting the righteous, and now smashing the proud and the wicked." Constance's rejection by the Islamic Syrians and her acceptance in England represent the beginnings of the rise of Christianity in England and the beginning of the corruption of Islamic civilization which prophetic thinkers expected to fall eventually. See C. A. Patrides, *The Grand Design of God* (London: Routledge and Kegan Paul, 1972), p. 19; cf. pp. 28–34.

Clerk's "first estate" conception of the ruler as an *imperfect* similitude for God in relation to whom his constant wife and subject acts as a similitude for faithful humankind. Walter is a cruel husband who professes to respect the inconstant "constance" which "yvele preeveth" of his more frivolous subjects (E, 995–1000) and fails to cherish his wife-subject's "constance and . . . bisynesse" (E, 1008, cf. E, 631ff.). He is, in short, a tyrant to all appearances. In contrast, his commoner wife, Griselda, comes down like justice from heaven (E, 440) and gives service to equity, peace, and the common profit when she assists in the rule of her land (E, 428–44). Yet when the Clerk interprets the story, Walter *as* unjust ruler and husband becomes the similitude for God (E, 1149–62), and he becomes so precisely because the logic of heaven and earth differ. If Walter rules by an arbitrary will, he evidences his fallibility and foolishness, but if God rules by what *appears* to be such a will, His action merely demonstrates humankind's tragic condition and gives evidence of human incompleteness while stretching humankind's limits and testing the love strong as death (Cant. 8.6; cf. E, 666–67). The ruler-husband cannot claim God's powers of arbitrary action and testing, for to do so would be unbearable (E, 1144). His action and Griselda's response only demonstrate that "For, sith a womman was so pacient / Unto a mortal man, wel moore us oghte / Receyven al in gree that God us sent" (E, 1149–51). The monarch who rules without regard to natural law at his own "divine" whim or the whim of his populace is only a mortal man.

In contrast, both Trivet and the Lawyer take for granted the God-like ruler and assign consultative or political government no power in creating just rule.[19] When the Sultan, as a consultative monarch, goes to his privy council and is told that he cannot "have" Constance save by marrying her and cannot do that

[19] Jones, *Royal Policy of Richard II*, pp. 164–85.

under Islamic law, he interprets the advice to mean that he must become a Christian and convert his liege lords. Though he mistakes his short-sighted decision to "baptize" his baronage in order to gain a wife for Christianizing his people, his mother knows that baptism, accepted without belief, is water and no more. A consultative decision foolishly understood destroys both the sultan and his design to Christianize the country. On the other hand, Alla easily becomes and remains a good king through supernatural intervention: he converts to Christianity, marries Constance, and Christianizes his country *because* of a miracle; he uncovers a crime by asking the culprit to swear on a Bible while waiting for the culprit's eyes to burst out and for a voice from heaven, and he finds Constance alive in Rome because she received supernatural strength to conquer her rapist on her return voyage to the imperial city and supernatural guidance to get her boat there alone. Finally, Alla discovers his son, Rome's future emperor who "lyved cristenly," by noticing him accidentally at a feast and asking after his origin. Indeed, I know of no more miracle-ridden story than the Lawyer's. If theocratic rule works, the story should certainly end as happily as every fairy tale. But the Lawyer does not show that to be the case.

Even though the tale shows England Christianized and the Empire stabilized, the narrator makes its end melancholy as death follows death. When Alla dies, the Man of Law cries out that conscience, anger, desire, and a whole series of sins destroy our *joie de vivre* (B,[1] 1135–38). Perhaps conscience has been the *Man*'s enemy, but his comment cannot arise from *Alla*'s death, since it is described neither as a tragedy nor as a defeat by conscience, anger, or any sin. Preceded by a life lived "in joye and in quiete" (B[1], 1131), it comes after a life of stabilizing, peacemaking, and setting the foundations for England and Rome.

The Lawyer does not consult providence, history, or eternity—only temporal hazard and opportunity. His whole work

treats God's providence as malevolent: the sultan's death for
love is written in the stars along with the deaths of the other
great heroes; the stars maliciously require dread events to hap-
pen (B¹, 295–308) as the Lawyer contradicts his source and re-
duces Bernard Sylvestris's complex view of the providential na-
ture of the universe to a direct contradiction of the Knight that
explicitly charges cruelty to the "firste moevyng," and denies
the Knight's paean to the "Firste Moevere" as author of the
"faire cheyne of love" (A, 2987–88).²⁰ Perhaps the Lawyer does
not understand how the natural successions properly read are
the source of positive law because his absolutist legal perspec-
tive requires no philosophic kings and councils to read God's
and nature's law.²¹ But that his incredible daisy chain of mira-
cles leading to a happy ending should lead him to attribute cru-
elty to the First Mover is preposterous. If the First Moving is
cruel, how does a theocratic ruler rule? Will he not also become
cruel as Walter has? Would it not be better to divorce kingship
from God as the Clerk does, and leave the problem of pain to
providence? The cruelty projected by the Lawyer's world view
both creates and is created by his hatred of poverty and love of
the Parvys and wharf, of robes and fee simple. His is the indif-
ference and cruelty of a person who sees the world from the per-
spective of a spoiled child without a sense of social responsibil-
ity. He creates a kingship that has about the same maturity.

At the end of his similar tale, Gower says:

> For [Alla] Constance hath in his hond,
> Which was the comfort of his lond.
> For when that he cam hom ayein,

²⁰ Wood, *Chaucer and the Country of the Stars*, pp. 209ff.

²¹ McCall (*Chaucer Among the Gods*, p. 164), suggests that Chaucer assumes
that a Christian perspective is impossible to characters who "lived under the law
of nature." This does not mean, in most of Chaucer's poetry, that a wise per-
spective under the law of nature is impossible for a temporal ruler before the
appearance of Christianity.

CHAPTER 3

Ther is no tunge it mihte sein
What joie was that ilke stounde
Of that he hath his qweene founde,
Which ferst was sent of goddes sonde,
Whan sche was drive upon the Stronde
Be whom the misbelieve of Sinne
Was left, and Cristes feith cam inne
To hem that whilom were blinde. (*Confessio Amantis*,
bk. 2, lines 1561–71)[22]

Gower has the right reading, for his story and for the Man of Law's.

Why does Chaucer create such dissonance in his tale and such misdirection in his moralization? Perhaps to undercut the royal lawyers' theocratic and absolutist views which, however correct, when narrowly interpreted endanger the realm and the king. Or perhaps he wants to show Richard or, more likely, his close advisors in the Chamber and among the royal clerks and

---

[22] All citations and quotations from Gower's *Confessio Amantis* are from the Macaulay edition as are those from his other works. The marriage and reunion of Constance, or Constancy, and England may also have reminded a medieval audience of the marriage of the Sergeant-at-Law who is supposed to declare himself constant to the estates of the realm of England through a ring-giving. Cf. Alexander Pulling, *Order of the Coif* (Boston, 1897), pp. 254–55; Fortescue, *De Laudibus Legum Anglie*, pp. 122–24. Since the story is a history, it probably should not be read as an allegory; "history" outside the Bible is never treated as allegorical or figural save when told out of its "natural order" in the epic or mingled with ..bled events; see Olson, "Chaucer's Epic Statement," pp. 62–66. For fourteenth-century reservations even about extensions of scriptural history to the figural, see Minnis, *Medieval Theory of Authorship*, pp. 103–7. Kolve's interpretation of Constance's ship as the ship of the Church appears to be an unwarranted extension of history into the figural which adds nothing to the tale since its letter clearly states that Constance brings Christianity with her to Syria and England. The Church already exists in the Rome to which she returns, and here the boat theme obscures the tale's concern with law and kingship, Empire and England, and trivializes its imperial conclusion; see Kolve, *Chaucer and the Imagery of Narrative*, pp. 297–358.

[102]

lawyers, that the leader's dignity and power derive more from consultation with the magnates and natural law than from miracle or superstition. Perhaps he wants to suggest that rule claiming direct sanction from God requires agents who practice constancy if it is to result in contented acceptance. The Lawyer is inconstant both in behavior and glossing (he ought to know how to do the latter from bench experience). Though Chaucer's immediate or topical thrust remains a mystery, his general direction does not, for when his Lawyer reinterprets the history of England and makes kingship miraculous, he says nothing that reduces the plausibility of the Knight's respect for natural law and such consultative kingship as derives law from constant, universal regularities and rules. He is the first of Chaucer's characters to misgloss history and kingship, but he is not the last.

4

Chaucer on Temporal Power and Art

THOPAS AND MELIBEE

Chaucer's own stories of Thopas and Melibee complete the tales giving full treatment to the temporal power and the consultative view of rulership developed by the Knight and by the magnates in the 1380s. The Monk and Prioress may intrude on the project, but ineffectively, since the Melibee provides its own complete picture of how the ruler who governs by Christian *and* natural law achieves sapience, a theme of the entire B² group in the *Canterbury Tales*.[1] Chaucer, in real life a poet, administrator, and occasional poetic counsellor through "ballades," illustrates the problems of the court poet in the tales assigned to him—the frivolously poetic Thopas and the lengthy prose Melibee, which details how temporal leaders ought to pick counsellors and analyze recommendations. Through two tales superficially dissimilar to the point of incompatibility, the poet subtly illustrates how peace and "political" monarchy may come to an England that must move from Theseus' pre-Christian "pitee" and righteous prudence to the full Christian forgiveness incarnate in Christ-as-Logos. Thus, the poet comments on the function of court literature as it examines the relationship between the two swords—between earthly power

[1] Past criticism has argued that B², particularly Chaucer's own section, concerns the philosophic nature of true art or topical political matters. Cf. Alan T. Gaylord, "Sentence and Solaas in Fragment VII of the *Canterbury Tales*: Harry Bailly as Horseback Editor," *PMLA* 82 (1967):226–35; Dolores Palomo, "What Chaucer Really Did to *Le Livre de Melibee*," *PQ* 53 (1974):304–20; Gardiner Stillwell, "The Political Meaning of Chaucer's *Tale of Melibee*," *Speculum* 19 (1944):433–44; Charles A. Owen, Jr., "The Tale of Melibee," *CR* 7 (1973): 267–80.

and the Christian wisdom that in the A section of the *Canterbury Tales* appears only as a vague "wise purveiaunce" and "thyng . . . parfit . . . and stable" which is the source of natural law (A, 3011, 3009).

First, Chaucer explores the hazards of misleading, fantastic art in the Thopas, then the benefits of properly directive philosophic and jurisprudential discipline in the Melibee. He begins his own section by stating his incompetence in tale-telling as he has earlier noted his incompetence in presenting the estates in order:

> "Hooste," quod I, "ne beth nat yvele apayd,
> For oother tale certes kan I noon,
> But of a rym I lerned longe agoon." (B², 1897–99)

When the poet follows the Man of Law and offers only a piece of used-over "hawebake" as his contribution, he surprises no one, for he always professes insufficiency. The *House of Fame* invites us to contrast its timid Geoffrey, afraid of apotheosis, with the *Commedia*'s Dante who remarks that he is not Aeneas or Saint Paul while conveying his sense that he is both. (While Dante sits with immortal poets in the *Inferno*'s circle of light, Chaucer barely gets by.) The narrator of the *Troilus* is almost a buffoon—ugly, incapable of love, the scribe and "pope" of successful lovers; the narrator in the *Parlement of Foules* awakens befuddled by his own dream; and the General Prologue poet comes to us as at best an insignificant, moderately affable pilgrim (A, 31), satisfied with modest accommodations (A, 28), a little uncertain of his society's structure (A, 744), and the victim of his teller's tales (A, 725–38; cf. A, 3167ff., B¹, 45–80). It is thus not surprising that the Thopas poet represents himself as of little consequence—a cardboard versifier willing to deliver the tale requested. Since the Prioress has just told her sentimental "Hugh of Lincoln" story, reducing the pilgrims to sobriety, the host is offended by the poet's being abstracted like the rest of

[105]

the pilgrims when he ought to be prepared to keep the entertainment flowing:

"What man artow?" quod he;
"Thou lookest as thou woldest fynde an hare,
For evere upon the ground I se thee stare." (B², 1885–87)

Always more interested in "solace" than "sentence," Bailey commands Chaucer to "looke up murily" (B², 1888), to "[t]elle . . . a tale of myrthe" (B², 1896), to lighten a world where childsaints end in privies,² an assault that attacks the attitude the group draws from the Prioress as egregiously as does the Miller's breaking in after the Knight. In telling Chaucer what to tell, Bailey also conveys his opinion of the poet as little more than a pedestrian versifier, and Chaucer acquiesces to the opinion.

As Chaucer earlier uses his tales of temporal lordship to tally the temporal power's responsibilities, he employs the Thopas to number the abuses implicit in the role of court poet—the provision of episodic trash that caters to the love of the "delicious" and says nothing to the ruler's moral imagination, the writing of ridiculous rhymes, and so on. On the other hand, the Melibee shows how linguistic discipline when controlled can serve the goals of good rule. To emphasize the point of the Thopas, the poet writes mumbo-jumbo and end-stops his lines to make rhyme dominate meaning while everything else is subordinated to the rocking-horse motion of his words. Charles Owen has put the sense of the prosody perfectly:

What happens to the word "forest" in the line,
    He priketh thurgh a fair forest (B², 1944)
happens also to the wildly unchivalrous elements, the hair and beard to his waist, the archery and wrestling, the bevy of maidens

² Arthur K. Moore, "*Sir Thopas* as Criticism of Fourteenth Century Minstrelsy," *JEGP* 53 (1954):532–45.

sleepless in vain for his love, the absurdly domesticated land-
scape.[3]

The rhythm of the verse masks the incongruities until one does
a double take and clutches at them. When one finally takes in the meaning of Chaucer's sen-
tences, one discovers that Chaucer is talking about a domesti-
cated puppet lord who is seized by a "love-longynge" so strong
that he goes after the queen of fairies, probably Proserpina,
with a sexual appetite so fierce that he rides his "horse" on soft
grass until it sweats blood. After he lies down to give his
"horse" hay, his sleep so wraps itself in love that he dreams of
an elf-queen under his "goore" as his mistress, his "heart" aris-
ing so bold from this that he rides out to meet his Goliath. But
he quickly rides back to town. Confronting the Oliphaunt, he
discovers that he is not David and that Oliphaunt has the equip-
ment, and he has to trot back for his armor and his pep-up of
minstrels and "geestours" with their royal romances of "popes"
and "cardinales" and "eek of love-likynge" (B², 2039–40). Re-
questing romances while arming, he gets only gingerbread, lic-
orice, sweet wine and mead (B², 2041–46), and, in the candy-
store of poetry missed, is arrayed in jewel armor to fight for no
common weal. Warriors who had fought in the Hundred Years
War with its disease, suffering, cold, and scorched earth would
have found our hero's solitary, empty career uproarious (even
more would those anticipating a crusade against the Turk), but
perhaps no more so than they found the well-known romances
to which Thopas is compared in Chaucer's text—*King Horn*,
Guy of Warwick, *Bevis of Hampton* (B², 2087–92)—overlong,

[3] Charles A. Owen, Jr., "Thy Drasty Rymyng . . . ," *SP* 63 (1966):540, 538–
43; cf. Walter Scheps, "Sir Thopas: The Bourgeois Knight, the Minstrel and
the Critics," *Tenn. Studies in Literature* 11 (1966):35–41; cf. Alan T. Gaylord,
"Chaucer's Dainty 'Dogerel': The 'Elvyish' Prosody of *Sir Thopas*," *Studies in the
Age of Chaucer* 1 (1979):83–104.

chaffy, and self-indulgent popular adventure stories full of fantastic episodes, endless riming, and verbiage without a hint of allegory or serious philosophic purpose. All contain innumerable forgettable battles, and the latter two, unnumbered episodes of trivial love.[4] None should be confused with the more serious allegorical romances in the mode of Chrétien, the *Queste del Saint Graal* or the *Estoire del Saint Graal*, that the Wife of Bath imitates.

Chaucer, in the prologue to the Thopas, presents himself as a teller of memorized rhymed tales—a kind of *gestour*. Since Bailey again asks for a "geeste" (B[2], 2123) immediately after the Thopas, he apparently has only heard the "rym dogerel" of the verse and not even identified its kind. But Chaucer is making a point about minstrelsy and poetry. The best account of medieval minstrelsy, that in Constance Bullock-Davies's *Menestrellorum Multitudo*, records a 1306 feast that Edward I held to rouse his forces to afflict the Scot. Minstrels were, from time to time, used to rouse knights for battle, as well as for court and city entertainments; the 1306 record lists the several kinds of minstrels that Edward used: musicians subclassified as *estivours*, citole players, and trumpeters; and minstrels in charge of miscellaneous entertainments subclassified as heralds, waferers, watchmen, messengers, acrobats, and fencers. It is not clear where poets fit in. The musicians might include poets who sang lyric poems or poets who told stories might be put in a separate class of *gestours*. Though jugglers, conjurers, and mimics were possibly also classes of minstrels, they do not appear at the 1306 ceremony.[5] Outside the House of Fame, whose pinnacles contain niches full of "mynstralles and gestiours, that tellen tales"

---

[4] See Ann S. Haskell, "Sir Thopas: The Puppet's Puppet," *CR* 9 (1975):253–59; cf. Lee C. Ramsey, *Chivalric Romances: Popular Literature in Medieval England* (Bloomington: Indiana University Press, 1983), pp. 26–68, 211–13.

[5] Constance Bullock-Davies, *Menestrellorum Multitudo: Minstrels at a Royal Feast* (Cardiff: Wales University Press, 1978), pp. 27–63, esp. 55.

(*HF*, 1197–98), Chaucer has fun with the same classes of entertainers—musicians who pipe like Robin and Marsyas the satyr (lines 1214ff.), watchmen-trumpeters like Joab who sound the call to war, heralds and "pursevants" who lather rich folks, and jugglers, magicians, and "tregetours" who know how to "fumigate" the brain (lines 1260ff.):

> Tho saugh I in an other place
> Stonden in a large space,
> Of hem that maken blody soun
> In trumpe, beme, and claryoun;
> For in fight and blod-shedynge
> Ys used gladly clarionynge.   (*HF*, 1237–42)

Indeed, on the outside of the House of Fame as on the inside, what is most hymned are the *lust* and *love* and *war* we later find as key elements in the Thopas.

Lust and love and war are the Thopas' tally. Minstrels still performed in Chaucer's day. For example, Chaucer's overseer in his responsibilities with the Petherton forest, Sir Peter Courtenay, took minstrels with him when he went to do battle in France in 1383; Richard II took them with him on his Irish expedition in 1399 as did Henry V when he embarked in 1415. Some of the minstrels of that time may have resembled Philip de Vitry or Jean de Condé and been serious poets, but Chaucer is not mocking these; and even the mockery of the less serious ones may be two-edged, for part of the fervor, the bawdiness, the oral liveliness, and the greatness of Chaucer's more "classicized" poetry—its escape from dullness and pedantry—may be attributable to the competition that he faced.[6] But his *Canter-*

---

[6] Edmund Faral, *Les Jongleurs en France au Moyen Age* (Paris: Librairie Champion, 1910), pp. 224–25; Creton, *French Metrical History of the Deposition of Richard II*, ed. John Webb (London, 1824), pp. 21–22; cf. M. T. Clanchy, *From Memory to Written Record* (London: Edward Arnold, 1979). Cf. Jacques Ribard,

bury Tale period, the late 1380s and 1390s, appears to witness a shift in court taste in directions useful for understanding the Melibee and the Thopas. One finds increasing criticism of the *gestour* or romancer for his empty feeding of emotion and his lies. For example, Gower in book VI of the *Confessio Amantis* has Delicacy, a species of Gluttony, speak with relish of feeding the appetite with meat, drink, "fair-looking," and the romance of *Amadis and Ydoine* (bk. 6, lines 875–82), a French work similar to the Thopas. In *Piers Plowman*'s C text, Active Life portrays himself as a minstrel who makes the people happy through the grain of his labor rather than through frivolous works such as lordly minstrels offer their rulers:

> Wolde y lye and do men lawhe thenne lacchen y scholde
> Or mantel or mone amonges lordes munstrals.
> Y can nat tabre ne trompy ne telle fayre gestes,
> Farten ne fythelen at festes, ne harpe,
> Iape ne iogele ne genteliche pipe,
> Ne noþer sayle ne sautrien ne syngen with þe geterne.[7]
>
> *(Piers Plowman*, C text,
> Passus 16, lines 203–8)

A Wycliffite speaks harshly of those who teach their children "jeestis of battaillis and fals cronyclis."[8] And the *Mirrur of Sermons*, a late fourteenth-century English sermon collection, says "loketh now to tristrem, to gy of werwik" and the reader will find "mani lesinges and grete ffor . . . ich man þat makeþ hem enfourmeþ hem efter þe wil of his hert."[9] The critics see *gestes*

Un Menestrel du XIVe siècle: Jean de Condé (Geneva: Librairie Droz, 1969), and James I. Wimsatt, *Chaucer and the Poems of 'CH'*, pp. 59–60.

[7] *Piers Plowman: An Edition of the C Text*, ed. Derek Pearsall (Berkeley: California University Press, 1979).

[8] Wyclif, *Select English Works*, 3:196.

[9] *The Mirrur of Sermons*, fol. 1^r. *Cursor Mundi* had earlier expressed the same objection.

or *romances*, even the Arthurian romances, as frivolous, self-in-dulgent or false. In particular, some versions of the *Lancelot* come under criticism in the period: Dante pictures Francesca saying that a *Lancelot* pimped her liaison with Paolo (*Inferno*, v.137), Chaucer has his Pandarus read an old romance as he contemplates the achievement of his purpose in Troilus' and Criseyde's mutual seduction (bk. 3, line 980), Philippe de Mé-zières, in his *Songe*, attributes to the *Lancelot* the fostering of un-faithfulness,[10] and Chaucer's Nun's Priest says that his fable "is also trewe . . . / As is the book of Launcelot de Lake, / That wommen holde in ful greet reverence" (B², 4401–3), hardly praise given the picture of "women" painted by the Nun's Priest. The pejorative emphasis is sharpened by the awareness that more serious Arthurian work was still appreciated and pa-tronized, particularly at north and west country courts.

The extant noble library lists describe a late fourteenth-cen-tury movement away from some of the chaffy romances popu-lar in earlier decades and toward the books of history, theology, philosophy, and the classics once recommended to courtiers by John of Salisbury, and such a movement probably explains why Chaucer moves from Thopas to Melibee. Mortimer and Edward III used Arthurian romance to mobilize martial senti-ment, and the love of romances continued among the old vet-erans of the French wars into the second half of the century: nineteen of forty-two books in Guy of Beauchamp's 1360 li-brary were romances as were twelve of Sir Simon Burley's nineteen volumes (1388), nineteen of Thomas of Woodstock's eighty-three books left at Plesley (1397), and all nine of Richard II's books (1399). Most of the other volumes were pious saints' lives, and only Thomas of Woodstock had a substantial number

---

[10] *Lancelot* and other romances which tell lies and attract people to "amer par amours" are dismissed; Philippe de Mézières, *Songe du Vieil Pèlerin*, 2:221.

of serious books about government—five books of law, six of philosophy, and nine chronicles.[11] In contrast, in the next generation raised in the 1390s, Henry V was taught Latin as a child and had a Latin library of 110 volumes including works by the Church fathers and books of legal theory and history, John of Salisbury's *Policraticus*, Seneca's letters, and works by Cicero, Aristotle, Valerius Maximus, and, significantly, Chaucer![12] His brother, the Duke of Bedford, had an 843-volume library taken over from Charles VI of France, and another brother, Humphrey Duke of Gloucester, put together one of the greatest classical libraries ever assembled. The movement toward classical and Latinate literature and serious works about government is reflected by the poets of the period: in Gower who abandons the flaccid Anglo-Norman of the *Miroir de l'Omme* to write the more focused Latin *Vox Clamantis* and the English neo-Ovidian *Confessio Amoris*, in Usk who writes his Boethian book of philosophic counsel for the out-of-favor, and in Hoccleve who produces his advice to princes. At this historical turning, Philippe de Mézières is also advising against Arthurian

[11] Henry J. Todd, *Illustrations of the Lives and Writings of Chaucer and Gower* (London: Rivington, 1810), pp. 161–62; cf. Clarke, *Fourteenth Century Studies*, pp. 120–21; "Inventory of the goods and chattels belonging to Thomas, Duke of Gloucester," *Archeological Journal* 54 (1897):300–303; Goodman, *Loyal Conspiracy*, pp. 80–81; Edith Rickert, "King Richard II's Books," *Library* 13, 4th ser. (1933):144–47. Green's implication (*Poets and Princepleasers*, pp. 91–99) that late fourteenth-century English noble libraries were larger than the extant inventories is speculative; Edward depended heavily on clerks for his administration, and the French war did not allow leisure for chivalric learning at his court.

[12] McFarlane, *Lancastrian Kings and Lollard Knights*, pp. 15–17, 233–38. Henry's books may have been captured in France and intended as a gift for an English center of learning. Of his Latin learning there can be no doubt. The education that Henry IV received may reflect an effort to redevelop a temporal lordship learned in the philosophy and technical arts of temporal rulership after the French wars. Cf. *Songe de Vergier*, 1:135–37. Wyclif argues that the king must be instructed because not all kings are endowed with infused sapience; John Wyclif, *De Officio Regis*, p. 47.

romance as "so full of lies that the history in it remains suspect" and in favor of the writers central to this book: Solomon's Wisdom books, Oresme, Giles of Rome, Augustine, John of Salisbury, Boethius, Seneca, Aristotle, the best of the Jewish and Roman historians, Josephus, Livy, Valerius Maximus, and the stories of the Christian emperors.[13] The exchanges of tapestries—some of them undoubtedly resembling the tapestry of Caesar presently in the Cloisters (fig. 24)—of the 1390 peace negotiations reflect the same transition. Some of them were romance tapestries, but others were clearly serious allegories and classical histories.[14]

Thus, in the Melibee, Chaucer, like others in his period, turns from romance to serious political-philosophic and juris-

[13] Cf. Léopold Delisle, *Recherches sur la librairie de Charles V* (Amsterdam: Gérard Th. van Heusden, 1967), 1:138–41, 396–98; Roberto Weiss, *Humanism in England During the Fifteenth Century* (Oxford: Basil Blackwell, 1957), pp. 61–69. Philippe de Mézières, *Songe du Vieil Pèlerin*, 2:222–23. The French lyric forms remained popular in Chaucer's circle as witness the poetry of the Earl of Salisbury, Odo of Graunson, Boucicaut, and Gower.

[14] Tapestry subjects also suggest a movement toward history and allegory. Philip the Bold sent the English court the following tapestries between 1390 and 1400 to further peacemaking efforts: *History of Octavius; History of Our Lady; History of Clovis; Clinthe* (sic); *History of Pharaoh and the Jews; Death of the Blessed Virgin; History of the King and His Twelve Peers* (Arthur?); *Seven Virtues;* and *Perceval Le Galloys.* The *Seven Virtues* included the virtues and seven virtuous emperors and kings who had served them, and the seven vices with seven rulers who had followed them. See W. G. Thomson, *A History of Tapestry* (London: Hodder and Stoughton, 1930), p. 74, citing Van Drival, *Les Tapisseries d'Arras* (Paris, 1878), pp. 88–89. Richard II's Crown tapestries in 1399 include twelve Biblical and classical historical tapestries, five subjects from medieval history, nine formal allegories, three romance subjects, and four unidentifiable subjects—e.g., Octavian, Alexander, a "histor. filie Regis Tiry," several items of Biblical history, a tapestry of English kings, two tapestries of the conquest of Alexandria (presumably the conquest by Peter of Lusignan), one tapestry titled "De Corpore et Anima vocat. Prest de Cipro," and one of Geoffrey of Bouloigne (Thomson, *A History of Tapestry*, pp. 84–85). See also fig. 23.

CHAPTER 4

prudential statement, from a fictive knight's pursuit of the elf queen and fleshy Oliphaunt to a quest for Sophia, the daughter of Prudence. Donald Howard has correctly indicated that "everything indicates that the 'Melibee' was taken seriously in its own time,"[15] and gives it an excellent interpretation, but he neglects what is, from a political-social perspective, the most important character in the work: Melibee's daughter, Sophia, or Sapience, wounded and left for dead by the three enemies of man. If we recall that sapience or wisdom is the power that makes a king sit among the silently musical orbs of the heavens and hear the law of nature, that Theseus exercising such wisdom makes a peace, then the drift of the Melibee as a peace work is clear.

Sophia, the character who is Chaucer's primary addition to his source materials in Albertanus of Brescia and Renaud of Louhans, traditionally represents the Heavenly Wisdom, contained in the descent of the dove, which the monastic seeks as the model for the rest of humanity. Here she is what a temporal ruler also seeks but in a mode different from the monastic's and from Theseus' search for Wisdom in his final speech. She is allied with and derived from Prudence: in Alanus' *Anticlaudianus*, she seeks the company of Heavenly Theology who supersedes and complements a more mundane Prudence;[16] in civic iconology, she emphasizes that the king's reason or knowledge of the law of nature is itself divinely created: for example, Ambrogio Lorenzetti's mural of "The Effects of Good Government" in Siena (fig. 27), makes Sapience hover above the head of Justice, inspiring her while Justice, in turn, inspires Concordia or Peace. Parallel with Justice in the painting, the good ruler man-

[15] Howard, *The Idea of the Canterbury Tales*, pp. 310–16.
[16] See Isidore of Seville, *Etymologiae*, 2.24.3; Giovanni of Genoa, *Catholicon* (Venice, 1495), sig. J4ʳ; Alanus of Insulis, *Anticlaudianus*, ed. R. Bossuat (Paris: Librairie Philosophique J. Vrin, 1955), pp. 124–39. Cf. also Donovan and Keen, "The *Somnium* of John of Legnano," pp. 331–37.

ifests justice, and above his head the figures equivalent to Sapience which inform his action appear as Christian Faith, Hope, and Charity. Beside him sit his associates in government, Prudence and Magnanimity, and beneath his feet stand the citizens of the peaceful city of Siena. Thus this Prudence, infused with Sapience, represents animate justice as the basis of peace.

Other civic illustrations represent the infusion of Sophia or Sapientia as the basis of the ruler's capacity to lay hold on reason and interpret natural law (fig. 25),[17] but, significantly, Chaucer does not present the loss of *sapience* by his Melibee's ruler as a loss of the power of the chrism, nor does he have the ruler bathe in oil to regain it.

Chaucer's view of rulership, like Dante's, detaches temporal government from direct dependence on clerics and clerical anointment for its authority, but it does not detach the monarch from dependence on divine law. The ruler has to learn privately the forgiveness and love required of the good man to become the good ruler.

Melibee, through the exercise of reason, does regain sapience though the story never says that his besieged daughter got up and walked. Lady Wisdom or Sapience, who makes the order of nature and the power of the ruler's rule in several books of the Old Testament, is clearly identified in the New Testament with Christ-as-Wisdom or Christ-as-Logos; and this tradition continues in medieval comment on Boethius' Lady Philosophia. If, as Donald Howard has indicated, the attack of the three enemies represents the Fall, it also represents the assault

[17] Kantorowicz, *King's Two Bodies*, pp. 112–73; cf. pp. 109–15; "Sapientia" as equivalent with "Faith, Hope and Charity" is an infused power. For further discussions of the visual and philosophic traditions, see N. Rubenstein, "Political Ideas in Sienese Art: The Frescoes by Ambrogio Lorenzetti and Taddeo Bartolo in the Palazzo Pubblico," *JWCI* 21 (1958):179–207; Chiara Frugoni, "The Book of Wisdom and Lorenzetti's Fresco in the Palazzo Pubblico at Siena," *JWCI* 43 (1980):239–41.

of vice on any commonwealth—the brigandage that Chaucer has previously embodied in the Miller and the Reeve and their tales. The remainder of the treatise then traces a civic redemption through which the spirit of Wisdom and Christ are recovered by a temporal government which originally rested only on violence but which may through grace rest on service, as the Parson observes (I, 770ff.).

Chaucer's Prudence is not worldly prudence or self-interest but a figure like Virgil in the *Commedia*: she comes to Melibee as an objective rational analyst after he has met the three beasts and provides maxims and analytic rules for examining (1) who offers counsel and who should offer it, (2) what special interests the counsel serves, (3) what emotions it panders to, and (4) what logical questions the ruler may ask of it. Prior to Prudence's entry, most of Melibee's counselors—physicians, old enemies, fearful neighbors, flatterers, and advocates—like the estates of birds in the *Parlement*, offer apparently useful but quite limited advice: the physicians note that diseases are cured by their contraries but interpret that to mean that war can be ended by a sudden vengeance; the fearful neighbor suggests that a quick war would help; the wise lawyers argue that a rapid military build-up and a slow search for retaliation would be good. The young want a war now, and the old wish for a search for peace, however slow. The perception of each response is limited by the profession and temperament of its advocate, and the ruler must put all the responses together in the realization that many of his subjects may be killed, whatever his judgment. As the wise old man says, "Lordynges . . . ther is ful many a man that crieth 'Werre! Werre!' that woot ful litel what werre amounteth. . . . [M]any a child unborn of his mooder . . . shal sterve yong by cause of thilke weere, or elles lyve in sorwe and dye in wrecchednesse" (B², 2227–31). Such a passage calls attention to the silliness of the Thopas' description of the soldier's "delicious" solitary life of easy questing, loving, and battling. In answering the proposals for war, Prudence describes for Melibee who his counsellors are, why they offer their plans, and what their logical fallacies are. For example, she points out that the physician's advice to have vengeance shifts categories and makes vengeance the opposite of war; the old advocates' analysis of defense, which is not exhaustive, also indulges in faulty definition; the old enemies, neighbors, and flatterers, who advise quick vengeance, fail to make a Ciceronian analysis of the rational concomitants and contexts for their advice, its motives, causes (formal, final, and so forth) and consequences.[18] Prudence, in contrast, as a sort of Inns of Court teacher, sharpens the analytic tools of jurisprudence in the medieval mode, and when her tools have exposed the deficiency of the counsel to war,[19] she increasingly speaks as Sophia in the form of Christ as she advances from the technical to the revealed and takes her student-ruler through examinations of his jurisdiction and his fortune, his obligation to leave vengeance to God and acquire wealth slowly while using it well, and his need to make peace with God and achieve reconciliation with his enemies.

As in the Virgil-Beatrice nexus of the *Commedia*, grace and love become an implicit part of the discussion only after rational

[18] For the wisdom tradition in Israel, see Gerhard von Rad, *Wisdom in Israel* (New York: Abingdon, 1972); *Aspects of Wisdom in Judaism and Early Christianity*, ed. Robert L. Wilken (Notre Dame: Notre Dame University Press, 1975); M. Jack Suggs, *Wisdom, Christology and Law in Matthew's Gospel* (Cambridge, Mass.: Harvard University Press, 1970); Fred W. Burnett, *The Testament of Jesus-Sophia* (Washington, D.C.: University Press of America, 1979); J. N. Birdsall, "Logos," *New Bible Dictionary* (Grand Rapids, Mich.: Eerdmans, 1975), pp. 744–45. This tradition is carried on by Boethian commentary and by Augustine and his tradition; in Boethian commentary, Lady Philo-Sophia is generally interpreted as the love of Wisdom in the sense described in the Sapiental books—Wisdom as creative principle of order in the universe, divine epiphany, source of kingly rule, and of the fearing and loving of God. I am preparing a study of the place of Wisdom in medieval educational theory and practice.

[19] Cicero, *De Officiis*, 2.5.

philosophy has explored their alternatives in the construction of human society. Asserting that unity and peace are the greatest things in the world, Prudence finally quotes Christ on peacemakers: "Wel happy and blessed been they that loven and purchacen pees, for they been called children of God" (B², 2869–70). Hence Melibee should initiate the reconciliation which will, figuratively interpreted, heal his wounded Sophia, eliminate his hardheartedness, and return peace:

> Thanne dame Prudence discovered al hir wyl to hym, and seyde, / "I conseille yow," quod she, "aboven alle thynges, that ye make pees bitwene God and yow; / and beth reconsiled unto hym and to his grace. / For, as I have seyd yow heer biforn, God hath suffred yow to have this tribulacioun and disese for youre synnes. / And if ye do as I sey yow, God wol sende youre adversaries unto yow, / and maken hem fallen at youre feet, redy to do youre wyl and youre comandementz. / For Salomon seith, 'Whan the condicioun of man is pleasaunt and likynge to God, / he chaungeth the hertes of the mannes adversaries and constreyneth hem to biseken hym of pees and of grace.' " (B², 2903–9)

When the enemies submit to Melibee and ask his judgment, Prudence again advises and secures his forgiveness of them.[20]

Whereas the sapient pagan Theseus describes a necessity governed by love as the basis of a peace, Prudence's word to Melibee glosses the road to peace in a more Christian way, like that proposed also by the Order of the Passion: the nobility of Europe are to take leadership in showing that God can turn hard hearts and make them seek forgiveness.[21] The Melibee does not exhibit the pacifism of the Wycliffites of the 1380s or

---

[20] In addition Prudence indicates in what emotional attitude the ruler must be to hear counsel, cf. Charles A. Owen, "The Tale of Melibee," pp. 267–80.

[21] Brown, *Mézières' Order*, pp. 56–58, 81–86. Philippe says that Christ, the "Wisdom of God," offers to the French and English kings, the "bread of life" as the seal of peace; Philippe de Mézières, *Letter to Richard II*, pp. 47–49.

of the 1395 *Conclusions*; rather, it allows for the possibility of just wars. But it also asserts that repentance, faith, prudence, and the wisdom of forgiveness can make the ruler God's representative through actions of the heart that, although not overtly miraculous, may be more effective than theocratic absolutism in creating peace.

Chaucer's allegory envelops both internal and external meanings: the internal concerning how to make peace with the passions through forgiving them and setting reason to rule over them; the external about limiting war within and without the realm through good counsel. Though the internal application, moving any "Melibee" away from his fall before the enemies, may be the paramount one, a strictly internal application makes jejune the talk about war preparations, choosing counsellors and analyzing what they say. The external application by itself would be superficial homily. Both are needed.

The complaint about royal acceptance of bad counsel or refusal to accept counsel at all extends from the appointment of the Lords Ordainers, the banning of some Despensers, and the hanging of others in Edward II's reign, to the dismissals of Latimer, Lyons, and Neville in Edward III's time to the 1386 and 1388 continual councils and, finally, to Richard's deposition.[22] England flopped back and forth between absolutist and consultative poles by turns, governed or controlled by king or magnates, and it knew a stable period only during Edward III's prime when he successfully harnessed the magnates to his cart in the wars and the parliament. Chaucer's work also resonates to older fights over the issue in Italy and in the Low Countries and interprets the English fights in terms of their precedents. When Albertanus wrote his Melibee in 1246, ten years after he

---

[22] Stillwell, in "The Political Meaning of Chaucer's Tale of Melibee," pp. 433–44, relates the tale to the 1386–88 situation, but bad counsel was a rather consistent problem in the period; cf. *RP* 3:379, 422–23.

had been captured at Brescia by Frederick II's forces, he was promoting an Italian urban ideology against an imperial one. Earlier, Frederick had promulgated, in his *Liber Augustalis*, the notion of an emperor, inspired by God, needing no counsel and no consent of the people. Bound by no human law, he acts as the mediator between reason as an abstract idea and positive law, and is the father of human, and the son of divine, justice. Frederick's notion appears in his Capuan Gate where the emperor sits among four figures—Wisdom, Clemency, Prudence, and Piety, none of whom signifies counsellors—and above his singular creation, the massive figure of Caesar's justice—positive law (fig. 26).[23] Albertanus of Brescia probably wrote his *Liber Consolationis et Consilii* after his work with the communal city states of the Lombard League opposed to Frederick, and to answer Frederick's Ghibelline theocratic absolutism glorified in the Capuan Gate.[24] Renaud of Louhans did the same thing with his Melibee in relation to Eudes IV of Burgundy, caught in the 1336–37 war with his barons and tenants-in-chief. For both works the issue is the consultative as opposed to the absolutist view of the prerogative of the King.[25] Whether Chaucer's audience would have known the historical resonances in his work is unclear. Clearly, Richard's absolutism had continental roots, and the Melibee would have been seen as answering such thought whether its precise derivation was known or not.

---

[23] See Kantorowicz, *King's Two Bodies*, pp. 97–143; cf. the introduction by James Powell to his translation of the *Liber Augustalis* (Syracuse: Syracuse University Press, 1971), pp. xxi–xxxiv, 7–9, 32–33, 42–64. C. A. Willemsen, *Kaiser Friedrichs II: Triumphtor Zu Capua* (Wiesbaden: 1953), pp. 61–75.

[24] Albertanus of Brescia, *Liber Consolationis et Consilii*, ed. Thor Sundby (London, 1873), pp. 83–84. Cf. Thomas Curtis Van Cleve, *The Emperor Frederick II of Hohenstauffen* (Oxford: Clarendon Press, 1972), pp. 321–22.

[25] Ernest Petit, *Histoire des Ducs de Bourgogne* (Paris: Picard, 1901), 7:126–241. Cf. "Le Livre de Melibee et de Prudence par Renaud de Louhans," *Histoire Littéraire de la France* 37 (1938):497–99.

Chaucer does not cast his sapient ruler as the monarch-isolate who seeks a private peace as Richard did in his 1387 negotiating, nor does he make him a public militarist like the magnate counsellors who sought renewed war with France in the same period. Chaucer's peace is based on a consultative process, a unity, and a forgiveness that both the magnates and Richard seem to have had difficulty mastering in the period from the Merciless Parliament to Richard's removal.

Chaucer appears to say, in his introduction to the Melibee, that the temporal tales that come earlier than the Melibee contain the same "sentence" as it does (B², 2141–56). Whether or not he says this, many of the section A and B¹ stories *do* treat the same themes. Melibee's Prudence is a feature of Theseus also, given the *Songe de Vergier*'s definition of prudence as exercising the memory, understanding, and foresight of a person and teaching the fragility of life, God's greatness, philosophy in office, and providential governing.[26] Both Theseus and Melibee begin their progress in rule with the discipline of this virtue and are ultimately governed by Sophia—Theseus in his advice to the wisdom which makes a virtue of necessity, Melibee in his forgiveness of his enemies. But whereas Theseus knows only an unrevealed perfection, Melibee knows it "revealed." As Melibee's sensuality and lack of discipline result in his abandonment of Prudence and his daughter's capture by the three enemies, so Robin's lack of discipline produces his abandonment of the Knight's and Theseus' chain of love and his reflection of the three enemies in his life and tale. Prudence also paraphrases the self-justificatory maxim with which Oswald begins his vendetta against Robin, "For leveful is with force force of-showve"

---

[26] *Songe de Vergier*, 2:148–50. Cf. V. J. Scattergood, "Chaucer and the French War: *Sir Thopas* and *Melibee*," *Court and Poet*, ed. Glyn S. Burgess (Liverpool: Francis Cairns, 1981), pp. 287–96. Oresme (*Le Livre de Politiques de Aristote*, pp. 311–12) notes that political prudence is the proper virtue of a king as sapience or contemplation is the proper virtue of a lord spiritual.

(A, 3912), but she frames it with the principle that vengeance belongs to God and earthly punishment to courts. Only immediate self-defense justifies the use of force unsupervised by law (B², 2720–25). Finally, Prudence demonstrates that Constance, rather than her author, understands how the struggle against evil is to be won. She sets straight the twisted version of the diatribe against poverty that the Man of Law draws from Innocent III (B¹, 99–121) and describes poverty as fundamentally a physical rather than a moral evil (B², 2751–59). She clarifies the question of wealth by urging its slow acquisition, and she would have her followers avoid the gambling in trade and the trafficking in hardship which the Man of Law praises in merchants (B¹, 124–30). Though Prudence's careful reasoning reminds one more of Theseus than of the Man of Law, she is like his Constance in one respect, namely that she ends by advocating trust in divine intervention: "for the victorie of a bataile comth nat by the grete nombre of peple, / but it cometh from oure Lord God of hevene." (B², 2851–52). Sophia! Sapience—not the chrism any more and not simply natural law but the oil of disciplined jurisprudential reasoning whose essence is mansuetude.

The technique of the Thopas-Melibee section moves daringly to create an art of anti-art. Its lavish Thopas confection mocks the "delicious" superficiality of kinetic art, art for art's sake or art for recreation's sake, the craft of pure entertainment now popularly claimed as the aesthetic of the fabliau. Chaucer has no respect for art that is only wish-fulfillment unconnected to the reality of the world outside. In a parallel statement, his Melibee exposes the ruler who seeks primarily wish-fulfillment from *placebo* counsellors, the ruler who cannot learn the tough logical disciplines that would allow him to see for himself how things are done with words, what consequences are likely to flow from his actions, and how understanding and reconciliation could be won from his adversaries. Unlike the Knight's Tale, which can be read for its "lovely story" without these disciplines, the Melibee makes no concessions to its audience. It requires that one deal with its linguistic and logical rigor, and comes with the sign, *Caveat lector otiosus*.

PART III

The
CANTERBURY TALES
*on the Spiritual
Power*

5

Stratford's Nunnery, Sapience, and
Monasticism's Critical Role

The tales of the Prioress and the Nun's Priest, which with the Monk's tale surround Chaucer's "own" tales, center on the monastic, as opposed to the royal, search for the sapience necessary to administer temporal courts. Together with the other Stratford tale told by the Second Nun, they define what contemplatives can do for the temporal ruler. The Melibee gives a normative account of the significance of the ruler's personal perfection and capacity for forgiveness and ignores structured public relations between Church and temporal court. The monastic tales study what contemplatives may offer temporal courts— whether they primarily model the ruler's approach to perfection, give him critical advice, offer him administrative help, or follow his court's fashions.

In the *Canterbury Tales*, Chaucer dedicates more of the tales to the Church and to clerics than to any other group, perhaps partly because clerks like Hoccleve and Usk were members of his audience. Certainly he must have done this partly because the Schism, Wycliffite controversy, and general controversy over the place of monastics and friars had made the royal court almost a second convocation for ecclesiological dispute. Reciprocally, each segment of the Church had its stance toward Richard's court and tended also to favor different policies toward France and Italy. The monastics followed a strong English alliance with the Roman pope and the Emperor and opposed a peace with France until quite late in the period. Some friars seem to have been close supporters of the Ricardian movement to put the war with France behind. Wyclif pretty much advocated John of Gaunt's international positions during his life-

CHAPTER 5

time. Clerics tried to influence court thought—in parliament, and through administrative action and advocacy. Of these, the most vociferous and visible was Wyclif until his death in 1384, and even after that the courts appear to have discussed the issues he raised at least until 1395 when several of the Chamber knights sponsored the *Conclusions*.

The preeminent issues that Wyclif directed to the court grew out of the intertwining of the temporal and spiritual swords by Christendom's four "sects": monks, canons regular, friars, and bishops. Wyclif attacked monastic temporal possession, canon regular endowment, friar conventualism, and episcopal exercise of the keys during the period of his greatest influence at London and Oxford. Late in his life, he turned to an attack on all papal authority, the theory and administration of penance, and the conventional doctrine of the Eucharist itself and, thus, placed himself outside the orbit of conventional academic interchange or ecclesiastical debate. Yet for most of the period, England was not so polarized as to prohibit civil discussion of many of Wyclif's issues; Chaucer's friend, Strode, addressed Wyclif in two friendly treatises, and the Chamber's court figures discussed his teachings long after his death. People could favor one or more of the reformer's points without adopting his credo. Indeed, the usual distinction between orthodox criticism of Church abuses and heterodox criticism of the Church is not terribly helpful in this period of two popes and confused authority. Also, Wyclif frequently began his criticism with an obvious Church abuse, then attacked Church authorities for not bringing it under control and showed that they could not bring it in tow, and finally attacked the doctrine that led both to "practice" and "abuse." Where does his heterodoxy begin? To what extent is he only echoing the clichés of the period's reformers in more violent language? How much of his analysis did a thinker in his period have to accept to become a Wycliffite? None of these questions were clear in Chaucer's period. It should be remembered that no discussions by the English hierarchy of Wyclif's teachings ever led to his excommunication, and the most serious warning that he received came in a 1382 "Earthquake Council" condemnation of Wycliffite techniques which led to the excommunication of Repingdon, Hereford, and Bedeman, but not of Wyclif. Not until Arundel's Preaching Constitution of 1407–1409 was the discussion of Wycliffite ideas seriously impeded by civil *and* religious authority acting in concert.

Too often Chaucer studies have sought only to define Chaucer as a Wycliffite or an anti-Wycliffite. The truth is far more complex. Wyclif, as a predestinarian in salvation psychology, a royalist in politics, and a direct polemicist could only advocate, or appear to advocate, a predestined radical royal reform of the institutions connecting Church and state. Chaucer, not bound by predestinarianism, one-sided royalism, or the hazards of direct polemic, could, on the other hand, accept a Wycliffite analysis of the problems of the institutions connecting Church and state without accepting Wycliffite solutions to those problems. Admitting the issues, the poet could push the analysis further back by showing how the confusion of temporal and spiritual swords in Wyclif's four sects derives ultimately from the "sect of Epicurus," from its materialism and substitution of temporal delight for discipline (see chap. 9 below). The confusion of the swords can only be straightened out by an affirmation of the very perfective and penitential disciplines denied by Wyclif's predestinarianism and individualism. It is meaningless to call such a position Wycliffite or anti-Wycliffite.

In the Stratford group, Chaucer ignores Wyclif on the surface and portrays a potentially Epicurean Prioress, with her *Amor vincit omnia*, and a similar Chantecleer who is attached to his "sisters" of the yard enclosed with sticks and loves them "[m]oore for delit than world to multiplye" (B², 4535). In the configuration of the Stratford tales, the poet prepares for his analysis of Wycliffite perspectives on the relationship of

Church and state by establishing how a false simulation of contemplation by the Epicurean person may create a "false sapience" and how true contemplative discipline finds a wisdom that can effectively challenge the princely courts. Though Chaucer was no theologian of the contemplative life, he translated Boethius' *Consolation*, which was seen to concern contemplation, knew Dante's work with its sophisticated presentation of contemplative theology, and dedicated the *Troilus* to Ralph Strode, who in 1378 and 1379 wrote his friendly rejoinders to Wyclif's attacks on monasticism, ecclesiastical property, and sovereignty—rejoinders that questioned the practicality of Wyclif's desired return from medieval monasticism to a primal apostolic state. The poet's friends, the Chamber knights—Stury, Clifford, Latimer, Montagu, and Cheyne—posted the 1395 *Conclusions* attacking monasticism's vows of chastity and all ecclesiastical (monastic?) holding of temporal wealth.[1] Chaucer had seen the Schism develop firsthand on his 1378 Italian trip and had encountered Giovanni of Legnano's elevation of the clerical life, dedicated to contemplative sapience and canon law, above all other lives.[2] Obviously the poet wrote in a cli-

---

[1] See chap. 6, n. 6, below, for citations and discussions. Zacharias Thundy, "Chaucer's Quest for Wisdom in *The Canterbury Tales*," NM 77 (1976):582–98 ignores the wisdom theme in B² save for the Melibee.

[2] The Clerk says that Legnano illumined all the realm of Italy with his philosophy, law, and other arts (E, 34–35). Philosophy is conventionally etymologized as philo-sophia, love of wisdom or *sapientia*, and Legnano's *Somnium* begins with five stars illuminating the papal throne, among them *Sapientia* and *Ars*, and goes on to explain the derivation of canon law from wisdom (*sapientia*) or revelation and its relation to the arts. See Donovan and Keen, "The *Somnium* of John of Legnano," pp. 325–46. The Clerk's phrase gracefully summarizes the *Somnium* that argues for the "essential harmony of all laws, founded upon a conception of the entire cosmos as an articulated and harmonious whole subjected to . . . God" (p. 335); Chaucer, unlike John of Legnano and like the *Songe de Vergier*, generally assigns the discovery of this also to temporal rulers such as Theseus.

mate rich with ecclesiastical controversy, particularly about monasticism. Section B², largely dedicated to Chaucer's own tales and the tales by and about monastics, forms the poet's bridge between his discusson of the temporal power and his representation of the cleric's force, and focuses on the birth of sapience first in private devotion and then its appearance in public courts.

Sapience, the power of seeing and harmonizing with the divine, was initially ascribed to bishops through the power of their anointment, but from the middle of the eighth century it was attributed also to kings because they too were anointed with chrism. In the later Middle Ages, the locus *par excellence* of sapience was the monastic institution. The monastery's members putatively meditated day and night on Christ-as-Logos, held continuous masses and devotions in the company of the angels, cleansed themselves from impurity as God's virgins, and saw His face in special contemplative experience.[3] Meditating in their cloisters between heaven and earth, brothers to angels, they knew the power of the divine court; in writing chronicles, they encountered the errancy of the earthly. By virtue of contemplation, the "heavenly" world of the clergy had claimed superiority to all kings and tyrants,[4] and St. Bernard, whom Chaucer's two nuns "use" in the form of the prayer cited by Dante, placed monks above knights and gave crusading commands to kings. This medieval sense that the virgin of God, the contemplative, has a special access to wisdom partially accounts for the use of monks as court advisors and administrators which prompted Wyclif to attack their temporal positions and Uthred of Boldon to defend the heavenly basis of their earthly rule. But Chaucer's Theseus has no "monastic" counsellor, nor

[3] Duby, *The Three Orders*, p. 235–37; Jean Leclercq, *The Love of Learning and the Desire for God*, trans. Catherine Misrahi (New York: Fordham University Press, 1961), pp. 253–67.

[4] Duby, *The Three Orders*, pp. 201–3.

does the poet ever countenance any monastic undertaking of daily temporal court business or life. To examine the claims of the monastic relationship to the court, he invents two parties, the Stratford nunnery group and the Monk and, in the former group, uses his Prioress to survey earthly attachment, his Second Nun to do the same for sapiential detachment, and his Nun's Priest to map the bumps and hard places on the penitential road between them. Chapter 6 will show that he uses his other cloistered party, the Monk, to extend this discussion to Wyclif's and Uthred's dispute over monastic administration of property and power away from the cloister.

Imagine a mother superior at a convent which is committed to the perfective life—the vision of God, poverty, chastity, and obedience—who is herself infatuated with love, finery, and court news, a priest to that convent infatuated with the mother superior, and another nun, probably a chaplain to the convent, "infatuated" with religious "work" in the medieval sense.[5] Imagine the plot of the Nun's Priest's tale played out in a cloister having a somewhat worldly and domineering prioress, an infatuated priest, and a stern female chaplain. You then have in outline the Stratford tales of the Prioress, the Nun's Priest, and the Second Nun. You can also anticipate the harmonies and disharmonies that the competition of the Epicurean and perfective lives creates in the Stratford convent's Canticle garden.

[5] For the tale as a projection of the Nun's Priest's situation at the nunnery, see Maurice Hussey, *The Nun's Priest's Prologue and Tale* (London: Cambridge University Press, 1965), pp. 5–10, 35–40. For the perfect life, see Jean Leclercq, *The Life of Perfection*, trans. Leonard J. Doyle (Collegeville: Liturgical Press, 1961); James Walsh, *Pre-Reformation English Spirituality* (New York: Fordham University Press, 1965), pp. 121–209; Mary Elizabeth Mason, *Active Life and Contemplative Life* (Milwaukee: Marquette University Press, 1961), pp. 78–108; Kenneth E. Kirk, *The Vision of God* (London: Longmans, 1931), pp. 235–74, 319–58; William A. Pantin, "Two Treatises of Uthred of Boldon on the Monastic Life," pp. 363–85.

Stratford was a "court" monastic institution, so understand-
ably its fictive prioress acts a little like a courtier. Madame
Eglantine's Stratford-at-Bow priory had its historical counter-
part on the Lea River which flowed into the Thames a few miles
east of London. It attracted court people such as Elizabeth of
Hainault and Philippa of Ulster (the daughter of Chaucer's
early patron, Lionel of Clarence) who took up residence there,
and the royal family who visited it on occasion. Richard II in
1380 excused it from paying taxes on lands flooded by the Lea.
Though a royal favorite, it lacked the great properties of other
monastic institutions—governing only the manors of Bormley
and Hastington, the livings of four London area churches, a
few London and Southwark tenements, houses, and shops, and
other minor property scattered about Cambridgeshire, Essex,
and Hertfordshire.[6]

Madame Eglantine, despite her institution's modest wealth
and important connection to the court, describes herself as a
helpless infant, weak in knowledge (B², 1671), through whom
only a kindly God can perfect praise (B², 1646–49, 1674–77).
She appears too naive or too disingenuous to be an effective
court-related prioress. Yet, the installation rite of Barking Nun-
nery, Stratford's sister, says to the incoming ruler of the insti-
tution, "Take the shepherd's staff," and the bishop instructs her
to "Take this power of ruling."[7] Again the Benedictine rule for

[6] J. S. Cockburn, et al. *A History of the County of Middlesex* (London: Oxford
University Press, 1969), 1:156–59. Cf. John Matthews Manly, *Some New Light
on Chaucer* (New York: Henry Holt, 1926), pp. 21ff. Manly has argued with
some plausibility that Eglantine may refer to Stratford's nun, Argentine, a con-
temporary who resided at the convent.

[7] *The Ordinary and Customary of the Benedictine Nuns of Barking Abbey: Sancto-
rale*, ed. J.B.L. Tolhurst (London: Harrison and Sons, 1928), 1:352. For the
relationship between the terms "prioress" and "abbess," see Lina Eckenstein,
Women Under Monasticism (Cambridge: Cambridge University Press, 1896), pp.
366–67.

women says "the prioress . . . is to be honored inside the abbey [sic] and out of it wherever she goes or rides, . . . shall be a law in herself, . . . shall have no pride in her heart but ever love God, and . . . is responsible as a shepherd or herdsman for the women given into her care."[8] The oath of installation and rule did not call for a prioress-child.[9] Indeed, the prioress's daily duties required that she have the administrative skill of a baron and the spiritual authority of a parson. She had the authority to see the liturgical services properly said, to oversee all management of the convent property, to supervise the education of convent novices, children, and youth, to supervise convent arts, crafts, and eleemosynary work, and to provide for the disciplining of sisters violating humility, continence, voluntary poverty, or the worship-and-work disciplines.[10] She also had ultimate responsibility for the physical upkeep and development of the convent properties. Joan Wigenhall, prioress of Crabhouse Nunnery from 1420 to 1444, in 1420 "drewe downe" the barn at the convent gate, had it rebuilt with new timbers and old tile, "made" the north end of her chamber, paid for "halfe chaunsel makynge" at Saint Peter's local church, and

[8] Eckenstein, *Women Under Monasticism*, pp. 366–67, paraphrasing the rhymed English version, *The Rule of St. Benet*.

[9] Childhood may be an emblem for humility or innocence as in Matthew 18.2–3: "Vel *parvulum*, id est, Spiritum sanctum posuit in cordibus eorum, ut humilitate superbiam vitarent" (*Glossa Ordinaria*, PL 114:116). Rabanus indicates that childhood here means simplicity without arrogance, charity without envy, and devotion without wrath (*Commentariorum in Matthaeum*, PL 107:1006). Cf. Anselm of Laon, *Enarrationes in Evangelum Matthaei*, PL 162:1227; S. Bruno Astensis, *Commentaria in Matthaeum*, PL 165:223. The *Glossa* interprets the children of Psalm 8 to be the foolish in the faith who do not know spiritual things and have to be fed spiritual milk; it sees those of Matthew 21.16 as the immature who witnessed the miracles of Christ but did not understand his full teaching (*Glossa Ordinaria*, PL 113:855–56, 114:153.

[10] *Three Middle English Versions of the Rule of Saint Benet*, ed. Ernst A. Kock (London: Trübner, 1902), pp. 112–13.

compacted that the nunnery would not remove its lead church roof unless repairs required it. Later she walled the nunnery, made a south end for it, repaired its chapel with the financial help of a local parson and others to be buried or honored in it, had a "large chaumbre" made, and completed the building of the chapel: "So with the helpe of God and of the good man before seyde [another parson]," the prioress "in the ix yere of hyr occupacion . . . arayed up the chirche and the quere and stolid it, and made doris, which cost X pownde, the veyl of the chirche with the auter-clothis in sute cost xls."[11]

Eglantine assumes other duties. She takes her brooch's motto from Virgil's young lover's phrase in Eclogue 10.50, *Amor vincit omnia*. A convent sister is married to Christ in Canticle terms, and in the *Dialogue between a Cluniac and a Cistercian*, the Cluniac exclaims that he is amazed that noble women going into the Cistercians can endure the harsh work and devotion of their nunnery life, whereupon the Cistercian replies, "Holy love conquers all."[12] But holy love does not conquer Eglantine's predilection for fine clothes, her courtliness and false courtesy (A, 139–40), or her false affection for dogs and true hatred for Jews. During Barking Convent's Feast of Innocents, a child prioress ruled and convent-school children performed the functions of the sisters in the services that referred to Psalm 8, Herod, Rachel crying in Ramah, and the Innocents of the Apocalypse—all also mentioned in the Prioress's Tale.[13] With

---

[11] Mary Bateson (ed.), "The Register of Crabhouse Nunnery," *Norfolk Archaeology* 11 (1892):60; see 57–62 for a more complete picture of Prioress Joan's activities. "Stolis" (stalls) is my emendation for "stol it" in the text.

[12] E. Martene and U. Durand, *Thesaurus Novus Anecdotorum* (Paris, 1717), 5:1639.

[13] *Ordinary and Customary of Barking*, 1:33–34. The liturgies for the day include readings or singings of the *Hostis Herodes, Angelus domini apparuit, O beati innocentes, Herodes iratus, Ex ore infancium*, and the *Vox in rama*. Passages from the Apocalypse that stress the theme of innocence are also used: *Ecce vidi agnum*

her baubles, Eglantine seems to reverse the Feast of Innocents by taking on a child's attitude, but her role-playing is all show.

Her central piece of showmanship is contained in a miraculous tale about a child, a tale which appears to advance her or others toward wisdom and to ascribe to her the innocence and spiritual ignorance of a child whose praise will be perfected (B², 1671ff.). Through the child-martyr whose praise *is* "perfected," the story appears to suggest that the Prioress is willing to suffer for Christ as did Herod's innocents and the child in her tale. (The Innocents may have been of special interest to the court as their relics were brought to England in 1396.)¹⁴ But being "estatlich of manere" and wanting to be held "digne of reverence" (A, 140–41), she denies the essential childlike heart expected of a prioress by her convent's rule:

> Al is scho be highest in degre,
> In hir-self lawest sal scho be.
> Hir aw to be gude of forthoght
> What thinges es to wirk & what noght,
> Chaste and Sober, meke & mild,
> Of bearing bowsum os a child.   (2:2263–68)¹⁵

---

stantem and *Centum quadraginta*. Compare B², 1769–75. Cf. Robinson, p. 735. Cf. John C. Hirsh, "Reopening the Prioress's Tale," *CR* 10 (1975):30–45; Marie Padgett Hamilton, "Echoes of Childermas in the Tale of the Prioress," *MLR* 34 (1939):1–8; J. C. Wenk, "On the Sources of *The Prioress's Tale*," *MS* 17 (1955):214–19.

¹⁴ For a discussion of the character of the little school to which the child goes, see Philippe Ariès, *Centuries of Childhood*, trans. Robert Baldick (New York: Knopf, 1962), pp. 286ff. Boys probably learned their ABCs, simple Latin and psalms at these "petty schools"; a similar function was performed for the young who led the services on the Feast of the Holy Innocents by convent education (see *Ordinary and Customary of Barking*, 1:33–34). For the two Holy Innocents supposedly brought to England in 1396, see *Anglo-Norman Letters and Petitions*, ed. M. D. Legge (Oxford: Basil Blackwell, 1941), pp. 67–68.

¹⁵ *Three Middle English Versions of the Rule of St. Benet*, p. 111. The "children"

Independent of work or action, no mere story can create the effect of such childlike humility.

However, Eglantine asks that she be allowed *in her story* to perfect the praise of the incarnate Christ-Wisdom (B², 1662) whose natural design Theseus praises in his final speech and whom the Melibee will soon praise as Sophia. The perfective life's completion in wisdom required an all-conquering love of God—*Amor vincit omnia.* Thierry of Chartres says that wisdom, the unified vision of the truth, can only be attained by love, and St. Bernard, whom the Prioress's prayer quotes in Dante's words, explains that wisdom (Psalm 110.10) can be created in the individual only by his fearing, thinking, and feeling God:

> Are you in fear of God's justice, of His power? If you are, you are experiencing the delectability of a just and powerful God, for this fear is delectable. . . . Fear comes first: it is only a preparation for wisdom. . . . The preparation is knowledge: it easily engenders presumptuousness unless fear represses it. He who combats this lack of wisdom from the very start, possesses in truth the beginning of wisdom. In the first step one arrives at the threshold of wisdom, in the second one enters upon it.[16]

The cloister's search for wisdom began with penance, as Bernard here makes clear, and ended in the mystical or contemplative experience. The movement from penance to rapture was embodied in the search of the bride in the Canticle for the bride-

---

entering the kingdom of heaven in Matthew 18.3–4 conventionally meant innocence or humility.

[16] Leclercq, *The Love of Learning,* p. 263; St. Bernard, "Super Canticum," 23.14, trans. Catherine Misrahi in *The Love of Learning,* p. 267. Cf. "Wisdom," in *The Late Medieval Religious Plays of Bodleian Mss. Digby 133 and E. Museo 160,* ed. Donald Baker et al. (London: Oxford University Press, 1982), pp. 116–40. For the characteristics of the sapiental *auctor* and his or her relation to simplicity, humility, lack of greed—the perfective disciplines—and to love, see Minnis, discussing Gower in *Medieval Theory of Authorship,* pp. 178–90.

groom who was to be found in the vineyard of the cloister, or in the innocent's pursuit of the Lamb in the Apocalypse who was to be praised in the new song. Art fused these images in, for example, Van Eyck's altarpiece with the mystic lamb where both sets of imagery are used and Mary appears as Wisdom (figs. 30–31).[17] Wisdom, the direct experience of God, was seen as helping the monastic advise the ruler to be just and equitable less through daily administration than through the prophetic voice of a John the Baptist or a St. Bernard (cf. Wisdom 9.1–12). Since, as Oresme argues, "Political prudence is the proper virtue of a King even as . . . sapience or contemplation is the proper virtue of a lord spiritual,"[18] the effective monastic lord spiritual had to be, above all, the alert critic of quotidian "secular" court assumptions about the conduct of things, which is precisely what most of Chaucer's monastics are not.

Sapience is not born in the cloister through the logical disciplines and the reading of natural law that instructs Duke Theseus and Leader Melibee—not even through the forgiveness and love that the latter learns from Christ in order to heal society. The cloister is preeminently the place of the direct adoration and love of God, completed in experiences like that which Dante encounters at the end of his contemplative *Paradiso*. Such an experience is what the Prioress seeks, or feigns to seek and express through her child-martyr singing the new song (B², 1774). The child-martyr singing this song is a self-conscious mirror of the child-Prioress singing her "song" (B², 1677). The technique resembles that used in illustrations to Alexander Laicus' *In Apocalipsim* where saints singing the new song in heaven are a mirror of monastics singing their songs of adoration (fig.

[17] See Lotte Brand Philip, *The Ghent Altarpiece and the Art of Jan Van Eyck* (Princeton: Princeton University Press, 1971), pp. 55–108. Cf. Erwin Panofsky, *Early Netherlandish Painting* (Cambridge, Mass.: Harvard University Press, 1953), 1:209ff.

[18] Oresme, *Le Livre de Politiques d' Aristote*, pp. 311–12.

28). As Wisdom historically was brought to human flesh in Mary's child (B², 1662), so it may be expressed in the Prioress's time in a child's song. Implicitly it may be born through a child-Prioress. The person who lives in the image of Wisdom experiences Christ's martyrdom, as the self is consumed by divine love—the martyrdom of Rachel's children (B², 1817; cf. Jeremiah 31.15), of the Holy Innocents, of the child of the tale.[19] Through martyrdom, the power of the abused temporal sword is overcome—the power of Herod (B², 1764), of Rachel's Old Testament enemies, and of the Jews in this story. And here the power to overcome tyranny expresses itself in the child's song perfected after his death, giving witness to the glory of Christ and his mother.

But is this true contemplation, true perfection of praise? The Prioress cannot weep over the destruction of Israel's children in her tale (B², 1818ff.) since she also makes the Jews "folk of Herodes" (B², 1762–65); these are the same people who in Matthew are Herod's victims. Whereas in Matthew, Christ's enemy, Herod, is responsible for the mass killing of Jews, in the Prioress's Tale Christians are responsible for a similar action, and with her approval. She remains the old-law figure of her story, preaching an eye-for-an-eye vengeance, unmoved by what her own words say: "Yvele shal have that yvele wol deserve" (B², 1822).

Her incompleteness comes to focus in her representation of the triumph over tyranny. Her "innocent," like the Biblical innocent, suffers martyrdom at the hands of Jews. His murder is revealed through an Abel-like voice which his mother pursues until she finds him singing. The child sings the *Alma Redemptoris* to Mary in his dead, mortal aspect, but in his live, immortal one he sings with the hundred and forty-four thousand inno-

---

[19] For Rachel as the Church and her children as the martyrs, see Hirsh, "Reopening the *Prioress's Tale*," pp. 33–35; Wyclif, *Select English Works*, 1:328.

CHAPTER 5

cents who figure perfection's life of direct knowledge of wisdom both in the Ghent altarpiece and in the glosses of the Wife of Bath's tale. The *Alma* only praises Mary as the mother of the Redeemer and asks for spiritual maturity amid persecution, for assistance in helping fallen persons stand.[20] The innocents' new song reflects the joy of all three estates as they encounter God and praise all-conquering love: "For thou wast slain, and hast redeemed us to God by the blood out of every kindred, and tongue, and people, and nation; and hast made us unto our God kings and priests and we shall reign on the earth." The child is God's agent in both songs but the new song to Christ, not the *Alma*, obviously completes the progress to wisdom. However, the *ending* of the *Alma*, and not the continued praise of the new song, appears a wonder to Eglantine's abbot (B², 1863). And after the martyrdom and earthly song are over, the Syrian convent praises only Mary—not Christ-Wisdom (B², 1867–70). No one sees the *visio dei* because the Prioress aspires to the courtliness of the temporal court and the ecstasy of the eternal without respecting either. However, in spite of herself, she may achieve a kind of wisdom through the structure of her plot in that the pilgrim or reader may imitate her child and become the innocent or new person. He may move from praising Mary as the vehicle of the divine to fulfilling Christ's "[w]il that his glorie

[20] Duby, *The Three Orders*, p. 239. For the text of the *Alma*, see Joseph Connelly, *Hymns of the Roman Liturgy* (Westminster, Md.: Newman, 1957), pp. 44–45. Martyrdom and monastic profession both relate to the death of an old, and the birth of a new, self; see Edward Malone, "Martyrdom and Monastic Profession as a Second Baptism," *Vom Christlichen Mysterium* (Dusseldorf: Patmos-Verlag, 1951), pp. 115–34. For the new song, see Robertson, *Preface to Chaucer*, pp. 127–30. For the 144,000 as meaning the life of perfection in *CT* glosses, see Geoffrey Chaucer, *The Canterbury Tales: A Facsimile and Transcription of the Hengwrt Manuscript*, ed. Paul Ruggiers (Norman: Oklahoma University Press, 1979), p. 230, gloss to line 105, "Virgynytee / is greet perfeccioun"; compare a similar gloss to the Prioress's Tale, line 1773, on p. 841. The Wife develops the Stratford tale themes dealing with perfection.

laste and be in mynde" (B², 1842–43) and sing perfection's song while rejecting the rest of the story. But his doing this does not mean that the Prioress herself is wise.

In late fourteenth-century terms, the Prioress's main failure in the temporal sphere is not anti-Semitism; it is injustice. It is urging the notion that the spiritual power can do the temporal power's work, a notion also suggested by Eglantine's courtly dress and manner. The Prioress would not have appeared depraved because of Innocent IV's and Gregory X's canons against Jewish ritual murder stories, since these earlier papal proscriptions lacked weight in Chaucer's England,²¹ and, though the French Avignon papacy depended on Jewish financial support, England's Roman pope did not. Neither Urban VI nor Boniface IX at Rome enforced the proscription against these stories as anti-Semitism rose in Spain and Germany (although Boniface did issue a bill forbidding the forcible conversion of Jews). And England was no paradise for Jews. England's Edward I had expelled Jews in 1290, the parliament in 1376 asserted that the Lombard merchants were Jews and Saracens in disguise,²² and Richard II gave grants only to converted Jews.²³ On the other hand, injustice and violation of due process were not popular in the same England, and Jews in medieval England had status before the law comparable to that of other citizens.²⁴ John C. Hirsh has incorrectly argued that the Prioress

²¹ Richard G. Schoeck, "Chaucer's Prioress: Mercy and Tender Heart," *The Bridge: A Yearbook of Judaeo-Christian Studies* 2 (1956):239–55. Cf. Hirsh, "Reopening the Prioress's Tale," p. 42.

²² *RP* 2:332.

²³ *C.P.R., 1381–85*, p. 491; cf. *C.P.R., 1388–92*, p. 158. The *Songe de Vergier*, which may give a French perspective on the Jews, argues that a king or lord may not justly deprive them of their goods or remove them from the realm but ought to let them live in peace (*Songe de Vergier*, 1:219).

²⁴ The Jews prior to their expulsion from England in 1290 had standing before the English courts, and those who remained, being converted Jews, had it after the expulsion period. Cf. Solo Baron, *A Social and Religious History of the*

possesses a proper "medieval" sense of law since the provost in her tale puts to death only those Jews "that of this mordre wiste" (B², 1820; cf. B², 1757).²⁵ But Eglantine tries to establish the complicity of all the Jews in the tale by having the widow-mother ask "every Jew" about her child's whereabouts (B², 1791). The terms of the tale make it highly improbable that all of the Jews could have heard a cry (B², 1759ff.). If they did, why did no Christians hear? Yet all the Jews appear to withhold their knowledge, and all that know of the murder and do not cooperate in the search for the child are killed (B², 1818ff.). Everyone in the Jewish section of the Syrian city must have been in the conspiracy in some way. Furthermore, for Hirsh's theory to be correct, all those who were killed would have to have been co-conspirators and equally involved in the killing, an idea denied in B², 1757. The persons who hired the "homycide" are accessories rather than perpetrators, but the Prioress fails even to raise the question of accessories. Though the law covering homicide was "wide enough to comprise him who gave the deadly blow and those who held the victim but also those who 'procured, counselled, commanded or abetted the felony' "²⁶ and recognized accessories before and after the fact, one could not try accessories until the principal was found guilty and then had to find them equally guilty.²⁷ Sometimes, where large groups of accessories acted, the government made distinctions between leaders and followers, especially in the Peasants' Revolt murders where Richard's pardon distinguished the "chiefs, leaders, inciters, approvers" who killed Sudbury, Hales, and

---

Jews, 2d ed. (New York: Columbia University Press, 1965), p. 115. This also is suggested by the entry at *C.P.R.*, *1388–92*, p. 158.

²⁵ Hirsh, "Reopening the Prioress's Tale," pp. 39–40 and notes, p. 45.

²⁶ Sir Frederick Pollock and Frederic W. Maitland, *The History of English Law Before the Time of Edward I* (Cambridge: Cambridge University Press, 1905, 1968), 2:509.

²⁷ Maitland and Pollock, *The History of English Law*, 2:509–10.

Cavendish from the revolt's other participants.[28] The Prioress's provost, a religious or a civic figure, oversees no two-step trial, however, but rounds up all the Jews, condemns principals and accessories alike, and shows no mercy to accessories (B², 1819).

The trial of the Jews is further irregular in that the punishment given them—drawing and quartering and hanging—goes beyond any conventional punishment for murder and includes the penalties for treason. The Prioress apparently views the Jews' martyrdom of the child as an act of treason to God and therefore requires no due process prior to judgment. English law, after the signing of the Magna Carta, required a careful identification of an accused felon's crime, a well-regulated inquiry and trial, and a penalty to match the crime which was fixed by statute—all features absent in the Prioress's "Christian" Syria (B², 1806–10, 1818–24). According to Bracton, when a person was accused of homicide, an inquest was to be held and the accused was to be summoned, given a *libellus*, and allowed to defend himself in front of a judge, or judge and jury, prior to verdict.[29] In contrast, the provost's punishment of the Jews, drawing with wild horses and hanging "by the lawe," is a substitute for a trial (B², 1824). Inspired by a miracle, the provost needs no inquest. And in punishing, he does not destroy his culprits for murder but for treason—for *lèse-majesté* or violating the dignity of the ruler—a crime that leads to drawing and then hanging.[30] Here the Jews, as God's betrayers, receive treason's punishment. They receive it precisely because the Prioress confuses the two courts, in her tale as in her dress, and compensates for her lack of vocation by positing a God who is a

[28] *RP* 3:98–103.

[29] Bracton, *On the Laws and Customs of England*, ed. George E. Woodbine, trans. Samuel E. Thorne (Cambridge, Mass.: Harvard University Press, 1968), 2:318, 340–54, and *passim*.

[30] Bracton, *On the Laws*, trans. Thorne, 2:318; J. G. Bellamy, *The Law of Treason in England in the Later Middle Ages*, pp. 17, 20–21.

superlatively powerful temporal ruler—*Domine, Dominus Noster*. She, like the Man of Law, believes in theocratic rule, force before wisdom. Her sense of vocation grotesquely links her meaning with that of the liturgical Feast of the Innocents on which her tale draws. The Innocents were interpreted as martyrs who did not will their martyrdoms, and their feast was linked with two post-Christmas feasts, the first dedicated to Stephen who willed and endured martyrdom and the second to John the Apostle who willed but did not endure it.[31] Clearly, Eglantine is an ironic "Innocent" who does not will death or spiritual suffering for herself, but for others. Her side has all the power, the miracle, and the glory. What need of discipline?

Eglantine would properly be instructed by "another Nonne . . . hir chapeleyne" (A, 163–64) who adopts her tale's idiom and also uses her devices—Bernard's prayer, musical imagery, martyrdom, the saint's life with imagery drawn from the Apocalypse and Song of Songs—to show how wisdom's journey may end in perfection when the two swords are separated. But the Second Nun has no power. Convent chaplains generally only recited minor liturgical hours with the choir and occasionally substituted for prioresses as religious teachers. Little administrative responsibility centered in them, though one Crabhouse Nunnery chaplain, William of Watlington, handled convent land.[32]

When the Second Nun imitates Eglantine in prefacing her tale with Bernard's *Commedia* prayer that Dante may have the

[31] Durandus, *Rationale Divinorum Officiorum* (Treviso, 1479), 7.42. Cf. Wyclif, *The Select English Works*, 1:328. The *Songe de Vergier's* Clerk speaks of those who strive too hard for secular success as "*martyres diaboli & non Christi.*" The martyr of the Prioress's tale may partly suggest her unwilling "martyrdom" in the nunnery as she seeks to project "cheere of court"; *Songe de Vergier* 1:141. For another view, cf. Sherman Hawkins, "Chaucer's Prioress and the Sacrifice of Praise," *JEGP* 63 (1964):599–624.

[32] Eckenstein, *Women Under Monasticism*, pp. 376–77; Bateson, "Register," p. 45; cf. pp. 43–48.

unitive experience, her prayer—closer in spirit to Bernard and to the *Commedia* as a whole—confesses that sin, not childlikeness, limits her capacity to see the light (G, 57–77); clearly, like Dante, she has been through the penitential journey (G, 57ff.; *Paradiso* XXXIII.22–24). Since in the Parson's analysis (I, 1076ff.), penance is the beginning of the discipline which ends in the vision and perfected love of God, we expect true contemplation here. Hence, the Second Nun does not protest her similarity to the Virgin through proclaiming her innocent bearing of the praise of Sapience but calls herself Eve, Mary's antithesis (G, 62),[33] and her Mary is not an alter-ego but one who grants access to Christ (B², 1667–73; G, 36–70), the "eterneel love and pees" that guides the threefold realms of sea, earth, and sky to make them cohere in praise (G, 43–47; *Boece*, bk. 4, met. 6). This Christ-Wisdom resembles Theseus' "thyng . . . parfit . . . and stable" (A, 3009), but is also incarnate as the flesh and blood that lets any Canaanitish woman eat the crumbs from his table (G, 57ff.).

Seeking contemplation, the Second Nun also properly prays for *works* as the culmination of her faith (G, 64–65), and her story is her "werk" (G, 77), directing itself to her spiritually idle Prioress, to the Nun's Priest, and to the Monk. In it, the verbal union of prayer and work, contemplation and action, central in the Second Nun's use of Jacobus de Voragine's allegorization of St. Cecilia's name (Ceci-lia), develops into the actual union of rapture and deeds in Cecilia's life. *Lia* or *lilia* the Second Nun takes to mean "hevenes lilie" (G, 87ff.) or innocent contemplation—honest in its white color, conscience-filled in its green, and full of good fame in its scent; *ceci* or *caecus*, road for the blind, refers to Cecilia's active life of teaching.[34] *Ceci-lia* also

[33] See Stephen Manning, *Wisdom and Number* (Lincoln: Nebraska University Press, 1962), pp. 71–72.

[34] See Robinson, p. 757. Osbern Bokenham's late fourteenth-century translation of the *Legenda Aurea*'s life of Saint Cecilia makes her the fusion of the active and contemplative lives and the model of *sapientia*; Osbern Bokenham, *Le-*

joins heaven and *Lia* (G, 96), heaven for the thought of holiness or contemplation and Lia after the Biblical Leah whose weak eyes figured the active life and its "lastynge bisynesse" (Genesis 29.17; G, 98).[35] Cecilia means absence of blindness (G, 100), the contemplative's light of Sapience (G, 101), but she is also the people's heaven as an exemplar of good works (G, 104). All of these etymologies reflect the idea of the contemplative life's leading one to Wisdom so that the active life can proclaim Him. All of them answer Eglantine's life of "delices" and sloth with an imagery of sight, lilies, and heavenward motion which anticipates the tale's description of the same emblems of contemplation as the basis for spiritual work (cf. G, 1–28).[36]

The story fuses contemplation and work by joining contemplative music and sight to active preaching. Like the Prioress's child and many contemplatives after St. John, Cecilia struggles with the tyranny of a Rome that worships the deaf and dumb idols of imperial power (G, 287) and does not follow Theseus in perceiving the love binding things together that limits temporal power and gives meaning to the fables in the temples and their statues. This temporal kingdom's idols are not fable-illustrated roads to knowledge, as Theseus' could be, but are ends in themselves.

However, Cecilia does not need metaphors or temples to lead her to God after her pure marriage since she sees God and his

---

gendys of Hooly Wommen (London: Humphrey Milford, 1938), p. 202. Bokenham was influenced by Chaucer.

[35] Rabanus Maurus, *Commentariorum in Genesim*, PL 107:595–96; Bruno Astensis, *Expositio in Genesim*, PL 164:210; Dante makes Leah an allegory for the active life in *Purgatorio* 27:94–114.

[36] For a discussion of related meanings of "Eglantine," see Chauncey Wood, "Chaucer's Use of Signs in His Portrait of the Prioress," *Signs and Symbols in Chaucer's Poetry*, ed. John P. Hermann and John J. Burke, Jr. (University, Ala.: Alabama University Press, 1981), pp. 82, 225; for idleness, see Jean Leclercq, *Otia Monastica* (Rome: Herder, 1963), pp. 40–41, 70–71, 94–95.

MONASTICISM'S CRITICAL ROLE

messengers directly. She does not begin as a contemplative bride of God but asks to become one. On the day of her wedding, the organs, celebrated in Dryden's famous ode and in baroque painting, play while she prays to remain innocent within her carnal marriage:

> And whil the organs maden melodie,
> To God allone in herte thus sang she:
> "O Lord, my soule and eek my body gye
> Unwemmed, lest that it confounded be."
> And, for his love that dyde upon a tree,
> Every seconde and thridde day she faste,
> Ay biddynge in hire orisons ful faste. (G, 134–40)

She asks for the perfective experience and is not simply God's vehicle as Reames argues (n. 40, below). Nicholas Oresme, in his translation of and commentary on the eighth book of the *Politics*, tells how the natural effect of organ music inclines but does not force the soul to contemplation:

By sacred music, [Aristotle] means the music which is used in divine worship because it was such that it calmed all evil passion in souls having a good nature. But it did not work so on others even as medicine is not able to do any good for a body born with an evil constitution or corrupted by accident. And it is similar with music in regard to the soul. . . .

Moreover, this sacred music inclines the soul to contemplation. And therefore, the Holy Scriptures say, "Sing to the Lord a new song" [Psalms 32.3]. And on this account Elisha had a psaltery played before him in order that he might be moved to devotion by this and have the inspiration of prophetic vision as is clear in the fourth book of *Kings*.

[Elisha] said, "Bring me hither a minstrel. And when the minstrel played, the hand of the Lord came upon him" [4 Kings 3.15]. And we read of St. Cecilia that while the organs sounded she chanted to God in her heart. And Saint Paul says and admonishes that one chant this spiritual music to which the perceptible music

[147]

inclines and leads one, "Speaking to yourselves in psalms, and hymns, and spiritual canticles, singing and making melody in your heart to the Lord" [Ephesians 5.19].[37]

The song of Cecilia's organ, the new song of the Prioress's 144,000 innocents, and the new song of the monks in Alexander Laicus' illumination, all rising to Wisdom's harmony, invite contrast with Eglantine's nasal singing and Chantecleer's arias (fig. 28).

If the relation between art and contemplation begins the Second Nun's work, that between instruction and perfective sight completes it. Cecilia, after learning the divine melody, sees divinity, but Tiburce cannot see the lilies and roses because he lives in a dream, unable to see truth (G, 267–68), and knows only Pascal's God "yhid in hevene pryvely" (G, 317). However, when Cecilia teaches him the mysteries of the Trinity, he also routinely sees God's angels, and a converted Maximus sees the souls of Valerian and Tiburce mount toward heaven. Cecilia can, given the terms of the story, appropriately accuse the Roman officer of blindness at her final trial:

> Ther lakketh no thyng to thyne outter yën
> That thou n'art blynd; for thyng that we seen alle
> That it is stoon,—that men may wel espyen,—
> That ilke stoon a god thow wolt it calle. (G, 498–501)

Instruction leads to sight, but sight also leads to instruction, and more than one of the senses come into play in Cecilia's instruction of her flock. Two sights and a scent disclose to man's three sapiences (G, 338) what the Trinity is: a visionary Saint Paul portrays God's general fatherhood through a vision-book echoing Ephesians 4.5–6 (G, 204–10), an angel promises

[37] Oresme, *Le Livre des Politiques de Aristote*, pp. 355–56. Cf. V. A. Kolve, "Chaucer's *Second Nun's Tale* and the Iconography of St. Cecilia," *New Perspectives on Chaucer Criticism* (Norman: Pilgrim Books, 1981), pp. 137–58.

Christ's kind of suffering through the sight of lilies and roses, purity and martyrdom (G, 239ff.), and the scent of these same lilies and roses tells Tiburce of the Paraclete's effects (G, 246ff.).[38] All of these extraordinary experiences celebrate the human connection to divinity rehearsed in Cecilia's instructions:

> Right as a man hath *sapiences three* [italics mine],
> Memorie, engyn, and intellect also,
> So in o beynge of divinitee,
> Thre persones may ther right wel bee.   (G, 338–41)

The Second Nun has a sense of the reality that transfigures human nature which her superiors cannot see. Cecilia's life of praise, musical contemplation, and second sight is empowered by her obedience to the evangelical counsels—to chastity in her marriage, to humility in her acceptance of martyrdom, and to poverty in her granting her property to Pope Urban. Her action may appear as mere Puritanism to modern readers, but as Mircea Eliade remarks of India's ascetics, "renunciation has a positive value" which permits the ascetic to become a vehicle for a divine action—precisely what Eglantine prays for and what the Second Nun shows to be possible.[39]

Chaucer, unlike his sources, makes his tale center on Cecilia's confrontation with temporal power. Her detachment about dying permits her to convert the first group of representatives of that power she confronts, Maximus and his associates including the first Roman executioners. And the same detachment gives her the strength to face Almachius, the Roman judge, and pronounce her judgment on him as having power only over

---

[38] Rabanus Maurus, *Allegoriae in Sacram Scripturam, PL* 112:1086 (explaining Cant. 1.4); Rupert of Deutz, *In Cantica Canticorum, PL* 168:841; Rupert of Deutz, *De Divinis Officiis, PL* 170:23.

[39] Mircea Eliade, *Patanjali and Yoga,* trans. Charles Lam Markmann (New York: Schocken Books, 1969), p. 106.

death (G, 463–92).[40] During her own death at the hands of the second group of executioners, she defies the Roman axe for a time and, "half deed" (G, 533), continues to teach her flock and assign her temporal goods. These she gives to a Pope Urban, quite unlike the Urban VI of Chaucer's period. He carries no metaphoric *Domine, Dominus Noster* on his banner but lives in shadowy catacombs on the edge of Rome—so far from temporal power that he fears for his life, a theme illustrated in Lorenzo di Bicci's illustration of Cecilia's pontiff (fig. 29). When Cecilia dies, she quietly initiates the institution of ecclesiastical property by giving her house to him to make St. Cecilia in Trastevere. (Honoré Bonet reminds us that "Saint Urban . . . was also the first who ever took rents and temporal possessions in the name of the Church, for aforetime the whole Church lived

---

[40] For the assumptions behind martyrdom, see Herbert B. Workman, *Persecution in the Early Church* (Oxford: Oxford University Press, 1980), pp. 9, 143. The notion that life after baptism as in Romans 6.3–4, is self-death and martyrdom is common in the Church fathers. Sherry L. Reames ("The Sources of Chaucer's Second Nun's Tale," *MP* 76 [1978]:128–29), notes that Chaucer's handling of his sources makes the trial scene achieve a new importance. The scene makes an important point about the prophetic function of the clerical and monastic orders and does not, prior to Cecilia's martyrdom, technically present grace as abolishing nature as Reames argues in "The Cecilia Legend as Chaucer Inherited It and Retold It," *Speculum* 55 (1980):38–57. The organ music, which induces the contemplation, the physical bodies of the characters, are "nature," and Cecilia's point that the Empire controls only death whereas God controls life and death suggests that grace completes nature. I fail to see the conversions as "imposed"; obviously, the Romans can resist Cecilia's preaching, and most of the conversions require human doctrinal persuasion as well as divine action. Furthermore, Reames's conclusion makes the tale Chaucer's and not the Second Nun's. The Second Nun is endeavoring to counter the fake all-conquering grace of the Prioress's tale and the submersion in "nature" of the Monk's. She shows the prophetic role of the contemplative as agent of God to the temporal prince, thereby limiting both the Monk's and Prioress's claims. If the Second Nun "abolishes nature," she does so in the face of the Knight's Tale and despite the Parson's respect for both nature and grace.

according to the doctrine of the apostles, and took nothing that was offered except alms by which to live and to give sustenance to poor pilgrims.")[41] But the new community's property apparently makes no difference to its spirituality because it is detached—a point relevant to my next chapter and to any discussion of Chaucer's relation to Wyclif.

The distance from Prioress to Second Nun, from pseudo-wisdom to wisdom, and from feigned to real contemplation requires that one travel with the Second Nun in penance. Penance is the office of the Nun's Priest—along with preaching and celebrating mass. Instead of sermonizing humility directly, the Priest tells a penitential fable about himself which is also applicable to Madam Eglantine, to Chaucer's Monk, and to all ecclesiastical Melibees. Chauntecleer images the Nun's Priest, as several recent critics have noted: nuns' priests lived in chambers outside the convent while prioresses lived within the main convent living area in their own chambers, served and watched by other sisters. Chauntecleer laments that his "perche is maad so narwe, allas" (B², 4359) that at night he cannot ride on the beautiful sister, Pertelote,[42] and if Chauntecleer is a rooster, Harry Bailey makes the Nun's Priest into a rooster at the end of the tale (B², 4637–50). While the Nun's Priest leaves the nunnery and travels to Canterbury with the sisters, Chauntecleer leaves his roost to nuzzle the hens. He is more than a conventional icon for any priest; he is this specific priest, now telling his "tale" in contrite comedy at his own expense.

[41] Bonet, *The Tree of Battles*, p. 84. Lampridius says that Urban bought property in Rome for a church.

[42] *The Rule of St. Benedict*, trans. Cardinal Gasquet (New York: Cooper Square, 1963), pp. 107–8. See D. Jean Leclercq, "Le Sacerdoce des Moines," *Irénikon* 36 (1963):11–19; Eileen Power, *Medieval English Nunneries* (Cambridge: Cambridge University Press, 1922), p. 144; for an account of local parish priests who appear also to have been nuns' priests, see Bateson, "Register of Crabhouse," pp. 57–60.

The character's name, Chant Clear, refers to his liturgical functions which recollect the singing of the Prioress, her martyr, and St. Cecilia. As mass-priests might sing the mass, so Chant Clear crows more merrily than the "murie orgon / On messe-dayes that in the chirche gon" (B², 4041–42) with a music that outdoes Cecilia's music of contemplation,⁴³ and he sings—presumably the hours—more predictably than an abbey clock such as Stratford probably would have had while measuring the movement of the sun with his inner "sundial."⁴⁴ An Epicurean, "loving" more for delight than for multiplying (B², 4535), he naturally explains the fall with the same flattery for the ladies that his narrator indulges (B², 4353ff., 4446–56) at the same time as he appeals to the songs of birds to call Pertelote into the yard to the "revel and solas" that prompt his song (B², 4388–93). When the hens come down from the roost and lie in the sand, he sings more happily than a mermaid (B², 4460). Later he learns from Russell Fox that he sings as pleasantly as the angels singing the divine praise (B², 4481ff.). After such praise, though he knows that his father has been to the fox's house to his "greet ese" (B², 4487), he rises to tiptoe, stretches his neck up high, and sings until his eyes close and "the fox" catches him, perhaps as he sings nasally like Eglantine. The Wycliffite treatise, *Of*

---

⁴³ Theoretically there should be no rivalry between the song of the organ and that of the rooster in that, as Durandus of Metz puts it, the rooster "tells of the light to come, preaching the day of judgment and future glory," precisely what the contemplative embodies tropologically in the present. See Durandus, *Rationale Divinorum Officiorum*, 1.1.22. For the symbolism of the rooster, see Charles R. Dahlberg, "Chaucer's Cock and Fox," *JEGP* 53 (1954):282–84. Wyclif, citing Chrysostom, makes the Church like a hen who calls her young, gentile and Jew, from carnal wandering; the widow, in her pursuit, has a comic version of that function for the rooster in this tale. Cf. Wyclif, *Opus Evangelicum*, ed. Johann Loserth (London: Trübner, 1896), 3–4:91–92; Durandus, *Rationale Divinorum Officiorum*, 1.1.22; Bromyard, *Summa Praedicantium*, 2:254ᵛ.

⁴⁴ Durandus interprets church clocks as symbols for preachers; *Rationale Divinorum Officiorum*, 1.4.4–7.

Feigned Contemplative Life, attacks such self-conscious monastic singing for drawing the worshipper away from charity and devotion "to knacke notis for many markis & poundis . . . & þus bi þis nouelrie of song is goodis lawe vnstudied & not kepte, . . . & pride & oþere grete synnys meynteyned."[45]

Chauntecleer's hen, Madame Pertelote (B², 4160), at the narrowest metaphoric level refers to Madame Eglantine in that the descriptions of both highlight their lovely eyes set in a kind of hood, their courtesy, companionability, and good bearing (B², 4061–62; A, 132–49), and, finally, their obtuse understanding of revelation whether through dreams or miracles. Stratford is probably not Cockaigne or Bel Eyse, where monks repose with the sisters[46]—the Prioress and the Nun's Priest do not roost together—but their spirit is not altogether different.

Chant Clear's humor derives from his repeating unwittingly the story of Adam and Eve but, with his seven-hen harem, he also reenacts the story of the senile Solomon, whom the Merchant's January also imitates and Proserpina decries (E, 2138–48, 2298–99). His henyard is "enclosed al aboute" exactly as is January's Canticle garden (E, 2143; B², 4037) because the *vinea* of the nun's cloister was commonly compared to the Canticle garden. His seven hens are "his sustres and his paramours" (B², 4057) not because Chaucer wishes to treat of incest and "phallocratisme," as André Crepin asserts, but because they are convent sisters and the Canticle bridegroom addresses the bride as sister and spouse (Cant. 4.10; 5.1).[47] Chant Clear imitates the

---

[45] Wyclif, *English Works*, pp. 191–92.

[46] Power, *Medieval English Nunneries*, pp. 535–38.

[47] André Crepin, " 'Sustres and paramours': sexe et domination dans les *Contes de Cantorbéry*," *Caliban* 17 (1980):3–21. Crepin recognizes the Nun's Priest's likeness to Chant Clear and that the sister idea may come from the Canticle but then ignores the implications of this. Canticle images are so insistently associated with the monastery and nunnery as to allow Chaucer to bring in the Canticle analogy with a very few strokes. Cf. Dahlberg, "Chaucer's Cock and

Canticle mode of those stupid fourteenth-century scholars who had asserted that the *Canticle* was Solomon's song to his pagan concubines and did not understand its praise of spiritual love.[48] His seven wives (B², 4056; Cant. 4.10; 5.1; 6.7–8), his playing at being a haremed lion-king, his pointing to the flowers and listening to the song of the birds (B², 4391–93; Cant. 2.12–13)—all come from Solomon misunderstood. For the "sister and spouse" of Canticle 5.1, whom the Canticle bridegroom has earlier commanded to arise since winter has ended (Cant. 2.10ff.), January substitutes a "wyf, . . . love, . . . lady free!" (E, 2138); for the same sister and spouse, the Nun's Priest, like the Solomon of the exegetes repudiated by Pierre d'Ailly, substitutes the "sustres and paramours" of his "yeerd . . . enclosed al aboute / with stikkes" (B², 4037–38). Chant Clear parodies the bride's song from Canticle 6.1, "Mi leef wente doun in his gardyn," by singing with Pertelote, "My lief is faren in londe!" (B²,

Fox," pp. 285–86. For monasticism and the Canticle, see Jean Leclercq, *Monks and Love in Twelfth Century France* (Oxford: Clarendon Press, 1979), pp. 27–61; McDonnell, *The Beguines and Beghards*, p. 414–15. For a like inverted use of the Canticle in the Merchant's Tale, see Douglas Wurtele, "The Figure of Solomon in Chaucer's *Merchant's Tale*," *University of Ottawa Quarterly* 47 (1977):478–87.

[48] The notion that the *Song of Songs* could have been addressed to Solomon's paramours must have been around in Chaucer's time since it is attacked by Pierre d'Ailly: "Intentio Salomonis est hortari sponsam ad oscula et amplexus et ab omni amore adulterino revocari: unde patet falsitas errorum illorum quo dicunt Salomonem hunc librum composuisse ab amorem, concubinae carnalis, quam fornicari dilegebat." Pierre d'Ailly, "Super Cantica Canticorum," *Opuscula Spiritualia* (Douay, 1634), pp. 468–69. January treats May as his mistress in the Merchant's Tale and sings Solomon's song to her. Cf. *Biblia Latina cum postillis Nicolai de Lyra* (Nürnberg, 1493), Pt. 2: Sig Em [1ʳ]. If the sisters and paramours of B², 4057 are taken literally, then Chantecleer's relation to them is incestuous, an obvious absurdity given the bird's worry about his narrow perch preventing fulfillment with Pertelote and the absence of any further suggestion that the sisters are blood sisters. Solomon performs the role of a priest in 3 Kings 8 where he leads the prayers and sacrifices for the people of Israel; cf. *Songe de Vergier* 1:53; 1:115–19; 2:33–34; 2:39–40; 2:125–27.

4069) in his gardenless land.[49] However, when like the Canticle groom, he reminds his beloved of the coming of spring, the song of the birds and the blooming of flowers (B², 4388–93; Cant. 2.12–13), he significantly fails to mention the Canticle's spring pruning from the same passage. It would remind his "convent" of the penance, which is the meaning of pruning, and recall the Nun's Priest's function (figs. 32–33).[50]

Since convents were thought to be particularly susceptible to temptation and heresy, medieval Church authorities made special provisions to protect the *vinea* of the convent from the little foxes of Canticle 2.15 (fig. 34). However, since this Solomon has forgotten who he is and what his enclosed place and sisters symbolize, the fox has an easy time. The Nun's Priest recognizes Chauntecleer's fault and his Epicurean temptation to confuse delight and joy, the temporal and spiritual courts, through style:

> Real he was, he was namoore aferd.
> He fethered Pertelote twenty tyme,
> And trad hire eke as ofte, er it was pryme.
> He looketh as it were a grym leoun,
> And on his toos he rometh up and doun;
> Hym deigned nat to sette his foot to grounde.
> He chukketh whan he hath a corn yfounde,
> And to hym rennen thanne his wyves alle.

[49] *Ms. Bodley 959*, ed. Conrad Lindberg (Stockholm: Almquist and Wiksell, 1965) 4:289; Jerome, in the commentary on the Canticle, which Chaucer knew, emphasizes that the "soror mea sponsa" of Canticle 4.9 excludes the possibility of carnal love, a concept that Chaucer plays with here in reference to Stratford's "sisters"; St. Jerome, *Adversus Jovinianum, PL* 23:265.

[50] *Glossa Ordinaria, PL* 113:440; Bruno Astensis, *Expositio in Cantica Canticorum, PL* 164:1248; St. Bernard, *Sermones in Cantica, PL* 183:1055–61. Chantecleer's "tragedy" also mirrors the Monk's inclination to temporal things while his escape from the fox mirrors the happy ending the Knight seeks; see Thomas J. Hatton, "Chauntecleer and the Monk: Two False Knights," *PLL* 3 (1967): 31–39.

Thus roial, as a prince is in his halle,
Leve I this Chauntecleer in his pasture.   (B², 4366–75)

To invert E. T. Donaldson, the morality of the Nun's Priest's Tale is that *style* is morality.[51] The Knight's epic devices—high language, foreshadowings, May 3 setting, and imperial rhetoric (B², 4528–91)—imposed on the priest's failure and appeal to Eglantine's pretense, become stylistic self-mockery and repentance for his contribution to his convent's imitation of the temporal court. When the little fox-devil, or friar, comes into the enclosed place, we know from the Canticle echoes that he will "spoil the grapes" and capture the rooster. Friars often sought and received special protective and teaching functions in beguinages and convents—ostensibly to keep out the foxes that spoil the grapes, the heretics and bad preachers who corrupted nunneries.[52] But Chaucer, always reversing, brings in Friar Russell to supplant the legitimate priest, Chant Clear, by heightening his temptation—praising the glory of his self-con-

[51] E. Talbot Donaldson, "Patristic Exegesis in the Criticism of Medieval Literature: The Opposition," *Critical Approaches to Medieval Literature*, ed. Dorothy Bethurum (New York: Columbia University Press, 1960), pp. 16–26. A recent effort to show that Chaucer's fable differs from other medieval fables which are not old wives' tales, in that it has no figurative meaning, is found in Joerg O. Fichte's *Chaucer's 'Art Poetical': A Study in Chaucerian Poetics* (Tübingen: Gunter Narr Verlag, 1980), pp. 113–16. Fichte confuses the literary fable and the sorts of fables and old wives' tales against which the Parson objects when he quotes Paul's advice to Timothy. Fichte also objects that no consistent allegory can be found in the tale, an objection that the referencing of the tale to Stratford and the temporal-spiritual controversy overcomes. Medieval critics beginning with Augustine compared allegory to a plow; as the plow's many parts which are not the plowshare give necessary structural support and exist to support the share, so the many parts of a story that do not "signify" beyond themselves exist for those which do. Cf. Myers, "Focus and 'Moralite' in the Nun's Priest's Tale," pp. 210–19.

[52] McDonnell, *Beguines and Beghards*, pp. 414–15; cf. Wyclif, *Opus Evangelicum*, p. 433.

scious singing before the "sustres and paramours." Eglantine understands fully the art of such song since it is also her art.

Through his use of the mock epic style, the Nun's Priest distances himself from Chant Clear and from the Prioress, the Monk, and all monastics who play the temporal court game. His fox captures his rooster by appealing to him as if he were a senile Solomon with all of that figure's vanity of power and concubinage. On the other hand, the Nun's Priest preaches the other Solomon, author of "Ecclesiaste":

> Allas! ye lordes, many a fals flatour
> Is in youre courtes, and many a losengeour,
> That plesen yow wel moore, by my feith,
> Than he that soothfastnesse unto yow seith.
> Redeth Ecclesiaste of flaterye;
> Beth war, ye lordes, of hir trecherye.   (B², 4515–20)

Ecclesiastes 7.1–6, defines temptation as failure to perceive the ephemerality of the human pilgrimage and preferring fools' flattery to wisdom's rebuke. Ellesmere applies the Tale's ending to "Dominus archiepiscopus Cantuariensis,"[53] perhaps seeing it as warning Courtenay against flattering friars serving as confessors to archdiocesan monasteries and convents. In any case, at the end, rooster and priest preach almost the same "moralitee": the rooster—

> Thou shalt namoore, thurgh thy flaterye,
> Do me to synge and wynke with myn ye;
> For he that wynketh, whan he sholde see,
> Al wilfully, God lat him nevere thee!"   (B², 4619–22)

the priest—

> Lo, swich it is for to be recchelees
> And necligent, and truste on flaterye.   (B², 4626–27)

53 Robinson, p. 755.

[157]

Being "reccheless" and "necligent" means violating monastic principles as the Prioress and Monk appear to do, the former with the Nun's Priest's help. To fail to see with the contemplative's sight in the enclosed garden or yard requires, in Chaucer's fiction, deliberate self-blinding. One must abandon the bride and bridegroom's nuptials, Cecilia's contemplative marriage, the virgin-martyr's processional and song; one must lose the holy love that conquers all. Though providence followed by penance's sight converts the rooster-tragedy of the Nun's Priest into the comedy that the Knight required before the tale began (B², 3957–69), this providence seems to have little effect on modern readings which, for the most part, have wished not to see what style or iconology, frame story or internal allusion, are doing in the fable or why it ends happily for Chant Clear and the Nun's Priest. The conceptual frame is too distant, too ridiculous, too fanatical for our taste.

The language of the three Stratford tales works toward what Leclercq has called "holy simplicity." If one looks back to the Prioress's Tale, one can partially understand why Chaucer mocks artfulness in the Thopas and holds up the logically disciplined approach to sapience in the Melibee, for the head nun is artful at every turn—in her motto, her dress, and in the sadistic tale that she tells—as she adopts her child's pose, with such lacy refinement and such contempt of all temporal court procedure. The Nun's Priest responds to the Monk's inadequate tragedies with a tragedy turned comic, but for the child-Prioress he provides child's fare—a mock-epic animal fable such as might be told to a child, a chicken story whose stylistic inflation mocks monastic and conventual affectation of temporal court styles and values. Rightly, things should go the other way. The monastic should model aspects of the court's search for perfection. As Mann interprets him the Knight seeks perfection in a quasi-monastic discipline. The Nun's Priest's fable does not mock either art or fable allegory so much as artful-

[158]

ness. It allows him to mirror what is not easily said. He comes home to such simplicity that the Second Nun can present the transparent, even naive, style of her tale without embarrassment. One moves from the pretend-innocent style of the Prioress playing at being a child, to the fable style of a "father" speaking to a "child," to the innocent style of the Second Nun combining work and wonder. Stylistic nuance creates the whole sense of what mystical experience may be and what it is not, leaving us with the sense of a silence unrendered save in Cecilia's deeds, for "of those things concerning which one cannot speak one must be silent." Chaucer's portrayal of monastic temptation, in short, establishes a norm for viewing the more explicitly controversialist Monk's Tale and the tales of the pilgrimage Epicureans, whether lay or clerical.

6

Monasticism's Royal Claim

UTHRED, WYCLIF, AND THE REALMS
BEYOND TRAGEDY

Monastics in Chaucer's time often did not remain cloistered. Yet few appeared before temporal court officials to announce a divine message as St. Cecilia does. Rather, like Chaucer's Monk, they often filled more public roles such as managing monastic or court properties or participating in the councils of the royal government. Chaucer's Monk manages temporal properties and tells princely tragedies that indirectly answer Wyclif's charges against the "sect of the monks" who abandon the contemplative life to act as temporal administrators. But his implicit claims for himself and his life also reflect unfavorably on Uthred of Boldon's opposite claims for monks as properly the best temporal rulers. In general, Chaucer resolves the Uthred-Wyclif controversy, and similar disputes, by returning to the original purposes of the monastic rule and to its earlier prophetic role. The Monk tells his tragedies—these particular tragedies—to count the cost of monasticism's assumption of temporal sovereignty in the form of large estates, important temporal offices, and a foreign policy position. The cost is a loss of an accurate sense of history and historical tragedy, the loss of St. Cecilia's full contemplative life and of her capacity for active prophetic testimony before princes. Chaucer's tragic muse requires that her "authors" achieve distance from history's events, compassion for its people, and a personal sense of vulnerability: Chauntecleer understands tragedy *and* the sources of his own vulnerability and fall when providence permits him to escape from the fox's mouth and fly to the treetops; Troilus after his death *understands* and *laughs at* his Trojan attachments from Scipio's contemplative eighth sphere; and Theseus interprets the meaning of Arcita's tragedy when he ascends in thought to the First Mover and the circling cycles of the heavens and nature. Medieval tragedy studies a historical subject— "a certeyn storie . . . of heigh degree" (B², 3163–66), and the monastery as the locus *par excellence* of chronicle writing, often designed to give advice to temporal rulers or to trace the hand of providence in history, should be the proper realm for tragedy. However, Chaucer's invulnerable Monk is no true contemplative, detached from history's currents. He finds no providence in his history and no meaningful suffering. Through his failure the poet defines how a civilization that follows Uthred and too generously encourages monastic temporal roles may fail by having only managers and no prophets and how a civilization that follows Wyclif and has no structured institution for contemplatives and their discipline may also fail by lacking rules to direct the contemplative effort. Chaucer, thus, through metaphor, allusion, and inverted philosophic statement, locates his Monk's Tale between the Wycliffites and their monastic opponents. He undercuts Wyclif's argument for monasticism's ultimate worthlessness, but he also opposes the monastic apologists' claims for their orders' importance to temporal administration, historical interpretation, and foreign policy formation.

Monasticism's royal claim begins with the Romanesque picture of the temporal court as the place where the monastic might play Nathan to David. As Duby has described it, Cluny aspired to be the colony of the "immaterial on earth" and bridgehead to the kingdom of heaven. Its monastic theology described a scale of perfection related to sexual abstinence in which the fully abstinent monastic was labeled as being even better than married folk or continent widows. Since monks were more perfect than married kings, they deserved to rule

[161]

them. Hence, at Cluny there developed a version of a perfected three-order society soaring between heaven and earth above the normal orders of society—a "priesthood" saying the perpetual sacerdotal mass, a "divine militia" fighting the principalities and powers spiritually and the heretics physically, and a group of monastic "agricultural laborers" providing food for the poor and food for the soul as well. Hugh, the abbot of Cluny, was able to dominate bishops and kings, claiming spiritual identity with the archangel Gabriel, exorcising knights and ordering the temporal nobility about.[1] Though Cluny's power had long since declined by the fourteenth century, monastic theology was again to make explicit monasticism's "sexual estate" claim to rule princes through Uthred of Boldon's clever analyses countering Wyclif's efforts to take the monastics out of temporal administration and then out of existence.

The Monk's portrait points to contemporary controversy. F. N. Robinson long ago observed that the Monk's "How shal the world be served?" (a, 187) refers to the "many secular positions of trust . . . held by the clergy," and showed that the comparable phrase in Gower's *Mirour de l'Omme* attacks parish curates who leave the parish to serve at the temporal court (lines 20,245ff.). He argued that "Chaucer ironically asks how these valuable services [performed in secular positions of trust] are to be rendered if the clergy confine themselves to their religious duties and manual labor," precisely one of the Uthred-Wyclif issues.[2] But Robinson explored the issue no further.

Behind the phrase to which Robinson called attention lay at least a decade of controversy about monasticism's right to temporal office and to large-scale temporal properties—together labeled temporal *dominium*, a controversy that began when the Black Prince and Edward III used monastic administrators in

[1] Duby, *The Three Orders*, pp. 195–97, 201–3.
[2] Robinson, p. 656.

the upper echelons of their bureaucracies. The Prince's brother, John of Gaunt, held a view, contrary to theirs, that temporal position properly belonged only to temporal rulers. These differences came into the open with the Good Parliament's reforms of 1376 aimed at John, at his senile father, and at their allies, reforms that received support from the Black Prince and William of Wykeham, Bishop of Winchester, who had been chancellor of England during 1368–1371 and an ally of the black monks throughout his career. The 1376 reforms did not give the monks more power, but they heightened Wykeham's influence and embarrassed John of Gaunt. When the Prince died (1376), Gaunt headed a caretaker government, since Edward was in his dotage and Prince Richard very young, and made that government support the principle that temporal matters should be administered by "knights" rather than by clergy (though he himself continued to use clerical administrators). He had Wykeham arrested for malversation during his chancellorship, perhaps to dramatize his position, and formed an alliance with Wyclif who defended the Lancastrian approach in a series of London sermons.[3]

Wyclif's London sermons applied theological positions to court politics which his Oxford controversies in the early 1370s with the monastic theologians, William Binham and Uthred of Boldon, had developed. In these, he had argued that God's sanction of temporal authority depended on the state of grace of the temporal ruler. Since God has not given monastics temporal power, in usurping it they may have lost their divine sanction. Theoretically, the state could then unburden monasteries and churches of their property for their good if it found them ruled

---

[3] McKisack, *The Fourteenth Century*, pp. 289–91; Sydney Armitage-Smith, *John of Gaunt* (Westminster: Constable, 1904), pp. 121–44, 160–83; Michael Wilks, "Predestination, Property and Power: Wyclif's Theory of Dominion and Grace," *Studies in Church History* 2 (1965):220–36.

by sinful clerics, too heavily immersed in temporal possession.[4] Wyclif surely knew that the prospect of seizing monastic properties would tempt a nation whose French war was going badly and whose royal treasuries were often strained by its cost. By 1375–76, he had gone from criticizing monasticism's temporal property to criticizing its temporal power by elevating the contemplative above the active life and thereby condemning the clerical or monastic entrance to active vocations such as temporal court administration. In short, he implied that monks are rightly too good to have power and ought to be kicked heavenward to the realms of pure contemplation; he was, however, later to attack the special perfective disciplines of the contemplative—penance and ascetic disciplines aimed at detachment from the temporal, the better to adore God and love neighbor—on a predestinarian basis.[5] Contemplation was granted to the elect on a predestined basis and needed no special institutions. Chaucer's friend, Strode, responded in a friendly way to Wyclif's arguments in the late 1370s, urging that his issues ought not to be clerical property or administration but the abuse of these, that wholesale reform might tear the garment of Christendom, and that predestination would render Christian responsibility and hope meaningless. Wyclif's replies to these ar-

---

[4] Herbert B. Workman, *John Wyclif: A Study of the English Medieval Church* (Hamden, Conn.: Archon, 1966), 2:321ff.; David Knowles, *The Religious Orders in England*, 2 vols. (Cambridge: Cambridge University Press, 1955), 2:65–67. For Wyclif's first responses to Uthred and William Binham, see *Opera Minora*, pp. 405–14, 416–30. Wilks ("Predestination, Property and Power," pp. 228–29, 233–35) argues cogently that Wyclif's theory probably portended no radical change. However, that several popes and councils condemned his theory suggests that they, rightly or wrongly, saw it as destroying divine sanction for the temporal property and offices of clerics. Cf. *Songe de Vergier*, 1:26–27.

[5] John Wyclif, *De Civili Dominio*, 4 vols., ed. Reginald Lane Poole (London: Trübner, 1885), 1:1–80, 124–38, 162–92; cf. John Wyclif, "De Perfectione Statuum," *Polemical Works in Latin*, ed. Rudolf Buddensieg (London: Trübner, 1883), 2:440–82.

guments also remained friendly. Later in 1395, other friends of Chaucer, the Chamber Knights, raised Wyclif's side of the argument again by attacking ecclesiastical property and some monastic disciplines such as the vow of chastity.[6] Chaucer was, by virtue of his friendships, in a position to ponder Wyclif's arguments from both favorable and unfavorable perspectives and probably was reflecting this position when he had his Monk ask, "How shal the world be served?"

Once Wyclif entered public political controversy, he encountered harsher opposition than Strode's. England's monastic leaders were not inclined to lose property and temporal position without a battle, and they successfully encouraged Archbishop Courtenay to schedule a hearing concerning the reformer's views in February of 1377. However, Gaunt, not to be outdone, secured four friars to defend the reformer, an easy enough task since, as one chronicler observes, it was "not difficult . . . to compel the friars . . . 'anxious to assist' one who had 'a natural hatred of the possessioners.' "[7] After the Lady Chapel debate broke off with a minor riot precipitated by Gaunt's protesting Wyclif's having to stand to defend himself, the monks forwarded Wyclif's positions to Pope Gregory XI who condemned several of them, especially those threatening the Church's temporal property and arguing that the Church's divine authority depended on the grace of the person holding it.[8] The English Church did little about Gregory's condemnation, since Gregory died shortly thereafter; Urban VI replaced him, and Wyclif appealed to Urban for relief. However, the monastic theologians busied themselves with giving local answers to

[6] Wyclif summarizes Strode's treatises and, further, replies to them in a friendly manner in *Opera Minora*, pp. 175–200, 398–404. For the *Conclusions*, see above, Introduction, n. 5.

[7] Workman, *Wyclif*, 1:286, quoting the *Chronicon Angliae*, pp. 117–34 (actually p. 116).

[8] *Hist. Ang.*, 1:353–55.

the reformer's attacks. Especially important in this respect were Uthred of Boldon, a Durham monastic theologian; Thomas Brunton, a black monk, court administrator, and bishop; and Adam Easton, the monk and cardinal who had had a hand in keeping England part of the Imperial-Roman papal alliance against France and its pope in the early 1380s.[9] Their arguments, reflective of the realities of Edward III's late reign, essentially said that monks are better temporal administrators than other people because their discipline makes them more secure in their offices—superior to the attachments of life—and that England ought to stick with the Empire and the Roman pope against France.

Chaucer speaks to the controversy by examining how monastic abandonment of the contemplative life affects monastic administration and historical understanding. First, the General Prologue explores an agricultural metaphor through which Wycliffites described monastic possession by making the Monk a steward of his monastery's farms—and a fat one, at that. In opposing monastic abandonment of the contemplative life, Wyclif, like Gaunt, had questioned the "outriding" tendency of the clergy to take temporal offices outside the monastery in "Chancery, Treasury, Privy Seal, and similar offices in the Exchange."[10] Sometimes the Wycliffites used an agricultural metaphor to reinforce this position—for example, "Against the Secular Lordship of Priests" argues for Origen's view that what separated the Pharaoh's priests who had land, and God's who had none, was that God wanted his priests to study and cultivate their souls rather than till the soil.[11] Other Wycliffite treatises assert that monastics are "fat cows" who primarily worship

[9] K. B. McFarlane, *John Wycliffe and the Beginnings of English Nonconformity* (London: English Universities Press, 1966), pp. 79–81.

[10] John Wyclif, *De Blasphemia*, ed. M. H. Dziewicki (London, 1893), p. 261; cf. pp. 188–202).

[11] Wyclif, *English Works*, pp. 396–404.

food, huge buildings, courtly positions, and property management instead of contemplation.[12] And Chaucer's Monk-outrider's portrait evokes exactly such fat-cow possession: "How shal the world be served?" How shall "venerie" be followed with the many dainty horses of his stable? How shall the horses' bells be made to ring as distinctly as the bells of the cloistered monks' hours? And finally, how shall Augustine's quest for divine work be abandoned and more practical chases substituted?

The poet elaborates the General Prologue's picture of upside-down monasticism in the Shipman's tale set at the beginning of the B² section which also includes the Monk's tale. The Shipman's "noble monk" (B², 1252) acts as the St. Denis monastery's outrider, supervising its barns and granaries. He borrows from a merchant engaged in "chevyssaunces" (B², 1519), usurious exchanges that require borrowing at Paris and lending at Bruges (B², 1519, 1459ff., 1539ff.), to produce a thousand-franc profit. He appears to assume that he could also lend to the merchant from the monastery treasury, were it in better shape. While the merchant neglects his wife's sexual needs and spends his chaste life contemplating the vagaries of Fortune's wheel in his upper-room counting house (B², 1404–28), the monk, never contemplating or worshipping, satisfies the woman and works at active-life pursuits. "[C]osynage" (B², 1599) and "bey[ing]" of "certein beestes" (B², 1462), con games and prostitution, make his world invulnerable. The poet elaborates the meaning of such monkish invulnerability in the Monk's tragedies.

He also elaborates the portrait of the Jovinian monks described by the Summoner's friar. This fictional friar shares with the historical Lady Chapel friars that Gaunt sent to defend Wyclif a natural hatred of monk-possessioners and describes monks as having a vow ("professioun," D, 1925) inferior to his

[12] John Wyclif, *Polemical Works in Latin*, 2:524–36, 531; cf. Wyclif, *English Works*, p. 190.

because they "swymmen . . . in possessioun." Hence, they deny the evangelical counsels to poverty, chastity, and obedience with their riches, gluttony, "lewednesse," and pomp—as the Monk denies Benedict's, Maurus', and Augustine's rules with his similar vices. Like the Christian Epicurean, Jovinian, they come fat as a whale and waddle like swans, while they belch forth their virginal hymn to God, the *cor meum eructavit* (D, 1923–37).[13] Coupled with the General Prologue's Monk in wealth and pomp, immersion in swan's flesh and fat, and defiance of monasticism's rules, they pray with belches (D, 1932–35) and, like Don John, happily forego contemplation and its direct sight of God (A, 184). Dante's Saints Peter Damian and Benedict also complain that the monks of Dante's day are so fat-laden that they require four persons, one in each direction, to support them as they walk, and are utterly unable to climb Jacob's ladder of contemplation (*Paradiso* XXI.121–35; XXII.69–96). With the pilgrim Monk's fat go his "eyen stepe, and rollynge in his heed" (A, 201), betraying a mind attracted to the "multiple and varied objects"[14] that Fortune offers. Such eyes are to be contrasted with the blindness to the world and the fixed eagle sight in spiritual matters of the conventional St. John and his eagle emblem, of Chaucer's St. Cecilia, or of the

---

[13] For profession as the vow taken by those in the regular orders, see *Vox Clamantis*, bk. 4, lines 389 ff., and OED, *Profession*, 1, 1, citing *CT*, B², 1345.

[14] Leclercq, *The Love of Learning*, pp. 253, 279–282. Cf. David E. Berndt, "Monastic *Acedia* and Chaucer's Characterization of Daun Piers," *SP* 68 (1971):435–50, esp. 439. St. Bernard speaks of the contemplative as "rapt" ("Sermones in Cantica Canticorum," *PL* 183:1193–94). Monastic hunting required special royal permission: *C.P.R., 1381–85*, p. 389; *C.P.R., 1391–96*, p. 101. Cf. Hatton, "Chauntecleer and the Monk," pp. 31–39; Rodney K. Delasanta, " 'Namoore of This': Chaucer's Priest and Monk," *TSL* 13 (1968):117–32. For the Monk's relation to the rule, see *Three Middle-English Versions of the Rule of St. Benet*, pp. 2–3; cf. Robert B. White, Jr., "Chaucer's Daun Piers and the Rule of St. Benedict: The Failure of an Ideal," *JEGP* 70 (1971):13–30.

conventional figure of Contemplation.[15] In short, Chaucer's General Prologue portrait and its elaboration in the Shipman's and Summoner's tales relate farming, fat, security in possessions, and contemplative failure in a fashion framed for late fourteenth-century England, in Wycliffite anti-monastic polemic and its continental predecessors.

Consequently, the monastic assumption of natural security in temporal office lies at the very center of the Monk's condescending tragedies and the Knight's interruption of them. Launched from earlier Anselmian three-order assumptions, Uthred's treatises contradicted Wyclif's claim that monks are too good to have power, and announced the philosophic absurdity that a monastic administrator can, unlike a prince, ride secure while managing Fortune's goods. To him, monks metaphorically still live in a stable Eden bound by the poverty, chastity, and obedience that Adam and Eve practiced. Instead of being inappropriate as secular governors, as Wyclif had argued, they are especially appropriate because, in their Edenic world, they come closer to God and his law and are, as Pantin puts it, "more spiritual, therefore . . . more discreet and suited to govern—Aristotelian natural rulers."[16] It would be unnatural to follow Wyclif's direction and remove monastics from government to create a heightened monastic insecurity through disen-

[15] Cf. Rabanus Maurus, *Allegoriae in Sacram Scripturam*, PL 112:862; Garner of St. Victor, *Gregorianum*, PL 193:70. St. Paul's blinding on the road to Damascus may also relate to this iconology; cf. *Glossa Ordinaria*, PL 114:448–49. Cf. Edmund Reiss, "The Symbolic Surface of *The Canterbury Tales*: The Monk's Portrait, Part II," *CR* 3 (1968):12–28. For Contemplation, see James Nohrnberg, *The Analogy of "The Faerie Queene"* (Princeton: Princeton University Press, 1976), pp. 155–57).

[16] W. A. Pantin, *The English Church in the Fourteenth Century* (Cambridge: Cambridge University Press, 1955), pp. 166–75; cf. *Studies in Medieval History Presented to Francis Maurice Powicke*, pp. 363–85.

dowment or to teach apostolic poverty and growth in contemplation.

Though common sense told people that individual monks might be disgraced in their handling of temporal office and power, whether as chancellors or outriders, Chaucer's Monk has no fear of Wyclif or common-sense considerations. As he flits from topic to topic, following the rolling of his eyes, he considers telling the tale of Edward the Confessor, Richard's favorite saint and a monk-king of sorts.[17] Or he may tell tragedies of "popes, emperours, or kynges" (B², 3176) from the hundred in his cell—perhaps the only works he has read (A, 184–87). He will please and instruct those lords and clerics wise enough to listen (B², 3165–80).

But he does not. He tells only stories of *emperors* and *kings*, not of *popes*—not the full three-estate tragic cycles of Boccaccio and Lawrence of Premierfait. What he tells are not tragedies at all but tales of Fortune's capricious betrayal of knights, emperors, and kings which are primarily implicit advertisements for the security of his own estate in temporal office. Proper tragedies, like epics, were to be told by rulers about rulers and in the high style; and as a forthcoming study by Roberet Haller will show, the two forms were often identified with each other. Tragedy included narratives of popes and monks as "stories of heigh degree."[18] Harry Bailey seems to think the Monk a lord spiritual

---

[17] For St. Edward as royal patron saint, see Jones, *The Royal Policy of Richard II*, p. 14; Gervase Mathew, *The Court of Richard II* (London: John Murray, 1968), pp. 21, 36, 48; cf. the Wilton Diptych scholarship, especially Francis Wormald, "The Wilton Diptych," *JWCI* 17 (1954):191–203. See also *Vita Aedwardi Regis*, ed. and trans. Frank Barlow (London: Nelson, 1962), pp. 40–50; Aelred of Rievaulx, "Vita S. Edwardi Regis," *PL* 195:746–53.

[18] See especially the portrait of Pope John XII in Giovanni Boccaccio, *De Casibus Illustrium Virorum*, ed. Louis Hall (Gainesville: Scholar's Facsimiles, 1962), sig. [c11ʳ–c11ᵛ]. Lawrence of Premierfait begins his version with an account of the three estates, and the frontispiece includes a picture of all three estates subject to tragedy's falls (see frontispiece above). Lydgate, as Bury monk,

and calls on him after the Knight ("sir Monk," A, 3118) in a three-order pattern; he also calls him "lord" (B², 3153) and speaks of him as "maister" at home (B², 3128). Even Chaucer says he could have been an abbot (A, 167), but Don Piers has chosen to rule the monastery's temporal part, not its spiritual. If he were to have peculiar authority in tragedy, he would have it through cherishing the very contemplation that he has rejected, the contemplation Wyclif elevated, so that he could see the significance of events with some distance. Contemplation, the vision of God, is partly a gift of grace. Wyclif argued that the graceless lack *dominium*—divinely sanctioned authority to rule. Though a person's state of grace cannot, in medieval culture, be generally known, his or her acceptance of the grace of contemplation could be represented in literature by external signs, precisely such signs as Chaucer denies the Monk. Cecilia's contemplative power gives her second sight and the security to command Roman officers. If lack of contemplative grace denies one security in rule, then Don Piers has so little security that, when he tells of the insecurity of others, their loss of Eden and fortune, he really tells of his own potential fall.

A true contemplative tells other kinds of tragedies, as Lydgate does in *The Fall of Princes*, all the while emphasizing his monastic role. Like the ascetic *bodhisattva*, the person who masters this life removes himself from immediate events, seeks unity in a divine realm, and looks back on time with detachment and on people with compassion. The great patristic Christian writers in this tradition, Boethius and St. Gregory commenting on Job, look at history's suffering with this detachment and compassion,[19] as do Boccaccio and Chaucer's Troilus. Anyone vulnerable who sees the tragic hero placing himself on Fortune's

---

asserts in *The Fall of Princes* (bk. 9, lines 3265–67) that monks can experience Fortune's fickleness and deals with clerics as well as princes.

[19] Cf. Chaucer's *Boece* in Robinson, pp. 319–84; cf. St. Gregory, "Moralia in Job," 1.32, 5.24–30, 9.50, 24.2, 24.4, 24.11, and *passim*.

wheel by the desire for some transitory good, rising for a time into Fortune's cap or midpart and knowing a painted paradise created by his achievement, cannot but feel sorrow at the expense of spirit. When a complex action, some of it outside the hero's control, results in the loss of what he has gained and worshipped, he may end in despair and blame Fortune and his former good, rather than his own choice. Or he may detach himself from his former good as Boethius does, as Nabuchodonosor does, as Arcita does, and as one would expect the heroes who are objects of praise in tragedy to do.[20] Indeed, tragedy in Boccaccio, Laurence of Premierfait, and Lydgate forewarns all estates and conditions that nothing temporal is as permanent or Edenic as Uthred had claimed the position of monks at the temporal court to be. The great tragic writers of the late fourteenth

---

[20] Lawrence of Premierfait's account of the philosopher Stilbon, who loses everything and yet retains his freedom of mind, illustrates the freedom of the tragic hero to resist fortune; cf. Lydgate's *The Fall of Princes*, vol. 1, pp. liv–lviii. For an analysis of the nonsense in the distinction between Boethian and *De casibus* tragedy, see Robert F. Haller's review of Mona E. McAlpine, *The Genre of Troilus and Criseyde* in *SAC* 2 (1980):172–79. Boccaccio's, Laurence's, and Lydgate's portraits of the heroes whose stories the Monk narrates emphasize each hero's choice of lust, pride, or avarice as basic to his degradation and fall before Fortune. In Lydgate, for example, see the portrait of Hercules in the *Fall*, bk. 1; lines 5216, 5153–5201, 4338–5523, 5529–33; again, in Boccaccio and Lydgate, Croesus dreams a conditional dream and, unlike the Monk's Croesus, still has a choice after he has dreamt it. Cf. Edward M. Socola, "Chaucer's Development of Fortune in the 'Monk's Tale,' " *JEGP* 49 (1958):159–71; Paul Ruggiers, "Notes Toward a Theory of Tragedy in Chaucer," *CR* 8 (1973):97; and Berndt, "Monastic *Acedia*," pp. 444–48. For the notion of tragedy as involving the praise of good rulers, see H. A. Kelly, "Aristotle-Averroes-Alemannus on Tragedy," *Viator* 10 (1979):161–209; cf. Allen, *The Ethical Poetic of the Later Middle Ages*, pp. 86, 121–23. The standard Aristotelian-Averroistic definitions of tragedy are not incompatible with the Boethian-Robertsonian sense of Chaucerian tragedy set forth in *A Preface to Chaucer* (pp. 38–44, 473ff.) if one assumes that some tragic heroes such as Nabuchodonosor detach themselves from false goods as a consequence of their suffering and are, therefore, deserving of praise.

18. St. Nicholas saving the storm-tossed. *Queen Mary's Psalter*; English, early fourteenth century

19. St. Nicholas raising the three dead in the pickling tub at the false innkeepers. *Queen Mary's Psalter*; English, early fourteenth century

20. St. Nicholas rescuing the maidens about to be made prostitutes with a gift. *Queen Mary's Psalter*; English, early fourteenth century

21. Absalom with hair spread like a fan. Guyart de Moulins'
translation of Peter Comester's *Historia Scholastica*; French,
early fifteenth century

22. Noah as an old man and carpenter. Guyart de Moulins'
translation of Peter Comester's *Historia Scholastica*; French,
early fifteenth century

23. Noah as husbandman supervising the harvest (*above*),
and drunk, exposed, and mocked (*below*). *Holkham
Picture Bible*; English, 1325–1330

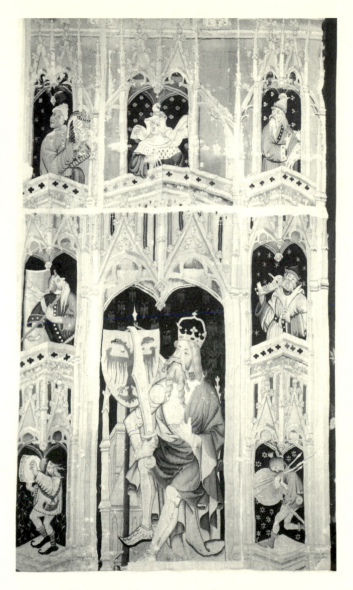

24. Tapestry of Caesar, resembling tapestries of
temporal lords exchanged in English-French peace
process. Flemish, late fourteenth century

25. Science leading to Prudence and mechanics; Entendement leading to Sapience (Christ), "the memory of hidden things and outstripping of present for future things." Oresme's translation of Aristotle's *Ethics*; Paris, 1367

26. Frederick II's Capuan Gate (reconstruction). Italian, thirteenth century

27. Ambrogio Lorenzetti's *The Effects of Good Government*. Palazzo Pubblico; Siena, 1340s

28. Monks (*right*) singing the New Song with the innocent in Paradise (*left*). Alexander Laicus, *In Apocalipsim*; German, late thirteenth, early fourteenth century

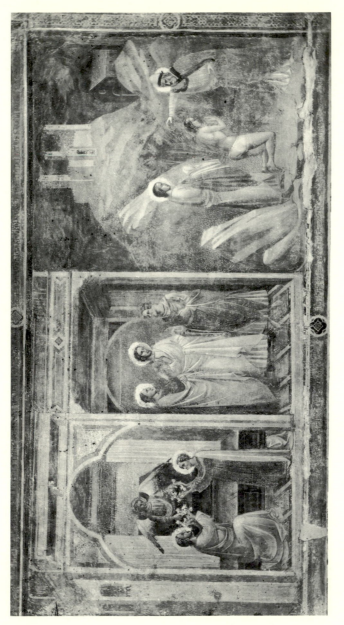

29. Lorenzo di Bicci's (?) life of St. Cecilia: (1) Cecilia and Valerian receive crowns of lilies and roses; (2) Tiburtius's conversion; (3) his baptism by Pope Urban in barren poverty on the outskirts of Rome. Santa Maria del Carmine, second half of the fourteenth century

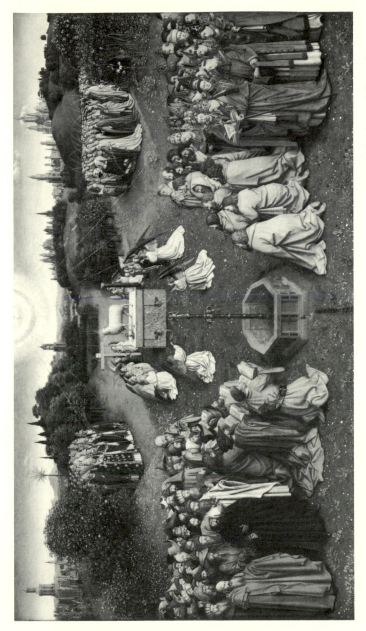

30. Jan Van Eyck's "Mystic Lamb" altarpiece, with Garden of Paradise, Apocalyptic lamb, and Canticle fountain surrounded by (*from lower right, counterclockwise*) apostles and martyrs, virgins, confessors, and prophets. Flemish, 1420s

31. Jan Van Eyck's "Mystic Lamb" altarpiece, with Mary as
Sapience crowned with lilies and roses, and with the inscription
from Wisdom 1.26–29 praising her as Sapience, the mirror of
God's majesty, more beautiful than the sun, stars, or physical
light. Flemish, 1420s

32. The enclosed Canticle garden centering in a fountain as the Church centers in baptism. *Bible Moralisée*; French, thirteenth century

33. The voice of the turtle as the voice of the preacher announcing the end of the law's night. *Bible Moralisée*; French, thirteenth century

34. Defending against the Canticle foxes as protecting
the weak against heresy. *Bible Moralisée*; French,
thirteenth century

35. The thrones of God the Father and Christ, with the orb of power surrounded by red cherubim. Guyart's translation of Peter Comester's *Historia Scholastica*; French, early fifteenth century

and fifteenth centuries, like Wyclif, had little doubt that loss of property and position could do as much for monks as for kings, for Don Piers as for Chauntecleer. Figure 1 in this book illustrates the significance of estate theory to tragedy.

The Monk, in contrast, creates tragedies that crush only lords temporal and deny the Knight's and Theseus' distanced sense of a providence operating through chivalric suffering such as Arcita's. His account reduces pagan "natural-law" rulership to a pitiable thing without assigning power to theocratic rulership. Hercules, Theseus' great friend and pattern prince, loses his Boethian status as a paragon of rulers who overcome vice through suffering (*Boece*, bk. 4, met. 7) and becomes a trivial victim.[21] Cenobia is no merciful Amazon Ypolita. The other classical protagonists—Croesus, Julius Caesar, Nero—all portrayed on the walls of the Knight's houses of Venus and Mars as having at least the dignity of freely followed appetite—here appear as the pitiful tools of a mechanical Fortune. Finally, Alexander—praised by the Monk as Chaucer praises his Knight, as a paragon of gentility and generosity—leads such an uncontrolled life as to make the epithets ludicrous.

When the Monk looks at the Bible, he sees the same kinds of scenes. Lucifer stumbles, and Adam misgoverns. Samson, Belshazzar, Holofernes, Antiochus, and Nabuchodonosor do not choose when they fall, or reflect Old Testament redemption

---

[21] Cf. Chaucer's "Boece," bk. 4, met. 7. Lydgate makes Hercules a "rightful juge" (*The Fall of Princes*, bk 1, line 5058), first in chivalry in his day (bk 1, line 5064), philosopher-knight (bk 1, line 5216) and friend and reflection of Theseus. Simon of Hesdin says that Theseus "fut ung trespuissant et vaillant chevalier et compaignon de hercules en telle maniere que quanques hercules fist fut attribue a theseus, et aussi les fais de theseus a hercules." Simon of Hesdin, *Valere de Grant*, sig. [B⁺ᵛ]. Cf. Marcel Simon, *Hercule et le christianisme* (Paris: Les Belles Lettres, 1955), pp. 171–73; F. Michael Krouse, *Milton's Samson and the Christian Tradition* (Princeton: Princeton University Press, 1949), pp. 31–62. Cf. Dudley R. Johnson, "The Biblical Characters of Chaucer's Monk," *PMLA* 66 (1951):827–43.

history, or model the actions of just crusaders and warriors like the Knight.[22] Even Nabuchodonosor's repentance and recovery from his wild-man episode appears as a free action only as an afterthought, in Daniel's warning to Belshazzar (B², 3400–12). In the ruler's own tragedy, God appears to release him for no reason.

Europe's monks writing in their monastic *scriptoria* compiled chronicles for several purposes, including prophetic instruction to the ruler,[23] but not this monk. Philippe de Mézières, the Celestine monastic, uses history to instruct the courts he addresses in the *Songe*, the *Ordo*, and the *Letter*, and the Monk's tragedies

[22] For Samson, see Judges 13–17; Holofernes, Judith 1–13; Nabuchodonosor and Balthasar, Daniel 2–6; and Antiochus, 2 Maccabees 9. Samson is generally seen as the savior of Israel and a type of Christ whereas the other figures, save for Nabuchodonosor in his period of repenting, are seen as "Babylonian" tyrants following Augustine's conception of Babylon. The Monk departs from medieval historiography which turns on two primary conceptions, history as providential and as made up of a succession of world empires; cf. Alan Richardson, *History: Sacred and Profane* (Philadelphia: Westminster, 1964), pp. 54–79, and Patrides, *The Grand Design of God*, pp. 13–46. For Nabuchodonosor's dream, correctly understood by Chauntecleer and acted out by him with a like recovery, see Richard Crider, "Daniel in the 'Nun's Priest's Tale,' " *AN&Q* 18 (1980):18–19.

[23] For the historical work of St. Alban's monastery during the period, see Knowles, *The Religious Orders in England*, 2:264–68. Thomas Walsingham's account of the period, 1382–1399, written at St. Alban's monastery, opposes the peace with France, favors the Lords Appellant, depreciates Richard II's accomplishments, but sees suffering (e.g., in Richard II's fall) as providential for the kingdom; *Hist. Ang.* 2:232–38, and cf. Leclercq, *The Love of Learning*, pp. 190–96. For tragedy as counsel, see Raoul de Presles's remark that Seneca's *Octavia* pictures Nero's cruelties and warns him to abandon them; Raoul de Presles, *Cité de Dieu*, 1:sig. [z5ᵛ]. Cf. Simon of Hesdin, *Valere de Grant* (Lyon, 1489), sig. [p5ᵛ]. Nicholas Oresme observes, "Item de ce nous lessierent exemple les contemplatifs qui furent jadis, comme Ysaie, Jeremie, et les autres sains prophetes, qui annoncierent as princes et as cités les perilz a venir, et enseingnoient les remedes et donnoient conseulz actifs et pratiques au salut du paiz" (Oresme, *Le Livre de Politiques d'Aristote*, p. 285). The Monk provides no remedy (B², 3974).

ought to be in the same way chronicles-advisory to lords, particularly since he directly addresses the lords with Balthasar's example (B², 3429). Instead, his contempt for knighthood unfolds in ancient histories which only mock the Knight's outline of history and providence. Whereas he hints that tragedy is often written in the heroic hexameter meter, associated with epic and the high style (B², 3169), his poem includes none of the high meditative style of the Knight's Tale or the *Troilus*, none of their elaborate metaphor, mythological allusions, dignity of diction or philosophic complexity, and none of the Knight's advice for peace. His little tales are so short as to have no middle, so to speak, and do not allow for the due praise or blame suggested by their subjects' natural characters.[24] The Monk is not, like Chaucer in the *Troilus*, the servant of the servants of love who wishes to pray for them and live in charity. Nor does he have fellow feeling for the servants of Fortune. Removed from Cecilia's tragic sense of the double meaning of death in the life of the "empire" and the life of the martyr, he can only arrogantly deplore death and physical loss in the life of the rival estate while he proudly prepares himself for the despairing end he assigns to others—his eyes ever circling with Fortune's wheel.

No wonder the Knight interrupts him. He does so after a particularly bitter pill—the modern instances. Like the Marshal Boucicaut of the Order of the Passion, the Knight relishes stories "of God, of the saints, of virtue, of the good that someone has done, of bravery, of knighthood, of good examples," of the books of the "deeds of the Romans and ancient histories."[25] He stops things precisely because his antagonist-pretend knight extends his diatribe from ancient to modern times, to the Knight's own crusading culture and then renders it meaningless

[24] Allen, *The Ethical Poetic of the Later Middle Ages*, pp. 122–25.

[25] *Histoire de Maréchal Boucicaut*, p. 379. Robert Haller's variorum edition will show that textually the modern instances belong at the end of the Monk's Tale.

CHAPTER 6

by treating its heroes and villains alike. By confusing recent history, Don Piers superficially legitimizes the monastic foreign policy devised by Adam Easton to keep England in the Imperial-Roman papal alliance by precluding a peace with France that might diminish the Roman pope and his power to support the monastic claims.[26]

The modern instances include the death of Bernabò Visconti in 1385 and could not have been written until after 1385–86. Possibly they were not set down until the 1390s. Three of the heroes were of particular concern to England as in the late 1380s and 1390s she shifted away from surrounding France with enemies in the German part of the Empire, and in Italy, Spain, and the Low Countries, and toward seeking a peace and a Turkish crusade.[27] The first modern instance, Peter of Lusignan, was the Knight's commander against the Turk in the Mediterranean and represented *par excellence* the model through whom the Order sought to urge the view that Christian warriors ought to be fighting in the East for Christian civilization rather than in France for booty:[28]

O worthy Petro, kyng of Cipre, also,
That Alisandre wan by heigh maistrie,

[26] Pantin, *The English Church in the Fourteenth Century*, pp. 175–81; Sister M. A. Devlin, "Bishop Brunton and his Sermons," *Speculum* 14 (1939):340–42. Walsingham as a monk takes the same position; cf. n. 21, above.

[27] For an account of the shift in policy, see Palmer, *England, France and Christendom*.

[28] For Leo of Armenia and Philippe de Mézières, see Palmer, *England, France and Christendom*, pp. 181–99; Clarke, *Fourteenth Century Studies*, pp. 287–88. Cf. Donald K. Fry, "The Ending of the *Monk's Tale*," *JEGP* 71 (1972):355–68. Fry and Hatton have anticipated some of my argument in this section, partly in consequence of work that I did in the 1960s; however, Fry's textual argument goes beyond anything that I had worked out and is extremely useful. Jorga confirms the general historical accuracy of the Order's view of Peter; cf. Peter Edbury, "The Murder of King Peter I of Cyprus (1359–69)," *Journal of Medieval History*, 6 (1980):219–33.

Ful many an hethen wroghtestow ful wo,
Of which thyne owene liges hadde envie,
And for no thyng but for thy chivalrie
They in thy bed han slayn thee by the morwe,
Thus kan Fortune hir wheel governe and gye,
And out of joye brynge men to sorwe.   (B², 3581–88)

The Monk has no leisure to detail Peter's greatness as visualized by Chaucer's court but only says that he was worthy and was killed for envy. What was envied—whether Peter's virtue, his prowess, or his wealth—is not clear. Nor does the Monk make clear how Fortune governed Peter, whether he means by his last two lines only that Peter was killed or also means that he was "attached" to the changeable goods of Queen Fortune rather than to the First Good.

Pedro and Bernabò, enemies of the Knight's "Order of the Passion" strategy, also receive ambiguous treatment. But they were perceived very differently from Peter by Chaucer's court. The reorientation of English military and diplomatic strategy toward France in the late 1380s and 1390s required a loosening of earlier affiliations with the Holy Roman Emperor, the neo-Ghibelline faction in Italy, anti-French forces in Spain, and the Roman pope; and this requirement grew more urgent as the ring of alliances created to foster Edward III's "Imperial" strategy disintegrated in Italy and Spain. Bernabò Visconti of Milan who was expected to control Italy for the English faction was murdered in 1385 by his "scholarly" Pavian nephew, Giangaleazzo, and Milan then pursued a less English policy.[29] Though the Monk praises Bernabò as, like Peter, an innocent victim of Fortune and a scourge of God—without the least sense of

[29] See Bueno de Mesquito, *Giangaleazzo Visconti*, pp. 31–34; cf. Giuseppe Marcotti and John Temple-Leader, *Sir John Hawkwood*, trans. Leader Scott (Lucy E. Baxter) (London, 1889), and Fritz Gaupp, "The Condottiere John Hawkwood," *History* 23 (1939):305–21.

irony—the English court by the period of the *Canterbury Tales* knew that Bernabò was no statesman and no divine scourge, that his reign as Epicurean Cupid ("God of delit"; B², 3590) made Milan into a sty of intrigue, poisonings, and institutionalized self-indulgence. Though he died a victim, overall he was as corrupt as his murderer-nephew from Pavia, Giangaleazzo, and as self-indulgent as Giangaleazzo's bourgeois Pavian semblance, January.³⁰ Ugolino's tale, a semi-modern instance, simply recapitulates the story of Bernabò by relating the fall of an "innocent" Italian city tyrant whom Dante treats otherwise.³¹ Finally, the fourth modern instance, Pedro of Castille or Pedro the Cruel, becomes the Monk's Roland betrayed by Guenelon ('Genylon-Olyver"; B², 3579). Pedro was one of Spain's crueler petty tyrants, disallied by the Black Prince over his treatment of prisoners (Chaucer probably fought against him in 1366), no longer a favorite as the father-in-law of Gaunt who once claimed to be the King of Castille. To Chaucer's court Pedro must have appeared either insignificant or evil.³²

The Monk's tragic rhetoric makes no distinctions. It represents all knights as equally done in by Fortune and the envy of their temporal lordship by those close to them. Anyone against

---

³⁰ There were suspicions that Lionel of Clarence was poisoned in Milan; for the Order's view of Milan and Visconti rule under Bernabò, see Philippe de Mézières, *Songe du Vieil Pèlerin*, 1:280–83. The complexities of English-Burgundian-Visconti negotiations, 1390–1399, are too intricate to record here; see Richard Vaughan, *Philip the Bold* (Cambridge, Mass.: Harvard University Press, 1962), pp. 182–87; Bueno di Mesquita, "The Foreign Policy of Richard II in 1397: Some Italian Letters," *EHR* 56 (1941):628–37.

³¹ The early Visconti were related to Ugolino by marriage.

³² On Pedro's reputation, see Philippe de Mézières, *Songe du Vieil Pèlerin*, 1:385–87; P. E. Russell, *The English Intervention in Spain and Portugal in the Time of Edward III and Richard II* (Oxford: Clarendon, 1955), esp. 13–148; Haldeen Braddy, *Geoffrey Chaucer: Literary and Historical Studies*, pp. 25, 31–33. Crow (*LR*, p. 65) notes that Chaucer may have fought with Henry of Trastamare against Pedro.

reconciliation with France, as the monks were because of their alliance with the Roman pope, would have had little reason to distinguish the lives of Peter, Pedro, and Bernabò or develop a discriminating rhetoric of praise and blame. Since the Monk cannot rise above history to see its direction, he cannot do more than flatter his own estate and predict the doom of the temporal one; he cannot praise and blame with justice, or distinguish himself from his party's old allies. Yet, medieval Aristotelian critics believed that poetry should praise or blame and that tragedy should praise good rulers and condemn tyrants.[33] Boethius' philosophy also separates tyrants and good rulers on the basis of their detachment from Fortune and their recognition of the role of providence in all histories of suffering. The Monk simply destroys the tragic function. Chaucer's Knight, having fought his fictive battles in Spain, perhaps under Pedro, and in the Mediterranean under Peter of Lusignan and having advocated peace in his tale, recognizes that Peter, Pedro, and Bernabò did not live only to adorn a fortunistic bromide. Hence, he interrupts the Monk's tale with his demand for an end to more than a "litel hevynesse" (B², 3959) in order to call for stories of men of poor estate who rise up and *remain* prosperous— as Chantecleer does in the next tale. Even our host knows that tragedy with "no remedie" is only "hevynesse" (B², 3973ff.).

The Knight, given his tale, has reason to expect the tragedian to see as much as he sees in Arcita or as Chaucer sees in Troilus. What offends the Knight in the modern instances should offend anyone having a sense of classical and Biblical history: men die meaninglessly,[34] no Zion is protected, no civilization saved,

---

[33] H. A. Kelly, "Aristotle-Averroes-Alemannes on Tragedy," pp. 161–209. Kelly argues correctly that Chaucer did not know Aristotelian-Averroistic tragic theory; however, Boethius uses the rhetoric of praise and blame, which late medieval Aristotelian tragic theory would recommend, in his portraits of Nero and Hercules.

[34] Cf. John Wyclif, *De Civile Dominio*, 1:94. Jean Leclercq observes that, in

and no providence in history displayed. All the "tragic" heroes live and die only to illustrate the tired maxim that ends Peter of Lusignan's tragedy.

> Thus kan Fortune hir wheel governe and gye,
> And out of joye brynge men to sorwe.
> (B,² 3587–88; cf. B², 3566–67, 3591–92, 3647)

In contrast, the Order of the Passion documents composed by the monastic Philippe de Mézières always emphasize how Divine Providence speaks to the nations—through the defeats of the Hundred Years War, through the assassinations, through the success of the Moslems—of another strategy necessary for European civilization.³⁵ He consistently employs the rhetoric of historical praise and blame to show the necessity of his programme. If the Monk presented in the General Prologue lacks the crucial monastic ascetic disciplines, the Monk presented through the tale lacks a crucial contemplative one—the focused distance from historical events, the vision of a Philippe, a Scipio, a dead Troilus, or a Theseus, that would permit him to perceive the events and suffering of history as a pattern in a mosaic, and yet feel compassion for its flesh-and-blood persons. The Monk's flat treatment of people shows, with devastating irony, the fallacy of monastic arrogance in temporal court administration, property management, and foreign policy. The Monk's art is art of the most difficult sort, bad art by a bad man

---

monastic history properly done, "[t]he individual story is always inserted in the history of salvation," and "[e]vents are directed by God who desires the salvation of the elect" (Leclercq, *Love of Learning*, p. 194). Diane Bornstein calls the Monk "an incompetent contemplative" failing to see divine control of events; "Chaucer's *Monk's Tale*, 2095–2142," *Explicator* 33 (1975):item 77.

³⁵ Brown, *Philippe de Mézières' Order*, pp. 16–36, and *passim*; providentialist rhetoric pervades Philippe's *Songe*. Richard II appears to pick up on Philippe's providentialist rhetoric in his letter about the 1396 marriage to Isabella (reproduced Legge, *Anglo-Norman Letters and Petitions*, p. 159).

to show what the good art of tragedy with "remedie" ought to be.

Chaucer's location of the Monk's problem in his denial of perfective discipline moves the tale's irony from Uthred to Wyclif to undercut Wycliffite attacks on monasticism itself and on the perfective disciplines. The answer to monasticism's Epicureanism and temporal wallowing is not disendowment but serious monasticism. The answer is St. Cecilia. Chaucer never advances Wyclif's late charges that monasticism, because of its temporal property and power, is a sect that destroys the Church and should be abolished in favor of a predestinarian evangelism and a universalized contemplation. Indeed the Monk is criticized in the General Prologue for ignoring the rule. For the poet, secularism, not sectism—idle fat, rolling eyes, that is, failure to develop a seriously spiritual tragic view that applies universally—constitutes the Monk's tragic flaw. Chaucer does not so much attack monasticism as give it a pre-Romanesque significance consistent with his living the last of his years in a house within the garden of the royal monastery at Westminster.

As if to reinforce what he says about the monastic rule, the poet repeats it in the Canon's Yeoman's Tale. Wyclif's charges against the "sect" of the Augustinian canons run parallel to Chaucer's charges against monasticism. The canons too are overly concerned with endowments. They also claim ridiculous miracles for their order which, even if true, would not substitute for charity but which may be only diabolic illusion.[36] The Canon's Yeoman's Tale, following the Second Nun's, repeats the Monk's Tale's ironies under an alchemical metaphor. Its canons contemplate the physical compounds and their mystical properties and a miraculous philosopher's stone as their salvation; their search is to pave the world with gold rather than

36 Wyclif, *Polemical Works in Latin*, pp. 247–51.

to seek a "golden" Jerusalem, and hence they, like the Monk, transform the world into a secular hell. The charge may be particularly appropriate to the Augustinian canons since they had both parish and conventual duties, but it also fits uncloistered monastics. In Chaucer's Canon's Yeoman's Tale, the search for a philosopher's stone substitutes for sapience and places mankind in an adversary relationship with God:

> Thanne conclude I thus, sith that God of hevene
> Ne wil nat that the philosophres nevene
> How that a man shal come unto this stoon,
> I rede, as for the beste, lete it goon.
> For whoso maketh God his adversarie,
> As for to werken any thyng in contrarie
> Of his wil, certes, never shal he thryve,
> Thogh that he multiplie terme of his lyve. (G, 1472–79)

The way of the philosopher's stone, marked by manipulation of Luna, Mars, Saturn, and Jupiter—"gods of stone" such as Cecilia overcame—makes one God's adversary as does, implicitly, monastic entanglement with Fortune. The stone gods are sought as ends, the philosopher's stone substituted for *Amor sapientiae* or *philo-sophia*. Thus both Chaucer's canons and his Epicurean Monk lose similar opportunities, benefitting neither themselves nor society as they destroy the good of their orders and lives in order to create a stable illusion. Ultimately such illusions explode in a tragic world.

7

The Hierarchy's Keys

SUMMONER AND PARDONER AND THE

ABUSE OF LOVE

No claim to power, not even the monks', surpassed that for the keys that locked and unlocked the gates of eternity. In earlier times princes had been brought to their knees by the prospect of a curse, or crusading armies to the field by the promise of a blessing. But Italy in 1378 saw the papacy brought low by the Schism and lower still by Urban VI's cruelty to his own cardinals. Decline at the hierarchy's apex also affected the authority of the bishops and their courts, and discipline at all levels declined in the conflicts between the *curia* and appointees of the two popes. Earlier in the century the keys had frequently come under fire from Spiritualist friars and temporal rulers. In the *Paradiso*, St. Peter declares his papal place empty and reddens to condemn the papacy's allocation of the martyr popes' blood, intended to "feed the spouse of Christ," to the traffic in indulgences. At the same time, the papal keys shine on the banners of crusades against the baptized (*Paradiso* XXVII.34ff.). In England, Wyclif and his followers challenged any administration of the keys that brought the temporal sword to support the spiritual through the *significavit* and indulgence-blessed crusade and also attacked the papacy and bishops who administered the keys for using the temporal sword.

In the portraits of the Summoner and the Pardoner which represent the excommunication curse and the indulgence, Chaucer reddens with satiric indignation to expose the Epicurean root of Wyclif's problem with the keys and turns his narrators' invective and sermonistic abuse into a flaying of vices.[1] Through this flaying, the poet places himself on the conservative side of Wyclif and the Chamber knights and to the left of the most conservative elements in the hierarchy. His fictive blessings and curses operate through, and in spite of, corrupt clerics, through, or in spite of, a visible church and sometimes through an invisible Church. The poet supports the Wycliffite claim of inappropriate mingling of the temporal and spiritual powers in the administration of the keys but would remedy the problem by appealing to the same faith that led to Peter's declaration of belief and Christ's delegation of the keys to the Petrine successors.

In the General Prologue, the poet links the two male lovers who administer the keys as the papal keys themselves were linked; the Pardoner who frees people from penalty for sin plays a female role while the Summoner who binds the recalcitrant plays a male, and in their love song, the Pardoner, "a geldyng or a mare" (A, 691), carries the soprano part of the "Com hider, love" while the Summoner adds the low stiff "burdoun" (also a phallic pun). This harmony figures how one rascal uncovers sins for his own and his lord's profit and the other absolves them for similar comic reasons. Though Wyclif and the Lollard knights spoke of clerics who combined the temporal and spiritual power as mules or hermaphrodites,[2] Chaucer narrows the metaphor to specify their combination of these powers in the specific summoning which precedes the unjust curse and temporal imprisonment, and the plenary pardon granting in-

---

[1] For the medieval distinction between satire and invective, see John of Garland, *Parisiana Poetria*, p. 103. Cf. Simon of Hesdin, *Valere le Grant*, sig. e7ʳ.

[2] Wyclif treats clerical "effeminacy" as symbol in the *De Officio Regis*, pp. 243–244; cf. the Lollard knights' use of the same image in Wilkins, *Concilia*, 3:22. For other aspects of the homophile image and Wycliffite critiques, see Terrence A. McVeigh, "Chaucer's Portraits of the Pardoner and Summoner and Wyclif's *Tractatus de Simonia*," *Classical Folia* 29 (1975):54–58.

dulgences to supporters of crusades against Christians. Since the "Com hider, love" reflects medieval lyrics based on the Canticle (one preserved carol does contain the requisite burden),[3] the soothing Pardoner, preaching while stretching his neck like a dove (c, 395–97), acts a ludicrously proper role as the Canticle dove or Church while the Summoner, as a cherubic, angry, redfaced messenger from the throne of judgment, plays the Spouse calling the Pardoner at pruning time and rejecting the remaining pilgrims (fig. 35). Irony can go little further.

The presentation of the Pardoner and the Summoner as grotesque parodies of the Church arises out of late fourteenth-century English theological disputes over the hierarchy and the keys parallel to those over the monks and their temporal power. The dispute about the keys ends somewhat one-sidedly since the popes and bishops responded to Wyclif in no extended way but only with their brief actions against him in 1377, 1379, and 1382. They did not have to answer; they had the power and the developed theology. Hence, the only theologian who contemplated replying to the reformer on this issue was Cardinal Adam Easton in his incomplete *Defensorium*.[4] Wyclif's, or the Wycliffites', analyses of the keys did not simply repeat conventional objections to harsh summoners, overstrict archdeacons, and false pardoners but made the administration of the keys a three-order issue and used it to attack the central power of the "sect of the bishops and pope," a position finally dealt with at the Council of Constance.

---

[3] *The Pearl*, ed. Sir Israel Gollancz (London: Chatto and Windus, 1921), p. 154, compares A, 672, to *Pearl's* "Cum hyder to me, my lemman swete" (lines 763–64), an echo of Cant. 4.7–8. One song based on the Canticle, "Come, my dere spouse and lady free," has a burden; the substitution of *love* for *spouse* or *lady* in the song of the Pardoner and Summoner is obviously required by their relationship. See Richard Leighton Green, *A Selection of Early English Carols* (Oxford: Clarendon Press, 1962), p. 262.

[4] Pantin, *The English Church in the Fourteenth Century*, p. 179.

Specifically, Wyclif opposed the *significavit* given at the re-
quest of the bishop because it required the temporal arm to im-
prison unrepentant excommunicates, and the papal plenary in-
dulgence because it used the spiritual power to push temporal
lords into papal crusades, especially against the French pope
and his allies—an action that prolonged the French wars. Chau-
cer also centers on these issues.

Wyclif first attacks the summons and *significavit* in the late
1370s, then the pardon or indulgence in the early 1380s.[5] In
1378, he reverses the usual three-order logic by placing the tem-
poral power above the spiritual. He derives episcopal power
from that of the crown, and obligates the crown to examine
both crime and sin since the latter also jeopardizes the realm.
Since in his view, excommunication only harms persons al-
ready cursed by their own sin and by Christ, and since many
curses are unjust, he holds that the state ought not automati-
cally to arrest unrepentant excommunicates on the basis of
chancery writs of *significavit* but allow for crown appeals as part
of its suppression of sin and injustice. Later he elaborates on the
same arguments by adding that, though Christ, when reviled,
did not revile in return (1 Peter 2.23), the bishops do return re-
viling constantly and curse the blessed, presumably Wyclif-
fites, for their obedience to God's law.[6] The reformer's related
objections to crusading indulgences develop after the 1378
Schism in connection with anti-schismatic efforts. By 1383 he
objects to the plenary indulgence offered to support the 1383
Despenser crusade against the antipope, Clement VII, as in-
tensely as he had objected earlier to the *significavit*, and he ob-
jects on essentially the same grounds—the use of spiritual

---

[5] Wyclif, *De Officio Regis*, pp. 169–76, 205; cf. *De Blasphemia*, p. 108. *Opera
Minora*, pp. 92–97, and Wyclif, *English Works*, pp. 95–96. No orthodox criti-
cism or satire directed against the *significavit* exists in this period.

[6] John Wyclif, *Sermones*, ed. Johann Loserth (London, 1889), 3:206–12; Wy-
clif, *Opera Minora*, pp. 92–97.

[186]

power to subsidize temporal causes, and the abuse of temporal power in disputes over the schism properly to be settled within the Church.[7] Obviously these positions did not endear the reformer to the prelates, but Conclusion Nine of the 1395 *Conclusions* repeats the objections to the concept of indulgences and the treasury of grace while *The Plowman's Tale*, usually dated at about the same time, repeats Wyclif's charges against the use of the curse.

Wyclif, like Chaucer, begins his probe at the lowest level by attacking the behavior of the functionaries who administer the offices of the keys to show that the system is out of control and cannot be put in order by the hierarchy, should it want to reform it. Indeed, most of Chaucer's General Prologue description of the Pardoner and Summoner which is not traditional to estate complaint portraits appears to come from Wyclif or others who echo him. For example, the reformer scores rural deans, summoners' bosses, and summoners themselves for citing and excommunicating people to scare them. To enlarge their fines, they tempt people to sin; they encourage whores with easy fines so as to increase their profits from whoremongers. These are also Chaucerian complaints not traditional to the estate satires (A, 642ff.). Wyclif's pardoners show that the pope cannot police them by violating the decretals that say they are to live "moderate and circumspect" lives and "not to frequent taverns or other degraded places," and Chaucer's homophile Pardoner, who obviously does not lead a circumspect life by medieval standards, preaches his sermon while tippling at a pilgrimage tavern (C, 320ff.).[8] Both Chaucer and Wyclif use

---

[7] For Wyclif on indulgences and the 1383 crusade, see *De Ecclesia*, ed. Johann Loserth (London: Trübner, 1886), pp. 522–86; *Opera Minora*, p. 386; *Polemical Works in Latin*, pp. 588–632. For orthodox attacks on false indulgences which differ from Wyclif's on true papal indulgences, see Muriel Bowden, *A Commentary on the General Prologue* (New York: Macmillan, 1967), pp. 281–82.

[8] Wyclif, *De Blasphemia*, pp. 172–73, 272–73.

CHAPTER 7

functionaries to scrutinize who is above them on the ladder of authority, namely bishops and the pope, the inheritors of the apostolic power. Chaucer explores the meaning of the apostolic story for his own time in fuller Biblical images than does Wyclif and comes to different conclusions as he raises up two Biblical apostles in grotesque form and makes them walk English parish roads: Judas as a summoner and Paul as a preaching pardoner.

Before Chaucer introduces the Judas-summoner in the Friar's Tale, he raises the issue of the curse and the *significavit* in the General Prologue's portrait of its Summoner, a pilgrim who, like the medieval Epicurus, believes in no afterlife and, hence, presents the discipline of the Church as entirely of this world: "Purs is the ercedekenes helle" (A, 658). However, Chaucer in his own voice says that the Summoner's opinion is false, that a guilty man should fear a curse since it slays, and should also beware of the *significavit*. That guilty persons should dread some kind of curse, divine or human, is obvious. The contemporary issue was the innocent cursed by the Church courts, and Chaucer does not say how such a person should take his curse or why the guilty should beware the *significavit*. If the guilty pay off the archdeaconal courts so as to avoid the curse, they would have no need to fear the conventional *significavit* which provided only for state arrest of the persistent excommunicate. No temporal *significavit* could operate where no unresolved sins appeared on the court books. However, the poet clearly distinguishes himself from Wyclif both by recognizing official curses which are valid *and* by pointing to some kind of *significavit* that the guilty should fear—presumably including the guilty who have paid off the ecclesiastical courts and escaped censure. The Friar's Tale defines what this *significavit* is.

The tale's summoner-Judas comes straight out of the keys-and-possessioner controversy and, through his action and

God's reaction, defines the full meaning of Chaucer's understanding of the summons, curse, and imprisonment:

> And right as Judas hadde purses smale,
> And was a theef, right swich a theef was he. (D, 1350–51)

The character partly mimics his friar-creator, Huberd, who uses the tale in continuation of the secular-regular controversy. Like his character, he has an affinity for academic position (D, 1516–22; A 261), exploits widows, and embraces the rich while rejecting "Lazaruses."[9] Chaucer's tales always mirror their tellers, but here the poet also uses Huberd's tale to explore the Summoner and the two-sword issues raised in his General Prologue portrait. The image of Judas with a purse was conventionally used in polemic to symbolize the Church's right, or lack of right, to temporal property: the Spiritual friars had claimed that no true apostle could hold property and that Judas, holding the apostolic purse, was not an apostle; Nicholas of Lyra, an orthodox Conventual friar, said that Judas' purse made him less than a full apostle—Christ's minor follower, perhaps a primitive Church deacon (fig. 36).[10] On the other hand, Wyclif, arguing for the right of the parish priest to hold limited property for charitable purposes, asserted that Christ owned two hundred pence which he assigned to Judas.[11] The Friar's

---

[9] Cf. Arnold Williams, "Chaucer and the Friars," *Speculum* 28 (1953):499–513, and *The English Works of Wycliff*, p. 45. The promise to the Summoner to be a master of divinity fits the Friar narrator since the friars, in the polemical literature, are said to want to be M.A.s and to be called "maister." Cf. D, 1300, and *Piers Plowman*, A text, Passus 9, line 9.

[10] *Biblia latina cum postillis Nicolai de Lyra*, Pt. 4: Sig. s4. The comment is on John 12.6; for Judas as a type of deacon, see Wyclif, *De Blasphemia*, pp. 62–63, and cf. *De Civili Dominio*, 3:56. Cf. William of Ockham, "Compendium Errorum Joannis XXII," *Opera Plurima* (Lyon: 1494–96), sig. AA4ᵛ; William of Ockham, "Opus Nonaginta Dierum," *Opera Politica*, ed. J. G. Sikes et al. (Manchester: Manchester University Press, 1963), 2:711–13.

[11] Wyclif, *Sermones*, 2:328–29.

CHAPTER 7

summoner has even more experience with money and power than had Judas. His blackmailed victims are willing to make "grete feestes" (D, 1349) to honor him, mimicking the Biblical feast honoring Christ where Judas criticized the harlot Magdalene for anointing Christ instead of contributing to the poor. Obviously Chaucer's Judas, having no Christ at his feasts, need not gesture toward the poor when he summons the widow's "mite" (cf. D, 1377, 1581), and his hermaphroditic conjoining of purse and curse continues until his comic conclusion when he is imprisoned by the *significavit* of a real spiritual power.

His hermaphroditism continues—in the disguise he assumes by casting himself as a bailiff, normally a role which belonged to the temporal power. In fact, a summoner acted for the ecclesiastical courts as a bailiff would for the royal. The Biblical Judas was something of a bailiff for the Old Law's courts. Though the Gospel accounts of Judas disagreed, by Chaucer's time they had been harmonized to interpret Judas's betrayal of Christ as originating in his avarice at the anointment feast and later furthered by his devil-companion until, out of desire for power and money, he attached himself to Caiaphas, the bishop of Old Law, for thirty pieces of silver and served as a guide or bailiff to those sent from Caiaphas's court to arrest Christ. Christ was arrested for the heresy of anti-Synagogue blasphemies.[12] After

[12] For differences in New Testament accounts of Judas, see Donatus Haugg, *Judas Iskarioth in den Neutestamentlichen berichten* (Freiburg: Herder, 1930); Gert Buchheit, *Judas Iskarioth* (Gütersloh: Rufer-Verlag, 1954). For medical accounts, see Peter Comestor, *Histoira Scholastica, PL* 198:1597–1626; Origen, *Commentariorum in Evangelium Matthaei, PL* 26:208, St. Augustine, *In Joannis Evangelium, PL* 35:1761–62; Wyclif, *Sermones*, 3:21; John Wyclif, *Opus Evangelicum*, 4 vols. ed. Johann Loserth (London: Trübner, 1896), 3–4:335–36. See also *La Vie de Nostre Benoit Sauveur Ihesucrist & la Saincte Vie de Nostre Dame* (circa 1390), ed. Millard Meiss and Elizabeth H. Beatson (New York: New York University Press, 1977), pp. 63–64; and Rupert of Deutz, *In Evangelium S. Joannis Commentariorum, PL* 169:499, 652. Peter Comestor, *Historia Scholastica, PL* 198:1598, 1614. For the devil, see Luke 22.3 and John 13.2–4. Nicholas de Lyra

accusing the innocent Christ, Judas cursed himself, hung him-
self in despair, and his familiar devil took his soul to hell (see fig.
36). As Caiaphas's bailiff, Judas was made to signify Old Law
literalism, materialism, and tyranny, characteristics applicable
both to the summoner in this tale and in the General Prologue.
Judas is also the central figure in the medieval curse. Since
Acts 1.20 refers Judas's end to Psalm 108, the standard excom-
munication ceremony used the Psalm to condemn the excom-
municate as the curser cursed, the Judas who persecuted the
poor without mercy, loved cursing, repaid evil for good, and
was, therefore, self-cursed (Psalm 108.4–19). So recited, the
Friar's story of his Judas is the familiar Biblical story of the
apostle who betrayed an innocent person, cursed himself, and
found himself taken off to hell by a familiar devil.

---

comments on Luke 22.3 where Satan enters Judas: "[Intravit autem sathanus in
iudam] . . . id est animam iudae non per illapsum quia hoc est deo proprium:
sed per effectum venditionem christi ei suggerendo" (*Biblia latina cum postillis
Nicolai de Lyra*, Pt. 4, Sig. o[1ᵛ]). Cf. St. Augustine, *In Joannis Evangelium*, *PL*
35:1785–86; *La Vie de Nostre Benoit Sauveur*, p. 64; Rupert of Deutz, *In Evan-
gelium S. Joannis Commentariorum*, *PL* 169:687–88; Peter Comestor, *Historia
Scholastica*, *PL* 198:1617. Caiaphas and Annas, bishops of the Old Law, send
Judas out to arrest Christ on charges of heresy; e.g., *Ludus Coventriae*, ed. K. S.
Block (London: Oxford University Press, 1922), EETS, e.s. 120:230 (for the
summoning, see pp. 265–70; the "canon law charging," esp. pp. 266 and 274–
80). Cf. *La Vie de Nostre Benoit Sauveur Ihesucrist* which calls Caiaphas "tout le
premier" of "les evesques et les maistres de la loy" of the Jews (p. 58); Annas is
also called "l'evesque" (p. 81). Caiaphas plans to have Christ cited to come be-
fore Pilate: "Faisons-le citer dava[n]t Pylate . . ." (p. 59, cf. pp. 61–83). Cf.
Glossa Ordinara, *PL* 114:234; Rupert of Deutz, *In Evangelium S. Joannis Commen-
tariorum*, *PL* 169:646; Wyclif, *Sermones*, 2:29–30. For Judas as a bailiff symbol,
see Bersuire, *Opera Omnia*, 3–4:294; *La Vie de Nostre Benoit Sauveur*, p. 68. The
doctrine that the evil act as God's agents (D, 1478–1503), announced by the
Friar's devil, described Judas' role in the passion story; cf. William of Ockham,
Tractatus de predestinatione et de praescientia dei, Q 1; cf. Wyclif, *Polemical Works in
Latin*, 1:361–62; *La Vie de Nostre Benoit Sauveur*, pp. 77–78; Wyclif, *De Ecclesia*,
pp. 441–43.

Chaucer's story of Judas comes disguised in a fourteenth-century ecclesiastical court costume. It culminates with a simulation of the fourteenth-century curse, then summons its devil to take both soul and body of the new Judas on a *significavit* trip to "prison." Finally, it mimics the procedures of Church courts in their relationship to the temporal arm to make Chaucer's comment on the curse and the *significavit*.

The tale's new Judas does not serve under Caiaphas but, supposedly, under a Christian archdeacon and a Christian bishop, and he supposedly brings people to penance and reconciliation by acting as policeman and citation officer to those committing such "spiritual" offenses as simony, usury, fornication, heresy, witchcraft, and injury to Church property.[13] Two court systems served the normal diocese—the bishop's court and the archdeacon's court. The bishop's court supposedly tried serious crimes leading to excommunication and had the larger and more formally constituted group of officials.[14] In actuality, both courts' systems handled cases that led to the curse, their minor officials might overlap, and both competed for arrests (D, 1317–18). When a summoner for either system heard a complaint against a supposed culprit, he was to have his court regis-

---

[13] Brian Woodcock, *Medieval Ecclesiastical Courts in the Diocese of Canterbury* (London: Oxford University Press, 1952), pp. 29–92, and *passim*, for canon law courts in England: for topical and historical reference in the Friar's tale, see Hahn and Kaeuper, "Text and Context: Chaucer's *Friar's Tale*," pp. 57–101.

[14] Woodcock, *Medieval Courts*, pp. 47ff.; cf. F. Donald Logan, *Excommunication and the Secular Arm in Medieval England* (Toronto: Pontifical Institute, 1968), pp. 116–17. (I am indebted to Father Logan for many suggestions as to research sources for this chapter.) Cf. also Lyndwood, pp. 225–26. An English diocese might have from one to eight archdeacons according to A. Hamilton Thompson, *The English Clergy* (Oxford: Clarendon, 1947), p. 58, and deans were expected to act as summoners for the bishop's court while the subordinate summoners attached to each deanery of the archdeanery were to serve both the archdeacon's and the bishop's benches. This may explain the consonance of Wyclif's remarks on rural deans and Chaucer's on summoners.

trar record it and draw up a *mandamus* ("mandement," D, 1284) summoning the accused to appear at a set time to answer charges. When he had delivered his citation, he informed the court of his action, and if the accused did not appear, he was to cite again in thirty and then sixty days, whereupon an unanswered charge might lead to a curse.[15] When the initial "instancing" or charge was made, generally by a priest, the registrar drew up a statement of charges (*libellus*) and informed the accused of his rights to prepare a defense and be represented by counsel (*proctor*).[16]

Hence, the widow of the tale, thinking herself cited under an *ex instancia* procedure, demands her proper rights of a statement of charges (D, 1595), representation by defense attorney (D, 1596), and excuse from immediate appearance on the grounds of illness (D, 1590–94).

However, a summoner not only cited at the urging of other people such as the parish priest but might also cite habitual offenders himself (*ex officio* citations) by asking the court registrar to issue a brief *mandamus* ("Cite so-and-so"). Then he could use a spoken instead of a written charge, eliminate the proctor, and peremptorily insist on an immediate appearance without giving time for the preparation of a defense.[17] The summoner in the

[15] Durandus warns that the peremptory citation should not be given at the first citation or "prematurely" and sets the three-citation formula which provides for a thirty-day period between the first and second, and second and third citations. William Durandus, "De Citatione," *Speculum Juris* (Frankfurt, 1668), 2.1.2–3 for time allotted after citation. Cf. Woodcock, *Medieval Courts*, p. 96.

[16] Ibid., pp. 47–51, 69–92.

[17] Ibid., pp. 69–70, 79–92, 133. Durandus says that even in peremptory citations the cause of citation should be expressed and that a peremptory summons ought not to be sent as a first command to appear in court; "De Citatione," *Speculum Juris*, 2.1.83. However, he also says that the following are not necessary in the securing of the peremptory citation: "Accusatio, vel denuncatio, vel inquisitio, vel exceptio, nec testes etiam, vel aliae probationes." "De Notoriis Criminibus," *Speculum Juris*, 2.81.1. A peremptory citation could be sent in

CHAPTER 7

Friar's tale treats his poor widow as a habitual offender, one guilty of repeated sexual misdeeds and long-term failure to pay the tithe fine (D, 1581–83, 1614–17); he eliminates the necessary brief registration of his charge and, relying on blackmail, makes himself policeman, registrar, proctor, and judge. Finally, he threatens the widow with a curse (D, 1587) which, since she is innocent, carries a threat only to her property or pan. Implicitly, were she unwilling to pay and were the summoner supported by his court, she could receive a *significavit* imprisonment in the temporal courts. The summoner must assume that if challenged, he will be protected by his eager archdeacon and bishop (D, 1424–34), though a summoner citing without a *mandamus* was supposed to be grievously punished according to canon law.[18] Were Chaucer writing a traditional critique of the canon-law courts, his tale's conclusion would have shown satirically how papal discipline of the summoner, archdeacon, or bishop could have amended things.[19] But he cuts off conven-

emergencies where notorious behavior was not involved but where speed of handling the problem was required; "De Citatione," 2.1.s3; see also 2.s1.1, concerning time for preparation of the defense in peremptory citations.

[18] Late fifteenth-century summoners made 4d. for each citation and 1d. for each mile traveled, about £5 per year as of the late fifteenth century; the guild artisan in the same period made about £7.10s. Apparitors could own property and may have derived some income from that or other jobs; Woodcock, *Medieval Courts*, p. 77.

[19] Ibid., pp. 69–70. Cf. Durandus, "De Citatione," *Speculum Juris*, 2.1.s4, 6 where Durandus makes clear that the summoner is to be believed as to procedure (i.e., when he says he has given a summons, etc.) but not as to his denunciations. For the "ex officio" summons, see William of Pagula, *Summa Summarum*, B.M. Royal MS. 10 DX, fol. 210ᵛ; for the bishop's responsibility, see Robert L. Benson, *The Bishop-Elect: A Study in Medieval Ecclesiastical Office* (Princeton: Princeton University Press, 1968), pp. 45, 48, 113. For archdeacon cursing, see Lyndwood, p. 352; cf. Logan, *Excommunication and the Secular Arm*, p. 25. The tale's summoner's archdeacon appears to have, or claim, the power to curse (D, 1347, 1587). See *C.P.R.*, 1388–92, p. 415, for a 1391 Great Council revocation of archdeacon powers over the *significavit* and *de excommunicatis capiendis*. For the

tional avenues of appeal, thereby creating an ecclesiastical tyranny of the kind that Wyclif's crown appeal against unjust charges was meant to prevent.

Chaucer rather employs direct divine intervention in the form of a divine *significavit* against the unjust official, which has the Biblical authority of the devil's carrying off Judas to hell. James Work has shown that the widow's malediction of the summoner in the Friar's Tale follows the formulae for the anathema and that D, 1628–29, reflects an anathematizing phrase.[20] If the procedures of the anathema are at work in this passage, connected procedures for summoning and securing the *significavit* inform the immediately preceding and succeeding passages. The *significavit* meant simply that, after the excommunication or curse went unheeded for a certain time, the Church would turn from the spiritual to the temporal arm and send a request from the bishop in the accused's territory to the King's Chancery calling for the writ of *significavit*. The Chancery then automatically sent such a writ to the local sheriff or bailiff for the royal courts asking him to imprison the excommunicate and "justice him in his body" until he made satisfaction for crime

---

responsibility of archdeacon to bishop for acts under his jurisdiction, see Thompson, *The English Clergy*, pp. 57–65, esp. 60; for that of bishops to the pope as to the keys, see Stanley Chodorow, *Christian Political Theory and Church Politics in the Mid-Twelfth Century* (Berkeley: California University Press, 1972), pp. 185–86. Lyndwood (p. 352) says that, under a canon of Boniface, a summoner summoning without a mandate was to be grievously punished and the defendant excused.

[20] James A. Work, "Echoes of the Anathema in Chaucer," *PMLA* 47 (1932):428. The request for the *significavit* at D, 1623, and its execution at D, 1634–40, is not a simple curse since curses do not punish the body but declare the separation of the soul from the Eucharist and the Church (cf. Logan, p. 14). The widow goes through the procedures of a trial and a *significavit* before damning because no one should be excommunicated without trial, charges, and proof; cf. St. Thomas, *Summa Theologicae*, 3a.81.2. Here Chaucer makes a point about correct procedures *and* correct spirit.

CHAPTER 7

and contumacy.[21] Since the Church theoretically did not exercise temporal power, it could not imprison, but the automatic granting of the writ meant that, in fact, the Church had temporal power, the basis of Wyclif's objection. Chaucer's widow follows proper procedure and issues three summonses, two accompanied by the threat of the curse and the *significavit*. Her first summons asks the Church official to show here some charity or common decency:

> Ye knowen wel that I am povre and oold;
> Kithe youre almesse on me povre wrecche. [the first summons]
> (D, 1608–09)

When her accuser refuses to show mercy and adds another lie to his blackmail to gain the "apostolic" twelve pence, she reminds him twice more of his sin and warns him of her *significavit*:

> "Thou lixt!" quod she, "by my savacioun, [the second summons]
> Ne was I nevere er now, wydwe ne wyf,
> Somoned unto youre court in al my lyf;
> Ne nevere I nas but of my body trewe!
> *Unto the devel blak and rough of hewe*
> *Yeve I thy body and my panne also!*" [threat of curse and *significavit*]
> (D, 1618–23,
italics added)

Her third summons, echoing the anathema (D, 1628–29), explicitly requests the summoner's repentance, gives a second re-

---

[21] For the procedure, see Logan, *Excommunication and the Secular Arm*. The king's writ dealing with imprisonment of the body usually went as follows: ". . . quod Radulfus de Brakeleg, clericus propter suam manifestam contumaciam excommunicatus est nec se uult per censuram ecclesiasticam iusticiari. Quia uero potestas regia sacrosancte ecclesie in querelis suis deesse non debet, uobis precipimus quod predictum Radulfum per *corpus suum* secundum consuetudinem Anglie *iusticiares* donec sancte ecclesie tam de contemptu quam de iniuria ei illata ab eo fuerit satisfactum . . ." (Logan, *Excommunication and the Secular Arm*, p. 195, italics mine). Compare *Piers Plowman*, A text, Passus 9, lines 86–96.

minder of his imminent damnation, and promises that the devil will fetch him. To this, the summoner, a Judas "hanging" himself, responds with heightened contumacy:

> "Nay, olde stot, that is nat myn entente,"
> Quod this somonour, "for to repente me
> For any thyng that I have had of thee." (D, 1630–33)

When the character remains contumacious, the bailiff-devil (D, 1396) as God's instrument (D, 1483) carries out the *significavit* arrest specified as possible in the widow's second and third summons:

> "I wolde I hadde thy smok and every clooth!"
> "Now, brother," quod the devel, "be nat wrooth;
> *Thy body and this panne been myne by right*.
> Thou shalt with me to helle yet to-nyght,   [the carrying out of
> Where thou shalt knowen of oure privetee   the *significavit* order]
> Moore than a maister of dyvynytee."
> And with that word this foule feend hym hente;
> Body and soule he with the devel wente.   (D, 1633–40, italics added)

Obviously the "superior" Friar wishes to show the materialistic Summoner that the curse of the invisible Church, disregarded by his Epicurean rival, can hurt more than the purse, and does so in the only terms the Summoner understands, physical terms. But in doing this he fortuitously echoes the *significavit*: "Thy body and this panne been myne by right" (D, 1635). The phrase in the chancellor's writ was, "We instruct you that you should punish X in his body following the custom of the English." Now we know the answer to the implicit question of the General Prologue: the *significavit* that the guilty who control the archdeacon's courts should fear has a divine origin.

The scene is unique in depicting the punishment of the culprit's body. Judas's soul is taken to hell by his devil but without his body (fig. 36). The culprit's body is never transported to hell in Chaucer's source stories but is reserved for Judgment Day as orthodox belief would require.[22] However, Chaucer's widow commits the summoner's body and soul to hell's prison, and the devil-bailiff takes both there in precise imitation of the *significavit* action of the royal bailiff. The devil-bailiff cannot act as God's instrument and take his prize until the summoner has been summoned and properly cursed by the widow, and his imprisonment requested from Christ as divine King, represented here as a champion of souls, delivering those "thral and bonde" from their prison (D, 1660–62). Christ, as king of kings and source of both the temporal and spiritual power (see chap. 10 below), assumes the offices of king and chancellor when ecclesiastical authority is unjust and no crown appeal exists.

Chaucer is obviously not proposing some new theory of bodily damnation prior to the final judgment but is using the echo of the *significavit* to call attention to the misplaced worry over both unjust *significavits* and failure to apply them when called for. If the function of the procedure is to produce repentance, then its application will not ultimately harm the good. The failure to apply it when called for only denies the cursed an opportunity for penance and will bring them to an eternal prison. The story substitutes, for Wyclif's attack on the *significavit*, a two-level system which advises the ordinary parishioner to respect the prescriptions and punishments of the juridical Church and admonishes the Epicurean guilty, who can bribe to control Church justice, to fear a divine justice that goes beyond that of the Church.

Chaucer includes one more turn in his dialogue with the reformer with his portrait of the widow, whose polemical role recalls that of Christ in Dostoyevsky's Grand Inquisitor scene. Though the Friar tells his tale in malice to consign the secular

[22] Bryan and Dempster, *Sources and Analogues of Chaucer's Canterbury Tales,* pp. 269–70, and *passim,* 269–74. Dante, *Purgatorio* XXVI. 1–36.

clergy to hell for their twelve-pence apostolic claims, Chaucer's widow controls terminology and actions that were the special domain of the medieval Church. The widow in the Nun's Priest's Tale chases the fox who takes her rooster-cleric from her enclosed garden, and the child Prioress's widow wanders through the city to find her praising child,[23] but the widow in this tale does not protect her cleric. She is the Church condemning the Church. She acts unseen by the Summoner to condemn him as her false representative, an invisible Church suggestive of Wyclif's. Her action should not surprise anyone who knows Chaucer's biography, given his association with the Chamber, or Lollard, knights.

The Lollards, like some Spiritualist friars, posited an invisible Church made up of those destined for salvation, implicitly and sometimes explcitly those of their own faction. This true or invisible Church opposed the visible Church with its prelates and curses. Wyclif had argued that a prelate in the visible Church cannot rightly excommunicate without being commanded by God—that is if he uses the *significavit* to bring in the secular arm, he places himself in mortal sin and loses authority because his curse becomes merely the tool of Judas and the Antichrist.[24] The widow is such an invisible Church, condemning false Judases.

[23] Charles R. Dahlberg, "Chaucer's Cock and Fox," pp. 277–90; Albert B. Friedman, "*The Prioress's Tale* and Chaucer's Anti-Semitism," *CR* 9 (1974):124–25. Cf. *English Wycliffite Writings*, ed. Anne Hudson (London: Cambridge University Press, 1978), p. 128; Wyclif, *De Ecclesia*, p. 6, and Thomas Hatton, "Chaucer's Friar's 'Old Rebekke,' "*JEGP* 67 (1968):266–71. Hahn and Kaeuper ("Text and Context," p. 73) remark that the old woman's knowledge "of the court, even to the use of specialized legal terms and legal representatives" testifies to the "local presence of the apparatus of correction"; however, the widow's specialized knowledge more likely testifies to her iconological significance since Kaeuper and Hahn bring forward no independent evidence that historical medieval villagers had detailed knowledge of canon law procedure.

[24] *English Wycliffite Writings*, p. 128; Wyclif, *De Ecclesia*, p. 6; *De Blasphemia*,

Yet the fiction may not have offended orthodox thinkers who occasionally made a similar distinction between the true and the untrue in the Church. Prior to the Council of Constance, the canonists recognized that people could be cursed by God and not by the Church, or vice versa.[25] Dante's angry Peter condemns corrupt popes, and the apostolic chariot which crosses the Purgatorio's Eden is later turned into the corrupt feathered cart that is tied to the tree of empire in post-Constantinian times. Holy Church also differs from the misguided clerics who seek to lead Will in *Piers Plowman*. Prior to Constance and Trent, the Church could still become the spiritual Synagogue, an implication of the 1380 parement of Charles V of France showing scenes from Christ's arrest and crucifixion (figs. 37–38).[26] In the scenes surrounding the crucifixion, which mark the

---

pp. 70–71. These precepts were condemned at the Council of Constance; C.M.D. Crowder, *Unity, Heresy and Reform, 1378–1460: The Conciliar Response to the Great Schism* (New York: St. Martins, 1977), pp. 85–86. For Wyclif on excommunication, including the precepts condemned at the Council of Constance, see *De Ecclesia*, pp. 111, 152–56; *De Civili Dominio*, 1:260; *Dialogus sive Speculum Ecclesie Militantis*, ed. Alfred W. Pollard (London, 1886), p. 56; *De Officio Regis*, pp. 169–76. For Wyclif's views on the invisible, or non-institutional, nature of the Church and the opposition between the "true" and the "institutional" Church, see Workman, *Wyclif*, 2:8–13.

[25] William of Pagula says that certain persons are excommunicate of God and given over to Satan without manifest ceremony. William of Pagula, *Summa Summarum*, B.M. Royal MS. 10 DX, fol. 246ʳ–246ᵛ; see Chodorow, *Christian Political Theory*, pp. 88–95, for Gratian's analogous views. Constance restricted excommunication to the official act; see Julius Goebel, *Felony and Misdemeanor: A Study in the History of English Criminal Law* (New York: Publications of the Foundation for Research in Legal History, 1937), p. 263. For the ceremony of cursing, see Henricus de Bartholomaeis, *Summa super titulis decretalium* (Lyon, 1517), fol. 418ᵛ.

[26] See Erwin Panofsky, *Studies in Iconology* (New York: Oxford University Press, 1939), p. 27; Millard Meiss, *French Painting in the Time of Jean de Berry: The Late 14th Century and the Patronage of the Duke* (New York: Phaidon, 1967), Plates 1–5 and discussion. Some Marian devotional literature argues that Mary

transition from the Old to New Law, Judas arrests Christ (fig. 37), and Christ is buried, harrows hell, and appears to the Magdalene. In the central crucifixion scene, David tells the Synagogue to see her lord in the crucifixion (fig. 38, *right*) and Isaiah points the Church to Christ (*left*). In the center, the crucifixion scene is rendered perennial through the use of the pelican figure and angels who carry Eucharistic cups from the cross while the King and Queen look to the crucifixion as if invited to see the divine element in the Eucharist and go beyond Synagogue to Church in cognition.

Chaucer invites a similar cognition. The Church is to be seen in the widowed and the poor, and its reform belongs neither to bishops and canonists nor to Wyclif's princes and royal lawyers but to laughter. Chaucer's laughter at the summoner summoned recalls Troilus' cosmic laughter at an evil that works out its impotent drama and scuttles off "this litel spot of erthe" with the psychopomps who do it justice. Chaucer's question anticipates Ivan's in the Grand Inquisitor scene. Both ask how institutions that reject the spirit of their martyr-founder and substitute police power for spiritual power can claim authority. Chaucer's conclusion ends with the comic faith that his widow, his body of Christ, will not ultimately be put out at the gate by the inquisitors, as Ivan's Christ is. The difference in fictive iconology defines the difference in culture separating the fourteenth from the nineteenth century.

Chaucer's Pardoner, companion to the Summoner, is tied to the Wycliffite critique of the indulgence in his hermaphroditism and tavern tippling, and he also continues the poet's serious satiric analysis of the keys. He sells true pardons, as Marie

alone retained faith through the passion (cf. P. Congar, "Incidence ecclésiologique d'un thème de dévotion mariale," *Mélanges de science religieuse* 7 [1950]:277–92); this leads William of Ockham to argue that the Church can exist in a single individual independent of the institutional Church (William of Ockham, "Dialogus I," *Opera Politica* 1:451, lines 12–13).

Hamilton long ago demonstrated,[27] and thus directly represents the pope, since only a papal legate could sell pardons through the pontiff's plenitude of power and open the doors to the "jewel of Christ's passion . . . and the merits of the saints in heaven," as the Chamber knights sarcastically put it in their 1395 *Conclusions*.[28] Appropriately the Pardoner has come straight from the court of Rome (A, 671), and though the Roncevalles house to which the Pardoner belongs, had once in the 1360s sold false pardons, by the *Canterbury Tales* period, it had reformed itself and received continued license to sell partial indulgences supportive of its charities. Though an alien priory whose mother institution's loyalty to the French pope led to its management by the King's clerks from the 1378 Schism until 1383, thereafter it ran its own affairs and came under no further suspicion of false pardoning.[29] The Pardoner's presence at Rome should relieve any schismatic suspicions as should his showing the requisite papal authorizing documents along with

[27] Marie P. Hamilton, "The Credentials of Chaucer's Pardoner," *JEGP* 40 (1941):48–72; cf. Alfred L. Kellogg and Louis A. Haselmayer, "Chaucer's Satire of the Pardoner," *PMLA* 66 (1951):273.

[28] Wilkins, *Concilia*, 3:221. Cf. Maureen Purcell, *Papal Crusading Policy: 1244–1291* (Leiden: E. J. Brill, 1975), p. 50. In 1369, "some rectors and vicars (in the province of Canterbury) complained to Urban V that the questors refused to show to the parish priest either papal or episcopal letters authorizing them to offer their indulgence in the church." Cf. William E. Lunt, *Financial Relations of the Papacy with England* (Cambridge: Medieval Academy, 1962), 2:478, and cf. 2:478–79; cf. also Wyclif, *Opus Evangelicum*, 1:38. That papal bulls carried the phrase *"Auctoritate beatorum Petri et Pauli"* is used by the Knight in the *Songe de Vergier* to argue that Peter and Paul were equally first among the apostles (*Songe de Vergier*, 2:73); the Pardoner as imitation-Paul reflects the emblemology of his bulls.

[29] The scandal that Manly posits at the house later in the century was not scandal at the house but scandal among people outside it pretending to use its right of indulgence; J. M. Manly, *Some New Light on Chaucer*, pp. 125–27; cf. Lunt, *Financial Relations*, 2:477–79; Sir James Galloway, *The Story of Saint Mary Roncevall* (London, n.p., 1907), p. 18; *C.P.R., 1381–85*, p. 196.

those required from more local authorities—cardinals, patri-archs, and bishops (c, 335–45). Clearly Chaucer wishes to treat the hazards of administering the indulgence key and not just its abuse. He treats both the partial and the plenary indulgence. That is, his gelding or mare Pardoner preaches the partial for-giveness of the Roncevalles' indulgence and the full remission of the 1383 crusading one which created so much consternation among both conventional writers and the Wycliffites. And he does this through preaching parts of two sermons, one for each kind of indulgence.

The Pardoner hawks the Roncevalles pardon, a partial indul-gence of the kind normally given for contributions to charities, at the end of his tale when he offers to sell a little pardon for each mile's sins on the road to Canterbury (c, 928). But at an-other point in his narration (c, 911–15), he offers plenary in-dulgences to wipe people's sin-slates clean and make the sinners as innocent as when they were born. He must mean "baptized" since children are not "clene" until baptized—though the irony of "born" should not pass, given the Pardoner's emphasis on man's incorrigibly sinful nature and the admitted inefficacy of his pardons (c, 916–18). Plenary indulgences wiping out the punishment for all past sins could only be given to people going on a crusade or contributing men or armor or money to one. Hence, the Pardoner's sermon must split into two parts, an old sermon or part of a sermon selling plenary indulgences to an imaginary crusade-related audience and a new one selling par-tial indulgences to the pilgrims. The new section preached to the pilgrims includes the tale's prologue telling the pilgrims how the narrator preaches his *radix malorum* sermon only to make money and the part beginning at c, 915, where he says, "Lo, sires, thus I preche" and goes on to offer partial pardons to the pilgrims to get them through the next miles (cf. c, 937ff.). The rest of the spiel, what the Pardoner is "wont to preche" (c, 461), begins with the tale proper and it ends with an appeal to wives to bring forward the wool that they would not be likely to carry on a pilgrimage and a promise to enter gift-givers' names in a roll that the Pardoner does not have in the General Prologue (C, 910–15). This part clearly comes out of the old sermon barrel in a form badly adapted to the pilgrims. In it, the Pardoner, without requiring a confession, promises the plenary indulgence (C, 914–15). The new section, on the other hand, stays within the Roncevalles warrant requiring confession (C, 377–84)—though the Pardoner forgets that at C, 923–40—and offers a limited indulgence (C, 923–30) in return for the monetary offerings usually given to Roncevalles and conceivable on a pilgrimage.

Since the old sermon's promise of a plenary indulgence requires a crusading context, one is not surprised by its adapting, to the pilgrimage-context, rhetoric of the kind associated with the indulgence preaching that supported the Despenser 1383 Low Countries crusade to overcome the antipope, the crusade mocked in the portrait of the Squire.[30] Few people would have missed the point in Chaucer's time. The Despenser venture so abused the plenary indulgence that both Wyclif and conventional writers questioned it and raised a storm which still reverberated in the 1395 *Conclusions* and in the Hus controversy,[31] and several features of the Pardoner's old sermon, imperfectly fitted to the Canterbury journey, obviously refer to the Despenser episode and its critiques. The Pardoner's request that

---

[30] For the rationale for granting plenary indulgences to crusaders, see Purcell, *Papal Crusading Policy*, pp. 52–56. For the 1383 crusades plenary indulgences, see Lunt, *Financial Relations*, 2:535–36. For the unpopularity of the 1383 crusade, see Vaughan, *Philip the Bold*, p. 28; *Eulogium Historiarum*, 3:357; *Piers Plowman*, B text, Passus 19, lines 407–56. Cf. the squire discussion, chap. 1 above.

[31] Lunt, *Financial Relations*, 2:535–37; cf. Edouard Perroy, *L'Angleterre et le grand schisme d'occident* (Paris: Monnier, 1933), pp. 175ff. Hus's critique of crusading indulgences derives from Wyclif's formulated at this time.

wives give him brooches, spoons, wool, rings, and other household valuables not ordinarily carried on a pilgrimage (c, 906–10) recollects Knighton's saying that the 1383 pardoners collected "incredible amounts of coin in gold and silver and jewels, necklaces, rings, dishes, cloth, spoons and other ornaments" and the remarks of most chroniclers that women especially contributed to the ingathering.[32] His not requiring confession of his hearers and his promising that his indulgences will make them fully clean recollect the 1383 preachment—actually it extended from 1382 to 1386—which promised the indulgence purchaser delivery from both guilt and blame, thus obviating the need for confession. So Wyclif and three orthodox chroniclers attest, the orthodox despite the fact that orthodox indulgence theology stipulated confession as necessary to the removal of the guilt of sin, since the indulgence removed only its *poena* or required satisfaction.[33] The Pardoner's promise that his product will make people go directly "into the blisse of hevene" (c, 912) recalls Froissart's remark that the 1383-period buyers were told by

[32] Henry Knighton, *Leycestrensis Chronicon*, ed. Joseph Lumby (London: Eyre and Spottiswoode, 1895), 2:198; *Eulogium Historiarum*, 3:357. Froissart (*Chroniques*, 10:207) does not particularly attach the giving to women but says that a "tun" full of gold and silver was collected in London alone.

[33] Knighton (2:198–99) says, "Habuit namque praedictus episcopus indulgentias mirabiles cum absolutione a poena et a culpa pro dicta cruciata a papa Urbano sexto ei concessas, cujus auctoritate tam mortuos quam vivos, ex quorum parte contributio sufficiens fiebat, per se et suos commissarios a poena et culpa absolvebat." The same assertion is made by the independent "Dieulacres Chronicle," in *The Deposition of Richard II*, ed. M. V. Clarke and V. H. Galbraith, *Bulletin of the John Rylands Lib.*, 14 (1930):166. Froissart says that those who had given money were absolved "de painne et de coupe"; Froissart, *Chroniques*, 10-205. Wyclif says that the people were absolved "a poena et a culpa"; Wyclif, *Sermones*, 4:39, 122; *Polemical Works in Latin*, 2:589. Lancaster's crusade to Castille also included the preaching of an indulgence but one less fervid and corrupt than that associated with the Despenser venture; see *C.P.R.*, *1385–89*, p. 134, and *Financial Relations*, 2:545–46. For the duration of the indulgence selling, see Lunt, *Financial Relations*, 2:542–43.

bulls and believed that they would die blessed, and the *Eulogium*'s statement that the pardoners ushered the dead into bliss by standing on graves and commanding Gabriel to come and conduct them heavenward.[34] Despite the fact that the Pardoner in the General Prologue carries no roll, the Pardoner's claim in his old sermon that he carries a roll to enter the names of contributors who will go straight to heaven (C, 910–11), recalls Despenser's preachment system, its sending friar-preachers to raise the parish sense of guilt, confessors to receive any confessions given, and clerks to record contributions in a roll forwarded to Despenser[35] (though the Pardoner is now an Augustinian canon, Skeat has suggested that he with his wandering past shows the characteristics of a friar).[36] Finally, the Pardoner's preaching against the extreme evil of a Flanders whose gluttonous devil-worshippers, afflicted with the plague, think that they can conquer Death, recollects common Urbanite rhetoric interpreting supporters of Clement VII as supporters of the Antichrist, antipope and so forth, dead in their excommunicated trespasses and sins.[37] Of course, the Pardoner does not

[34] Froissart, *Chroniques*, 10:207; *Eulogium Historiarum*, 3:356–57. These claims were not sustained by the bulls issued by Urban. However, there is no evidence that Urban or Despenser endeavored to control the *quaestors*.

[35] Knighton, 2:201–13; cf. Lunt, *Financial Relations*, 2:539.

[36] *The Complete Works of Geoffrey Chaucer*, ed. W. W. Skeat, 6 vols. (Oxford: Clarendon, 1900), 5:274. The friars feigned a "lady dreem" in which an English woman received assurances that the Norwich Crusade indulgences would be efficacious, a feigned miracle parallel to the Pardoner's manipulation of gullibility; Wyclif, *Select English Works*, 2:166. The Augustinian canons who controlled Roncevalles may also have had a role in the crusade, for Wyclif attacks them for saying that brothers killed in France on the Norwich crusades are martyrs; *Polemical Works in Latin*, 1:250.

[37] Robert of Geneva is commonly called "antipope" in the chronicles which suggests Antichrist; for both popes as Antichrist, see Wyclif, *Polemical Works in Latin*, 2:595. St. Vincent Ferrer also compares the antipope to Antichrist; cf. Melanie V. Shirk, *Royal Reaction to the Black Death in the Crown of Aragon* (Lawrence: unpublished University of Kansas diss., 1976), pp. 21, 69ff., and *passim*.

mention the crusade—perhaps because he continued to preach the sermon after the crusade was over (one wonders what the preachment sermons which went on for three years after the crusade said about it), or perhaps because Chaucer wishes us to see the Pardoner making a crude adaptation for his pilgrimage audience. The sermon even recalls imagery quoted from Augustine by Wyclif in one of his attacks against the 1383 crusade and its indulgence which makes the pope a sterile tree bearing no fruit and a wolf in sheep's clothing.[38] However, Wyclif goes on to argue that the passage in Matthew 7.16 which describes a corrupt tree as incapable of bearing good fruit is predestinarian. Because human beings are predestined, the indulgence is not effectual.

In contrast to Wyclif's predestinarian attack on the 1383 and like indulgences, Chaucer's black humor is implacably "free willist," particularly when read against the Parson's treatment of the concepts it introduces. Its fundamental point is that the indulgences externalize the penitential act, spiritual discipline, and the whole economy of sin and grace. The Pardoner appears to preach against sin, but actually he preaches against original

---

Jeame d' Agramont speaks of a moral pestilence causing robberies and denial of natural feelings in human beings analogous to the physical plague; cited by Dominick Palazotto, *The Black Death and Medicine* (Lawrence: unpublished University of Kansas diss., 1974), pp. 33–34; Charles F. Mullett, *The Bubonic Plague and England* (Lexington: Kentucky University Press, 1956), p. 15; "The Diabolic Element in the Plague," *The Black Death*, comp. Johannes Nohl (London: Unwin, 1926), pp. 161–80; Jean-Noel Biraben, *Les Hommes et la Peste en France et dans les pays européens et méditerranéens* (Paris: Mouton, 1976), 1:415. For Chaucer and the plague, see D. W. Robertson's "Chaucer and the Economic and Social Consequences of Plague," forthcoming manuscript.

[38] Wyclif, *Opus Evangelicum*, 1–2:433. The *Catholicon* says that a *questor* is a mercenary preacher or shepherd who, unlike the true shepherd (John 10.1–14), preaches for money; if he preaches falsehood, he becomes a thief from the sheepfold. Cf. Giovanni of Genoa, *Catholicon*, (Strassburg, n.d.), no sig., entry under *questor*.

sin, the "radix malorum" that his text defines as avarice,[39] a preachment as futile as behavioristic efforts to deny instinct. He places the root of evil in Flanders where the three rioters live out the precepts of the three enemies of virtue by remaining luxuriously drunk and gluttonous, avariciously gambling on Fortune's wheel, and proudly blaspheming. Confronted with Death's presence in the land and its destruction of their friend, they set out to kill the pestilential fellow. For them there is no spiritual promise that "Death once dead there's no more dying then," but the drunken prospect of a physical conquest; they will hazard Death's "peril" (C, 693). Even as they set out, they again succumb to the three temptations (C, 692–710), and, full of evil, go to destroy its first consequences. The Pauline Old Man directs them up a crooked path where they believe they will find a Death to kill and instead find their own deaths near the tree in bushels of gold which substitute for the root of evil. In conventional iconology, the skull beneath the tree of the cross reminded the medieval believer that the cross was made of Adam's tree (fig. 38), but the Pardoner does not bother to remind his audience of that. The rioters create the death that they want to destroy when the glutton, with his bread and wine, poisons his fellows while the oathtaker and gambler rouse themselves enough to murder him (C, 808–34) by remembering their former oaths and prospects of gambling.

[39] The Parson at I, 739–40, cites Timothy 6, the "roote of alle harmes is Coveitise," and attributes to this "coveitise" the fall from God-as-comfort to the "solas of worldly thynges" (I, 321–46, associates this movement to the "firste coveitise" with the first fall). The Parson's section on avarice then goes on to the definition of avarice in the normal sense of seeking many earthly things and not giving to the needy (I, 742ff.). The Parson also defines pride as the root of the seven sins from which springs "Avarice or Coveitise (to commune understond-ynge)," that is, avarice in the narrow sense (I, 388). The notion that pride is the root of all evils was used interchangeably with the notion that *cupiditas* is, since they were both seen as referring to the phenomenon of denying primary love to God and substituting other goods or self-satisfactions, cf. B², 3021–58.

The Pardoner concludes by preaching that avarice is very bad, but its wrong can be undone by the "warice" of a few nobles, spoons, and bags of wool (c, 904–9). We are back in an Epicurean world. Purse is the Pardoner's heaven.

In a useful parallel description of the growth of the root of evil or "firste coveitise" (I, 337), the Parson presents an internal psychomachic or spiritual process which will never entirely uproot the root of evil but also will not inevitably terminate in death beside it (I, 321–49). The Parson's Adam brought Death to all, following Romans 5.12 through Satan's suggestion that Adam and Eve could become gods through carnal disobedience, through Eve's or the flesh's delight in the sight of the forbidden, and Adam's or the reason's consenting to its eating. The first sin produced physical death, but also brought to mankind both the guilt of original sin, which would have to be removed by baptism, and its punishment in the form of "firste coveitise"—concupiscence or libido—which draws humankind to repeat the first fall. In Eden began the covetousness of the flesh, the fleshly eying of earthly things, and the pride of heart (I, 335) that are the three enemies basic to the Edenic and all successive falls. Failure to stop these enemies leads to spiritual Death (I, 354–70). Though the primal avarice as the root of the other sins is weakened by baptism and penance (I, 339), the life of humankind pits the spirit against the flesh, discipline against languor, as all of the great saints beginning with St. Paul testify (I, 341–49). The Parson's message thus posits a root of evil that can be weakened, three enemies who can be resisted with the help of grace, a human spirit that can struggle to resist delight and consent, and a spiritual Death that can be overcome (I, 321, 1080). In the Pardoner's account of his presumptuous rioters and his presumptuous self, no spirit wrestles, nothing resists suggestion and consent. The "old man" or flesh points to a path automatically taken, the three enemies encounter no reason to overcome, and death at the root of the evil tree appears almost automatic.

The Pardoner, like all pardoners, would have carried St. Paul's image on his papal seal, and he acts as an inverted St. Paul, taking his text from 1 Timothy 6.10 and also citing Phillipians 3.18 (C, 529ff.), 1 Timothy 5.6 (C, 547), 1 Corinthians 6.13 (C, 521ff.), Hebrews 6.6 (C, 472ff.), and Ephesians 5.18 (C, 483-84). His catalogue of sins, including drunkenness, gluttony, gambling, oaths, and avarice, sounds like the Pauline catalogue of sin, and Robert P. Miller has argued that the Pardoner's old man (C, 720) directing the rioters to their crooked path and final death represents the Pauline "old man," sterile as the eunuch Pardoner in offspring other than death.[40]

The Pauline material also defines the failure of the Pardoner's theology. The *radix malorum* text makes no sense in an indulgence sermon since it refers to that "firste coveitise" (I, 336) against which, as the Parson explains things, neither baptism nor penance is wholly efficacious. If such a permanent force is intractable in the face of legitimate discipline, how much more will it be in the face of indulgences? However, one of the Pauline concepts that the Pardoner inadvertently uses is the creation of death and crucifixion by the self and the necessity for a constant recrucifixion and resurrection in those who are part of Christ (C, 474, 532, 548)—the Parson's Pauline struggle of spirit against flesh (I, 341). When death as the plague comes into the story, Chaucer has already prepared his readers for a dual understanding of the figure as the physical plague and as sin, located at the tree of death at the end of the crooked path with gold near its root (C, 760-71). Inwardly, the three enemies, in the Parson's theology, do find the old man and the root of evil and create death, and no crusading indulgence undoes that,

---

[40] Robert P. Miller, "Chaucer's Pardoner, the Scriptural Eunuch," *Speculum* 30 (1955):180-99.

only the permanent penitential struggle. The rioters' purchase of death contrasts with the Pauline concept of Christ's purchase of mankind mentioned at c, 900ff., a passage marked *Auctor* in Ellesmere. Dying and living, crucifying and resurrecting, are in Pauline theology, tropological inward actions repeated daily which grow out of an orientation of the spirit, not a simple sin-count (Ephesians 4.22; Romans 6.3ff.; Colossians 3.9). The pilgrims do not rush to buy pardons because they recognize that the Pardoner's cures do not reach to the root causes of evil and death. Harry Bailey is willing to risk Christ's curse before he offers payment to the Pardoner (c, 946). The fiction's satiric objection to the indulgence, and particularly to the plenary indulgence, is that it confuses the swords, not by using the spiritual sword to support temporal wars, but by externalizing and temporalizing the whole spiritual journey. Between the helplessness of Wyclif's eternal predestination and the helplessness of endless temporal payment to summoners and pardoners lies the road of choice and discipline.

The Pardoner's perversion of Paul's message goes with a distortion of his life. Though the Pardoner preaches and carries letters patent from the high priest as St. Paul does in *Queen Mary's Psalter*, (fig. 39) he sees no blinding light of grace, and preaching in "sondry landes" (c, 443), he refuses to follow Paul in the active work of making baskets (or tents) for a living.[41] Preaching pardon which supposedly allows people to make satisfaction and recreate the world which their wrong has undone, he does no work in the Second Nun's sense (c, 447–55). No new

---

[41] John V. Fleming, "Chaucer's Ascetical Images," *Christianity and Literature* 28 (Summer, 1979):21–22, shows that basket-weaving was posited as the common apostolic mode of self-support. Cf. *Chaucer's Major Poetry*, ed. Albert C. Baugh (New York: Appleton-Century-Crofts, 1963), p. 492, n. on line 446. The Pardoner collects "gifts" from the poorest widow even though her children might die of hunger, a detail inverting Elijah's treatment of the widow of Zarephath (3 Kings 17.8–24).

Church like that emblemized by Mary, the garden, and the fall of the Synagogue in the *Grandes Heures'* illustrations of St. Paul preaching, emerges from the Pardoner's world of poisoned and murdered rioters, false relics, and castration threats. Nothing redemptive appears save the accidental lines that constitute the benediction attached to the old sermon (fig. 40):

> And Jhesu Crist that is oure soules leche,
> So graunte yow his pardoun to receyve,
> For that is best; I wol yow nat deceyve.   (D, 916–18)

For a moment, the Pardoner falls into a pat tale-teller's conclusion that recognizes Pauline forgiveness as the medicine for the tale's deep plague. The formulaic benediction, like the devil's carrying the summoner off to hell, allows Chaucer to open up, momentarily, a happy solution, recalling the final comedy of the Friar's Tale. It is as if Chaucer were to say, "If God pardons according to a predestined intent, as Wyclif claims, indulgence reform makes no difference. On the other hand, if God grants the level of pardon that people choose through their spiritual discipline, then reform may be less necessary than scathing laughter and satiric indignation at material pardons that produce no renewal of the human spirit." Those who, after hearing Harry Bailey's mockery (D, 946–55) and the Knight's efforts to cheer up the Pardoner, continue to substitute the indulgence for repentance and true satisfaction know that they are purchasing second best. So the comedian's vision. Interestingly the papacy apparently attempted no reforms of pardoning practice until the mid 1390s.[42]

---

[42] J. J. Jusserand (*English Wayfaring Life in the Middle Ages*, trans. Lucy Toulmin Smith [New York: G. P. Putnam, 1930], pp. 443–44) notes a later effort at reform of pardoning by Boniface in 1390. Boniface appears to direct his bull at both false pardoners and authorized pardoners making excessive claims such as were made under Urban VI. Lunt observes that a Durham chronicler says that 1383 money was collected fraudulently in that the confessors gave absolution in

Chaucer's satires constitute his most indignant "Juvenalian" work. His Summoner and Pardoner represent his most grotesque creations, more grotesque than the Reeve and the Miller, their "temporal" counterparts. Only in these tales does the poet's rhetoric and plot seem governed by a Swiftian *saeva indignatio*, as if the poet, recognizing an absolute inversion of an absolute claim, feels a need to turn from the Parson's "fairnesse" to the grossest ugliness he can imagine to describe the "verray filth and shame" of dishonest summoning where no sin exists and of pardon's glaring harelike look where no grace is offered. To feel the power of the satire, one may need to feel, in imagination at least, the power of the positive values that launch it—the power of the curse of a poor widow and the force of a "soules leche" rooted in lifetime struggle and sacrifice.

---

cases not authorized by the bulls. Boniface orders discipline both for false pardoners and for authorized pardoners, who offer indulgences to those who are not penitent and make frivolous and excessive claims for their power, claiming the right to give easy penance for serious faults. It is not clear whether Boniface's order was enforced by the English Church.

8

Summoner Wrath on Friar Perfection

THE APOSTOLATE OF FRIAR JOHN AND
LAY BROTHER THOMAS

Against the summoner-Judas, Chaucer pits his Friar and the apostolic friar of his Summoner's Tale, guilty of many of the faults that Wyclif assigned to his sect of friars, but again culpable for different reasons. Like the Prioress and Chant Clear, like the Monk and the Summoner, he is an Epicurean materialist, more obviously materialistic than Epicurean.

No figure expressed the "divine gifts" more fully in the eyes of medieval churchmen than did St. Francis, who embodied the medieval conception of charismatic spiritual power. He and his twelve friars set about to transform Europe through poverty, healing miracle, and a literal imitation of the life of Christ and the apostles. However, the friars blew out their flame in internal controversy, lapsed discipline, and fights over privilege and jurisdiction with the monastics, the parish clergy, and the papacy. Chaucer appeared long after things had gone awry, but he reaches back toward the primal Franciscan vision by inverting it in his Summoner's Tale. His critique of the friars in that tale and in the General Prologue has been related, in the work of Arnold Williams, Bernard Levy, John Fleming, and Penn Szittya,[1] to anti-fraternal critiques, originating with William of

---

[1] Cf. Bernard S. Levy, "Biblical Parody in the *Summoner's Tale*," *TSLL* 11 (1966):45–60; John V. Fleming, "The Antifraternalism of the *Summoner's Tale*," *JEGP* 65 (1966):698–99. Some of my arguments are anticipated in Penn R. Szittya's "The Friar as False Apostle: Anti-Fraternal Exegesis and the *Summoner's Tale*," *SP* 71 (1974):19–46. Szittya does not work with the passages from Matthew 10 and Luke 9 as central to Spiritualist-Conventual, Wyclif-friar contro-

St. Amour, which were carried along by Jean de Meun, Fitz-ralph, and Wyclif. These portrayed the friars as parish interlopers, ruining the penitential discipline developed by the local priests.² However, as this chapter shows, the friars also criticized one another on the basis of Francis's original vision. The Summoner, in Epicurean malice, attacks his fictional friar and Huberd with the tools that the friars had created to assault one another as materialistic and fraudulent Franciscans rather than

versy. Cf. also Alan Levitan, "The Parody of Pentecost in the *Summoner's Tale*," *UTQ* 40 (1971):236–46.

² Arnold Williams, "Chaucer and the Friars," pp. 499–513. Cf. Charles R. Dahlberg, *The Secular Tradition in Chaucer and Jean de Meun* (Princeton: unpublished Princeton University diss. 1953). Anti-fraternal satire probably required Chaucer's complex strategies of indirection since Richard issued a patent letter on November 4, 1384, defending the friars against verbal attacks on their founding and apostolic privileges and physical attacks of various sorts (*C.P.R.*, *1381–85*, p. 480; for other royal favors to friars, see *C.P.R.*, *1381–85*, pp. 527, 599; *C.P.R.*, *1385–87*, p. 208; *C.P.R.*, *1388–92*, p. 227; *C.P.R.*, *1396–99*, p. 425). Throughout this chapter, I will treat the subject of the tale as a Franciscan or friar-in-general on the basis of the Holderness reference and the references to the Franciscan rule; some scholars have regarded him as a Carmelite since he asserts Elijah's foundation of the friar orders (D, 2116), an official Carmelite claim. However, Bonaventura also made claims for the Franciscan Conventuals that holy mendicancy began with Elijah; see his "Apologia Pauperum," *Opera Omnia*, ed. Aloysius Lauer (Quaracchi: Coll. of St. Bonaventura, 1898), 8:324, hereinafter Bonaventura. See fig. 40, showing the upper church at Assisi: after Francis receives the *Regula Bullata* from the Pope, his chariot of vision is borne up to heaven like Elijah's; Alistair Smart, *The Assisi Problem and the Art of Giotto* (Oxford: Clarendon Press, 1971), p. 21. For the Franciscan building program in the Holderness area, see *The Victoria History of the County of York*, ed. William Page (London: Constable, 1913), 3:264–65. For fraternal and anti-fraternal polemics in Chaucer's England, see Aubrey Gwynn, *The English Austin Friars in the Time of Wyclif* (London: Oxford, 1940), pp. 93–94; Jacobus, *Omne Bonum*, B.M. MS. Royal 6E, VII, 526ᵛ, and *passim*; cf. Pantin, *The English Church in the Fourteenth Century*, p. 164 (a monastic attack on friars); Pantin, "Two Treatises of Uthred of Boldon on the Monastic Life," pp. 363–85; Wyclif, *Polemical Works in Latin*, 2:449–82, 524–36, esp. 456 and 527. Richard of Maidstone, "Protectorium Pauperis," ed. Arnold Williams, *Carmelus* 5 (1958):132–80.

with the tools of his own secular clerics' party. In particular, the
Summoner uses the gimmicks of the Spiritualists, and of Wy-
clif as their heir, to show how Francis's apostolic spiritualizing
has been mechanized and materialized by the Friar Johns and
Lay Brother Thomases of his day. Thus, he creates a satire as
subtly "Horatian" in tone as the Friar's is indignantly "Juve-
nalian."

Chaucer's rhetorical technique in the Summoner's Tale
points in many directions, as in all of his churlish tales, but
mainly toward the friars. Like the Friar, the Summoner, in nar-
rating, exposes himself as a false cleric and a materialist. His
friar's sermon against wrath mocks that friar's own later, wild-
boar wrath (D, 2156ff.), which in turn mocks the Summoner-
narrator's earlier misdirection of the divine wrath that upright
summoners were to represent (D, 1667). The tale's critique of a
materialism that denies the world of the Spirit also falls back on
the doubting Summoner (A, 654–58). But the Summoner's sa-
tiric force falls as much on his friar as Huberd's falls on him.
Even such issues as the relative claims of monastic and friar per-
fection (D, 1904–41; see chap. 5 above) diminish in importance
as Chaucer scrutinizes the Conventual friar's efforts to claim a
Francis-like spirituality and perfection through using the lan-
guage of a Spiritualism whose practice he has rejected.[3]

Friar John can lay claim to "spirituality" only through a sys-
tematic violation of Christ's apostolic commands in Luke 9.1–5
and 10.1–12, Matthew 10.6–15 and Mark 6.7–13 echoed in the
Franciscan rule and rhetoric. These commands dominated the
polemic between rival Franciscan parties throughout the thir-
teenth and fourteenth centuries and also played a role in the sec-
ular clergy's anti-fraternal critiques. In the passages cited,
Christ magnificently sends out the twelve and the seventy, two

---

[3] *Summa Theologica*, 2.2.186a7; Leclercq, *The Life of Perfection*, pp. vii ff., and
passim.

by two, to preach his coming kingdom, to heal the sick, and to cast out devils. He orders them to take none of their journey's necessities along—no staff, scrip, bread, money, gold, or silver, not even two coats—but to depend on the houses that accept them. When they find such a house, they are to wish it peace and take whatever is offered there. If they are rejected, they are to shake the dust from their feet and go to the next town, unafraid to be brought before the governors of society for Christ's sake because the Spirit will speak in them. As Szittya and others have pointed out, the Summoner simply makes his tale picture how friars systematically violate these mandates. Brother John goes out with "scrippe and tipped staf" (D, 1737); his two-by-two group includes a third "harlot" who comes behind to carry the possessions that the group is given.[4] Though Friar John claims to be a workman worth his hire (D, 1973; Luke 10.7), his only work is to chase the cat from his seat. He goes to every house instead of to those worthy to receive him and greets people not with a "Peace be to this house" but with an ostentatiously belched "*Deus hic!*" that is, God in the form of a friar is here. Instead of accepting what is given, he asks for a trinity of delicacies, and after Thomas insults him, becomes so angered that he neglects to shake the dust from his feet as he leaves. When he comes before the governor of the little village in which the apostolic drama occurs, nothing speaks in him, so the lord's squire has to tell him, literal-minded dunce that he is, how to fulfill his oath. Appropriately, none of the promised gifts of the Spirit come to him: his preaching misfires as he creates in himself (D, 2161) and in Thomas (D, 2121) the rage against which he has preached. He heals no one and casts out no demons (though his lord holds the Thomas who gives him the problem in *arsmetrik* to be a demoniac), and obviously no person becomes more Christ-like because of his efforts.

4 Szittya, "The Friar as False Apostle," pp. 19–46.

CHAPTER 8

The Luke 9 and 10 passages and related passages in Matthew and Mark were crucial to both friar and anti-friar claims to the apostolic mantle. In anti-friar polemic, the basis of most previous analyses of this tale, William of St. Amour had argued for the secular clergy that the twelve apostles sent out in Luke 9 meant bishops, and the seventy sent out in Luke 10, the parish priests and presbyters.[5] Friar rhetoric, following the Franciscan rule, argued that the twelve and the seventy foreshadowed the friars because they lived like the apostles, had apostolic powers, and had been told by St. Francis, when he wrote Chapter 14 of his First Rule between 1210 and 1221, that they were to follow literally the apostolic charges from Luke 9 and 10. To these Francis added passages from Mark 5 and Luke 6 commanding friars not to resist attempts to steal from them and ordering them to give what they have to any who ask for help.[6]

Francis's radical First Rule was modified toward the "center" in the official Franciscan rule confirmed two years later by Pope Honorius III in 1223; at his insistence and that of the governing Pentecost chapter of the order, the official rule deleted the passage from Luke 9 that required friars to take nothing on the road. It modified the requirement that probationers sacrifice all of their property, making good intentions suffice (compare Chapter 2 of the 1221 and 1223 rules). And it rendered insignificant the rule requiring the order to have no property.[7]

[5] William of St. Amour, "De Periculis Novissimorum Temporum," *Opera Omnia* (Constance, 1632), 2: Sig. c4ᵛ (p. 24); cf. Godefroid de Fontaines, *Le huitième [dixième] Quodlibet*, ed. J. Hoffmans (Louvain: Institut supérieur, 1924), in *Les philosophes belges* 4:38–39.

[6] David Flood et al., *The Birth of a Movement: A Study of the First Rule of St. Francis*, trans. Paul Schwartz and others (Chicago: Franciscan Herald Press, 1975), p. 85. For the Franciscan aesthetic and use of materials modeled on the life of Christ, see Smart, *The Assisi Problem*, pp. 17–29. Cf. David L. Jeffrey, *The Early English Lyric and Franciscan Spirituality* (Lincoln: Nebraska University Press, 1975), pp. 66–68.

[7] John Moorman, *A History of the Franciscan Order From its Origins to the Year*

Though the 1223 rule, like the earlier one, mentioned that the group should have nothing, its interpretation permitted a communal holding of property so long as its possession was assigned to the pope and only its "use" given to the friars.[8] Though St. Francis's testament, dictated shortly before his death, again elevated the ideals of the First Rule, Gregory IX declared it not binding on the order and left the Franciscans split between Spiritualists who gave to Francis's words a strict interpretation and Conventuals who gave them a more liberal one. Thus was created a division in the friars of which both friars and secular-order polemicists took advantage. This split in turn allows Chaucer to use mock-Spiritualist rhetoric to expose Spiritualist rhetoric, Conventual practice, and the alliance of the two in his England.

The Spiritualist group, which opposed friar property, buildings, and bureaucratization at first, included Brother Leo, Francis's friend and biographer, Bernard of Quintavilla and Brother Giles who were among Francis's earliest disciples, and Masseo, his principal counsellor.[9] Holding out for the radical position, the group carefully passed down its practice of living in hutches instead of convents, as well as its own lore, different from the official version of what St. Francis and his original order were. The Spiritualist party received a sympathetic hearing from John of Parma who headed the order between 1247 and 1257, but he, simple in heart and generous in devotional life, also came to trust in Gerard of Borgo San Donnino's Joachimite

---

1517 (London: Clarendon Press, 1968), pp. 53–61. For the *Regula Bullata*, see *Expositio Quatuor Magistrorum Super Regulam Fratrum Minorum*, ed. L. Oliger (Rome: Storia et Letteratura, 1950), pp. 173–93, or Henry Bettenson, *Documents of the Christian Church* (London: Oxford University Press, 1963), pp. 179–84 (English trans.).

[8] Cf. the 1241–42 "four masters" exegesis of the *Regula Bullata; Expositio Quatuor Magistrorum Super Regulam Fratrum Minorum*, pp. 141–58.

[9] *Analecta Franciscana* (Quaracchi: Coll. of St. Bonaventura, 1897), 3:35–121.

heresy which posited an evolving revelation guided by the Holy Spirit through the friar orders: a first age under the Father extending from creation to the birth of Christ, a second under the Son going from the time of Christ to the thirteenth century, and a third under the Holy Spirit and the friars which was to go from 1200 to the end of the world and require no coercive institutions since all people would spontaneously follow God's spirit.[10] Obviously, John's and Gerard's views further challenged hierarchical rule, and during John's master generalship, the divisions between secular and regular clergy at the University of Paris broke into the open, culminating in William of St. Amour's publication of his attack on the friars for their Joachimism and pseudo-apostleship and his own secular cleric's explanation of the apostolic charge.

Though John of Parma quickly retired to be replaced by the Conventual St. Bonaventura, the Spiritualists continued to emphasize the strict version of Francis's apostolic charge, and in 1312 Clement V was still trying to reconcile differences within the order by restricting the Conventuals in their buildings, land purchases, and financial machinations (*Exivi de Paradiso*). By 1317, Michael de Cesena, the Spiritualist general of the Franciscans, worked further to restrict excesses in Conventual building, clothing, and money-raising while John XXII cracked down from the other side on the extreme Spiritualist "Fratricelli." However, just as a compromise appeared possible, John took from the Conventuals the old fiction that the friars were not possessioners by declaring that the pope did not own their property (*Ad Conditorem*, 1322). He also took from the Spiritualists the doctrine of Christ's lack of possessions (*Cum Inter Nonnullos*, 1323). Conventuals had to admit to having possessions and Spiritualists to misreading Christ's precedent. Shocked at the Pope's action, the Spiritualist Michael de Ces-

---

[10] Moorman, *History of the Franciscan Order*, p. 115; cf. pp. 146–54.

ena and his associate, William of Ockham, fled to the court of the Emperor, William of Bavaria. There Ockham developed his extensions of Spiritualist teaching into the doctrine of the invisible Church, freedom and grace, and the power of councils which made him a force in Wyclif's writing, in the conciliar movement, and in early Protestantism.[11]

Though apparently dead in the late fourteenth century, the Spiritualist party still influenced Chaucer's England as stories about St. Francis condoned by the Spiritualists, as well as those encouraged by the Conventuals, circulated and found their way into the popular *South English Legendary*. Ockham's works were known in England and France and influenced Wyclif, Pierre d'Ailly, Jean Gerson, and the conciliar thinkers. Though David Jeffrey argues that the Spiritualists essentially died out after the Black Death,[12] Moorman shows that the Observants, allowed Spiritualists founded in 1373, did not come to England for a hundred years because English Franciscanism was already strict.[13] The English Provincial Minister during Chaucer's later life, John Zouch, endeavored to impose an even stricter rule and got in trouble with Henry IV for doing so, perhaps because the Zouch group was associated with the friars who encouraged insurrection on Richard's behalf after his disposition.[14] Certainly Wyclif knew and was influenced by Spiritualist thought: Workman posits early-life sympathies based on his praise of the

---

[11] *Bullarium Franciscanum*, ed. Conrad Eubel (Rome: Vatican, 1898), 5:257–59 (for *Exivi de Paradiso*, see 5:80–86; *Ad Conditorem*, 5:233–46).

[12] Jeffrey, *The Early English Lyric and Franciscan Spirituality*, pp. 273–75.

[13] Moorman, *History of the Franciscan Order*, p. 444; A. G. Little, "The Introduction of the Observant Friars into England," *Proceedings of the British Academy* 10 (1921–23):458; cf. pp. 455–71.

[14] D. W. Whitfield, "Conflicts of Personality and Principle," *Franciscan Studies* 17 (1957):321–62, esp. 358. Whitfield interprets Zouch's efforts after 1395 as efforts to impose a strict rule, partially the product of Wyclif's criticisms, partially a response to an internal faction of the Franciscans who wanted reform.

Lady Poverty, his reading of Juan de Peretallada's *Vade Mecum in Tribulatione* which located the Joachimite prophecies in the fourteenth century, his call for poverty in the Church for monks, friars, parish clergy, and the hierarchy, and his contempt for friar buildings.[15] His program prior to 1377 continues the Spiritualist program by denying Church rights to significant possession, positing an invisible or true Church without property, and emphasizing the state's power to discipline the visible Church. Early Wycliffite writing also reasserts Francis's First Rule and his Testament, and the four friars who were to defend Wyclif's anti-possessioning position at the Lady Chapel must have shared his Spiritualist assumptions.

The use of Spiritualist rhetoric as a critical weapon was continued by Wyclif after he had abandoned the friars and by other writers who never supported them. Wyclif's alliance with the friars was not to last long as they deserted him in the early 1380s when he began to attack the doctrine of transubstantiation. With his usual sweetness, he in turn called them one of the four divisive sects of Christendom—as guilty as the monks of possessioning, guilty of the charges made against them by their Spiritualist wing, and guilty of the secular clergy's charges against them also, particularly those developed by Richard Fitzralph. Yet the Spiritualist strain in Wycliffite rhetoric continued and evidences itself in a translation of, and commentary on, the *Rule and Testament of St. Francis* which argues that the friars were bound to the First Rule because God gave it to Francis. The pope could not release the Franciscans from it since Francis reaffirmed it in his final will. The Francis of this work further says that *God* showed him that he should live according to the gospel, that his early friars had one coat and only one, and that they worked with their hands, stayed in people's houses as they traveled and greeted them with peace as Luke 10

[15] Workman, *Wyclif*, 2:100–02.

commanded. Finally, the St. Francis of this document reminds his audience that he ordered the friars, all living as pilgrims and guests, to receive no buildings or churches and to give his words no "glosis" or explanations in the Bonaventuran tradition that would make his discipline easier. The extended Wycliffite explanations of the *Rule and Testament* that follow reaffirm the Franciscan obligation to practice apostolic poverty, eschew buildings, and avoid the fiction that the pope holds their property. It urges the ordinary, possessioner friars to abstain from persecuting the Spiritualists ("trewe pore freris"), and its most entertaining passages describe Conventual friar pretenses of obedience to the strict Franciscan letter that deny its spirit: for example, the Conventuals take with them a "scarioth" who has been stolen from his parents (the equivalent of Chaucer's harlot—D, 1754) to do their begging for them because they know mendicancy is condemned by the Bible (i.e., as the Spiritualists claimed) and they count their money with a stick or with gloves to avoid touching "possessions" while they drink wine from gold cups and wear cloth finer than that of any emperor or king.[16]

The Wycliffites had company in their use of Spiritualist anti-Conventual ideas in satiric attack in the work of a conservative Gower who, in the *Vox Clamantis*, recalls the friars' use of "spiritual" words to justify their physical indulgence. They call themselves poor when they own everything including the pope, preach fearful public sermons while they gloss over sin in the private chambers of the rich, speak always of God but love gold, and blow about as if they were God's spirit when their

[16] Wyclif, *English Works*, pp. 46–51. For Wycliffite influence on the Summoner's Tale's picture of friar use of the Bible and opposition to translation, see Roy Peter Clark, "Wit and Witsunday in Chaucer's *Summoner's Tale*," *Annuale Mediaevale* 17 (1977):48–57. David Fowler has pointed out to me that Fitzralph, defending the secular clergy in *Defensio Curatorum*, had also argued that the Franciscans were bound by the First Rule.

real purpose is to stop at the parish bedrooms when the husbands are gone. Their piety creates a "redemptive" decoration of their church buildings which fails its salvation purpose:

> Ad decus ecclesie deuocio seruit eorum,
> Et veluti quedam signa salutis habent. *(Vox Clamantis,*
> bk. 4, lines 1141–42)
> (Their devotion seeks to adorn their churches
> As if adornment constituted a sign of salvation.)

Since they make visual representations of Christ that attach them to the world, Gower accuses them of going from heaven to earth in aesthetic perception, the reverse of the Bonaventuran process of moving from earth to heaven. They fail as true brothers ("fratres," friars), faithful to the love of Christ's Church ("amore fideles / Ecclesie Cristi"), and live as the fallen, the Synagogue, as Agar's offspring rather than Sarah's, the children of furor and hatred rather than of the original friars' love (bk. 4, lines 1091–1112).[17] Gower specifically recognizes that the First Rule ("regula prima," bk. 4, line 712) has been overwhelmed and lost in the luxuriant growth of his own period. Chaucer's Summoner's Tale assembles just such critiques of Conventual hypocrisy and lack of discipline from the perspective of the strict rule and Francis's original design. Chaucer's critique of the friars derives from the Spiritualist Franciscan rhetoric, perhaps because he always lays such emphasis on the founders' visions, perhaps because the Spiritualist critique is so clearly rooted in the apostolic life, perhaps because he wishes to deal with all of Wyclif's four sects in Wyclif's own terms, and perhaps also because irony is made easier if one can use an institution's members to testify against the institution itself.

The Summoner's Tale addresses itself to the use of Spiritu-

---

[17] *Vox Clamantis*, bk. 4, lines 1091–1110, draws on St. Paul's Agar-Sarah allegory from Galatians 4.22ff.

alist apologetic and polemic to justify Conventual friar prop-
erty-centered practices, a mode of argument developed by St.
Bonaventura to move Francis's followers into more conven-
tional paths. Chaucer gets at the excesses of both wings by par-
odying Conventual abuse of Bonaventura's method for resolv-
ing problems between the left and right in his order. The good
saint's method, developed shortly after he took over from John
of Parma, sacramentalizes the controversy by allowing any-
thing physical, material, or propertied that leads to spiritual
perception, while retaining Francis's emphasis. Bonaventura
allows the substitution of spiritual work—the activities charac-
teristic of the clergy—for the manual labor which Francis re-
quired of his followers, if such clerical effort resembles activity
which Francis undertook. If the friars are to fulfill clerical func-
tions, they need regular support from somewhere, not merely
the casual offerings given the Spiritualists or the returns of
manual labor. Hence, Bonaventura permits the friars to have
property if they "use it" for God and do not "seek it" for pur-
poses of prideful sovereignty or *dominium*. Hence, they can sub-
stitute aggressive mendicancy, the hearing of confessions, and
preaching for Francis's self-support. Bonaventura also tolerates
the carrying of material possessions on the road if they are
brought for "spiritual" ends. His life of St. Francis describes
St. Francis hearing Luke 9 and Matthew 10, and throwing
away his shoes, staff, money, and all.[18] But after his conver-
sion, he first acts to repair the material fabric of three churches,
and this work, following Bonaventura's conception of the
mind's journey to God, shows that Francis began with the
"things perceived by the senses" and went on to those "per-
ceived by the understanding."[19] Through his rebuilding of ac-
tual church structures, Bonaventura's Francis signifies the re-

[18] Bonaventura, 6:510.
[19] Bonaventura, 6:509.

building of the spiritual Church by his pattern of life and rule and by Christ's teaching. Thereafter, he receives the *Regula Bullata*, a "more orderly" revision of the First Rule, directly from God. It is confirmed by the Pope and sealed with the stigmata. Bonaventura nowhere admits that the 1221 and 1223 rules are different in content or that the First Rule, not the *Regula Bullata*, was commonly said to have come from God. Though his Francis feels inspired by God, the Holy Spirit, and vision, his life also legitimizes the possession of church buildings, other property, scholastic theological tools, and academic titles so long as these "material things" have a "spiritual" significance.[20] Though not a great deal of controversial Conventual friar literature from Chaucer's court has been published, Richard of Maidstone's two defenses of mendicancy and parish work follow the Bonaventuran rhetorical model.

To fight against the Bonaventuran compromise, the Spiritualist party early in the fourteenth century created its own alternative rhetoric of strict adherence, sudden inspiration, and divine outpouring. Early in the Franciscan visual tradition, Giotto, possibly influenced by the Spiritualists, had shown Saint Francis carried into the heavens in Elijah's vision chariot (fig. 41). The *Actus Beati Francisci* (1322–1328) and the *Fioretti* or *Little Flowers* (after 1328) both emphasize the wonder, wildness, and unpredictability of the wind of the Spirit as well as the absolute poverty of Francis and his early followers.[21] The *Fioretti* and like friar storybooks emphasize the four features of Franciscan life parodied in the Summoner's Tale: first, Franciscan obedience to the apostolic charges of Luke 9 and Matthew 10; sec-

---

[20] Bonaventura, 6:536.

[21] For the history of the *Fioretti* and Spiritualism, see Moorman, *History of the Franciscan Order*, pp. 288–89; cf. *Actus beati Francisci et sociorum eius*, ed. Paul Sabatier (Paris: Librarie Fischbacher, 1902), p. 6 and pp. i–xxiv. Cf. *The Little Flowers of St. Francis*, trans. Raphael Brown (Garden City: Hanover House, 1958), p. 44; further citations in the text are from this edition.

ond, Franciscan conformity to the more general apostolic mandate requiring healing the sick or casting out demons; third, Franciscan claims of special gifts and inspiration by the Holy Spirit; and fourth, Franciscan views showing God, Christ, or St. Francis benefiting the Spiritualists. This rhetoric must have been powerfully effective, for it was adjusted and also adapted to the Bonaventuran compromise by Conventuals.

The Summoner's Tale shows what allowing the material which points to the spiritual can result in. The fourfold Spiritualist claim becomes only wind and farts without Spirit, like the monkish belches which, in Friar John's description, come out in the *cor meum eructavit* of the cloistered virgins of God (D, 1934). Chaucer's Friar John inverts each of the four main Spiritualist rhetorical strategies and does so only to pay for a convent for his group. First, he systematically violates the apostolic charge, as we have noted. Secondly, he cannot heal old Thomas and mistakes his sickness or idleness for anger because the wife sets him on. Thirdly, he literal-mindedly obeys his oath requiring a pentecostal fart(h)ing divided in twelve for his convent without understanding the apostolic spirit of the common property of the first twelve (Acts 4.32). Finally, he punishes his monk enemies with his visionary superiority while his Summoner-narrator, in imitation of Spiritualist punishing visions, tells of a vision in which his enemy friars swarm like bees from the devil's behind. The comparable *Fioretti* stories, under the first category, show Francis and his early followers strictly following the First Rule, Luke 9, and Matthew 10. Those in the second group display him and his twelve "apostles" healing numerous sick people and saying the exactly right words in their sermons to the fallen. Those in the third category represent Francis and the Franciscan receiving divine fire and the Holy Spirit in numerous special ways. And, finally, those in the fourth group describe Francis's Spiritualist followers seeing visions in which Christ or St. Francis reward the good Spiritualists such as John of Parma and punish their enemies such as Bonaventura (see fig. 41).[22] Though the *Fioretti* are confined to Italy in their subjects, Thomas of Eccleston, the thirteenth-century English Spiritualist who chronicled the spread of Franciscanism in England, applies the same rhetorical modes to his English subjects, and the *South English Legendary* mixes Conventual and Spiritualist formulae in its life of St. Francis.[23] In short, Chaucer had available a fourfold Spiritualist rhetoric of obedience to the apostolic First Rule, inspired healings and sermons, visitations by special charismatic gifts, and visions of special punishments for enemies and rewards for friends. He also had at hand a related tradition that mocked the Conventual retention of this rhetoric and pretenses to poverty, First Rule asceticism, and charismatic gifts under radically changed conditions of group discipline. Like Gower and the Wycliffites, Chaucer shows how the fusion of the two traditions destroys the values of each and makes the inspiration of the Spirit become only material flatulence. The brilliance of Chaucer's satire lies, however, in its execution rather than in the traditions from which it derives.

The center of Spiritual Franciscanism is wonder. Friar John has wonder enough, all of it calculated to raise money for his group's building.

> "God woot," quod he, "laboured have I ful soore,
> And specially, for thy savacion." (D, 1784–85)

---

[22] E.g., *The Little Flowers*, pp. 67, 151–54, 293–97, 315–16; cf. *Actus beati Francisci*, p. 46.

[23] Thomas of Eccleston, *Tractatus de Adventu Fratrum Minorum in Angliam*, ed. A. G. Little (Manchester: Manchester University Press, 1951), pp. 32–39; cf. Thomas of Eccleston, "The Coming of the Friars Minor to England," *XIIIth Century Chronicles*, trans. Placid Hermann (Chicago: Franciscan Herald, 1961), pp. 177–78; Horstmann, *The Early South English Legendary*, pp. 177–78. Manfred Görlach, *The Textual Tradition of the South English Legendary* (Ilkey, Yorkshire: Leeds School of English, 1974), p. 194; cf. pp. 73–106.

"O Thomas, *je vous dy*, Thomas! Thomas!
This maketh the feend; this moste ben amended.
Ire is a thyng that hye God defended,
And therof wol I speke a word or two."   (D, 1832–35)

"His deeth saugh I by revelacioun,"
Seide this frere, "at hoom in oure dortour."   (D, 1854–55)

The frere answerde, "O Thomas, dostow so?
What nedeth yow diverse freres seche?
What nedeth hym that hath a parfit leche
To sechen othere leches in the toun?"   (D, 1954–57)

The leech's spontaneity and robotic "spirit" climax in "tendre groping" (D, 1817, 2148), in a tireless sermon against wrath, and in a mechanical Pentecost (D, 1954–2093). The "wonder" goes with Friar Thomas's art of sinking from the heavenly to the earthly in a reversal of the Bonaventuran pattern. Collecting money to finish building his group's convent, he develops the fourfold rhetoric to destroy Bonaventura's material world as an apt metaphor for the spiritual and makes the parish "spirit" serve only the material of his building program. To set the theme, the Summoner begins by placing his friar enemies in the most "material" of places, the devil's ass in hell, in parody of Spiritualist rhetoric stationing dead friars next to God in heaven or in His side or representing dead enemies directly chastised by Christ and St. Francis.[24] He then attacks his character's Luke 9 and Matthew 10 claim to live like Christ and the apostles and his marriage to poverty which parallels St. Francis's *Sacrum Commercium* marriage to the Lady Poverty, abandoned for eleven hundred years:[25]

[24] For hell as "material," and the devil as quintessential materialism in Dante, cf. Francis X. Newman, "St. Augustine's Three Visions and the Structure of the *Commedia*," MLN 82 (1967):61–64; for the fart as drawing on friar characterization of money as excrement and, therefore, mirroring friar materialism, see Fleming, "The Antifraternalism of the *Summoner's Tale*," pp. 698–99.

[25] The *Sacrum Commercium* indicates that Lady Poverty left the earth from

CHAPTER 8

we sely freres,
Been wedded to poverte and continence.   (D, 1906–7)

But we know that poverty-wedded John's harlot carries all the loot of his begging. His vision of the ascent to heaven of Thomas's son can be summoned only after the wife has told him of her boy's passing. Then it becomes a sign that contributions to the friars for friar prayers will cure Brother Thomas's physical illness (D, 1942–47), that all the money for prayers ought to come to friars so that the "ferthyng" need not be "parted in twelve" (D, 1967).

Friar John, were he attentive to the model of the apostle John, would preach of love and of the contemplation of final and spiritual things, but Conventual John, afraid of Christ's coming, invents his own "Joachimite" prophecy to promote building friar libraries to forestall the Johannine world's end and Christ's return:

And if yow lakke oure predicacioun,
Thanne goth the world al to destruccioun.
For whoso wolde us fro this world bireve,
So God me save, Thomas, by youre leve,
He wolde bireve out of this world the sonne.   (D, 2109–13)

When the world comes apart and the sun darkens, the Church Militant's "building" will be complete and the Church Triumphant will return as in the Apocalypse, but for John that disaster will not happen or happen only if friars lack buildings, libraries, proper books, and proper resources to go on preaching their building sermons.

John directs his speeches to a skeptical lay brother, Thomas (D, 1942), to whom he appeals by his name saint, doubting

shortly after the time of Christ until St. Francis; see *Sacrum Commercium S. Francisci Cum Domina Paupertate* (Quaracchi: Coll. of St. Bonaventura, 1929), pp. 50–54; cf. Dante, *Paradiso* XI. 58–75.

Thomas or Thomas of India (D, 1980). The apostolic Thomas, instead of building a palace for the king of India, gave the money to the poor out of love so that he might build for the king a spiritual mansion in paradise.[26] However, John appeals to St. Thomas as one knowledgeable "Of buyldynge up of chirches" (D, 1979), and he means the physical buildings which St. Thomas eschewed out of love for the spirit. The apostle's name means *division* or *parting*, and the parting to which Friar John should urge Brother Thomas is that attributed to his name-saint who separated the "world" from the "spirit" and, thus, was able to "[separate] his love from the love of the world." Though Brother Thomas is a doubter—appropriately doubtful of Friar John who wishes him to confess again after he has confessed to his curate—he remains in bed because he is old (D, 2182) and physically sick or, perhaps, because he is intended to suggest Sloth. In any case, he does not become wrathful until provoked by John's sermon on the vice. To gather the "fruit" of this wrath, Friar John reverses Thomas's namesake's act of placing his finger in Christ's side, referred to in the other meaning of Thomas's name, "wallow" or "abyss." This meaning, according to the *Legenda Aurea*, reflects Thomas's "materialism," his desire to know the spirit of Christ after the resurrection through the avenues of sight and touch (Thomas is, as it were, the apostolic Bonaventura). But Friar John fails to stand for Christ as a *Deus hic* and allow his doubting Thomas to reach into his side to know the spirit through the flesh. He does the reverse by reaching for Thomas's material goods through playing on his spiritual fears and entering his lay brother's material wallow to gain his "ferthyng." He receives the flatulent "spiritual" gift or "fart(h)ing" he so richly deserves, one whose *division* he, not Thomas, has to mastermind (D, 2129ff.). The action obviously inverts that in Giotto's Bardi Chapel picture of St. Francis

---

[26] Jacobus de Voragine, *Legenda Aurea*, pp. 32–39.

which shows the saint on his deathbed while a friar, modeled after St. Thomas, reaches into the wound in his side to experience Francis's spirit; the *Little Flowers* has a parallel description of a Brother Jerome who places his hand in Francis's side to relieve himself of doubt at the time of the saint's death (figs. 42–43).[27]

The ending turns from the subtly "Horatian" to the magnificently "Rabelaisian" in the inverted Pentecostal scene. Spiritualism culminates in Pentecost where perfected love moved the twelve apostles to speak in many languages. Previous scholars have shown how the final scene with its twelve "apostles" about the wheel resembles Pentecost and refers to the *Fioretti* rhetoric of the twelve first friars as like the twelve apostles, to the emphasis in such literature on friar Pentecostal inspiration, to Franciscan meetings at the time of Pentecost and at the original Pentecost chapter center, and to the Pentecostal expectations in Spiritualist Joachimite literature. But the scene also continues Chaucer's indictment of friar "love of material dung" and dependence on the division of temporal goods.[28] Friar John learns from a squire, the lowliest member of the estate that deals with material protection (D, 2243ff.), how to create his scatological Pentecost through the use of a wheel, as he earlier has had to be reminded by the squire's temporal lord to be the salt of the earth (D, 2196). Apparently the squire, since he can solve the problem, has studied Pentecost iconology better than his "maister," and one shudders to think what the convent buildings of such "maisters" are like in their symbolic statement.

The Summoner should feel no glee at his character's humiliation. After all, he also is a materialist and a possessioner. He presents the Franciscan friars at Holderness as representative of

[27] Cf. "The Considerations on the Holy Stigmata," *The Little Flowers of St. Francis*, p. 206.
[28] Jacobus de Voragine, *Legenda Aurea*, p. 32.

all friars—particularly Huberd—who speak of the Spirit but act the body's demands, confusing the domains and rhetorics of the two ruling orders. His Friar John's literal-minded acceptance of the task of distributing his "gift" equally but not in common, even after he has shown that he can "spiritually" gloss any part of Scripture to mean the friars, suggests that a "just" Franciscan division of common property can only be achieved mechanically—by *ars-metrike* on a still day. The wind cannot blow where it lists (D, 2254). But *ars-metrike*, given the scatological pun, is also the geometry crucial to Gothic building which could use the quadrivium discipline to lead to perfection and wisdom.[29] Masters of *ars-metrike* and the mechanical operation of the spirit, the Summoner's friars only make stones and mortar while they claim to build up Pentecostal love. Their materialism, perhaps reflective of the materialism of Conventional friars who formed an easy alliance with the propertied merchant classes, also summarizes the Epicurean Summoner himself and the materialism of his diocesan historical counterparts, particularly the archdeacons who so often ruled from great cathedrals also built from *ars-metrik*.

The General Prologue Parson provides the normative mirror for friars. Like a friar, he walks about his parish, yet carries his pastoral staff in his hand neither to blandish the rich nor to oppress the poor. He does all by apostolic "fairnesse." The Summoner presents the friars as the culmination of Chaucer's cycle of apostolic inversions by representing an ideal gone hollow at every level, so hollow that even the language of the ideal can be used for the obverse of its original purposes. In contrast, the Parson's speech and his actions are one (A, 496–528).

[29] Otto von Simson, *The Gothic Cathedral* (New York: Pantheon, 1956), pp. 13–39. Recent history has traced a pronounced association between the rise of the friars and the commercial classes. For the "firste fruyt" (D, 2277) as the English subsidy to the pope, sometimes collected by the friars, see Pantin, *The English Church in the Fourteenth Century*, p. 90; Wyclif, *De Mandatis Divinis*, p. 380.

The Summoner's friars may at first glance appear to be Wyclif's sect of the friars, departing from Francis's First Rule and owning property, but actually they are sectaries primarily because they do not believe in their own rule and spirit and follow the Epicurean sect of the Wife of Bath. Chaucer's clerics, aside from the Parson, the Second Nun, and the Nun's Priest, all live as Epicureans. They live for whatever "delight" they can conceive of and secure for themselves. Indifferent to the spiritual significance of the apostolate and to the evangelical counsels to perfection, they ignore the curlew call of Chaucer's afterworld. Caught up in imitating princely courts and in accepting money as penance, they pretend to an apostleship that they do not feel. Their jurisdictional battles require that, to condemn others, they pretend to know a divine law in which they do not believe. Though their appeals to the types and symbols of eternity tell us only of their own malice, at another level these appeals evoke a symbolic world which their lives deny. Thus, the satire moves us beyond the Epicurean waste land to the imagination of places where the types and symbols may have validity, places where Reason and Wisdom can dramatize the comedy of the expense of spirit in a waste of shame. However, we must return to the waste land one more time to observe how the Wife encapsulates Chaucer's technique in the clerical tales before we look at the Parson's spiritual world. She, with her loyal laity and clergy, epitomizes the grand *commedia* of the new sects changing England far more than Wyclif or the theologians who opposed him were ever able to imagine.

9

The Sect of the Wife of Bath and the Quest for Perfection

THE WIFE, THE MERCHANT, AND THE FRANKLIN
AND THEIR NEW MATERIALISM

The Wife of Bath appears first as an extraordinarily vigorous representative of the married estate and the commercial West Country. She has a life and followers of her own which she will not allow to be put down by more "perfected" orders.[1] She also exists "in another country," that of comical satire. Comic or Menippean satiric writing in the Christian tradition often invents alternative worlds that are governed by vices having their own philosophic statements, rituals, and mock solemn religious-rule systems. Hence the origin of the monasteries of Cockaigne and Bel Eyse, Breughel's Cockaigne with its three-estate gluttony, sausage fences, gruel mountain, and sleepy worship of food, Pope's descriptions of Belinda's rites of Pride and the epic games and battles associated with the protection of her beauty, and Swift's land of the Yahoos. The Yahoos, as humankind's fallen libido, fight with terrible claws, lust for shining stones, devour everything—herbs, roots, berries, and corrupted flesh—that comes in their way, and discharge their excrement *en masse* on retired leaders. Viewing them, Gulliver concludes that European civilization is different from the Yahoo's only in its "reason"-created refinement of the depravity of the flesh.[2] The same principle operates in the *Roman de la*

[1] Mann, *Chaucer and Medieval Estates Satire*, p. 121; Duby, *The Three Orders*, pp. 32, 81–82, 133–34, 210–11.

[2] Roland Mushat Frye, "Swift's Yahoo and the Christian Symbols for Sin," *JHI* 15 (1954):201–17.

Rose, where love deprived of reason creates the garden of earthly delights which comically simulates the garden of the temporal power and the celestial garden, or in the *Inferno*, where Lucifer's three comic heads signify impotence, ignorance, and hate, and imitate the trinity of Power, Wisdom, and Love—Father, Son, and Spirit.[3] Chaucer develops a similar world in rendering the Wife of Bath and her Epicurean sect which includes, among clerics, the Friar, Summoner, Pardoner, and the pilgrimage's Epicurean monastics and, among laity, the acquisitive Merchant and Franklin. The "sect" inverts old political traditions that placed the sexual estates of virgins and widows above the married one, and turns upside down the doctrine of perfection by asserting a new final good or wisdom consisting in the self and its accoutrements. It creates a new perfective discipline of the three enemies replacing the old discipline of the three evangelical counsels. The Wife of Bath expresses the sect's hilarious "theology," the Merchant, its "ecclesiology," and the Franklin, its social ethics, while the Clerk defines what is wrong with its picture of the present world.

Wyclif, in his critique of the orders of friars, monastics, canons, and hierarchy, had called them Christendom's sects;[4] Chaucer, drawing on the *Roman de la Rose*, creates his parodic sect of the Wife of Bath, ruled like Swift's Yahoos by carnality

[3] Cf. Bruce Kent Cowgill, "The Parlement of Foules and the Body Politic," *JEGP* 74 (1975):321–24; John V. Fleming, *The Roman de la Rose: A Study in Allegory and Iconography* (Princeton: Princeton University Press, 1969), pp. 17ff.; *Chess* gloss, 4:693–94; Benvenuto da Imola, *Comentum Super Dantis Allligherii Comoediam*, ed. G. W. Vernon (Florence, 1887), 1:18.

[4] For Wyclif's *sects*, see "De Fundacione Sectarum" and "De Quattuor Sectis Novellis," *Polemical Works in Latin*, 1:13–80, 241–90, and vols. 1 and 2 of this title, *passim*. For Lollard English usage: "It is seid comounly þat in tyme of Crist weren þre sectis of religions, Pharises, Saduceis, and Esses," see *Select English Works of Wyclif*, 1:44; "þe þrittenþe synne of fleishe ben sectis, as we mai now see of foure sectis þat ben now brouȝt in, aftir þe secte of Cristis ordre" (Wyclif, *Select English Works*, 2:349).

and governed like Swift's Europe by a depraved Yahoo reason. It has its own theology, philosophy, education, and fictional landscape full of gardens and dancing ladies, and its own legerdemain. Chaucer assigns the instruction of this sect to a West Country clothier and female preacher, perhaps as a dig at Wyclif who had a good following among West Country clothiers and had been accused of hypocritical Jovinian Epicureanism. After all, Wyclif had made the temporal lords' material reform of the Church the keystone of his reform efforts.[5] The poet makes the Wife and her followers teach the carnal, Synagogue truths which only laughter, such as that of her clerk husband, can penetrate and only the love of God and neighbor, made possible by the evangelical counsels, can transform.

When the Clerk prays, in solemn irony, that the Wife and all hers may be maintained in sovereignty ("maistrie," E, 1172), he gives her a "secte" and a "lyf" (E, 1171). As a clerk of this sect, she is decorated with "seinte Venus seel" (D, 604) and schooled in many erotic schools (D, 44a-44f.). She is an arch wife,[6] a

[5] For the Wife's Sermon as a mock-Lollard lay sermon, see D. W. Robertson, " 'And for my land thus hastow mordred me?': Land Tenure, the Cloth Industry, and the Wife of Bath," *CR* 14 (1980):415; for Lollard concentration among west-country clothiers in the period, see K. B. McFarlane, *John Wycliffe and the Beginnings of English Nonconformity*, p. 127. The Wife, as a lay preacher, preaches a Jovinian sermon, and Gower associates Wyclif with Jovinianism both in his *Vox Clamantis* bk. 6, line 1267 and in his "Carmen Super Multiplici Viciorum Pestilencia," line 32. Cf. Gower's *Works*, 4:346–54 and p. 417, n. 32. Gower's treatment of Wyclif as Jovinian probably points to hypocrisy as had early *Roman de la Rose* treatments of the friars as leagued with *La Vielle*; Chaucer probably points to Epicurean hypocrisy in general, including Wycliffite Erastianism and opposition to conventional notions of the life of perfection, in making his portrait of the Wife include some Lollard details. For *Roman de la Rose* and other connections of the idea of a sect or school, see Giovanni Boccaccio, *The Corbaccio*, trans. and ed. Anthony K. Cassell (Urbana: Illinois University Press, 1975), pp. 48–49 and n. 222 on pp. 130–31.

[6] "Archewyves" (E, 1195) may come from Dante's "eresiarche" applied to the Epicureans; Giovanni della Serravalle makes it "ab archos [quod] est princeps

preacher (D, 165), a schoolman (D, 1272), and, like the friars, a perambulator (D, 837). In combining sect and life, she preaches the ideals of the Epicurean sect which advocated the voluptuous life, unlike the other classical philosophic sects which promoted the active or the contemplative lives. In describing the three lives, Macrobius says that some people may choose to live contemplatively, seeking for "heavenly truths," others to devote themselves to family and commonwealth, protecting justice, and others to surrender to sensual pleasure and flout "the laws of gods and men."[7] This choice Fulgentius describes as Paris's choice of Venus, the voluptuous, before Minerva, the contemplative, or Juno, the active.[8] Later Albericus of London made Venus symbolize Epicurean "sectatores" as well as the voluptuous life,[9] and his description of the followers of Epicurus as a sect recurs in John of Salisbury, Dante, Simon of Hesdin, Jacques le Grand, and Nicholas Trivet.[10] Moreover, Paris's choice of his flesh and the voluptuous life is repeated by the dreamers in many late medieval poems such as the *Roman de la*

---

et heresis"; Giovanni della Serravalle, translation of Dante's *Commedia* with commentary, B.M. MS. Egerton 2629, fol. 46ʳ (early fifteenth century, trans. for English ecclesiasts). The pun on archbishop is obvious.

[7] Macrobius, *Commentary on the Dream of Scipio*, pp. 120–21, 244; Olson, *"The Parlement of Foules*: Aristotle's Politics and the Foundations of Human Society," pp. 56–57.

[8] Fulgentius, "Mitologiarum," *Opera*, ed. Rudolph Helm (Leipzig: Trübner, 1898), pp. 36–38. Interpretations of E, 1171, which do not account for the joining of "lyf and al hire secte" include Lillian Hornstein, "The Wyf of Bathe and the Merchant: From Sex to 'Secte,' " *CR* 3 (1968):65–75; William Matthews, "The Wife of Bath and All Her Sect," *Viator* 5 (1974):413–43; John Mahoney, "Alice of Bath: Her 'secte' and 'gentil text,' " *Criticism* 6 (1964):144–55.

[9] Albericus of London, "Mythographus Tertius," *Scriptores Rerum Mythicarum*, ed. G. H. Bode (Cellis, 1834), pp. 228, 241.

[10] Dante, *Inferno* x. 10ff.; Simon of Hesdin, *Valere le Grant* (1489), sig. g4ᵛ; Benvenuto, *Comentum*, 1:332; Jacques le Grand, *Sophologium* (Lyons, 1495), xv; Nicholas Trivet, Commentary on Boethius' *De Consolatione*, B.M. Add. MS. 27,875, fol. 7ᵛ.

Rose or the *Chess of Love* and with more comic consequences than Helen's rape or Troy's fall. Chaucer portrays himself as rejecting Paris's choice in the *Parlement* and rejecting it again, through comedy and irony, in the *Canterbury Tales* in the image of his "Venerien" Wife (D, 609).

The medieval sect of Epicurus constituted a habit of daily life in an increasingly materialistic age—John of Salisbury and Benvenuto call it the most common heresy. Because its appeal was intuitive, it needed no formal philosophers. Its tenets rarely were elaborated save in jest,[11] though the *Chess of Love* gloss tries to describe the intellectual basis of one of its two commonly ascribed tenets, namely that the physical pleasures represent life's chief good:

> Some also follow the voluptuous life in order to live more freely, and to pursue physical delights more according to their will. And there are those who want to argue that all delights are good and praiseworthy and that one should pursue them as much as one can, without qualification. And they prove it by the fact that nature orders nothing for evil, but all for good, as she is directed in her works and in her rules by God and the intelligences, in whom no error can be found, or any malice whatsoever. And that nature has given us a natural desire, called the concupiscible appetite by philosophers, to desire and pursue the delectable things that we see with delight when we can. It seems that this delectation should be a good and laudable thing and that one cannot do wrong in delighting himself. For this and several other reasons some of the ancients maintain and demonstrate that all delectations generally are good and lawful, and thus they wished to conclude that the voluptuous life was good and commendable among the others to the degree in which they wished to place true felicity in it.[12]

---

[11] *Pol.*, 8.24; Benvenuto, *Comentum*, 1:332.

[12] *Chess* gloss, 4:541–42. For the Ciceronian and medieval conception of Epicureanism, cf. Cicero, *De Finibus Bonorum et Malorum* 2.22.70–71; 2.7.21–22; Lactantius, *Divinarum Institutionum*, PL 6:398–405; Boethius, *De Consolatione*

The Epicurean faith in the "intelligences" and in "natural" desires, undirected by any cleric or prince, explains why the Wife attributes so much to the planets.

Dante describes the second common tenet of Epicureanism—that the soul dies with the body—in the heretic's circle of the *Inferno*. There the Epicureans, as the exemplars of all heretics because of their denial of the afterlife, endure eternal tombs. Benvenuto da Imola says that Dante chose this sect to represent all error because it had more followers than any other and its view of the afterlife "destroyed the foundation of faith and all of the good of human life," an analysis similar to that of Bradwardine, who treats Epicureanism as related to Sadducism or Averrosim.[13] Positing physical pleasure as the end of life and denying the spiritual world and the afterlife are complementary positions which may have had a certain popular appeal during the spiritual and social crisis of the fourteenth century.

January's conversion to Epicureanism clarifies how positing physical pleasure as life's chief good and denying the afterlife relate intellectually:

> Somme clerkes [i.e., Epicureans] holden that felicitee
> Stant in delit, and therfore certeyn he,
> This noble Januarie, with al his myght,
> In honest wyse, as longeth to a knyght,
> Shoop hym to lyve ful deliciously.

Philosophiae, bk. 3, pr. 2; Simon of Hesdin, *Valere le Grant*, sig. g4ʳ; Nicholas Trivet, Commentary on Boethius' *De Consolatione*, bk. 3, pr. 2 in B.M. Add. MS., 27, 875, fol. 33ᵛ; Dante, *Inferno* X.10ff.; Benevenuto, *Comentum*, 1:335–36; Raoul de Presles, *Cité de Dieu* (Paris, 1531), 1:sig. q³⁽ʳ⁾–[q³ᵛ]; Antonius Thomas, *De Joannis de Monsterolio* (Paris, 1883), p. 63; Don Cameron Allen, "The Rehabilitation of Epicurus," *SP* 41 (1944):4–5; Mario Fois, *Il Pensiero Cristiano di Lorenzo Vallo nel Quadro Storico-culturale del suo ambiente* (Rome: Libraria Editrice dell'Universita Gregoriana, 1969), pp. 122–23.

¹³ Benvenuto, *Comentum*, 1:332; Thomas Bradwardine, *De Causa Dei Contra Pelagium*, ed. Henry Savile (London, 1618), p. 76.

His housynge, his array, as honestly
To his degree was maked as a kynges.   (E, 2021–27)

January then constructs a garden which offfers a heaven on
earth set over against the true paradise (cf. E, 1647–48) and
which resembles John of Salisbury's Epicurean garden set over
against Wisdom's garden traversed by the four rivers of vir-
tue.[14] It is the garden chosen by the lovers in the *Roman de la Rose*
or the *Chess of Love* gloss. The place allows January to substitute
temporal felicity for the joy of the afterlife (E, 1635–54), his
pleasure garden for the Church's Canticle garden,[15] and to
marry one of Chaucer's numerous variants of the Wife of Bath
instead of Solomonic or Canticle Wisdom (cf. E, 1685–87). Like
the Wife, he concludes his "ful delicious" life in a comic wor-
ship of delight's goods.

Chaucer's wasteland clerics follow the same sect and its two
principles. They explicitly deny the afterworld or implicitly ig-
nore it, and they merchandize forms of penance that give sanc-
tion to hedonism and ignore the meaning of true contemplation
and selfless action. Several of the clerics directly flatter the
Wife. The Pardoner finds her to be a noble preacher who warns
him against "marriage" (D, 164ff.), the scholastic Friar praises
her scholasticism (D, 1270ff.), and the Summoner, who uses lo-
cal "Wives of Bath" for his spies, attacks the Friar for so rudely
interrupting the Wife's "disport" (D, 833ff.). In fact, the Monk,
Chantecleer, the Prioress and the materialistic Canon of the
Canon Yeoman's section are also her sectaries and raise the
question of why Chaucer substitutes the sect of Epicurus for
Wyclif's four sects that confuse the temporal and spiritual
swords. He does so, I think, because he sees this new kind of
"lyf," combined with the commercialization of penance and the

[14] *Pol.*, 8.16.
[15] Ibid.; cf. Olson, "Chaucer's Merchant and January's 'Hevene in Erthe
Heere,' " pp. 206–12.

[241]

erosion of perfection's quest by predestinarianism, as more threatening to his civilization than the jurisdictional issues raised in Wyclif's criticism of the four sects, more central to the immediate abuses criticized by Wyclif and reflected in the clerical tales.

In leading the other clerics the Wife begins with a theological introduction (D, 1–187) that preaches Epicureanism's present pleasure as humankind's final good and treats eternal goods as uncertain. Systematically, she shows how pleasure—sexual delight, wealth, social respect, and the liberty these confer—takes precedence over other things. Insouciant about the heavenly prize set up for virginity (D, 75ff.), she later observes that moths and mites have not affected her treasures laid up on earth (D, 560ff.)[16] and rejoices, "I have had my world . . . in my tyme" (D, 473). She defines virginity in a narrow, literal sense when she cites 1 Cor. 9.23–24. Speaking of its dart (D, 75) or prize, she neglects to mention that the prize is the "incorruptible crown" of immortality, which is offered to those who practice a *variety* of disciplines,[17] not just celibacy. Her interpretation indirectly supports Jovinian, the Epicurus of the Christians, by pretending to distinguish the evangelical counsels from divine commands and solve theological quibbles. She also recalls the *Chess* gloss's Epicureans in arguing that as Nature created nothing in vain, the genitals were made for a purpose (D, 119–50). And she ticks off *luxuria*'s rationalizations from John Bromyard's *Summa Praedicantium*—that God commanded sexual luxury when he told human beings to increase and multiply, that it is natural and required for the conservation of the species, that it overpowers everyone or almost everyone, and that cer-

[16] For clothes, as quickly devoured by pests and inferior to the soul's goods, see Bromyard, *Summa Praedicantium*, 1:108.

[17] For an account of the range of meaning attached to virginity, see John Bugge, *Virginitas: An Essay in the History of a Medieval Ideal* (The Hague: Nijhoff, 1975).

tain complexions or temperaments preclude anything else.[18] Since Epicureans had a reputation for sophistry,[19] Chaucer makes the Wife's introduction offer comical sophistry that goes beyond that described by Bromyard: she misses Christ's meaning when he said that the Samaritan woman's present consort is not her husband (D, 16–20), coarsely alters the spirit of Paul's permission to widows to remarry in God (D, 49–50; 1 Corinthians 7.29), misuses Biblical example to make Job into an exemplum of the husband necessarily patient before the wife (D, 431ff.), and argues that experience tells Nature's created purpose (D, 115–34) as if Venus or libido could not also use experience to teach Nature's abuse.

In speaking for carnality in her theological introduction, the Wife holds the Old Law above the New and muddles with outrageous gusto the latter's command that one dedicate body and spirit to the love and admiration of God and the love and care of neighbor.[20] Her *ordo* (D, 147ff.) requires that the New Law's—i.e., Wisdom's—counsels to perfection through poverty, cleanness, and obedience or humility be replaced by Epicurus' counsels to avarice, luxury, and vainglory as interpreted by Boethius and John of Salisbury.[21] In the Bradshaw order, she tells of her many husbands immediately after the Nun's

[18] John Bromyard, *Summa Praedicantium*, 1:462–62ᵛ. Bromyard's popularity is attested by his numerous manuscripts; J. Th. Welter, *L'Exemplum dans la Littérature Religieuse et didactique du Moyen Age* (Paris: Occitania, 1927), p. 34.

[19] For Epicureans as sophists, see Cicero, *De Finibus*, 1.19.2, 2.9; *De Natura Deorum*, 1.23; *Chess* gloss, 4:538–46.

[20] Cf. Robertson, *Preface to Chaucer*, 317–31; Graham B. Caie, "The Significance of the Early Chaucer Manuscript Glosses (with Special References to the Wife of Bath's Prologue)," *CR* 10 (1976):350–60; Doris Myers, *The "Artes Praedicandi" and Chaucer's Canterbury Tales*, pp. 140–76.

[21] *Boece*, bk. 3, pr. 2; *Pol.*, 7.15. Chaucer uses a series of exempla from *Pol.* 1.5 in the Pard. T., C. 591ff. (cf. Robinson, p. 731); cf. *Pol.*, vol. 1, pp. 36–38 (notes). The *Policraticus* is recommended as standard fare in the education of rulers by Philippe de Mézières; cf. chap. 4 above.

Priest has told his tale of a "recchelees" many-wived convent's loss of wisdom and penance. Whatever the order of the tales, the Wife clearly engages the Nun's Priest's themes of delight and multiplying (B², 4535), joys and sorrows, in Solomon's multiple marriages (D, 35ff.), and woe in marriage caused by "strutting one's stuff." Whereas the Nun's Priest can speak of the convent's marriage to delight or wisdom only through fables and authorities—from the Bible to Bradwardine, including "Launcelot de Lake, / That wommen holde in ful greet reverence" [B², 4402–3]—the Wife can speak of actual marriage from experience (D, 1). She disputes the authorities and tells a tale of Arthur's realm without the Lancelot beloved of women. Germaine Dempster argues that Chaucer canceled the Nun's Priest's epilogue because he decided to have the Wife of Bath break in uninvited after the Priest.[22] If the Nun's Priest speaks of what brought Chant Cleer and Pertelote to become "recchelees" in the *Miroir de Mariage*'s spiritual marriage, then the Wife speaks of what makes for and what eliminates woe in carnal marriage after temptation has become a fall.[23]

The Wife's theological introduction also confutes the gospel counsels to humility, cleanness, and poverty through a systematic "feminine" rhetoric. John of Salisbury's discussion of the Epicurean garden speaks of three of its rivers as desire, avarice, and vainglory—the triad of the Miller's Tale and Melibee—and adds to these three a fourth river, the desire for freedom. He contrasts the Epicureans of his time with the monastic Carthusians and other reformed orders who avoid the attachments of these "rivers" and live according to their rule.[24] In a later age,

---

[22] Germaine Dempster, "A Period in the Development of the *Canterbury Tales*," pp. 1149–50.

[23] Deschamps, *Oeuvres Complètes*, 9:245ff. ("Miroir de Mariage," lines 6717ff.). The "Miroir," one of Chaucer's primary sources for the Merchant's Tale, essentially praises the life of perfection; cf. lines 7532–7884, 8383–8410.

[24] *Pol.*, 7.15–23; 8.16.

St. Thomas, omitting the explicit reference to the Epicureans, makes essentially the same equation in saying that the New Law, which commands perfection or the full love of God and neighbor, also counsels detachment from other, impeding loves. Hence, the evangelical counsels to perfection—to poverty, chastity, and obedience—urge the faithful on the path to complete love through rooting out the incomplete loves which aspire only to possessions, pleasures, and self-aggrandizement—avarice, luxury, and vainglory. He then shows how persons in various conditions may follow these counsels to some degree under the freedom of the New Law as their condition, discipline, and grace permit.[25] St. Thomas's equation reappears in Chaucer's time in Gower when, early in his discussion of the monastic vow, he says that it implies that the proud should live humbly, the wanton chastely, and the seekers after riches as if they were poor (*Vox Clamantis*, bk. 4, lines 405ff.). And in a passage already mentioned, Philippe de Mézières illustrates the flexibility of the perfection to be followed by the Order of the Passion by saying that, since the three "grans pechies" have taken "seignorie" or "maistrie" over Christians, the remedy for pride is obedience and humility in the "sainte chevalerie," for luxury a faithful marriage, and for avarice the fire of charity and poverty of spirit.[26] Programmatically, the members of the Order's "estat de grace et de perfection," after the battle with the Turk and establishment of a Christian kingdom, will obey their sovereigns, practice chastity through respecting the sacrament of marriage and taking their wives with them to the Orient (where the heat of the weather and the stimulation of the crusade would make pure asceticism difficult) so that they can bear children ("multipliee") to increase the faith in the new land.[27]

[25] *Summa Theologica*, 2.2.186a7.
[26] Brown, *Mézières' Order*, p. 95–100.
[27] Ibid., p. 177.

They will possess the conquered lands administered by loyal "marchans et buorgoys" so that no one suffers from a famine or poverty or rebels out of confidence in excessive riches.[28] Uthred of Boldon in his *De Substantialibus regule monachalis* argues that the disciplines of perfection began in Eden, and that all human beings are bound to practice the perfection of poverty, cleanness, and humility appropriate to their role in society. He elaborates this argument in his *De perfectione vivendi in religione*.[29] Again, the popular *Abbey of the Holy Ghost* also extends this view of the pursuit of perfection to the laity.[30] In short, Chaucer's period had conceptualized an extension of perfection's pursuit to all social orders. It is this movement that the Wife counters in her first one hundred and eighty lines.

The central metaphor of these lines is the Samaritan woman's well and her five marriages. Jean Leclercq has shown that marriage, in the image of Christ's love of the Church or the Canticle Bridegroom's of the Bride, represents the usual metaphor for perfection's quest, the completion of the human person in a divine one.[31] "Woe in marriage" represents imperfection or disunity, the disunity of the Samaritan woman before she meets Christ, the Synagogue before the coming of the New Law. However, the Samaritan hears Christ and becomes a preacher, characteristically a theme of the *Bible Moralisée* illumination (fig. 45). Recalling the Biblical contrast between the Samaritan's water and Christ's water of wisdom, the Wife mentions both

[28] Ibid., p. 179.

[29] Pantin, "Two Treatises of Uthred of Boldon on the Monastic Life," pp. 363–85.

[30] This fourteenth-century book addresses those who would like to be in "relygyon" but may not, for one or another reason, be in bodily religion, yet can pursue "ghostly relygyon"; *Abbaye of the Holy Ghost* (Westminster, 1496), sig. a3r–a4v. For the three temptations and this pursuit of perfection, see sig. c2v–c3r.

[31] Leclercq, *Monks and Love in Twelfth Century France*, pp. 27–61.

that Jesus reproved the Samaritan "Biside a welle (D, 15) and that He is "of perfeccion . . . welle" (D, 107; cf. John 4.7–26). In urging folk to obedience or "folw[ing] hym," she observes that Christ's counsel to virginity was not absolute (D, 107ff.) and His counsel to poverty which prescribes selling all and giving the proceeds to the poor was not expected of everyone (D, 109). Rather He reserved such high demands for those virgins who sought to live perfectly—that is, contemplatives. In short, the Wife recognizes only one monastic order of perfection in love, and it does not apply to her. Though her extremely narrow idea of perfection had been rejected even by the ascetic Uthred, she continues the Samaritan metaphor of "bath" and "well," taken from her Biblical source, when she says that she will offer the Pardoner another "tonne" (D, 170) tasting worse than ale and, at the end, describes her surrogate, her tale's old hag, giving her knight a "bath of blisse" (D, 1253). The Wife's "well" or "bath" happily requires that one thirst again and again for *quoniam*, wealth, or "maistrie," depending on one's role and proclivities. Somewhat deaf (A, 446; D, 795), "grotesque" of ear like the original Midas who got his ass's ears from insensitivity to Apollo's music and a preference for Pan's,[32] she appears to reject only extreme asceticism. Actually she rejects all perfective counsel on the grounds that it was given by a Christ-Wisdom whom she cannot precisely understand (D, 20). She will not "lyve parfitly" (D, 111–12).

If the theologial introduction (D, 1–187) sets down the Wife's principles as well as those of the Franklin and the Merchant, the remainder of the Wife's prologue recounting her experience with her five husbands, and her tale set down the practice or discipline of her sect, followed faithfully by the Franklin, the

---

[32] See D. T. Myers, The *"Artes Praedicandi" and Chaucer's Canterbury Preachers*, pp. 175–76. Cf. D. W. Robertson, Jr., "The Wife of Bath and Midas," *SAC* 6 (1984):1–20.

CHAPTER 9

Merchant, and her clerics. Alysoun of Oxford has three lovers figuring the love of avarice, luxury, and vainglory, and Alysoun of Bath has three types of husbands—three rich old ones, a young lecher, and an upstart clerk. These attempt in turn to satisfy the Wife by providing her with material wealth, sexual bliss, and the satisfaction of marrying a clerk—wealth, pleasure, and pride. The most interesting of the group is the fifth husband, the clerk. After Alysoun has eased perfection out in her theological introduction (D, 1–192), she proceeds to ignore the counsel to poverty followed by Chaucer's Church-as-widow figures through gaining the wealth and lands of her three rich old husbands (D, 197ff.), the counsel to chastity through her marriage to and betrayal of her lecherous fourth husband (D, 453, 563ff.), and the counsel to obedience through assuming comic sovereignty over her fifth clerk husband. What disturbs the Wife most about her fifth husband is that he laughs at her as if she were comic. He reads "for his desport" (D, 670) about wicked wives in the book "cleped . . . Valerie and Theofraste" (D, 671), and "lough alwey ful faste" (D, 672) at Jerome's *Against Jovinian*, Ovid's *Art of Love*, Walter Map's *Valerius Ad Rufinum*, and related works not widely regarded as hilarious today. Young "joly clerk, Jankyn" enjoys these works though the Wife says that old impotent clerks—Jerome? Ovid?—wrote these "anti-feminist" treatises accusing women of incapacity to remain faithful in their marriages only after they could no longer do an "olde sho['s]" worth of Venus' work (D, 706ff.). Jankyn enjoys them, not because he is impotent but because they give him power over the Wife. The *Adversus Jovinianum* and the *Valerius Ad Rufinum* describe precisely the behavior that the Wife indulges in and then attributes to the husband's projection. But the "Valerie" with its standard commentary is kinder to women than Chaucer's Wife, for it says that it intends no attack against actual women, who may, like men, be saints

[248]

THE SECT OF THE WIFE OF BATH

or sinners. Its *woman* represents the flesh, its *man* the reason.[33] While the clerk husband laughs at the tales of Delilah, Dianira, Xantippe, and the rest in these books (D, 721ff.), he does not learn anything new to laugh at about the violence and lust of Alysoun of Bath, for he knew it all before he married her (D, 503–626). He can only laugh at the comic self-delusion of the flesh, especially his own. As a clerk, he is, as the Wife recognizes, a child of Mercury who loves Widsom (D, 699). Reason's comedies, wisdom's battles in the works he reads, deliver him from his wife until pride has its way and she burns his book and takes his bridle to ride him like Phyllis astride Clerk Aristotle (D, 813). As in Dunbar's *Twa Mariit Women and the Wedo* or many *Gesta Romanorum* stories, the three marriages become unions in which luxury, pride, and avarice destroy any movement to perfected love, replacing it with "preambulacioun" (D, 837) and "wandrynge by the weye" (A, 467).[34]

---

[33] Ruth J. Dean, "Unnoticed Commentaries on the *Dissuasio Valerii* of Walter Map," *Medieval and Renaissance Studies* 2 (1950):135–37; Trivet, Commentary on *Dissuasio Valerii*, Bod. Add. MS. A. 44, fol. 17. For Jerome's *Adversus Jovinianum* not intending blame to marriage or good women, see Jacques le Grand, *The Book of Good Manners* (London, 1494), sig.[e4ʳ] ff.; Simon of Hesdin, *Valere le Grant*, sig. [g4ᵛ]; Antoine de la Salle, "La Sale," *Du Reconfort*, ed. Joseph Neve (Brussels, 1881), pp. 80–81; A. Coville, *Recherches Sur Quelques Écrivains* (Paris: E. Droz, 1935), pp. 159–60. Cf. Pierre Col's remarks on La Jaloux's unreasonable "anti-feminism" in *The Epistles on the Romance of the Rose and other documents in the debate*, trans. Charles F. Ward (Chicago: Chicago University Press, 1911), pp. 65–68. Lee Patterson's useful analysis of the Wife's dilation also endeavors to define the "medieval idea of the feminine" without looking at these conventional glosses and rhetorical interpretations of the sorts of sources on which Chaucer draws ("For the Wyves love of Bathe: Feminine Rhetoric and Poetic Resolution in the *Roman de la Rose* and the *Canterbury Tales*," *Speculum* 58 [1983]:656–95).

[34] Olson, "Vaughan's *The World*: The Pattern of Meaning and the Tradition," p. 31. Cf. *Gesta Romanorum*, ed. Hermann Oesterly (Berlin, 1872), pp. 322, 331, 392 (paired with evangelical counsels), 632.

CHAPTER 9

The Wife's tale explores the role of fantasy in the surrender to the three enemies and the creation of the "freedom" of John of Salisbury's fourth. In commenting on the Wife of Bath's Tale, Brathwait calls it an old wives' tale and speaks of the Wife's gaining sovereignty through her use of private opinion, apostolic doctrine (to her own gloss), and "Fabulous Tradition."[35] Actually the old Wife's tale is nothing but an "old wives' " Arthurian fable. The Wife of Bath is an old woman full of astrological superstitions like the Old Superstitious of whom Philippe de Mézières writes in the *Songe*,[36] and she tells a tale about an "olde wyf" (D, 1046) set in an Arthurian world full of superstitions. It is against her kind of fable, which forsakes "soothfastnesse," that the Parson warns the pilgrims, quoting the passage from 1 Timothy 4.7 where Paul enjoins Timothy against heeding "ineptas . . . et aniles fabulas," translated as "vncouenable fablis, and elde wymmens fablis" in the Wycliffite Bible. The Parson calls them "fables and wrecchednesse" (I, 34) and says that he refuses to sell bran (I, 35), what the Wife says that she must sell now that her flour is gone (D, 477ff.). Her old wives' tale—according to the exegetes, oral tradition handed down—concerns an old wife, supposedly a witch or hag,[37] who mirrors herself. Robert Haller has identified the hag of the tale with the elf queen who dances with her company at D, 860, and, therefore, with Proserpina as the queen of the fairies in the Merchant's Tale and one aspect of the triple-aspected Diana-Lucina-Proserpina of the Knight's Tale (A, 2075ff.,

[35] Brathwait, *Comments*, p. 39.
[36] Philippe de Mézières, *Songe du Vieil Pèlerin*, 1:595–597.
[37] Cf. *The New Testament in English*, trans. John Wyclif and John Purvey, ed. Josiah Forshall and Frederic Madden (Oxford, 1879), p. 418. "Anilas fabulas" Augustine interprets as "traditiones suas, quas non scriptas, habent, sed memoriter tenent, et alter in alterum loquendo transfundit" in his *Contra Adversarium Legis et Prophetarum*, PL 42:637. Sarah Disbrow first discovered this and has an article forthcoming in *SAC*.

[250]

2296ff.).[38] The *Chess of Love* gloss makes Diana surrounded with nymphs (or in French, *fees*, "fairies") represent the natural powers of her various realms so that she, presumably in her Lucina aspect, influences human generation.[39] The *Songe de Vergier*'s clerk adds that old women describe rides on beasts with Diana when they have power of instant travel and metamorphosis. The knight in the same work ascribes such phenomena to superstitions and false belief caused by the devil's illusions when he comes as an angel of light.[40] The Wife further accepts the notion of incubi (D, 880), creatures whom Raoul de Presles associates with the fallen angels, who "came in to the daughters of men" and bore the mighty men of old who became giants of pride, and with the "Spirits called fairies who appear in cattle sheds and trees."[41] That all of this supernatural machinery is "old wives' " flimflammery is relatively obvious. Even the Wife knows that, as regards her own time, she is telling an old wives' tale for she avers that the *freres* have driven out the *fayeres* (italics mine) in their preambulations and become the new incubi doing "dishonour" to women (D, 860–81).

What then is the function of the tale in her eyes? To show how she can "enchant" her next lover with the enchantments she attributes to her fifth husband (D, 575)? To suggest that she is the new succubus to anyone who will submit to her? To say that those who do can have both Carnival and Lent, both the Epicurean bath of bliss and the bliss of perfected love for Wis-

[38] Robert Haller, "The Wife of Bath and the Three Estates," *Annuale Mediaevale* 6 (1965):58.

[39] *Chess* gloss, 3:380–83. Cf. the descriptions of Diana-Proserpina in the Knight's Tale at A, 2051–88 and A, 2297–2330.

[40] *Le Songe de Vergier*, 1:241. Jean Le Fevre's translation and explanation of the *De Vetula* says concerning its hag that "l'entencion et la final cause est que par l'exemple de lui, il entend a nous retraire et rappeller de fole amour et illicite"; Jean Le Fevre, *La Vieille*, ed. Hippolite Cocheris (Paris, 1861), p. 9.

[41] Raoul de Presles, *Cité de Dieu* (Paris, 1531), 2:sig. kk6r.

dom? At least the surface of the tale so speaks. As Robert Miller and Bernard Levy have demonstrated, the miracle of the old hag and Saint Venus at its end resembles the miracle of the *Commedia*'s Siren who transforms herself through the power of lust until Virgil intervenes, and this miracle is repeated by Chaucer in different forms at the end of the Merchant's and the Franklin's narratives.[42]

However, the Wife of Bath's tale provides its own antidote through its appeal to Arthurian tradition; that is, not to popular romance tradition such as the Thopas parodies but to "theological" romance such as the Cistercians prompted. Such Arthurian romance includes characters who theologize, philosophize, and explain the higher meaning of what has happened—as the old wife of the Wife's Tale does in her final sermon (D, 1106ff.). Even as the irony and comedy of the prologue is elucidated in its upside-down appeal to exegesis, perfection theology, and "Valerie," the irony of the tale is elucidated through its inversion of the "theological" Arthurian tradition. The Wife may intend to appeal to such deliciousness in literature as the Thopas parodies or as the Nun's Priest's "women" must enjoy when they read the *Lancelot*. But she does more.

"Theological" Arthurian stories often tell of a challenge presented to Arthur and taken up by one of his knights. The knight ventures forth, whereupon he encounters fabulous experiences and old hermits who explain the iconological meaning of these experiences to prepare him to meet his challenge. He either succeeds or does not succeed, depending on how he takes the advice, and carries back to Arthur's court the token of his success or failure. Often, as in the *Queste del Saint Graal* and the *Estoire*

---

[42] Robert P. Miller, "The *Wife of Bath's Tale* and Medieval Exempla," *ELH* 32 (1965):442–56; Bernard S. Levy, "Chaucer's Wife of Bath, the Loathly Lady and Dante's Siren," *Symposium* 19 (1965):359–73, and "The Wife of Bath's *Queynte Fantasye*," *CR* 4 (1970):106–22.

del Saint Graal, the meaning has to do with a Cistercian perfection theology for knights. In *La Queste del Saint Graal*, Perceval—in a scene that anticipates the first book of the *Faerie Queene*—meets a lion and serpent fighting, and assists the former against the latter. He then has a vision of an old woman, reminiscent of Alysoun's old wife, mounted on a serpent, and of a younger one, mounted on a lion. The younger requests his protection and the older reproaches him for killing the serpent. Awakening, he meets a priest who explains that the woman "vielle & anchiene" whom he has met is the Old Law and her serpent, the word of God badly understood and explained, which "spoke" to Eve and created a train of later intellectual errors derived from misreading scripture.[43] Later in the work Perceval again encounters the same serpent in the form of a beautiful lady like the beautiful woman promised at the end of our tale (D, 1223) who captivates him in the pavilion of the World but declines his advances unless he will submit to her commands. When Perceval makes the sign of the cross, she vanishes, leaving a foul-smelling cloud.[44] In the next episode, the hermit reminds Lancelot that he once possessed the virtues necessary to escape from the world to perfection—humility, chastity, charitableness: *Lors estoit li feus dou Saint Esperit chauz et ardanz en toi* ("then was the fire of the Holy Spirit warm and fervent in you").[45] However, the devil has used Guinevere to transform him so that he does not see the grail and its wedding feast. The grail quest in this work is the quest for purgation from the enemies of man, which in turn leads to the vision of God associated with the grail. In the light of these subtexts from glossed romances available to Richard's court, Alysoun, who in her prologue has explained scripture badly, now tells of

[43] *La Queste du Saint Graal*, ed. Albert Pauphilet (Paris: Librairie Ancienne Honoré Champion, 1923), pp. 94–103.

[44] Ibid., pp. 104–15.

[45] Ibid., p. 125.

a knight who encounters an old woman—the Old Law or Epicureanism again. She, like the serpent woman in the *Queste*, becomes beautiful as she tempts; the knight, unlike Perceval, submits to her, and because he makes no effort to solve her conundrum—attempts no "sign of the cross"—she does not vanish.

The whole tale preposterously inverts Camelot: a knight rapes a "mayde" (D, 888), receives the death penalty, and is saved by Queen Guinevere's suit, whereupon Arthur surrenders his royal responsibility to her. Thereupon Guinevere and the ladies of the court ask him to go on a quest that is neither a physical nor a moral challenge. He is to discover what women most desire, hardly a fitting topic for a character who cared little what the woman desired when he committed his crime. But figuratively, "woman" means the carnal side of human nature, the appetites, both in the Wife's contrasting of "clerks" and "women" (D, 697–706) and in standard commentary on the "Valerie." The appetites seize this or that, but what do they really want? The knight predictably finds that "women" love the Wife's three "husbands," Alysoun of Oxford's three "lovers": riches, honor, and jollyness (D, 925–26); in an alternative formulation of avarice, vainglory, and luxury, they love rich array, to be widowed and wed often, and "lust abedde" (D, 927–29). In yet another formulation of the three, they love to be flattered (D, 930–34); they want the luxury to be allowed "oure vice" (D, 937) without reproof and told that they are "wise" in it (D, 938); and they want to be held stable and trusted with such secrets as were given the wife of Midas, prince of avarice and lover of Pan's music. Since these three are, as 1 John 2.16 puts it, what is in the world, it is not surprising that a rapist hears that they are what women want.[46]

[46] Cf. chap. 4, and Olson, "Vaughan's *The World*: The Pattern of Meaning and the Tradition," pp. 26–32.

But they want more. The twenty-four dancing women, suggesting Diana's attendants in the Wife's conceit but the allurements of the flesh in Chaucer's, disappear as the knight nears the end of his somewhat desperate search. Then only an old wife is left who whispers her "pistel" in his ear, wisdom enough to answer Queen Guinevere.[47] John of Salisbury whom Chaucer quotes in the Pardoner's Tale (C, 591ff.) says that the fourth Epicurean river, flowing in same direction as the three temptations, seeks personal power, autonomous freedom, and primacy (cf. A, 449ff.). Actually, its efforts to forestall the disturbance of its dream culminate in a vulnerable, enslaved tyranny.[48] Whether Chaucer had this *Policraticus* passage in mind in writing the answer that the old woman whispers to the knight is irrelevant. The perception is a common-sense one. The Wife is a tyrant. She and her hag counterpart are sure that women want "maistrie" or "sovereynetee" (D, 1037).

The process of getting the freedom the woman wants requires that the knight again choose between the Epicurean goods and perfection—a beautiful, unfaithful wife or an ugly, faithful one, with the Vulgate symbolism reversed. When the old wife demands her marriage reward, the rapist offers only a tautology: "Taak al my good, and lat my body go" (D, 1061). Since his body has been his good, his distinction is impossible—the proper plea of a woman being raped but not of a rapist. The wife refuses the offer and calls attention to the marriage debt; she taunts the "lawe of kyng Arthures hous" (D, 1089) that apparently makes knights thus skittish and complains of her particular knight's "dangerousness" on his first night, immediately after her completion of his salvation (D, 1090–92). The

[47] Robertson has called my attention to Boccaccio's gloss on the dancing ladies in the gloss on the house of Venus in the *Teseida* as stimulations to the lustful; Giovanni Boccaccio, *Teseida delle Nozze Emilia*, ed. A. Roncaglia (Bari: Laterza, 1941), p. 418.

[48] *Pol.*, 8.16.

knight responds with a grandiloquent complaint against her low birth, loathliness (indicating poverty), and old age or ugliness. To this, she replies, with Dante's and Boethius' argument, that gentility does not mean arrogance of possessions or blood but humble dependence on God (D, 1125–49), poverty may be Christ's voluntary poverty which leads to sapience (D, 1177ff., 1197), and ugliness may be a guarantor of chastity. In short, she implies that she personifies the evangelical counsels to humility and dependence on God, poverty, and chastity, and will be "a trewe, humble wyf" (D, 1221). Still resisted, she offers to "fulfille" the knight's "worldly appetit" (D, 1218) by being either foul (i.e., poor), old (i.e., chaste), and "trewe" (D, 1220–21), or young, fair, and possibly unfaithful. Here youth implies license, fairness means imperial appearance (D, 1245–48), and unfaithfulness carries with it jealous cuckoldry. Thus, the knight is asked whether his worldly appetite will be satisfied by obedience to the three evangelical counsels or by marriage to the luxury, vainglory, and avarice that Miller displays and Philippe de Mézières savages. "Worldly appetite" cannot choose between perfection and Epicurus. When the knight has a choice between the two gardens and their rivers put to him so baldly, his appetite gives the choice to the wife, who adds John of Salisbury's fourth river—mastery or tyranny. After his submission, she promises to embody Eden *and* the Epicurean garden and to create a second sight that is an inversion of St. Cecilia's: "I wol be *to yow* bothe" (D, 1240, emphasis mine). In Arthur's fairyland, one can have both Eden and the Epicurean garden, follow both Widow Holy Church and the Synagogue (or Saint Venus), and obey both the evangelical counsels and the three enemies simultaneously—but only there. Only in fairyland can one choose the latter in each of the pairs and declare it the former—like Humpty Dumpty defining glory.

Epicurean tyranny can construct its own definition of society, the good, and perfection. Though the Wife is old, and in spirit like the Synagogue or the allegorical hag of romance, the Church's materialists, as members of her sect rather than of Wyclif's four sects, substitute a fantasy of salvation through her as a young and fair bride for dependence on the old woman who is her opposite, the Widow Church. Hence the Friar's summoner's widow is not seen for what she is, the Summoner's friar's Pentecost offers only material flatulence, the Pardoner remains an unpardoned old man, not a chaste eunuch "for the kingdom of heaven's sake," and the Monk can only see how temporal fortune turns. The iterative connection of these figures to Epicurus, to the Synagogue, makes them a sect of Epicurus both more comic and more pervasively a threat to medieval civilization than Wyclif's four sects.

*　*　*

The tales of the lay figures connected to the Wife, the Merchant and the Franklin, expand on the significance of the Wife's commercial culture and her promise of an Epicurean garden for the laity after the Clerk has stipulated how love relates to perfection and how the imagination ought to operate in relation to God. Perhaps because the Clerk's story was regarded as history and therefore expected to be exemplary and not allegorical in content, he attaches to it a statement of the similitude that he wishes it to illustrate:

> For, sith a womman was so pacient
> Unto a mortal man, wel moore us oghte
> Receyven al in gree that God us sent. (E, 1149–51)

As a master of logic, Aristotle, and philosophy (which I take to mean the love of Wisdom, not simply the technical discipline), the Clerk could answer the Wife, schoolmaster for schoolmaster and dialectic device for dialectic device; but since, as Prudence knows, in the mind's journey to God, patience leads to perfection, he rather tells a simple tale culminating in the similitude quoted, which underlines the serious implications of the Wife's tale. He begins by reminding his audience that Italy's greatest clerks, Linian and Petrarch, are dead and that what he tells was left by one of them—thereby making the face of death set the limits to Epicureanism. He then sets Griselda's story where the Wife's ought to be located and where the Samaritan woman's is iconologically placed—at a well. Walter, as a ruler, finds Griselda at the well preparing to fetch water as Christ finds the Wife's model. She dwells with "povre folk" (E, 200), no "likerous lust" (E, 214) runs through her heart, and she assists her father with "everich obeisaunce and diligence" (E, 230)—thereby fulfilling the evangelical counsels in a lay role. Since the quest for perfection depends upon grace, the Clerk is accurate when he says that God sometimes sends His "grace into a litel oxes stalle" (D, 207), given the echoes of the incarnation of Wisdom and medieval pictures of the nativity in that phrase.

After Walter marries Griselda, he tests her poverty, obedience, and chastity in turn. He puts away their daughter first, reminding Griselda of the "povere array" (E, 467) and "povre estaat" (E, 473) from which he chose her and that peace with his people requires his action; Griselda responds "with hertely obeisaunce" (E, 502) that nothing that Walter likes could displease her since she desires to have nothing and dreads to lose nothing, save him. He then puts away the son and says that the people fear having the blood of Janicula as their lord—he acts like the Wife's knight rejecting the hag for her low birth—and Griselda says, "Naught greveth me at al . . . At youre comandement" (E, 647–49) and further avers that she left her "wyl and al [her] libertee" (E, 656) when she married him and would have obeyed his will prior to his expressing it had she known it (E, 659ff.). Finally, he puts Griselda herself away and threatens to substitute another wife, and she, recalling her poverty (E, 816) and obedience to Walter's lordship (E, 820–26), further adds that she will remain a "wydwe clene in body, herte, and al" since she has given Walter her maidenhead (E, 836). The tests are incremental: poverty first, then poverty and obedience, and finally all three. She reminds us again of the principles of obedience, poverty, and chastity in her final speech to Walter before leaving his house where she says she brought to him "feith (obedience), and nakednesse (poverty), and maydenhede (chastity)" and like Job she came naked out of her father's house to return there naked again (E, 866ff.). In short, Walter tests not only love and patience but obedience to the counsels, and Griselda has only the imagination of love to keep her alive during her dark night. Walter's similitude emphasizes the principles of poverty, cleanness, and humility stated indirectly in the Wife's comedy, but even more, with an austere and strange beauty, dramatizes that these acquire their meaning from love and the detachment that such love requires:

> For wiste I that my deeth wolde do yow ese,
> Right gladly wolde I dyen, yow to plese. (E, 664–65)

The Clerk refers his Job story to the epistle of James (E, 1149–55):

> Blessed is the man that endureth temptation: for when he hath been proved, he shall receive the crown of life, which God hath promised to them that love him. Let no man, when he is tempted, say that he is tempted by God: for God is not a tempter of evils, and he tempteth no man. But every man is tempted by his own concupiscence, being drawn away and allured.
> (James 1.12–15)

No one should mistake Walter for God, or Griselda for perfected humankind for that matter. The similitude is in the relationship. St. Augustine, in treating of the figural implications of the Bible, indicates that what is an unattractive earthly situation may figure an attractive spiritual one and vice versa, so that God may be treated as like a jealous husband by way of similitude: God *righteously* jealous for the virtue of his wife, the soul; the husband *foolishly* jealous to possess the body of his wife.[49] A similar principle operates when Chaucer indicates that Walter is to Griselda as God is to "us" (E, 1142–62). Though Griselda's humility does not provide a model for proper wifely relations to husbands—such would be unbearable ("inportable")—it does show how human beings should accept God's tests in the form of temporal suffering, imaging and expecting a crown of life to emerge from them. Hence the Clerk launches into his bitter envoy to the Wife of Bath and her sect whose wandering makes the divine equivalent of their Walter "care, and wepe, and wrynge, and waille" (E, 1212).

* * *

The Merchant's and the Franklin's tales continue the battle of Carnival and Lent instituted by the Wife and the Clerk and once more treat the function of fantasy in creating a material world beyond tragedy. The Merchant, cuckolded by his commercial transactions, pushed into usury and its euphemistic substitutes, and still in debt, has also been deceived by his "marriage." When he hears the Clerk ironically encouraging the Wife's sect to let whatever husbands they have "care, and wepe, and wrynge, and waille" (E, 1212), he sees himself abused by the Wife's followers and makes the Clerk's last line the basis of his first (E, 1213). As if to avoid further description of his hurt he turns to January's commercial marriage in Pavia, the misery and illusion in it.[50] As I have earlier argued, the Merchant's malice against January derives from historical malice against

---

[49] St. Augustine, "Contra Adimantum," *PL* 42:138–42. The Walter-Griselda story resembles the history of Solomon and the Pharaoh's daughter which William of St. Thierry posits as the argument of the Canticle; see Minnis, *Medieval Theory of Authorship*, p. 48.

[50] Olson, "The Merchant's Lombard Knight," pp. 259–63. Cf. Bernard S. Levy, "*Gentilesse* in Chaucer's *Clerk's* and *Merchant's Tales*," *CR* 11 (1977):306–18.

Italian merchants active in the English wool market and banking, going back to before the bankruptcy of the Bari and Peruzzi in the first half of the century and culminating in the murder of Janus Imperiale. January, double-faced like his calendric counterpart, fears that his marriage's Epicurean perfection ("parfit felicitee," E, 1642) may interfere with his achieving eternal perfection since no person may have "parfite blisses two" (E, 1638), but Justinus reminds him that a Wife may be a purgatory to lead one to grace (E, 1665–70), that a "proper" marriage will not provide such felicity, that no one loses his salvation if he uses it properly, and, finally, that the Wife has made clear that the Epicurean marriage's perfection requires self-deception. The Merchant, attempting to outdo the Clerk, places his story in Pavia near the Clerk's Saluzzo, names his main character January after Griselda's father, Janicula, and has him, like Walter, marry a simple girl. Ignoring the meaning of the Clerk's story, he shows that such marriages as Walter's end as any educated medieval person would expect them to—with the goods getting away, this time in a pear tree which, at least in French poetry, stood for the phallus.[51] Ignoring what the Clerk has meant in speaking of spiritual marriage, he confirms it through his upside-down Canticle.

The whole story begins and ends in the imagination. The construction of a full Epicurean good requires an elaborate process beginning first with January's imagination seeking its own icons and finding May through engaging in high fantasy and curious "bisynesse," going to bed, and parading the local beauties through his mind's "commune market-place" until he condescends "on" one of them (E, 1577–1606). The Pygmalion of found art, he looks for and finds in the external world his imagination's living likeness with whom he celebrates an epic

---

[51] Thibaut, *Li Romanz de la Poire*, pp. 45–47; cf. the "Lidia," lines 510ff. and n. 2 (1:245) in Cohen, *La "Comédie" Latine en France au XIIe siècle*.

marriage including more ceremony and machinery than in the Knight's Tale and outdoing even the clerkish marriages of Mercury and Philology, eloquence and wisdom.[52] Since his marriage requires heroic stimulation to consume its marketplace good, January resorts to the wine and honey of the *De Coitu* and works all night with "houndfyssh" bristled kisses to achieve his "perfection":

> "Ther nys no werkman, whatsoevere he be,
> That may bothe werke wel and hastily;
> This wol be doon at leyser parfitly."   (E, 1832–34)

Failing at his secular efforts, January now tries in a religious way to possess May tyrannically and exclusively by building a grand Epicurean garden (E, 2021–41). This garden both imitates the Canticle garden of the Church and provides a place for the epic's divine councils to meet. In this merchant's paradise, the god of avarice in the form of Pluto appears, and abundance in the form of Proserpina and her "fayerye" come to dance like the hag and her attendants in the Wife of Bath's tale.[53] In the enclosed garden, January is able to pay his marriage debt to his wife and find pleasure not available "abedde" (E, 2051–52). In true merchant-financier manner, he keeps the key to its little gate. But becoming blind and covetous or "jealous,"[54] he so isolates himself as the god of his *hortus conclusus* that May becomes his Canticle church—his dove with "columbyn" eyes, white spouse, woman of the "gardyn . . . enclosed" (E, 2138–48). A personal appropriation of the imagery of the Canticle is not unheard of in Chaucer's period. One of the illustrations in the

[52] For Pygmalion, see Fleming, *The Roman de la Rose: A Study in Allegory and Iconology*, pp. 328–38.

[53] Olson, "Chaucer's Merchant and January's 'Hevene in Erthe Heere,' " pp. 208–13.

[54] Cf. Gower's *Confessio Amantis*, bk. 5, lines 595–610, and Olson, "Chaucer's Merchant and January's 'Hevene in Erthe Heere,' " p. 206, n. 4.

Duke of Berry's translation of the *Historia Scholastica* makes what appears to be a parallel claim by having the spouse of the Canticle wear Berry's swan insignia. But the intention is quite the opposite. Berry becomes part of the bride or Church, through his insignia (fig. 44), and remains subordinate to the bridegroom, or Christ, as the Church's gesture in the picture illustrates. In contrast, January becomes the bridegroom in his garden, the god who creates his own paradise and manufactures his final good. Unlike young Solomon who sang the Canticle, but like the old Solomon described by Proserpina, he follows the three temptations, beginning as luxurious lecher in creating May, then becoming the avaricious *jaloux* in his Pluto-garden and finally the prideful idolater as his own god singing to his own new church: "in his elde he verray God forsook" (E, 2299).[55] As the Wife's old wife can only by illusion be both Carnival and Lent, Synagogue and Church, so the May who cuckolds January and takes his goods can be both his chick and church only by an act of the imagination. His garden's destruction creates in him no sense of guilt or isolation from God. When he loses his good, Proserpina, the goddess of abundance, gives May a ready answer to provide January with eyes, which, however open, do not see. Serpent Damyan (E, 1786) reflects only the trivial evil of his "culture" and his phallic pear tree will never test obedience or poverty or chastity.

When the sponsoring gods debate Solomon's remark that he found one good man but no good women among a thousand, they do not recognize that Solomon's intent was, as Prudence has it, to define how all *creatures* lack the "perfeccioun of God" (B², 2265–70). The Solomon "fulfild of sapience" (E, 2243) who recognized perfection and built the temple, "Goddes hous" (E, 2293), and the one who made a "temple of false goodis" (E, 2295)

---

[55] For the various medieval Solomons, see Leclercq, *Monks and Love in Twelfth Century France*, pp. 27–29.

should not be conflated as Chauntecleer's life illustrates. When January, like Chauntecleer, sings the songs of the Canticle but does so in delight's garden, he does not notice his own winking but winks to recover the happy, happy world in which he and his mate remain forever dancing and forever young:

> This Januarie, who is glad but he?
> He kisseth hire, and clippeth hire ful ofte,
> And on hire wombe he stroketh hire ful softe,
> And to his palays hoom he hath hire lad.   (E, 2412–15)

Cuckolded and double-faced, January at the end knows through imagination once more the perfection of a "hevene in erthe heere" (E, 1647) which reverses that of the garden chosen by Franc Voloir in Chaucer's source poem—a heaven for those who choose suffering, containing the fountain of compunction flowing in the valley of humility with its lily of chastity and rose of martyrdom.[56]

*   *   *

Through a discipline of social imagination, Chaucer's Franklin finds John of Salisbury's fourth river of Epicurean freedom, apparently without the tyranny that accompanies it in the Wife's and Merchant's tales. Bearing the *franc* of freedom in his title, he is well placed to speak of freedom. The equivalent of a *libertinus* or *franchilanus*, he is by definition a villager holding a larger area of land than would most peasants, perhaps 30 to 60 acres, in free tenure and socage for swearing fealty and payment of specified rents for life or for his life and the lives of his heirs.[57]

---

[56] Deschamps, "Miroir de Mariage," lines 6119ff.; 7202–7215 in *Oeuvres Complètes*, 9:200, 234–35.

[57] For the franklin as *libertinus*, Galfridus Anglicus, *Promptorium Parvulorum*, ed. A. L. Mayhew, EETS, e.s. 102 (London: Trübner, 1908), col. 173. For the legal definition of a *libertinus* as a person manumitted from bondage, see Bracton, *On the Laws and Customs of England*, 2:31. For discussions of the franklin in

His land held in free tenure in *fee tail* would not revert until his male heirs ran out, in *fee simple* until all lineal and collateral heirs had died out. Thus he is freer of his lord's immediate commands than a villein,[58] since, according to Bracton, land held in free tenure cannot be subjected to the immediate will of the lord in charging labor or rental services. Franklins as freedmen also had status before the king's courts—before the assize of novel disseisin where they could resist irregular distraint by their lord or others, before the Justices of the Peace where they might serve as justices or plaintiffs, and before the Hundreds where they owed suit.[59] They might bring suit at the manor hallmote but their complaints against other freedmen, unless settled easily, would normally be carried over to the royal courts. After *Quia Emptores*, they could alienate parts of their holdings by substitution, though not by subinfeudation, and might have several servants or villeins under them. They were generally under the supervision of the lords and their stewards, though not a day-to-day basis, and still owed their lords fealty, rents, and occasional duties such as overseeing the harvest. They could be distrained for wasting woodland or abusing farmland held from the lord, or could be asked to represent their villages to the Hundred Court, the Justices of the Peace, or Parliament. Though less obviously under the dominion of their lords than

the medieval village, see Robertson, *Essays in Medieval Culture*, pp. 274-79, and George Caspar Homans, *English Villagers of the Thirteenth Century* (Cambridge, Mass.: Harvard University Press, 1941), pp. 248–50. Since the franklin held all or part of his land in free tenure, the laws governing free tenure generally define his role. For an alternative view of the franklin which emphasizes franklin gentility, see Henrik Specht, *Chaucer's Franklin in the "Canterbury Tales": The Social and Literary Background of a Chaucerian Character* (Copenhagen: Akademisk Forlag, 1981), but see also the review of the book by George D. Gopen, *JEGP* 82 (1983):436–39.

[58] Bracton, *On the Laws and Customs of England*, 3:126–33.

[59] Aside from Chaucer's portrait, see Homans, *English Villagers*, pp. 249–50; Robertson, *Essays in Medieval Culture*, pp. 275–77.

neighboring villeins and possibly self-defined as gentle, they still owed fealty to their lords and king, and their status was lower than that of a squire or belted knight who held more land, owed both fealty and homage, performed military duties, and stood on the lowest rungs of the ladder of temporal lords.[60] If, as St. Thomas remarks, being free means avoiding coercive legal restraint, then the ordinary franklin was only half-free, living like all other medieval people under the complex system of oaths, traditional obligations, and contracted ones which explains the obsession in the Franklin's tale with the "troth," obligation, and freedom in each of the estates.

However, the only serious obligations that exist for the Franklin are to make things pleasant. Chaucer presents him as free with his food, the saint of the loaded Epicurean table with his own frank for fattening guests. As the St. Julian of his Epicurean country, he pairs with the Wife's Saint Venus as inverted saint. In the conventional accounts, St. Julian, returning home while his wife was at Mass, discovered his parents in bed; thinking them to be his wife and a paramour, he killed them. Then, shamed by his discovery of his own crime, he left his home country accompanied by his wife. His penance was to set up a hostel beside a great river. There, after years of service to the poor and to travelers, he rescued a dying man whom he heard call out in a great storm from across the river, and found him to be Christ accepting his penance (fig. 46).[61] In contrast,

---

[60] Homans, *English Villagers*, pp. 233ff. and 335; Donald W. Sutherland, *The Assize of the Novel Disseisin* (Oxford: Clarendon, 1973), pp. 32ff., 86, 95, 135–38; Robertson, "Chaucer and the 'Commune Profit,' " p. 249. Specht (*Chaucer's Franklin*, pp. 118–41) argues that the franklin is a gentleman. He may be, but the title may be a relatively meaningless one when a group assigns it to itself; to be significant in application to franklins, it would need some generally accepted legal definition, which Specht's book does not show it to have had.

[61] Jacobus de Voragine, *Legenda Aurea*, pp. 142–43.

the Franklin's St. Julian "hostel" brings down snows of hospitality which extend less to the poor than to the Squire and the Man of Law who know "gentilesse" (F, 694) and can do favors. In his tale, the husband is not so gauche as to kill out of a sense of honor and no one does penance by serving the poor. The Franklin's living calendar, humorously distinct from the Church's calendar of saints' days or the elaborate astronomical calendar of his tale, consists in the changes in "mete" and "soper" (A, 348) to fit the seasons' food supply. His ludicrous aspirations to knighthood, apparent in his praise of the gentility of the squire (F, 673ff.), cause him to equip his loaded table, sharpen his sauce rather than his spear, and keep his cutlery gear always ready for the fray (A, 351–54; cf. A, 2180). His "table dormant" (for table round?) is always prepared. He lacks the intellectual freedoms (for example, the freedom of the seven liberal arts, even of rhetoric) and, therefore, overpraises the Squire's showy rhetoric and overdecorates his own story with rhetorical colors—improbable classical gods set in the Brittany of the Breton lais and with characters experiencing events which have improbable durations and difficulties. The Franklin also lacks the prospect of creating a truly noble succession because his heir apparent remains a wastrel unwilling to study even the squire's gentility or manners, preferring gambling and acting like the old hag's unworthy lord's son while ignoring her gentility based on virtue (D, 1150ff.; F, 682–94). Clearly, the personal life the Franklin has lived to secure nobility for his heritage is foredoomed, whether one considers blood, manners, or learning.

He can rise above such limitations through imagination. His tale celebrates a group of people who can act decisively without imposing tyranny or sorrow, who eliminate suffering and evil through a tolerance, a generosity, and an insouciance that fulfill the dream of the Epicurus in Dante's *Convivio*, namely delight without pain.[62] Like the Franklin's village world, the world of the tale appears to recognize strictly delimited but complex patterns of domination or "maistrie," although some in the tale are more confused than complex. Because love should be—implicitly, like franklinhood—free, Arveragus arranges a marriage in which as husband he pretends to be Dorigen's sovereign, but as lover acts as her servant or thrall (F, 792–93). The role of Arveragus as lover *and* servant conflicts with the Franklin's earlier statement about inconsistency between love and thraldom and indicates that Arveragus does not love Dorigen, an idea which the conclusion of the tale supports. However, the Franklin equivocates and denies his new love hierarchy: Arveragus made Dorigen his chivalric wife, not his ruler or, more nervously, he made her his love, his mistress, his lady or his mistress-ruler-wife. The semantic fun gets rather complex:

> Servage? nay, but in lordshipe above,
> Sith he hath bothe his lady and his love;
> His lady, certes, and his wyf also,
> The which that lawe of love acordeth to.   (F, 795–98)

As D. W. Robertson has pointed out, the marriage's premise that friends must obey each other is patently impossible without some ruler or spirit of adjudication as to when and what for.[63] Arveragus can no more be both lord and servant to Dorigen than the Franklin or the Reeve can be lords of their lords and servants also. The alternative to sovereignty in marriage is not wifely thraldom but wife-as-counsel as Prudence makes clear (B², 2252–2306). The ordinary franklin knew that his freedom did not derive from the lord's having only "the name of

[62] *Opere di Dante Alighieri*, ed. Fredi Chiappelli (Milan: I Classici Italiano, 1967), p. 235.
[63] Robertson, *Essays in Medieval Culture*, p. 281. Cf. Robert P. Miller, "The Epicurean Homily on Marriage by Chaucer's Franklin," *Mediaevalia* 6 (1980):151–86.

36. Judas returns the money received for Christ and hangs himself while his companion devil escorts his soul to hell. *Holkham Picture Bible*; English, 1325–1330

37. The arrest of Christ. Charles V of France's Parement de
Narbonne (*left section*); French, 1380s

38. The crucifixion with the Church and the Synagogue; Charles V
and his wife. Parement de Narbonne (*central section*); French, 1380s

39. St. Paul requests letters to allow him to persecute Damascus Christians. *Queen Mary's Psalter;* English, early fourteenth century

40. St. Paul preaches to Timothy and women; Mary with the Holy Ghost dove banner; text below reads: "He is the head of the body of the Church" (*upper detail*). The Synagogue falling with the prophet Micah and the Evangelist Matthew (*lower detail*). *Duc de Berry's Grandes Heures;* French, early fifteenth century

41. Francis, in contemplation, carried into heaven in Elijah's vision-chariot. Giotto, upper church at Assisi, late thirteenth century

42. St. Thomas reaches into Christ's side to touch a wound
that suggests Brother Thomas's secret place (D, 2140ff.).
Tweyere Psalter; North of England, around 1320

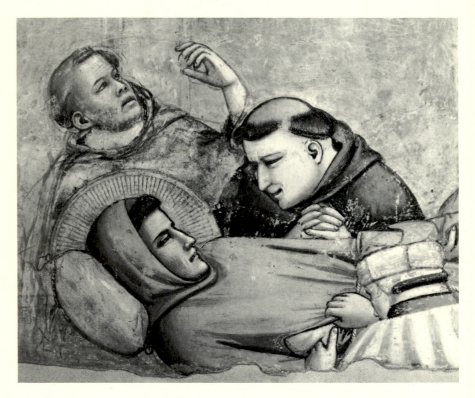

43. Giotto's *Funeral of St. Francis* (*detail*), with Friar Jerome imitating
Thomas's action by lifting Francis's robe to place his hands in his
side. Bardi Chapel, Santa Croce, thirteenth century

44. The Canticle bride wearing the Duke of Berry's insignia (the swan) to symbolize Berry's identification with the Church; in contrast, January plays groom and God. Guyart de Moulins' translation of Peter Comester's *Historia Scholastica*; French, early fifteenth century

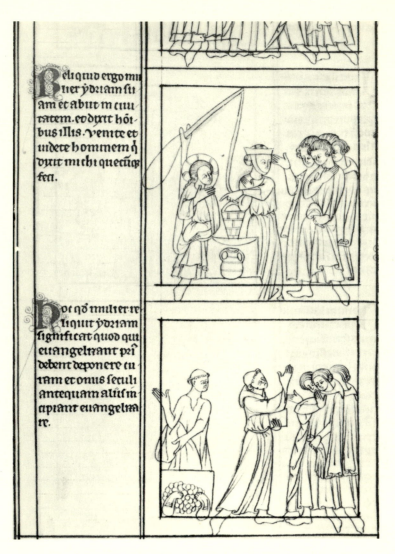

45. The Samaritan, a model to preachers, leaving her water pots to tell others, instructs the preacher to abandon worldly cares and proclaim Christ. *Bible Moralisée*; French, early fourteenth century

46. Scenes from the life of St. Julian. Rouen window; French, thirteenth century

a. St. Julian kills his parents

b. Wiping his sword, St. Julian meets his wife returning from Mass

c. St. Julian leaves home to set up a hospice for poor travelers

d. St. Julian ministers to travelers

e. St. Julian and his wife hear a man crying in a storm

f. St. Julian rows to help

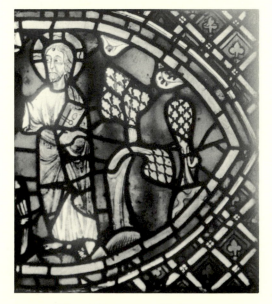

g. The crying-man-as-Christ accepts
Julian's penance

soveraynetee" (F, 751) but on both lord and man pledging and keeping a lifetime fealty or troth.

Deprived of legal husband-lord by mutual pledge (F, 738–59) and of servant-lover by the English tests of arms, Dorigen, walking by the sea for sport, posits a lack of troth and a malice in the God of wisdom and perfection who, in making the world (F, 871), incorporated fiendish rocks in Brittany's coast:

> Now stood hire castel faste by the see,
> And often with hire freendes walketh shee,
> Hire to disporte, upon the bank an heigh,
> Where as she many a ship and barge seigh
> Seillynge hir cours, where as hem liste go.
> But thanne was that a parcel of hire wo,
> For to hirself ful ofte, "Allas!" seith she,
> "Is ther no ship, of so manye as I se,
> Wol bryngen hom my lord? Thanne were myn herte
> Al warisshed of his bittre peynes smerte."   (F, 847–56)

> But, Lord, thise grisly feendly rokkes blake,
> That semen rather a foul confusion
> Of werk than any fair creacion
> Of swich parfit wys God and a stable,
> Why han ye wroght this werk unresonable?   (F, 868–72)

Her speech at first questions only the general providence that Theseus describes in his final speech, but it later attributes divine malice to such special providence as tested Job or Griselda (F, 881ff.). Its comic melodrama undercuts its surface Faustianism: Dorigen regularly says her despairing words sitting down lest she faint; she knows the rocks have destroyed a hundred thousand *bodies* though she can't bring them to mind (F, 877–78). Though clerks may put her down by claiming to know best about the rocks, she doubts their word while committing her lord to the "God that made wynd to blowe" (F, 888), apparently forgetting that rocks without wind would kill no one.

Finally, she asks God to sink the rocks in hell for Arveragus' sake, an idea explicated indirectly in Aurelius' prayer appealing to the sun to ask the deity of the other Epicurean tales—Diana, the moon, addressed as Lucina—to help him. At first Aurelius asks the sun to keep pace with the moon for two years so as to collaborate with her in bringing two-year tides to cover the rocks—a patent impossibility.[64] Then he implores the sun to ask the moon to bring the rocks down into "hir owene dirke regioun" (F, 1074), Lucina's hell where she dwells with Pluto (A, 2082ff). In the Merchant's Tale, Lucina-Proserpina represents earth, avarice, and the desire for things that lead to January's blind despair and self-deception; in the *Chess of Love* gloss, despair is said to go with Pluto's hell which is a figure for desiring impossible goods such as a human being's desire to fly or Narcissus' love of his own reflection. The *Chess* gloss makes clear that such impossible desires ultimately produce loss of faith in God's goodness.[65] Concomitantly, Dorigen exemplifies how desiring to put the rocks in hell means only despair. Fearing for the loss of her ready servant in love, she imagines the impossible good of a world without Breton rocks, a world where Theseus' chain of love, which requires death and decay as well as birth and growth, binds no one. She does so on the basis of the *possible* death of an Arveragus whom the rocks do not kill, on the basis of a *possible* relationship between wind and rock on the Breton coast, and on the evidence of the hundred-thousand bodies reputedly killed by the rocks (E, 865–93). She cites no specific cases. In a like circumstance, Theseus looks at a particular death, Arcita's, to discern its providence, and observes the inevitability of death and decay. The fulfillment of Dorigen's desire to place the Breton rocks in hell may solve Epicurean material problems, but hell's rocks are also dangerous. Conven-

---

[64] Wood, *Chaucer and the Country of the Gods*, pp. 245–71.
[65] *Chess* gloss, 4:475–80.

tionally, Sisyphus rolls hell's rocks in punishment for his inconstancy or lack of "trouthe," and Dante's prodigal and miserly souls roll hell's boulders toward each other. The threat of physical suffering and death helps one to be wary of spiritual suffering and death. To put it in another way, it may assist pilgrims sailing in search of the ABCs, "Haven of refut, of quiete, and of reste," to find help before their "ship tobreste" (11.14–16).[66]

Dorigen's denial of the divine troth represented by the existence of pain, whether Brittany's rocks or Griselda's tests, reflects the Franklin's general confusion of genuine troth and its polite semblance. When Aurelius seeks to seduce Dorigen, she recognizes that he is asking her to be an "untrewe wyf" but in "pley" gives Aurelius her "troth" that, if he will manage the removal of the rocks, she will love him "best of any man" (F, 997), whatever that means. The Orléanais magician carries out his "contract" by predicting tides that temporarily cover the rocks only *after* Arveragus has come home. Dorigen spends a day or two reciting examples from the *Adversus Jovinianum* of women who committed suicide rather than accept rape (Aurelius' proposal is not even legally binding, let alone a rape). Then, having postponed enough, she appears ready to go to Aurelius. Her poor fool husband, as eager to please as his Franklin creator, requires Dorigen to keep her "trouthe" to Aurelius and make him a wittol but not a public wittol—she will be killed if she tells.

---

[66] Ibid., 4:486. "[D]ures pierres" are, in Pierre d'Ailly, a symbol for "Epicurean" physical temptations; in escaping the black rocks of one kind, Dorigen places herself on others. Pierre d'Ailly, "Le Jardin D'Amour de l'Ame Devote," B.M. Add. MS. 32, 623, fol. 138ᵛ. Robert P. Miller observes that "the desire to remove [the black rocks], as well as their 'magical' disappearance, are both emblematic of the Epicurean imagination"; "Allegory in the Canterbury Tales," in *A Companion to Chaucer Studies*, ed. Beryl Rowland (London: Oxford University Press, 1979 rev. ed.), p. 343. See also Miller, "Augustinian Wisdom and Eloquence in the F-fragment of the Canterbury Tales," *Mediaevalia* 4 (1978): 245–75.

He conveniently forgets that oaths to break the moral or the civic law are not binding, neglects to ask whether Dorigen's oath was made in jest, and ignores her oath of marriage troth which under law takes precedence over all other contracts, particularly contracts to sin.[67]

If the black rocks cannot be physically removed, they can, like January's cuckolding, be eliminated through a recasting of events in the human imagination. The nice husband surrenders his marriage troth out of "gentility" (F, 1542–44), the nice lover for the same motive quits Dorigen of her adultery bond (F, 1533), and the kindly clerk-magician for like motives releases the adulterer of his money-troth. All are "fre" to each other (F, 1622), free or liberal in the sense of not compelling others to behave in a given way because of an oath, free of constraint in Epicurus' world where only the surfaces matter.

But such "fredom" is finally neither free nor liberal. Boccaccio's Queen Biancefiore, in answering question twelve, reminds her group of its Epicurean quest by telling one of her interlocutors with straightfaced irony: "You answer . . . as though we reasoned of eternal joys, for the purchasing whereof there is no doubt that all troubles ought to be accepted and all worldly wealth and delight abandoned, but at present we do not speak of them."[68] The Queen has earlier defined love as of three sorts: honest love which implies suffering but links the creature to the Creator, maintains the physical world, orders provinces and cities, and grants eternal life—essentially the love described in Boethius's *De Consolatione* (bk. 2, met. 8); love for delight without suffering (Epicurean love) which the *Filocolo* company worships and which no virtuous person ought to aspire to; and love for utility, essentially the love of fortune.[69] Love for delight be-

[67] Alan Gaylord, "The Promises in *The Franklin's Tale*," *ELH* 31 (1964): 352–57.

[68] Giovanni Boccaccio, *Decameron: Filocolo: Ameto: Fiametta*, ed. Enrico Bianchi et al. (Milan: Letteratura Italiana, n.d.), p. 892.

[69] Ibid., pp. 871–77.

gins for her as with Chaucer in the sight, develops in idleness and pleasurable thought, and culminates in the consent of the reason, the culminating steps for January, the Wife's husbands and knight, and the beginning step for Arveragus. Generally Biancefiore uses this ironic frame when she decides the questions of love. However, when she answers the question of who was most "fre" posed by Chaucer's source tale, she does so with a reference to the three enemies and the discipline of the evangelical counsels, straightforwardly indicating that Chaucer's magician's counterpart gave up only such riches as are a hindrance to a virtuous life, and was therefore wise in beginning voluntary poverty (since Chaucer's magician gains his claim by the chicanery of predicting tides and pretending magic, he gave up nothing to which he had a claim). Aurelius's counterpart gave up only lascivious desire, but Arveragus's counterpart gave up something real, that is, his honor—the pride in virtue that one should have, not mere pridefulness. When Menedon objects to Biancefiore that Arveragus's counterpart shows no liberality in giving away his wife since he is bound by her oath, the Queen replies that the wife is a member of the husband and could not lawfully make an oath to be unfaithful since her marriage oath would take precedence. Therefore, the Arveragus figure was genuinely free with his valuables. He gave away real honor in sending his wife to her lover.[70] His freedom is not the freedom described by the Theseus presented by Chaucer's Knight, the freedom to use one's will to make an inward virtue of suffering's necessity. It is the freedom to avoid painful contradictions by painless politeness. By interpreting troth or fealty as keeping immoral, socially acceptable private obligations rather than moral public ones founded on the law or sacraments, Arveragus as the Franklin's hero defines his narrator's sense of honor: the honor of the "good old boy" who can play

[70] Ibid., pp. 855–59.

St. Julian in Epicurus's country where every human prospect pleases and only Truth is vile.

The Franklin forgets or conceals what the Physician, who follows him and should know only the external man, observes in his tale:

> The worm of conscience may agryse
> Of wikked lyf, though it so pryvee be
> That no man woot thereof but God and he. (C, 280–82)

Aurelius's "gentility" to Dorigen prevents his drinking any real "penaunce" with a cup of satisfaction (F, 942); so does the magician-clerk's generosity of Aurelius, and hence conscience, the inner equivalent of the rocks metaphorically sunk into Proserpina's hell, remains covered by the goddess who keeps illusion thriving in the Wife's and the Merchant's tales.

The Epicurean Wife, Merchant, and Franklin form a "commercial" group: the Merchant a representative of the international wool traders who formed the Stapler group of royal financiers; the Wife a West Country representative of manufacturers, later the Merchant Venturers, moving England away from raw, and toward woven, wool export;[71] the Franklin a representative of an expanded group of somewhat wealthy country gentry. Chaucer presents them all as Epicureans, capable of living for material goods rather than for active service to the commonwealth or contemplative service to God. They turn aside from the pursuit of perfection and through a trick of poetic imagination eliminate self-perception and the sense of tragedy.

More recent economic historians treat the groups represented as the forerunners of a new acquisitive or capitalistic society. These lay figures and the Epicurean clergy whom Chaucer presents connect to each other in the richly imagined desert

---

[71] For an account of this industry, see Robertson, " 'And For My Land Thus Hastow Mordred Me?,' " pp. 403–20.

of Venus (cf. *HF*, 48off.) which makes up the *Canterbury Tales*. Chaucer's Huberd prefers wives to Lazarus and is "famulier" with franklins (A, 215ff.); his Summoner is kind to good fellows and teaches the legend of the monetary hell; his Pardoner tries to sell his pardon, especially to wives who have wool to offer (C, 91off.). The characters who administer penance in the tales can all be bought off because they believe in nothing. In the Shipman's tale the merchant is the commercial brother of the sensual monk in the life of "taillynge." The commercialization of penance and the secularization of the contemplative life both go with Chaucer's comic picture of the "socializing" of the Epicurean life. Though the development of a full-fledged commercial culture required considerable relaxing of the prevalent penitential disciplines, especially as regards usury, Chaucer makes the point that divine wisdom manifests itself to the disciplined in the material world—through natural law, visible revelation, contemplative symbols revealing to people their obligation in nature and history. Where no one seeks anything behind the material surfaces, life loses its divine purpose. Penance becomes a payoff and humankind's final good a garden centered in a pear tree. Wyclif has not so much chosen the wrong abuses to attack as attributed them to the wrong sect. The love of *temporalia* is the problem lying behind the confusion of the temporal and spiritual swords. The four sects are organized institutional entities, but the sins attributed to them will not be cured by the royal action sought by Wycliffites so much as by the very perfective disciplines which the Wycliffites increasingly rejected as they turned to predestined grace as the source of all perfection. The "sects" go beyond institutions. They go to the individual actions which create a culture. Their answer lies in individual and corporate action to create another "regne." Hence, the Parson's Tale.

10

In Conclusion

THE PARSON'S TALE AND REASON'S
RECONSTRUCTION

When Chaucer indicates that the Parson in the General Pro-
logue first follows "Cristes loore" (A, 527) and then teaches it,
he gives him Christ's qualities in John 1 where the Word be-
comes flesh and embodies what He also reveals in speech. The
Parson is not Christ, but Chaucer's description in the General
Prologue requires one to regard him as a figure of great author-
ity and to see his tale as Chaucer's normative statement on pen-
ance and the clerical life and, ultimately, on social organization.
Chaucer gives to the tale a setting, a description of law and so-
cial structure, and an aesthetic process for individual and social
reconstruction that allow it to represent the Parson's authority.
To understand it, one must first see what it is not—namely, as
has sometimes been assumed, a tale fundamentally different in
kind from the other tales. It is not an "anti-tale" which implicitly
rejects tale-telling. Like the other tales, it responds to earlier
tales, and comments on them. In particular, it gives the tally of
the rejection by the Wife of Bath's sect of the penitential and
perfective, but it also touches issues raised by most of the other
pilgrims.

In a recent article on the Parson's Tale, Lee Patterson argues
that the work does not gloss the preceding tales save in the areas
of marriage, gentility's responsibility to the poor, blasphemy
and perjury, and the penitent's obligations to confess all sins to
the same priest (I, 1008–9).[1] Assuming the reading that this

---

[1] Lee W. Patterson, "The 'Parson's Tale' and the Quitting of the 'Canterbury
Tales,' " *Traditio* 34 (1978):361–69.

book has given the *Canterbury Tales*, any treatment that defined marriage, gentility, oaths, and penance would do about all that "glossing" can do. However, Patterson further argues that the late date of the tale and the commonplace character of its passages which are paralleled in other tales indicate that Chaucer did not use it to create his other tales or think of it as his gloss,[2] and he may be correct. Though glosses are commonly written after texts, the gloss concept also, to some extent, makes one tale more or less than others. Since all the tales gloss each other in the tale-telling competition, one does better to regard this particular tale as the Parson's clerical reminder of commonplaces that his audience of "pilgrims" already know or should know. Dismissing these commonplaces also requires that one dismiss the whole fabric of the *Canterbury Tales*, for Chaucer's poetry is built of commonplaces—commonplaces that are manipulated, inverted, and finally brought home to the particulars of the time. Much of the idiom of the *Tales* is an idiom that was commonly known, here utilized with uncommon grace. Chaucer's humor, irony, and comedy arise out of the recognition of a tale's violation of commonplaces. When January says that one cannot hurt himself on his own knife (and then does so at the end of his tale), the Parson's affirmation that one can indeed do so defines the specific character of the comedy of January's ending (I, 859; E, 1839–40; E, 2366). One can easily multiply the examples from the thirty-five parallel passages that Patterson cites.[3] Since the General Prologue assigns the Parson the norm-

---

[2] Ibid., pp. 353, 356–61.

[3] Ibid., pp. 356–59. The binding together of riches and women's charms as passing as "a shadwe upon a wal" (I, 1068; E, 1315; B², 9) supports the general metaphor of wife and money as symbolically interchangeable possessions which I and others have observed in the Shipman's and Merchant's tales. The passage indicating that swearers like the revelers in the Pardoner's Tale tear Christ's body defines the conditions of truthful oath-taking, oath-taking in court, and oath-taking expressing worship to God and help to fellow Christians;

[277]

ative role for the clerical estate, one must interpret echoes unit-
ing his tale to other tales to function exactly as do the echoes
that relate the tales of the Clerk and the Knight to other tales.
The Knight's Tale, through being echoed in later tales, places
all of the narration's temporal rulers in perspective. The Clerk's
Tale, echoing earlier and later D, E, and F tales, interprets the
pilgrimage's false learning. The Parson's Tale no more acts as
an anti-tale than do the Knight's and the Clerk's stories.

Patterson, however, does not treat the Parson's tale as the
Parson's estate tally among the other tallies. He sees it as swal-
lowing up the frivolously aesthetic world of the other tales
whose "fables" display the dubious "moral integrity of poetic
language." His Parson rejects "all personal speaking that does
not confront, in the sacramental language of penance, the sin-
fulness of the human condition."[4] However, if Lydgate and Jill
Mann are correct, if the tales are told of "estates in the pilgrim-
age," their telling is not "personal speaking" at all save for the
superficial fiction that personifies estate roles as speaking and
confronting in the language of epic, comedy, history, satire,
tragedy, and romance, the comic "sinfulness" of each estate's
human condition, a sinfulness that is hilarious precisely be-
cause its disorder violates expectations of constructive service.
Patterson argues that the Parson's rejection of fables in I, 31–34,
rejects all of Chaucer's Tales. However, the fables that the Par-
son rejects when he quotes Timothy can only be the "elde
wymmens fablis" of the I Timothy 4.7 passage that he cites
(I, 34).

The rejection only indicates that he will not follow the Wife
of Bath and tell old wives' "bran" (I, 35; cf. D, 478), or the Man-

---

it then cites the Pardoner's proper saints, Peter and Paul, on oath-taking (I, 590–
600). In general, Patterson tends to be too quick to dismiss echo-passages as
merely conventional without looking at the particular functioning of the pas-
sage in the poetic tales and in the Parson's Tale.

[4] Ibid., pp. 378, 379.

ciple and tell the "wrecchednesse" (1, 34) of an Ovidian fable misglossed to spite a fellow pilgrim.[5] He does not despise fables but fables-and-wretchedness, the "ineptas . . . et aniles fabulas," against which Paul warns Timothy. If his tale's introduction condemns the fictive mode of the other Canterbury tales, he comically and unwittingly, condemns himself since he later tells histories aplenty, albeit Biblical ones, numerous verisimilitudinous "arguments" to illustrate the various sins, and even offers several instructive fables about the ships sunk by huge waves or small drops of water (1, 361–65), the modern shepherd (1, 720), the devil's wolves (1, 767). Reason cannot endorse any implicit muddle-headedness in a character whom Chaucer makes a learned clerk and true teacher who knows what he is about (A, 480, 528).

The Parson uses his commonplaces of estate expectation to remind the pilgrims and Chaucer's audience of the upright versions of ideas that appear in inverted or jumbled form in earlier tales, and the evening setting of his discourse integrates his tale

[5] Patterson (p. 378) takes the Manciple in relation to lawyers as the image of the poet in relation to courts; however, the Manciple's drunken tale no more defines Chaucer's view of poetry than does the Miller define his view of peasants. The Manciple obviously intends to intimidate the Cook with his sermon against jangling, and Chaucer's source, Ovid's Apollo-Coronis story moralized, made Apollo signify Sapience and Coronis humankind so degraded by sin and slandered by Satan (the crow or raven) that Sapience abandoned it. It appears to have abandoned both drunken Cook and waspish Manciple. However, in the original Ovidian story, the sun god rips Aesculapius from Coronis' womb after he kills her, allegorically suggesting Christ-as-Wisdom beginning the work of healing or reconstruction. The *Ovide Moralisé*, the source of the Manciple's Tale, allegorizes the birth of Aesculapius as God's granting grace to humankind; cf. "Ovide Moralisé," ed. C. de Boer, *Verhandelingen der Koninklijke Akademie van Wetenschapen*, *Afd. Letterkunde*, N.S. 15 (1915–38), 2:2549–2606. Bersuire also makes Aesculapius symbolize Christ in his *Metamorphosis Ouidiana Moraliter*, ed. J. Th. Minderaa (Utrecht: Instituut voor Laat Latijn, 1960), 1:58–59. The Parson's Tale, told as the sun darkens, provides the "Aesculapius," so to speak.

to the larger work's exploration of penance through the Wife and her sect. The themes of their tales—excommunication and indulgence, penance and perfection, theology and marriage and asceticism—constitute the themes of Raymund of Pennaforte's *Summa de Poenitentia et Matrimonio*. Penance had long been related to the coming of night, and Richard Alkrynton, in an early fifteenth-century sermon, recalls the evening setting of the Parson's Tale with his admonition that every pilgrim ought to seek the road to the spiritual Jerusalem, the sight of peace, be marked with the cross of penance, and hold to the way of the commandments. Even with such discipline, the pilgrim should say to God as the night of death and endtime draws near: "Lorde dwelle you here wiþ us, for it draweþ to niȝt."[6] The Parson begins as the scales of justice which have been Chaucer's constant poetic concern appear in the sky. The time is ripe for a character conscious of death and of the end of time to interpret the way of the Canterbury pilgrimage as the way of Jerusalem's penance and renewal (I, 49ff., 75–82).[7]

The tale shows the way of penance and the scales to be the way of the recovery of law, and bases its prescriptions, as Patterson notes, on its defining sin ontologically as a violation of the eternal law "ordeyned and nombred" (I, 218) by God. Since eternal law produces natural law, from which issues positive law declared by the king, as well as divine law, from which issues revelation and ecclesiastical law declared by popes and

---

[6] Richard Alkrynton, *English Sermons*, B.M. Add. MS 37,677, fol. 58ᵛ.

[7] Wood, *Chaucer and the Country of the Stars*, pp. 292-97; Raymund of Pennaforte, *Summa de Poenitentia et Matrimonio* (Farnborough, Eng.: Gregg Press, 1967), 3:33, 34; 4:1–25; cf. Judson Allen, "The Old Way and the Parson's Way: An Ironic Reading of the Parson's Tale," *JMRS* 3 (1973):255–71 which argues that Hugh of St. Cher's exegesis of the "old way" passage from Jeremiah 6 undercuts the Parson's penitential view. However, Hugh's comment is only directed against newfangled penances and religious modes of all sorts, practices against which the Parson also warns at I, 1052, and elsewhere.

bishops, the Parson implicitly speaks of the two laws controlling the body and spirit of humankind and connects his work to Chaucer's other tales about royal and ecclesiastical law. When the Parson defines sin as a violation of God's law and man's own nature, he explicitly calls attention to the two ladders of law treated in the *Canterbury Tales* as a whole.[8] And when he creates a tale so intellectually ordered that the disordered can, in the cognition of its structural order, find the beginnings of true order,[9] he lays the foundation for a movement toward reason and law. The Parson bases his most explicit societal statement, in I, 753–73, on ideas taken from the *City of God* which are only partially reflected in his basic source for this section, *Primo/Quoniam*. If one refers the Parson's statement to its source in St. Augustine, one finds that it, like *The Former Age*, describes early men who did not rule each other, and who did not seek to do so. They ruled only irrational animals. Before the Fall, no servitude was necessary. Even after the Fall, the early patriarchs were shepherds, not rulers (I, 759–66),[10] but Canaan's sin

[8] Patterson, "The 'Parson's Tale,' " p. 341, and cf. pp. 341–45. My disagreement with details of Patterson's argument accompanies respect for much of his article.

[9] Ibid., pp. 341–47.

[10] The Parson mistakenly ascribes the material to "Augustinus, de Civitate, libro nono," but the actual reference for the idea is 19.14–17; the notion that sovereignty did not exist before Canaan's sin appears in Augustine, *De Civitate Dei*, 16.2 and 19.15, and the material asserting this (I, 759–66) does not appear in *Primo/Quoniam*; cf. Siegfried Wenzel, "The Source of Chaucer's Seven Deadly Sins," *Traditio* 30 (1974):368. Chaucer also refers to the Augustinian concept of the origin of domination in Nimrod in *The Former Age*, lines 58–59, a poem that seems to answer "golden age" expectations during the Peasants' Revolt by asserting the Fall; for Nimrod, see Augustine, *De Civitate Dei*, 16.4–5. Cf. *Glossa Ordinaria*," *PL* 113:112–113; John Bromyard, *Summa Praedicantium*, 1:326ʳ. Wyclif disagrees with this view in his "De Servitute Civili et Dominio Seculari," *Opera Minora*, p. 146. For the association of the golden age with the prelapsarian period in political theory, see A. J. Carlyle, *A History of Medieval Political Theory in the West* (Edinburgh: Blackwood, 1930–36), 1:117 and 5:442;

against his father led to Noah's curse making him his brother's servant: '[T]he condicioun of thraldom and the firste cause of thraldom is for synne. . . . This name of thraldom was nevere erst kowth til that Noe seyde that his sone Canaan sholde be thral to his brethren for his synne" (I, 755, 765). The common villein, Noah-like Carpenter John, looks forward to following his antecedent and to being the "lord" of all the world, but he does not recognize that selfish men cannot all hope to be lords of all the world and any natural sense of society remain. Guilt, specifically the unnatural guilt of Canaan, requires servitude. Hence, post-Nimrodic (FA, 58), post-diluvian government forcibly controls behavior and seeks by habituation to restore the race to an outward obedience to natural law.

But the Christian commonwealth may go even further in restoring God's law and man's nature. It may transform the necessary police power of the state to a mutual service defined by estate roles: "[S]ith the time of grace cam, God ordeyned that som folk sholde be moore heigh in estaat and in degree, and som folk moore lough, and that everich sholde be served in his estaat and his degree" (I, 770). The Chaucerian form of this passage derives from Primo/Quoniam, but its ultimate source is Augustine's description of the proper Christian household in the City of God:

> [H]is own household are his care, for the law of nature and of society gives him readier access to them and greater opportunity of serving them. . . . But in the family of the just man who lives by faith and is as yet a pilgrim journeying on to the celestial city, even those who rule serve those whom they seem to command; for they rule not from a love of power, but from a sense of duty they owe to others—not because they are proud of authority, but because they love mercy.[11]

for the "golden age" ideas of the Peasants' Revolt, see Hilton, Bond Men Made Free, p. 222, and compare The Former Age," lines 1–55, as a possible response.

[11] Augustine, De Civitate Dei, 19.14, from the trans. of The City of God by Marcus Dods (New York: Random House, 1950), p. 693. For differences be-

The Parson, in extending Augustine's logic from the household to the whole society, may violate modern conceptions of Augustinian political theory but he creates a thoroughly Chaucerian political understanding:

> [T]he lord oweth to his man that the man oweth to his lord. / The Pope calleth hymself servant of the servantz of God; but for as muche as the estaat of hooly chirche ne myghte nat han be, ne the commune profit myghte nat han be kept, ne pees and rest in erthe, but if God hadde ordeyned that som men hadde hyer degree and som men lower, / therfore was sovereyntee ordeyned, to kepe and mayntene and deffenden hire underlynges or hire subgetz in resoun, as ferforth as it lith in hire power, and nat to destroyen hem ne confounde.   (I, 771–74)

In the Parson's society, everyone is properly a servant. Reason, lost in the Fall, as I, 325ff., asserts, is law in the medieval understanding.[12] Hence the powers temporal and spiritual—the latter exemplified in the Pope—must serve others by helping recreate the reason lost in humankind's forsaking the order and number of eternal law. They must give to their underlings the three recreative services of the Church's sustaining, the common profit's protection, and everyone's defense against violence ("pees and rest in erthe," I, 773).

The Parson's conception of sustaining Church discipline places him beside those conservative theologians who respected Innocent III's and Raymund of Pennaforte's penitential theol-

---

tween Augustinian and Aristotelian political thought, see Ewart Lewis, *Medieval Political Ideas* (New York: Knopf, 1954); H.-X. Arquillière, *L'Augustinisme politique* (Paris: J. Vrin, 1934). The Parson obliterates the difference between Augustine and Aristotle by extending Augustine's household logic of the law of nature and service in rule to the three estates.

[12] Robertson, "Chaucer and the 'Commune Profit,' " p. 239, quoting Sir John Stoner, Chief Justice. For *ratio status* or *ratio publicae utilitatis* as social rational control, see Gaines Post, *Studies in Medieval Thought: Public Law and the State 1100–1322* (Princeton: Princeton University Press, 1964), p. 301; and cf. pp. 241–309.

ogy requiring contrition, confession to a priest, and satisfaction as necessary preliminaries to the Eucharist's normal action of grace. On the other side, the nominalists, Wyclif and the Chamber knights, held confession to a priest to be unnecessary since grace operated through true contrition alone, rendering the sacramental system useless.[13] The Parson clearly upholds the ecclesiastical structure which enforced penance and included popes, bishops, holy orders, and the concept of contumacy. In his description of simony or benefices for the unworthy, he comes close to visualizing the institutional Church as something other than the true Church because simony puts in ecclesiastical places of power persons who steal "the soules of Jhesu Crist and destroyen his patrimoyne" (1, 789), sell the stolen souls to the wolf, and destroy respect for the sacraments. Yet, even this evil never explicitly raises the issue, emphasized by Wyclif and by the Friar's and the Summoner's tales, of what happens when agents of the institutional Church destroy what they were created to preserve and deny their original discipline.

However, the Parson's Tale does illuminate more detailed theological questions raised by other tales. For example, understanding the comedy of the Pardoner's Tale requires that one understand the difference between the *culpa* or guilt of individual sins removed by confession and the *poena* or "peyne" of sin removed by satisfaction. The Parson explains that though the guilt of original sin is removed by baptism, its punishment, the sting of concupiscence or "firste coveitise," remains—perhaps weakened by baptism and penance, but always latent (1, 335–48). Since original sin cannot be entirely removed, even by legitimate penance, the Pardoner's preaching a sermon on *Radix Malorum est Cupiditas* to get people to buy pardons that will

---

[13] Patterson, "The 'Parson's Tale,' " p. 348. I extend Patterson's remark to include persons such as the Chamber knights close to Chaucer who questioned aspects of the system.

make them clean as when they were born is ludicrously apt; by definition, they will remain as unclean as when they were born. The same function may be ascribed to the Parson's remarks, directed to the friars, advising confession to one curate (I, 1008–9); his counsel, directed to the Wife and her sect, reinforcing obedience to Perfection's apostolic counsels (I, 1078–80); and his explanations, directed to the same group, of marriage theology and the discipline of holy orders (I, 916–50). In a more precise case, though Patterson can find no precedent for the Parson's "bizarre" interpretation of Nabuchodonosor's tree of penance,[14] the interpretation may not be bizarre inasmuch as the tree that Nabuchodonosor saw cut down and that yet retained life in its root is said to be Nabuchodonosor himself (Daniel 4.16–25)—cut down, turned to a beast, and, after recognizing his nothingness in relation to God, restored to understanding (Daniel 4.26–34). Since the root of penance as the Parson describes it is contrition and Nabuchodonosor's contrition allows him to recover the "tree" of his humanity, mind and throne intact, the comparison developed in the Parson's Tale (I, 111–25) is a fairly logical extension of Daniel's metaphor. The interpretation also forms a palinode to the Monk's ignoring Nabuchodonosor's contrition as a model for humankind's freedom to escape from fortune (B², 3357–72; 3403–12).[15]

Going beyond detailed correction of the Chaucerian upside-down, the Parson also provides a structure and an aesthetic for the recovery of reason and law in both ruling orders through images. Patterson correctly lays out the structure through which this is done—text, explication or protheme (I, 1–84), division of the theme, analysis of the nature, etymology, action, and species of penance (I, 85–106), analysis of penance's helps

[14] Ibid., p. 352.
[15] Bersuire makes the tree and its history stand for a variety of cycles of pride and uprightness, fall and ultimate redemption; Petrus Berchorius, *Liber Bibliae Moralis* (Strassbourg, 1473), no sig; comment on Daniel 4.

(I, 107–1056) and hindrances (I, 1057–75).[16] The section on helps further divides into considerations of contrition, confession, and satisfaction, and the section on hindrances closes with the winning of the Celestial Jerusalem by progress through penance and toward perfection and wisdom on the path of the apostolic counsels that Chaucer has also discussed in the Melibee and the other clerical tales. Though Patterson finds the contrition section, which deals with the origin of sin in man's fall from reason and the disordering of his faculties, unique for this genre of work (I, 254ff.), he does not note that the passage also introduces the relationship between aesthetic and social order basic to the *Tales*.[17]

The contrition section includes two sets of past-present-future topics, the most important of which describes Christ's suffering the consequences of sin's inversion of the faculties in the process of the Fall. The topics pair as follows:

		Thought of evil embraced		*Thought of good shunned*
PAST	(A)	Shameful remembrance of past sin (I, 132–40)	(D)	Remembrance of lost good (I, 231–53)
PRESENT	(B)	Abhorrence of present thralldom (I, 141–56)	(E)	Present consideration of Christ's suffering the faculties' thralldom (I, 254–81)
FUTURE	(C)	Fear of future judgement (I, 157–230)	(F)	Hope of future forgiveness, grace, and glory (I, 282–90)

---

[16] Patterson, "The 'Parson's Tale,' " pp. 347ff.
[17] Ibid., pp. 344–45.

[286]

According to the chart's section E, innocent humankind, whether before the Fall or before individual indulgence in mortal sin, maintains an inner hierarchy attaching its mind and soul to the mind and soul of God, which allows God to rule the reason, sensuality (sensorium and imagination), and body in order—the lower faculties through the higher. The Fall, described above in chapter 7, allows the body and sensuality to seduce the individual reason away from God with the prospect of enjoying an individual, temporal good as if it were God or man's perfection (I, 325ff.), a seduction also described in the passage that introduces the Parson's account of the crucifixion (I, 260–66). Since the Fall seeks private benefits through a rebellion of the faculties, any restoration of what was lost in the Fall requires an imaging of how the crucifixion restores humankind to God and, implicitly, to unselfish society responding to the revolt of each faculty:

> And certes this disordinaunce and this rebellioun oure Lord Jhesu Crist aboghte upon his precious body ful deere, and herkneth in which wise. / For as muche thanne as resoun is rebel to God, therefore is man worthy to have sorwe and to be deed. / This suffred oure Lord Jhesu Crist for man, after that he hadde be bitraysed of his disciple, and distreyned and bounde, so that his blood brast out at every nayl of his handes, as seith Seint Augustyn. / And forther over, for as muchel as resoun of man ne wol nat daunte sensualitee whan it may, therfore is man worthy to have shame; and this suffred oure Lord Jhesu Crist for man, whan they spetten in his visage. / And forther over, for as muchel thanne as the caytyf body of man is rebel bothe to resoun and to sensualitee, therfore is it worthy the deeth. / And this suffred oure Lord Jhesu Crist for man upon the croys, where as ther was no part of his body free withouten greet peyne and bitter passioun. / And al this suffred Jhesu Crist, that nevere forfeted. (I, 266–72)

Reason's rebellion against God receives its answer in Christ's deliberate subjection to his bonds. Its shameful refusal to con-

[287]

form "sensualitee" to itself and God finds its reply in Christ's conformity to the shame of the sensual spitting in his face. And the body's uprising against both reason and "sensualitee" which produces death, finds resolution in the divine subjugation to death. Each falling step has been answered by the imaging of a divine response.

In like manner, the images and counterimages in the Knight's/Miller's/Reeve's tales, the "marriage" group, the Stratford group, and the tales dealing with penance work to mirror the inverted and fallen in their upright counterimages introduced as a subtext (e.g., Nicholas, Samson). The counterimages in the comic tales function like the images in the book of the Wife's fifth husband—as vehicles of detachment and reason. Nothing more clearly separates Chaucer from Wyclif than his aesthetic of images. Whereas Wyclif and the Lollard knights would sacrifice the logic of images, saints, and pilgrimages, for Chaucer this logic is central to the whole process of social construction and reconstruction. For example, his cult of Epicurus creates its paradise through an act of imagination that wipes out "reality"; his Miller defines the greatness of his Knight with images that invert those his pilgrims respond to when they say the Knight's tale is a "noble storie" worthy to be held in memory (A, 3111–12). Likewise, the clerical tales' Judases and Johns invert the true apostolate of his pilgrim Parson. Chaucer is the supreme poet of memorable images and counterimages. As in Boethius's *De Consolatione* (bk. 5, met. 4), the imagination, correctly used, moves the mind away from the material and toward reason's comprehension of ideas; so in Chaucer, the image of social good, upright and inverted, defines and celebrates the perfective society toward which Chaucer would woo the inner life.

But more than the contemplation of imagery is required in the reconstruction of society, for images taken seriously imply a discipline. The Parson differs from previous tale-tellers in that he spells out fully the discipline required by his images. For general reason to be recovered, the two ruling orders compose a juridical system embodying reason or law. Hence the Parson gives particular attention to the sins of rulers, as the General Prologue says he will in indicating his unwillingness to wait after "pompe and reverence" (A, 525). He dissects pride based on gentle birth; inveighs against spiritual homicide which involves the levying of heavy taxes on the poor or simony and sale of the sacraments by priests and curates—all as if the practitioners of these faults might hear him. He speaks to the fraud of merchants as if defrauding merchants were among his audience (e.g., I, 776ff.). In contrast, he touches churls and thralls only as exemplary of proper lordly action (e.g., I, 415ff.; I, 756ff.). Chaucer, in framing the Parson's Tale, did not forget that his audience was a court audience, much concerned with reason and law, and those who owned manuscripts of the *Canterbury Tales* in the fifteenth century for the most part held temporal or spiritual power.[18] Following *Primo/Quoniam*, the Parson speaks to rulers by dividing the sins roughly into offenses against body and spirit, nature and grace, temporal and spiritual rule—though other divisions are also present.[19] Readers can spell out for themselves how he speaks to rulers by examining passages specified in the chart below:

[18] Of thirty-nine manuscripts of the *Canterbury Tales* from the fifteenth century, twenty-three were clearly owned by spiritual or temporal lords. The remainder were primarily of unclear ownership. Seventeen manuscripts belonged to temporal lords. See Manly and Rickert, *The Text of the Canterbury Tales*, 1:29–544.

[19] Many of the distinctions between sins against nature and grace or temporal and divine law which the Parson gives are also included in *Primo/Quoniam* as reproduced in Wenzel, "The Source of Chaucer's Seven Deadly Sins," pp. 354–76, especially the sections of *Primo/Quoniam* analogous to the chart sections.

Nature; Body; The Temporal Power	Grace; Spirit; The Spiritual Power
I. PRIDE: pride of goods of nature, especially health and gentility (I, 450–52, 455–68)	pride of goods of grace—"science," power to suffer, virtuous contemplation—goods that ought to produce goodness or spiritual health (I, 455, 469)
REMEDY: humility, meekness, self-knowledge	
II. ENVY: envy as a sin against nature ("kynde," I, 491); sorrow at others' prosperity	envy as "lyk to" the devil (I, 492); joy at others' harm
REMEDY: love of God and neighbor	
III. ANGER: anger as bodily homicide: killing, and counsel to kill (I, 570–78)	anger as a spiritual homicide: hatred, backbiting, bad counsel to heavy taxes (I, 564–69)
REMEDY: gentleness, patience	
IV. SLOTH: bodily sloth which makes no provision for temporal necessity (I, 685)	spiritual sloth which avoids penance and good works (I, 688–725)
REMEDY: fortitude	
V. AVARICE: the avarice of exploitive temporal lords (I, 749–55)	the avarice of spiritual lords: simony and sale of sacraments (I, 781–90)
REMEDY: mercy and pity	
VI. GLUTTONY: drunkenness distempering the body (I, 826)	gluttony as destroying the reason and troubling the spirit (I, 820–25)
REMEDY: abstinence, temperance	
VII. LUXURY: luxury as sin against natural law (I, 904ff.; cf. I, 865 and I, 920)	luxury as spiritual sin: breaking faith, the sacrament of marriage, the vow of priests, etc. (I, 871–901)
REMEDY: chastity, continence, matrimony	

The analysis of the sins of rule specified in the chart must be set against the definition of proper rule in an estate society incorporated in the section on avarice.

As if to answer Chaucer's Epicurean clerics, the Parson requires that penitential repair extend beyond monetary satisfaction to the acts of service to neighbor which Christ mentions in his judgment of the sheep and goats (Matthew 25.34–40), namely providing food, clothing, and shelter to the needy, counsel to the troubled, visits to prisoners, all "with thy persone" (1, 1030) if possible and otherwise with messages and gifts. No monetary sorrow or satisfaction offered to "hermaphrodites" will do. But even the works of love drawn from Matthew 25 do not complete the tale's movement, for one may do the "right thing for the wrong reason." Only the discipline of perfection moving toward the Plowman's love can reach the right reason of divine order and number and answer the fantasies of the Wife, the Merchant, and the Franklin which promise perfection indifferent to tragedy—to the suffering implicit in the creation. Pantin remarks that "all the treatises on confession and on penance . . . cannot be ignored or passed over, because they were the necessary preparation or groundwork, without which one could not have had the exquisite flowering of the mystical literature"[20]—more properly the literature of the life of perfection. The Parson's Tale as a treatise on penance prepares for such a life, but whereas Dante and most modern mystical works evoke individual, private experiences of the vision of God, medieval thought for the most part assumes that the mind journeys to God in company—in search for a general Reason in monasteries, guilds, lay and chivalric orders. Chaucer is no exception. At the beginning of his tale, his Parson treats the infernal punishments that go with the three temptations that create society's evil (1, 185–230); at the end he treats perfection as compensation for the apparent suffering of detaching oneself from the pleasures of these three tempters—the better to know Jupiter, Sophia, "Walter." In the world where human beings are completed, "every soule [is] replenyssed with the sighte of the

---

[20] Pantin, *The English Church in the Fourteenth Century*, p. 250.

parfit knowynge of God. / This blisful regne may men purchace by *poverte espirituteel*, and the glorie by *lowenesse*, the plentee of joye by *hunger* and *thurst*, and the reste by travaille, and the lyf by deeth and mortificacion of synne" (I, 1079–80; brackets and italics mine). In the final good society, a "blissful regne" replaces the rule of avarice, "glorie" replaces vainglory, and "plente of joye" replaces luxury's delight. The Parson's journey cannot end with the completion of travel by the Southwark "compaignye" (A, 717), full of malice and comic bickering. It ends in Jerusalem, visualizing the good society of "the blisful compaignye that rejoysen hem everemo, everich of otheres joye" (I, 1076). Since Chaucer, in limning his Parson, does not, like Dante, evoke a personal mystical experience but rather a rejoicing society to ratify his vision, he does not at the end put himself in God's mind and claim perfection as his own. In his personal confession and leave-taking (I, 1081ff.), the maker of the fictional world of the *Canterbury Tales* thanks the Maker of all things for what He has made well and prays Christ to forgive him any elements that "sownen into synne" (I, 1086). He addresses his prayer to "hym that is kyng of kynges and preest over alle preestes,"[21] using a phrase drawn from three-estate controversial documents emphasizing the final sanction and limitation on each of the ruling estates. Obviously a good this-worldly society moves toward the condition of the Parson's good other-worldly one.

The Parson's Tale makes clear that, though Chaucer accepts the superficies of the Wycliffite indictment of the four sects of the Church, in his tale he turns to imaginative and spiritual rather than power-based, royal or lord temporal solutions to their Epicurean problems. He does not accept the Wycliffite call for abolition and disendowment because sectarian institutions confusing the two swords, commercializing penance, and

---

[21] Duby, *The Three Orders*, p. 33.

mechanizing perfection reflect the pervasive power of the sect of the Wife of Bath. The answer to this sect's materialism and dismissal of the afterlife cannot be a new materialism of royal reform or a new astrology of predestinarian salvation. Chaucer's Wife receives her answer from the Clerk's and the Parson's experiences of the divine through penance and the perfective disciplines that empower individuals within society—commoner Griseldas as well as monarchs and bishops—to find their "parfit felicitee" in the First Mover and their work in serving each man in his degree.

Chaucer has always been claimed by the parties of reform and reaction and with some cause, for late in his life, he still had dealings with the Chamber knights who supported the *Conclusions* and with the future heretic hunter, Archbishop Arundel. John Lydgate, through his creations appended to Chaucer's, makes him a poet of the estates, peace, and perfect holiness. As a skinny monk, he also writes proper contemplative tragedies to answer the inverted ones told by Chaucer's fat Monk. On the reformist side, the anonymous author of the *Plowman's Tale*, written about 1395, endeavors to pull Chaucer into the Lollard orbit by echoing the *Canterbury Tales* as if they were describing Wyclif's four sects.[22] His claim against the "sect[e]" that includes the pope and bishops is that they try to wield both swords, abuse the keys, and like January, "here . . . have hir blisse" (lines 232–35). The pope, in developing his sect, farms his powers out to pardoners and summoners (lines 325–32), sells bishoprics to great lords, and curses to create crusades against the rival pope. Pope's and bishop's functionaries threaten the righteous poor with cursing and with prison—that is, the *significavit* imprisonment. They fuse the two swords (lines 556–88); Judas-like, they betray Christ for money, damn

²² *Chaucerian and Other Pieces*, ed. Walter W. Skeat (Oxford: Clarendon, 1897), pp. 147–90; see p. xxxiv for dating.

Him to die, and condemn His teachings as heresy. Through the use of the *significavit* ("prison," line 642), they also curse people without giving them an opportunity for proper reply and, through the clerical fine, tax without consent of the Commons (lines 645ff.). The canons rob the people—recall Chaucer's canons—and depend on plural livings and absentee benefices. The monks despair of following the rule of St. Benedict, live like temporal princes with hawks and hounds, claim lordship over man and town, and oppress their tenants (lines 990–1060). And the friars, who have been treated by the same author in *Pierce the Ploughman's Crede*, apparently display similar faults (lines 1065–68). The Griffin in the *Plowman's Tale*, who personifies the four sects and the visible Church, combines the features of a proud bird of prey, representing the Church's clerical functions, and the lion, representing its confused temporal ones (lines 1303ff.). The bird contrasts with the Pelican who speaks for Lollards. Though professing respect for the Pope and St. Benedict, the tale turns for remedy, at its end, not to the perfective way but to Christ's (the Phoenix's) apocalyptic vengeance against the Griffin and to the contritionist hope that Christ will amend each man. Though Chaucer does not so easily surrender to party as the *Plowman's Tale* would have him do, it is clear that the author of that work, writing in the period 1395–1400, had studied Chaucer's clerical tales closely and recognized the Wycliffite basis of their diagnosis of the Church's diseases. As a Lollard, he simply denies Chaucer's perfective remedy.

Much ink has been spilled over what the *Canterbury Tales* would have been like, had they been completed. But, as to central theme they *are complete* in their celebration of a world of decorum and renewed discipline in art and in life. As part of this celebration, they explore, through their interlaced structure, the ramifications of a few ideas fundamental to Chaucer's concept of the renewal of his society. In the A section, the poet establishes the legitimacy of the pagan ruler and the possibility of a non-theocratic rule leading to peace, based on natural law and the acceptance of consultation with magnate and parliament. The pagan ruler glimpses perfection through seeing natural law but knows only the wisdom that makes a virtue of necessity, not the wisdom of freedom and grace. In the Man of Law's (B¹) section, the poet exposes the limitations of the theocratic rule promoted by royal lawyers who neither understood what it must be to be effective nor took it seriously by living governed by constancy. In the B² section, Chaucer goes beyond natural law to explore how revelation and grace may affect the spirit of the ruler of a human commonwealth through Prudence's ethic of consultation, analysis, and forgiveness, leading to Sophia. These qualities, privately learned, affect the king's public exercise and empower the only "theocratic" leadership Chaucer visualizes—that of the good man. The same section explores the sapiential or contemplative aids to wise temporal government. Monastics who usurp court roles appear incapable of providing sapient understanding as they destroy peace, justice, and their own capacity to recover St. Cecilia's prophetic court role. They are helped on the way by Epicurean monastic priests and flattering friars. The perfective society depends not only on the perfected king but on a perfected *parlement*, on "parfitness" in each estate. Therefore, the poet's D, E and F sections examine the apostolic wells on perfection's way, draughted through penance and the discipline of the evangelical counsels, and the alternative "wells" whose draughts belong to the Wife of Bath's sect.

Chaucer never appeals to Eden as the paradigm of the reconstructive process—not even in *The Former Age*—as did many polemicists from John Ball on the left to Uthred of Boldon on the right. The existence of libido means that reconstruction under post-Edenic conditions requires hierarchy, coercion, and structure, at least initially. But the poet does appeal to the founding spirit of post-Edenic institutions: Theseus, Hercules, and perhaps Samson for temporal lords, Christ and the apostles for spiritual, Solomon and St. Cecilia for contemplatives, St. Francis as reflected in his First Rule for friars, Pope Urban for popes. Each created a structure whose spirit must be recovered for Europe and England to move toward the good society, and the effective reconstruction of its upright image, to replace its upside-down one, requires a recovery of the version of perfection appropriate to it, the "marriage" that will complete each pilgrim. This does not mean monastic poverty, chastity, and obedience, and it may not even mean direct knowledge of New Testament revelation since Theseus also knows a version of perfection. It certainly does not mean being a ruler since the Plowman is Chaucer's fully perfected character. If the *Canterbury Tales* reach backward to earlier times to mirror the potential reconstruction of English and European institutions, they do so in order to reach upward to "a thyng that parfit is and stable" (A, 3009).

Chaucer unites his tales through examining the relationship of perfection and the three temptations in many settings: the still point of perfection surrounded by the circling of the creation ending the Knight's Tale, Nicholas' tubs "circling" to watch the heavens, the Prioress' child's round "greyn," the circling of the Monk's eyes with Fortune's false circles in the Monk's sections, the Wife's circle of dancers, the Pentecostal wheel in the Summoner's Tale, the Parson's "sighte of the parfit knowynge of God" (I, 1079)—all remind one of the still point in the turning world. Drawing one away from focusing on such stillness and stability, the three enemies appear in the Miller and the Reeve and their tales' characters, Melibee's enemies, the Wife's and her sect's characters, and the forces to which the Parson attributes the Fall. Chaucer makes his characters comically responsible for their follies and crimes, not predestined as Wyclif held. They do not reconstruct the world through mere

private contrition as Wyclif held, but through public speech—
penance as a public act, *parlement*, council, deliberation.

Almost every Chaucerian tale directly or by implication
raises three-order issues through including characters from
each of the orders, through referring to jurisdictional problems
between the orders—such as the *significavit*, commoner revolt,
monastic secular administration—or through specifically
speaking only to one order's responsibilities, as the Knight's
Tale does, explicitly leaving other questions to divines. The
tales admit, even detail, the contemporary problems attributed
to the orders in the reform literature of the Order of the Pas-
sion, the Wycliffites, and their respondents. But almost all turn
to two related models of reconstruction, the discipline of per-
fection and the recovery of the original spirit of institutions, as
a way of solving the crises of Chaucer's civilization.

In a broad sense social "tales" both create and interpret social
structure. Chaucer's *Canterbury Tales* may appear to many read-
ers of this book to offer a reactionary rhetoric that only post-
pones the arrival of the dream, "the image of a society no longer
riven by class distinctions, and yet still ordered."[23] Other read-
ers will point to Chaucer's respect for parliament and for eccle-
siastical reform to make him a pre-modern or post-feudal figure.
But he is neither reactionary nor modern. He is preeminently
the poet of perfection and discipline not only of the mind but of
the imagination and affections, perfection and discipline in a
world where Robin does not threaten and Alysoun of Bath does
not shock. Few civilizations have practiced both order and
equality for long periods, and Chaucer commonly sacrifices
theoretical equality to order conceived as a system of roles de-
fining how people are to serve and "love" each other in the hope
that the system and penitential discipline within it will lead to
the service of even society's poorest. Such a view outrages post-

---

[23] Duby, *The Three Orders*, p. 356.

Christian thinkers who cannot understand how wide-eyed medieval legal thinkers, monks, and chroniclers could visualize a history in the hands of God, a universal Reason that is law, a human action powered by something other than self-interest, or a role system not oppressively and reductively stereotypical.[24] From almost any modern perspective, this book's view of the *Canterbury Tales* makes them appear as a brilliant and dangerous superstructure legitimizing unacceptable social practice. However, even the groups that rebelled in 1381 visualized the ideal social world only as a modification of the three orders; practical people trying to put a world back together do so in terms of visions that they know. The work of reconstruction and adjustment attempted by the Order of the Passion failed at Nicopolis, but some of the needed internal and European reconstruction was accomplished by the deposing of Richard for tyranny, by Chaucer's son's leadership in parliament, by the negotiations of Constance and Troyes, and by the gradual modification of the bondage of rural peasants.[25] Much of the civilization so reconstructed was identifiably "Chaucerian" with his system of roles, laws, and divine sanctions. It may not have been a good society, but it was what its creators were able to shore up. To understand why fifteenth-century society was reconstructed so, one has to have some sense of why sane persons, including Chaucer, felt that the *ancien régime* was worth both preserving and laughing at. Amid our anomie and destruction of nature, we may find some intelligence not only in Chaucer's rhetorical brilliance but in his sense of what is obligatory, rea-

---

[24] Cf. Albert O. Hirschman, *The Passions and the Interests* (Princeton: Princeton University Press, 1977); Homans, *English Villagers of the Thirteenth Century*, p. 395.

[25] For Thomas Chaucer's career as speaker and leader in Lancastrian governments, see Martin B. Ruud, *Thomas Chaucer* (Minneapolis: Research Pub. of Univ. of Minnesota, 1926).

sonable, and serviceable in a community order with its head in the stars and its feet in the soil of the open fields. That is another task, beyond this book, but ready-made for those who wish to study what Chaucer lends himself to in our time as opposed to what he said to his own.

A Note on the Relationship of Meaning
and Historical Forms of Life

Ludwig Wittgenstein explains the relationship between meaning and context fully in his greatest work (*Philosophical Investigations*, trans. G.E.M. Anscombe [New York: Macmillan Co., 1953], pp. 8, 20, and 193ff.). For a useful account of the relationship between Wittgenstein's explanation of meaning and the forms of life of a people, see Henry Le Roy Finch, *Wittgenstein: The Later Philosophy* (Atlantic Highlands, N.J.: Humanities Press, 1977), pp. 89–102 (especially discussions of *Philosophical Investigations* I, 206 and 207). See also John W. Cook, "Solipsism and Language," *Ludwig Wittgenstein: Philosophy and Language*, ed. Alice Ambrose and Morris Lazerowitz (New York: Humanities Press, 1973), pp. 37–72. Cf. Wittgenstein's *Remarks on Frazer's Golden Bough*, ed. Rush Rhees (Retford, Nottinghamshire: Brynmill Press, 1979) on Frazer's analyzing another group's "practices" as "stupid actions," failing to understand how each language works within its form of life. For Wittgenstein's general understanding of how language-games work, see Garth Hallett, *A Companion to Wittgenstein's "Philosophical Investigations"* (Ithaca: Cornell University Press, 1977). For a useful example of a historical analysis of Chaucer's language placed in its institutional context and a useful riposte to ahistorical structuralist and semiotic studies, see Thomas Hahn and Richad W. Kaeuper, "Text and Context: Chaucer's *Friar's Tale*," *SAC* 5 (1983):67–70. This is not to derogate all structuralist studies, particularly those where the social, literary, and linguistic structures posited are also recognized by the society whose poetry or language is under study, as in the *emic* studies done by Kenneth Pike and the tagmemicists; see Ruth M. Brend and Kenneth L. Pike, *Tagmemics*, 2 vols. (The Hague: Mouton, 1976), pp. 87–90, 100–114; for a general description, see Kenneth L. Pike, *Language in Relation to a Unified Theory of the Structure of Human*

APPENDIX

Behavior (Glendale: Summer Institute of Linguistics, 1954), 3 vols. The analysis of the language-games of a society from within, and how the language "works" in the specific social structures for which it is made has become a major concern of ethnomethodology which draws on the work of Wittgenstein and Austin from philosophy and Pike from linguistics; Harold Garfinkel has argued that natural language as a whole is indexical—depending for its meaning on its context—and that to understand an utterance one must know in general its circumstances, its place in the stream of discourse, the relation between speaker and listener; see also Harold Garfinkel and Harvey Sacks, "On Formal Structures of Practical Actions," *Theoretical Sociology*, ed. John C. McKinney and Edward A. Tiryakian (New York: Appleton-Century-Crofts, 1970), pp. 337–66. Moreover, Garfinkel argues that members of a society are constantly engaged in creating accounts of their society and what is happening in it, which he calls glosses, and that these accounts are definitive; sociological descriptions are practical activities like any other descriptions of social structure and have no "scientific" character. Thus "society" does not exist independent of accounts of its character and actions by members, "saying-in-so-many-words-what-we-are-doing." Medieval poetic language is consistently characterized by medieval critics as performative, not "constative," to use Austin's description; Chaucer by identifying genre and mode says in so many words what he is doing, if one attends to the relationship between his language and common usage. The account of Chaucer's society and of his language-games must come from medieval people. Obviously context is not so readily retrievable for medieval language as it is for modern, but much that was said-in-so-many-words can be understood through attention to common usages, reflexive formulations, and glossing practices. See Douglas Benson and John A. Hughes, *The Perspective of Ethnomethodology* (New York: Longman, 1983), pp. 26–29, 99–153, for theory and analysis of the functions of telling stories. Most recent sociological analyses of Chaucer have been Marxist or Parsonian analyses which do not look closely at context or self-characterization. Chaucer's use of genre should also be examined in tagmemic terms as involving rough slot-filler systems manipulating traditional expectations through extension, inversion, and substitution.

[302]

Index

All forms of figurative language are listed as symbols in the index. The distinction between, for example, the Knight's tale as the Knight's account of his estate and the Knight's Tale as a structure seen in relation to itself is lost. Sets and editors are not indexed, and only the titles of anonymous works are given. Chaucerian topics are indexed under the tales or Chaucer life-record events.

[303]

INDEX

Cambridge, 70
Canaan, 55; and servitude, 281
Canaanitish woman, 145
canons, 181–82; and 1383 crusade,
206; in *Plowman's Tale*, 294
Canon's Yeoman's Tale, 181–82
Canterbury pilgrimage, fictive date, 4
Canterbury Tales, 239; completeness
of, 294–95; function for court, 26;
Group A, 49, 60, 105; Groups A
and B, 121; Group B2, 131; oral
character, 26; as *parlement*, 25;
structure of, 45, 294–95; structure
of pilgrimage, 26; unity of, 296;
written character, 26
Canticle of Canticles, 78, 137, 151–
56, 185, 241, 246, 262–64
Capgrave, John, 95
capitalism, 274
Carlyle, A. J., 281
Carmelite friars, 215
Carthusians, 244
Cecilia, Saint, 145–53, 158, 160, 175,
181, 295–96
Cenobia, 173
Chamber knights, 6, 10, 60, 102, 128,
165, 184; *Conclusions*, 8; as contri-
tionists, 284; on invisible church,
199. *See also* Lollard knights
chancery, royal, role in *significavit*,
195. See also *significavit*
chaplain, convent, 144
Charles V, 200
Charles VI, 14, 57, 59, 61
chastity, 58, 253. *See also* perfection
Chaucer, Geoffrey, 15; dealings with
William Beauchamp, 52; as Justice
of the Peace, 56; as peace negotia-
tor, 52. *See also* tales, historical
events

Chaucer, Thomas, 298
Chaucer-as-pilgrim, 105–6
Chauntecleer, 129, 151–56, 160; and
January, 264
Chess of Love gloss, 33, 239–43, 251,
270
"chevyssaunces," 167
Cheyne, Matthew, 12
Chodorow, Stanley, 195, 200
Chrétien de Troyes, 108
Chrimes, S. B., 21, 36, 88
chrism, 85, 115
Christ, arrest by Judas, 200–1; and
poverty, 256
Christ-as-Logos, 115, 131
Christ-as-Wisdom, 115, 137, 145–46.
See also Christ-as-Logos
Christian commonwealth, 282
chronicle, monastic, as advisory to
lords, 175
Church, debate over nature of, 128
Cicero, 112, 117, 239, 243
Cistercian order, 135
city group, General Prologue, 40
civil rule, Parson's account of, 288–90
Clanchy, M. T., 109
Clanvowe, John, 7, 52. *See also* Cham-
ber knights
Clanvowe, Thomas, 7. *See also* Cham-
ber knights
Clark, Roy Peter, 223
Clarke, Maude, 13, 112, 176
Clement V, 220
Clement VII, 5, 186, 206
Clerk, 30, 34–36, 130, 237, 259, 278
clerks, Dorigen's view of, 269
Clerk's Tale, 36, 257–62, 278; as com-
ment on theocratic kingship, 99
Clifford, Lewis, 7–8, 31, 52–53, 59,
130. *See also* Chamber knights

[306]

iconography, 93
idolatry, 263
image of God, in society, 36
images, aesthetic of, 288
imagination, and Epicureanism, 261
Imperial strategy, English, 177–78.
   See also Anglo-French negotiations
indulgence, 201–13. *See also* pardon
Innocent III, 122, 283
Innocent IV, 141
Innocents, Herod's, 136, 139, 144
Inns of Court, 117
invisible Church, 197–99, 222
Isidore of Seville, 73, 114
Islam, 32, 93, 97, 100

"Jack the Miller," 54, 75, 79. *See also*
   Peasants' Revolt
Jacob, E. F., 90
Jacobus, 215
Jacobus de Voragine, 78, 145, 231,
   266
Jacques le Grand, 238, 249
Janicula, 261
Jankyn, 248
Janson, H. W., 76
January, 14, 153–54, 260, 277; and
   Canticle, 264; conversion to Epi-
   cureanism, 240; his Epicurean gar-
   den, 241, 262
Janus Imperiale, 13–14, 261
jealousy, 263
Jeame d'Agramont, 207
Jean, Duke of Berry, 54
Jean de Condé, 109
Jean de Meun, 33, 215
Jean Gerson, 221
Jean le Fevre, 251
Jeffrey, David, 218, 221

Jehan de Courcy, 33
Jerome, 155, 248–49
Jerusalem, 292; as symbol, 280
Jews, in late fourteenth-century Eu-
   rope, 141–44; status before Eng-
   lish courts, 141
Joachimite heresy, 219, 222
Job, 171, 243; and Dorigen, 269; and
   Griselda, 259
John, Carpenter, 70, 77, 79, 81
John, the apostle, 35, 77, 144, 146,
   230, 288. *See also* apostles
John the Baptist, 138
John of Garland, 42–43, 184
John of Gaunt, 31, 51–52, 163;
   Spanish Crusade, 205
John of Parma, 219–20, 225
John of Salisbury, 21, 35, 85, 111–
   13, 241, 243–44, 250, 255; and Ep-
   icurean freedom, 264; on Epicu-
   reans, 238–39; his Epicurean gar-
   den, 241–44
John XXII, 220
Johnson, Dudley R., 173
Jones, Joan Morton, 33. *See also*
   Chess of Love gloss
Jones, Richard H., 85, 99, 170
Josephus, 113
Jovinian, 167, 237, 248; Epicurus of
   Christians, 242
Juan de Peretallada, 222
Judas, the apostle, 10, 35, 188–203,
   214, 288; in *Plowman's Tale*, 293.
   See also apostles
Julian, Saint, 266–67, 274
Julius Caesar, 67, 173
Juno, 238
Jupiter, 182, 291
Jusserand, J. J., 212
justice, 114

LIBRARY OF CONGRESS CATALOGING-IN-PUBLICATION DATA

Olson, Paul A.
The Canterbury tales and the good society.
Includes index.
1. Chaucer, Geoffrey, d. 1400. Canterbury tales.
2. Chaucer, Geoffrey, d. 1400—Political and social
views. 3. Social problems in literature.
4. Literature and society—England—History. I. Title.
PR1875.S6304 1986   821'.1   86–42852
ISBN 0–691–06693–0 (alk. paper)